THE BIG OTTER

CONTENTS

CHAPTER ONE.

Sleeping in Snow.

Cold comfort is naturally suggested by a bed of snow, yet I have enjoyed great comfort and much warmth in such a bed.

My friend Lumley was particularly fond of warmth and of physical ease, yet he often expressed the opinion, with much emphasis, that there was nothing he enjoyed so much as a night in a snow-bed. Jack Lumley was my chum—a fine manly fellow with a vigorous will, a hardy frame, and a kindly heart. We had a natural leaning towards each other—a sort of undefinable sympathy—which inclined us to seek each other's company in a quiet unobtrusive way. We were neither of us demonstrative; we did not express regard for each other; we made no protestations of undying friendship, but we drew together, somehow, especially in our hunting expeditions which were numerous.

On holidays—we had two in the week at the outpost in the American backwoods where we dwelt—when the other young fellows were cleaning gulls or arranging snow-shoes for the day's work, Lumley was wont to say to me:—

"Where d'you intend to shoot to-day, Max?" (Max was an abbreviation; my real name is George Maxby.)

"I think I'll go up by the willows and round by Beaver Creek."

"I've half a mind to go that way too."

"Come along then."

And so we would go off together for the day.

One morning Lumley said to me, "I'm off to North River; will you come?"

"With pleasure, but we'll have to camp out."

"Well, it won't be the first time."

"D'you know that the thermometer stood at forty below zero this morning before breakfast?"

"I know it; what then? Mercurial fellows like you don't freeze easily."

I did not condescend to reply, but set about preparing for our expedition, resolving to carry my largest blanket with me, for camping out implied sleeping in the snow.

Of course I must guard my readers—especially my juvenile readers—from supposing that it was our purpose that night to undress and calmly lie down in, or on, the pure white winding-sheet in which the frozen world of the Great Nor'-west had been at that time wrapped for more than four months. Our snow-bed, like other beds, required making, but I will postpone the making of it till bed-time. Meanwhile, let us follow the steps of Lumley, who, being taller and stronger than I, *always* led the way.

This leading of the way through the trackless wilderness in snow averaging four feet deep is harder work than one might suppose. It could not be done at all without the aid of snow-shoes, which, varying from three to five feet in length, enable the traveller to walk on the surface of the snow, into which he would otherwise sink, more or less, according to its condition. If it be newly fallen and very soft, he sinks six, eight, or more inches. If it be somewhat compressed by time or wind he sinks only an inch or two. On the hard surface of exposed lakes and rivers, where it is beaten to the appearance of marble, he dispenses with snow-shoes altogether, slings them on his gun, and carries them over his shoulder.

Our first mile lay through a clump of pine-wood, where snow had recently fallen. When I looked at my comrade's broad back, and observed the vigour of his action as he trod deep into the virgin snow at every stride, scattering it aside like fine white powder as he lifted each foot, I thought how admirably he was fitted for a pioneer in the wilderness, or for the work of those dauntless, persevering men who go forth to add to the world's geographical knowledge, and to lead the expeditions sent out in search of such lost heroes as Franklin and Livingstone.

My own work was comparatively light. I had merely to tread in the beaten path. I was not, however, thereby secured from disaster, as I found when, having advanced about half a mile, my right shoe caught a twig to which it held for a moment, and then, breaking loose, allowed me to pitch head down with such violence that I almost reached mother earth four feet below the surface.

This kind of plunge is always awkward owing to the difficulty of rising, and usually disagreeable, owing to the manner in which snow stuffs itself into neck, ears, nose, eyes, mouth—if open—and any convenient crevice of person or garments. The snow-shoes, too, which are so serviceable when you are above them, become exasperatingly obstructive when you are below them. After a struggle of two minutes I got my head clear, winked the snow out of my eyes, blew it from my mouth and nostrils, and looked up. Lumley was standing there with a bland smile on his amiable face; he seldom laughed, though he sometimes chuckled!

"What do you mean by grinning there like a Cheshire cat?" I exclaimed, "why don't you lend a hand?"

"What do you mean by tumbling there like a Christmas goose?" he retorted, "why don't you look out for stumps and twigs as I do?"

He made some amends for this reply by extending his hand and helping me to rise.

In a few minutes we were clear of the pine-wood, and came out upon a piece of swampland, where the stunted willow bushes just showed their tops above the surface of the snow. This led us to a bend of the broad river near to which, further down, stood our outpost—Fort Dunregan.

For four months there had been neither sight nor sound of water in that river. It was frozen to the bottom, except in the middle where its dark unseen waters flowed silently under six feet or more of solid ice through many a river-channel and lake to the distant sea. In fact, save for the suggestive form of its banks, the river might have been mistaken for an elongated plain or piece of open land. The surface of the snow here was, from exposure to wind and sun, as hard as pavement. We therefore took off our snow-shoes, and, the necessity for maintaining the Indian-file position being removed, we walked abreast.

"The air is keen here," remarked Lumley, pulling the thick shawl that was round his neck as far up over his mouth as his well-developed nose would permit.

"It is," said I, following his example with greater success, my own nose being a snub.

There was no wind; not even a breeze—there seldom is at such temperature—but there was a very slight movement of the air, caused by our own advance, which was just sufficient to make one appreciate the intensity of the cold. It became necessary now to pay frequent attention to our noses and cheek-bones and toes, to prevent frostbite. But the sun was brilliant and the air invigorating. So was the aspect of nature, for although there was no grandeur in the character of the scenery, there was extreme beauty in the snow lacework of the trees and leafless shrubs; in the sky, whose bright blue was intensified by the white drapery of earth; and in the myriads of snow-crystals which reflected the dazzling sun with prismatic splendour.

Indeed, the scene was too dazzling, and as there was a tendency in it to produce snow-blindness, we soon returned to the friendly shelter of the woods.

"Tracks!" exclaimed Lumley, in a low voice, pointing to the ground, where footmarks were clearly visible, "and fresh," he added, turning up the snow under the track with the butt of his gun.

"Ptarmigan!" said I in a whisper, pointing towards a little knoll, not quite a gunshot ahead of us, where some dozens of the beautiful snow-white creatures stood gazing at us in motionless surprise. Their plumage was so white that we had not observed them at first, almost the only black specks about them being their sparkling eyes, and the tips of their wings and tails.

Our guns were pointed instantly. I am ashamed to say that we were guilty of shooting them as they stood! In that land we shot for food as much as for amusement, and, some of us being poor shots, we were glad to take our game sitting! Nay, more, we tried to get as many of the birds in line as possible, so as to make the most of our ammunition. We were not sportsmen in the civilised sense of that term.

The extreme stillness of the woods was broken by the report of our guns in quick succession. A very cloud of pure white birds arose, as if Nature had taken to snowing upwards in rather large flakes, and seven victims remained behind.

"A good supper," remarked Lumley, as we bagged the game and re-loaded.

It is not my intention here to describe a day's shooting. Let it suffice to say that a little before nightfall we arrived at a place where was a snowy mound capped by a clump of spruce firs of small size but picturesque appearance.

"Behold our camp!" said Lumley.

"Not inviting at present," said I, as we slowly toiled up the mound, for we were weary, having walked about twenty miles, weighted with heavy flannel-lined deerskin-coats, blankets, and cooking utensils, besides a small quantity of pemmican, sugar, tea, and ship's biscuit, axes and firebags. It is true, the cooking utensils were few and simple, consisting of only two tin kettles and two tin mugs.

Dreary indeed—lonesome, desolate, and eerie was our mound when we got to the top of it. By that time the sun had set, and a universal ghostly grey, fast deepening into night, banished every sensation of joy aroused by the previous lightness. Although the scene and circumstances were nothing new to us we could not shake off the depressing influence, but we did not allow that to interfere with our action. Silently, but vigorously—for the cold was increasing—we felled several small dead trees, which we afterwards cut into lengths of about four feet. Then we cleared a space in the snow of about ten or twelve feet in diameter until we reached the solid earth, using our snow-shoes as shovels. What we threw out of the hole formed an embankment round it, and as the snow lay at that spot full four feet deep, we thus raised the surrounding wall of our chamber to a height of six feet, if not more. Standing on the edge of it in the ever-deepening twilight, and looking down into the abyss, which was further darkened by the overspreading pines, this hole in the snow suggested a tomb rather than a bed.

At one end of it we piled up the firewood. Extending from that towards the other end, we spread a carpet of pine-branches, full six inches thick. To do all this took a considerable amount of time and labour, and when Lumley stood up at last to strike a light with flint, steel, and tinder, we felt pretty well exhausted. The night had by that time become profoundly dark, insomuch that we had to grope for the various articles we required.

"We've been rather late of beginning to make the camp," said I, as I watched the sparks.

"Never mind, Max, my boy, we shall soon be all right," replied my friend, as one of the sparks at last caught on the tinder. In a few seconds the spark was blown into a blaze, and placed in the midst of a handful of dry moss and thin chips. This was applied to some dry twigs under our piled-up logs, and a vivid tongue of flame shot upward.

Blessed fire! Marvellous light! It is a glorious, wonder-working influence, well chosen by the Almighty as one of his titles. There is no change in Nature so intense as that from darkness to light as well in physical as in spiritual things. No sudden change from heat to cold, or from calm to storm; no transformation ever achieved in the most gorgeous of pantomimes, could have the startling effect, or produce the splendid contrast that resulted from the upward flash of that first tongue of fire. It was a vivid tongue, for the materials had been well laid; a few seconds later it was a roaring tongue, with a host of lesser tongues around it—all dancing, leaping, cheering, flashing, as if with ineffable joy at their sudden liberation, and the resulting destruction of dismal darkness.

Our snow-abyss was no longer black and tomb-like. Its walls sparkled as though encrusted with diamonds; its carpet of pine-branches shone vividly green; the tree-stems around rose up like red-hot pillars, more or less intense in colour, according to distance; the branching canopy overhead appeared to become solid with light, and the distance around equally solid with ebony blackness, while we, who had caused the transformation, stood in the midst of the ruddy blaze like jovial red-hot men!

"There's nothing like a fire," I remarked with some enthusiasm.

"Except supper," said Lumley.

"Gross creature!" I responded, as he went about the preparation of supper with a degree of zest which caused me to feel that my epithet was well deserved.

"Gross creature!" he repeated some time afterwards with a pleasant smile of intense enjoyment, as he sat in front of the blaze sipping a can of hot tea, and devouring pemmican and biscuit with avidity. "No, Max, I am not a gross creature. Your intellects are probably benumbed by the cold. If phrenologists are right in dividing the human brain into compartments, wherein the different intellectual powers are said to be located, I should think that some of those chambers lying nearest to the top of the skull are apt to freeze at a temperature of forty below zero, in which case the perfect working of the half-paralysed machine can scarcely be looked for. Hold your head to the fire, and thaw it while I expound this to you."

"Stay," said I, holding out my tin pannikin for more tea; "inward heat as well as outward is necessary to my thorough comprehension of *your* expositions."

"True, Max, all the faculties of such mind as you possess, in their most active condition, are required to enable you to take in the simplest proposition. Just give my bird a turn, like a good fellow."

17

He referred to a ptarmigan which, plucked, split open, roughly cleaned, and impaled on a stick, was roasting in front of the fire. I turned his bird and my own, while he continued:—

"To gratify the appetite with thorough and hearty appreciation after working hard for your food, or walking far to find it, is not gross. Grossness consists in eating heavily when you have not toiled, and stimulating with fire-water, pepper, or mustard, your sluggish appetite. To call me a gross creature, then—"

He stopped short, and, looking up, performed that operation with the nose which is styled sniffing.

"What do I smell?"

"My bird—burnt!" I shouted, snatching at the stick on which it was impaled. In doing so I capsized our can of tea. Lumley looked at it with a sigh, while I regarded with a groan the breast of my bird burnt to a cinder.

"Max, you should remember that a fire strong enough to subdue forty degrees below zero is intense—also, that our supply of tea is limited. All this comes of your unwisely calling me a gross creature."

"No, it comes of the intense application of my unthawed intellect to your absurd expositions."

"Whatever it comes of," returned Lumley, "we must remedy the evil. Here, fall upon my ptarmigan. I'm not quite ready for it, being still engaged with the pemmican. Meanwhile, I'll replenish the kettle."

So saying, he took up the kettle, went to the margin of our hole, and filled it with fresh snow well pressed down. This being put on the fire, soon melted; more snow was added, till water enough was procured, and then fresh tea was put in to boil. We were not particular, you see, as to the mode of infusion. While my friend was thus engaged, I had plucked, split, cleansed and impaled another bird. In a marvellously short time— for our fire was truly intense—the tea and ptarmigan were ready, and we proceeded with supper as comfortably as before.

18

"Now I shall continue," said Lumley, with a satisfied clearing of the throat, "the exposition of grossness,—"

"Oh, pray spare me that," said I, quickly, "but tell me, if you can, why it is that such a tremendous fire as that does not melt our snow walls."

"Put your head nearer to it, Max, for some of the phrenological chambers must still be frozen, else it would be clear to you that the intensity of the cold is the reason. You see that only a small part of the snow quite close to the fire is a little softened. If the fire were hotter it would melt more of it—melt the whole hole and us too. But the cold is so great that it keeps the walls cool and us also—too cool indeed, for while my face and knees are roasting my back is freezing, so I shall rise and give *it* a turn. Now," he continued, rising and turning his back to the blaze as he spoke, "I will resume my remarks on gross—"

"You've no objection to my making our bed while you lecture?" said I, also rising.

Lumley had not the least objection, so, while he held forth, I spread a large green blanket over our carpet of pine-brush. A bundle of the same under the blanket formed a pretty good pillow. Wrapping myself tightly round in another blanket (for physical heat evaporates quickly in the frozen regions) I lay down. My friend lay down beside me, our feet being towards the fire.

After a silent interval, while lying thus, gazing up through the overhanging branches at the stars that twinkled in the clear frosty sky, our thoughts became more serious. The grandeur of creation led us to think and speak of the Creator—for we were like-minded friends, and no subject was tabooed. We conversed freely about whatever chanced to enter our minds—of things past, present, and to come. We spoke of God the Saviour, of redemption and of sin. Then, with that discursive tendency to which most minds are prone, we diverged to home and civilised lands, contrasting these with life in the wild-woods of the Great Nor'-west. After that we became sleepy, and our converse was more discursive—at times even incoherent—in the midst of which Lumley reverted to his

19

unfinished exposition of grossness, and, in the enthusiasm of his nature, was slowly working himself back into a wakeful condition, when I put an abrupt end to the discourse by drawing a prolonged snore. It was a deceptive snore, unworthy of success, yet it succeeded.

My friend turned round and, with a contented sigh, went to sleep. After a brief space the snore which had been a fiction became a reality, and thus, on our bed of snow, in the depths of an Arctic night, in the heart of the frozen wilderness, and while the mighty fire burned slowly down, we unitedly took our departure for the land of Nod.

* * * * *

married, born, laid low by sickness, banished to the ends of the earth like ourselves, or even removed by death!

Is it surprising, then, that we caught our breath and flushed, and that our hearts leaped when we came unexpectedly upon the track of the two men who had dragged news from home for hundreds of miles over the snow? We knew the tracks well. Our intimate acquaintance with every species of track that was possible in that particular region, rendered a mistake out of the question. There was the step of the leader, who wore a snow-shoe the shape of which, although not unknown, was somewhat unfamiliar to us. There was the print of the sled, or toboggan, which was different in pattern from those used at Dunregan, and there was the footprint of the man in rear, whose snow-shoe also made an unfamiliar impression.

"The packet!" exclaimed Lumley, opening his solemn grey eyes to their widest as he looked up from the track to me.

"At last!" I returned, unconsciously betraying the prolonged state of suspense with which my mind had been afflicted.

"Come along!" said my companion, starting off homeward at a pace that was almost too much for me.

We soon reached the outpost, and there stood the makers of the track which had roused in us so much excitement.

Two strong men, chosen expressly for a duty which required mental endurance and perseverance as well as physical vigour. They stood at the door of the entrance-hall, talking with Mr Strang, the one with his snow-shoes slung over his shoulder on the butt of his gun, the other using the same implements as a rest for his hands, while Spooner, in a state of great excitement, was hastily undoing the lashings of the sled, to get at the precious box which contained "the packet."

"Well, gentlemen, here it is at last," said our chief, with a genial smile as we came up.

"Yes, we followed the track immediately we struck it," said Lumley, stooping to assist Spooner in his work.

We soon had the box carried to our chief's private room, while the two strangers were had off by our men to their own house, there to be feasted on venison, ptarmigan, salt-pork, fish, and pease-pudding to satiety, and afterwards "pumped" to a state of exhaustion.

I followed our chief, who had a provokingly deliberate way of opening the packet and examining its contents, while my feverish agitation and expectancy increased. There was a humorous twinkle in his eye, I thought, which told of mischievous purpose, while he kept up a murmuring commentary.

"Hm! as I expected—no news from Macnab. What's this?—ah! The Governor! A voluminous epistle, and—hallo! Lumley's friends must be fond of him. His packet is the biggest in the box. And Spooner too, not so bad for him. Here, take these to them. Stay—here is a bundle of letters for the men. You'd better deliver these yourself."

I hesitated, while a mist of great darkness began to descend on my soul.

"Nothing for me, sir?" I asked faintly.

"There seems to be—nothing—stay! what's this?—why, I thought it was a big book, but, yes, it *is* a packet for you, Mr Maxby—there!"

My heart leaped into my mouth—almost out of it—as I received a thick packet wrapped in newspaper.

Hastening to what was called the clerk's winter house with these treasures I distributed them, and handed the men's packet to one of themselves, who was eagerly awaiting it. Then I went to my room and barricaded the door to prevent interruption.

In Bachelors' Hall, as we styled our apartments, we had an inveterate habit of practical joking, which, however interesting and agreeable it might be at most times, was in some circumstances rather inconvenient. To guard against it at such times we were in the habit of retiring to our respective dens and barricading the doors, the locks being sometimes incapable of standing the strain brought to bear on them.

24

On this particular occasion I made my barricade stronger than usual; sat down on my bed and opened the packet from home.

But here I must let the curtain fall. I cannot suppose that the reader, however amiable, will sympathise with the joys and sorrows of an unknown family, interesting though they were to me. I may state, however, that before I got through the budget it was so late that I turned into bed and read the remainder there. Then, as the fire in the hall-stove sank low, the cold obliged me to put on above my voluminous blankets (we dared not sleep in sheets out there) a thick buffalo robe, which, besides having on the outside the shaggy hair of the animal to which it had belonged, was lined with flannel. Thus nestled into a warm hole, I read on until a shout arrested me and brought me suddenly back from the hills of bonny Scotland to the frozen wilderness.

"I say," shouted Lumley at the back of the door, which he saluted with a kick, "my sister is married!"

"Poor thing!" said I. "Who to?"

"Open the door."

"I can't. I'm in bed."

"You must."

"I won't."

"No! then here goes."

He retired as he spoke, and, making a rush, launched himself against my door, which, however, withstood the shock.

"Here, Spooner," I then heard him say, "lend a hand; let us go at it together."

They went at it together. The lock gave way; the chest of drawers went spinning to the other side of the room, and Lumley tumbled over Spooner as both fell headlong to the floor.

As this was by no means an unfamiliar mode of entering each other's rooms, I took no notice of it, but proceeded to inquire about the married sister; and Lumley, sitting down on my bed with Spooner, for neither of them had yet undressed, began to tell me of home and friends with as much eagerness as if I had been a member of both families. Young Spooner interrupted Lumley now and then when a touch of coincidence struck him with reference to his own family affairs, and I could not resist the pleasure of occasionally making some such remark as, "How odd! that's very like what happened to my little brother Bob," etcetera, whereupon Spooner would immediately become excited and draw a parallel more or less striking in regard to his own kindred and so we went on far into the night, until we got our several families mixed up to such an extent that it became almost impossible to disentangle them; for, being three families, you know, we became inextricably confused as to which was which, though each was perfectly clear in regard to his own! Thus, to me, Jane Lumley became confused with Janet Spooner, so that Janet Lumley and Jane Spooner were always tripping over each other in my brain, while my dear cousin Maggie Maxby became a Maggie Spooner to Lumley, and a Maggie Lumley to Spooner, and to each sometimes a Janet or a Jane respectively. If the reader will multiply into this question two mothers and three fathers, four brothers and six sisters, besides numberless aunts, uncles, and cousins, male and female, he will easily perceive how between mental perplexity and a tendency to slumber, we at last gave the matter up in a sort of jovial despair.

We were startled suddenly from this condition by a crash and an exceedingly sharp and bitter cry.

It must be remarked here, that, in order to subdue King Frost in those northern strongholds of his, we had, besides double doors and double windows and porches, an enormous cast-iron stove from the famous Carron foundry. It stood in the centre of our hall, so that its genial favours might be distributed with equal justice to the various sleeping-rooms that opened out of the hall all round. From this stove an iron pipe arose, and, turning at a right angle when within a couple of feet of the ceiling, proceeded to the chimney at the upper end of the hall. When the thermometer stood much below zero, we were accustomed to raise the stove and part of its pipe to a dull-red heat, which had the effect of partially melting the contents of the water-jugs in our bedrooms, and of partially roasting the knees of our trousers. To keep this stove up to its work was the duty of an Indian youth, whom we styled Salamander, because he seemed to be impervious to heat. He was equally so to cold. When I first went to Dunregan I used to pity Salamander, on hearing him every morning enter our hall with a gust of air that seemed cold enough to freeze a walrus, and proceed to strike a light and kindle our fire. My own nose, and sometimes an eye, was all that protruded from the buffalo robe at such times. But Salamander never shivered, and always grinned, from which I came to understand that my pity was misplaced. About nine o'clock each night he left us to look after the great Carron stove ourselves, and we were all pretty good stokers. Self-interest kept us up to duty. Sometimes we overdid it, raising the dull-red to brightness now and then.

On this particular occasion, in the exuberance of his feelings, Lumley, before bursting into my room, had heaped on as much dry wood as the stove could hold. It chanced to be exceedingly resinous wood. He also opened the blow-hole to its utmost extent. Being congregated in my bedroom, as I have described, deeply engaged in eager comments and family reminiscences, we failed to observe that the great Carron stove roared like a wrathful furnace, that it changed from a dull to a bright red in its anger, and eventually became white with passion. As "evil communications" have a tendency to corrupt, the usually innocent pipe became inflamed. It communicated the evil to the chimney, which straightway caught fire, belched forth smoke and flames, and cast a ruddy glare over the usually pallid snow. This chanced to meet the eye of Salamander as he gazed from his "bunk" in the men's house; caused him to bounce up and rush out—for, having a taste for sleeping in his clothes, he was always ready for action—burst open our door with a crash, and rudely dispel our confusedly pleasant intercourse with the exceedingly sharp and bitter cry before mentioned.

"Hallo!" shouted Lumley and Spooner simultaneously, as they bounded rather than rose from my bed. Before they had crossed the threshold I was out of bed and into my trousers.

There is nothing like the cry of "Fire!" for producing prompt action—or paralysis! Also for inducing imbecile stupidity. I could not find my moccasins! Thought is quick—quicker than words. Amputation at the knee joints stared me in the face for a certainty if I went out with naked feet. In desperation I seized my capote and thrust both feet into the sleeves, with some hazy intention of tying a knot on each wrist to protect the toes. Happily I espied my moccasins at the moment, pulled them on—left shoe on right foot, of course—and put the coat to its proper use.

By this time Salamander, contrary to all traditions of Indian stoicism, was yelling about the fort with his eyes a flame and his hair on end. The men were out in a few seconds with a ladder, and swarmed up to the roof of our house without any definite notion as to what they meant to do. Mr Strang was also out, smothered in winter garments, and with an enormous Makinaw blanket over all. He was greatly excited, though the most self-possessed among us—as most chiefs are, or ought to be.

"Water! water!" shouted the men from the roof.

A keen breeze was blowing from what seemed the very heart of King Frost's dominion, and snow-drift fine as dust and penetrating as needles, was swirling about in the night-air.

Water! where was water to come from? The river was frozen almost to the bottom. Ice six feet thick covered the lakes and ponds. The sound of trickling water had not been heard for months. It had become an ancient memory. Water! why, it cost our cook's assistant a full hour every day to cut through the result of one night's frost in the water-hole before he could reach the water required for daily use, and what he did obtain had to be slowly dragged to the fort by that slowest of creatures, an ox. Nevertheless there *was* water. In the warmest corner of the kitchen—at that hour about zero—there stood a water-barrel.

"Run, cook—fetch a bucketful!" cried our chief.

Cook, who had "lost his head," obediently ran, seized a big earthenware jug, dipped it into the barrel, and smashed it to atoms on a cake of thick ice! This had the effect of partially recovering his head for him. He seized an axe, shattered the cake, caught up a bucket, dipped it full and rushed out spilling half its contents as he ran. The spillings became icicles before they reached the flaming chimney, but the frost, keen as it was, could not quite solidify the liquid in so short a space of time.

Blondin, the principal bearer of the winter packet who was a heroic man and chief actor in this scene, received the half-empty bucket.

"Bah!" he exclaimed, tossing bucket as well as water contemptuously down the wide chimney. "Bring shuvill, an' blunkits."

Blondin was a French-Canadian half-caste, and not a good linguist.

A shovel was thrown up to him. He seized it and shovelled volumes of snow from the house-top into the chimney. A moment later and two blankets were thrown up. Blondin spread one over the flames. It was shrivelled up instantly. He stuffed down the remains and spread the second blanket over them, while he shouted for a third. The third came, and, another bucket of water arriving at the same moment, with a large mass of snow detached from the roof, the whole were thrust down the chimney *en masse*, the flames were quenched and the house was saved.

During this exciting scene, I had begun to realise the great danger of fire in the chimney of a wooden house, and, with the aid of my comrades, had been throwing the contents of Bachelors' Hall out into the snow. We now ceased this process, and began to carry them back again, while the men crowded round the iron author of all the mischief to warm their half-frozen bodies. I now observed for the first time that Blondin had a black patch on the end of his nose. It was a handsome feature usually, but at that time it was red, swelled, and what may be termed blobby.

"What's the matter with it, Blondin?" I asked.

"My noz was froz," he replied curtly.

"You'd better have it looked to, or it'll be worse than froz, my man," said Lumley.

Blondin laughed and went off to attend to his nose in the men's house, accompanied by the others, while we set to work to clean ourselves and our abode. Thereafter, with moderated fire, we again got under our buffalo robes, where we spent the remainder of a disturbed night in thinking and dreaming about the thrilling contents of the winter packet.

* * * * *

CHAPTER THREE.

Deeper Desolation.

Eight months of winter! Those who have read and entered into the spirit of Arctic voyagers, may have some idea of what that means, but none save he or she who has had experience of it can fully understand it.

To us who dwelt at the little outpost in the Great Nor'-west, snow and ice had become so familiar—such matter-of-course conditions of existence—that green fields and flowers were a mere reminiscence of the remote past. The scent of a rose was a faded memory—indeed the scent of anything belonging to the vegetable kingdom had not once saluted our nostrils during those eight months. Pure white became one of the chief and most impressive facts of our existence in regard to colour, if we may so call it—white, varying in tone, of course, to pearly grey. Cold, of varied intensity, was the chief modifier of our sensations. Happily light was also a potent factor in our experiences—bright, glowing sunshine and blue skies contrasted well with the white and grey, and helped to counteract the cold; while pure air invigorated our frames and cheered our spirits.

"I tell you what, boys," said Lumley, one afternoon as he entered the hall with gun and snow-shoes on shoulder, and flung down a bag full of ptarmigan, "winter is drawing to a close at last. I felt my deerskin coat quite oppressive to-day; does any one know what the thermometer stood at this morning?"

"Yes, it was twenty-two above zero," answered Spooner, who was attempting to smoke a pipe beside the stove; "I went to register it just after breakfast."

"I thought so—only ten below freezing point; why, it feels quite summery, and the snow has a softness that I have not noticed since last autumn. I hope dinner will soon be ready, for I'm very sharp set. Why, Spooner, what are you making such faces for?"

"Am I making faces?" said Spooner, blushing and trying to look unconcerned.

"Of course you are, a marmozette monkey with the toothache could scarcely make worse."

Spooner attempted to laugh, and I felt it difficult to refrain from joining him, for I knew well the cause of his faces. He was the youngest of us three and exceedingly anxious to imitate Lumley, who was unfortunately a great smoker; but Spooner, like myself, had been born with a dislike to smoke—especially tobacco smoke—and a liability to become sick when he indulged in the pipe. Hence, whilst foolish ambition induced him to smoke, outraged nature protested; and between the two the poor fellow had a bad time of it. He had a good deal of determination about him, however, and persevered.

The dinner-bell rang at the moment, and put an end to further badinage.

Lumley was right. Spring was in truth at hand, and a host of new anticipations began from that day to crowd upon our minds.

About the same time there came another break in the monotony of outpost life which had, if possible, a more powerful and exciting influence on us than the arrival of the winter packet.

Now at this point I must beg the reader's pardon for asking him to go with me to a still more desolate and remote outpost than our own. Between one and two hundred miles nearer to the pole the little post of Muskrat House lay under a beetling cliff, near the banks of an affluent of the great Saskatchewan river. It was in charge of Peter Macnab, before mentioned, who, in command of his army of six men and two women, held the post against all comers—the chief comers there being the North Wind and Jack Frost.

Poor Macnab was a jovial and sociable Scottish Highlander, who had been condemned to worse than Siberian banishment because of being one of the most active, enterprising, and pushing fellows in the service of the Fur-Traders. His ability to manage men and Indians, and to establish new trading-posts, excelled that of his fellows. He regarded it as a complimentary though trying circumstance when Mr Strang sent him to establish the post which was named by him Muskrat House, but he faced the duty—as he faced everything—like a man; did his best for his employers, and made the most of the situation.

But it is not easy for even the strongest mind and lightest heart to be jovial when buried for eight months in snow more than twelve hundred miles beyond the influences of civilised life; and it is hard to be sociable with six uneducated men and two Indian women for one's companions. Macnab tried it, however, and was in a measure successful. He had his Bible with him—the one given him long ago by his mother—and a bound volume of Chambers's Edinburgh Journal, and three copies of the *Times* newspaper nearly two years old, and a few numbers of an American paper called the *Picayune*.

With these materials he set to work—after each day's labour of water-drawing, firewood-cutting, and trapping was done—to educate his army in religion, politics, political economy, and the varied ramifications of social life. He had intelligent and grateful scholars. If they had not been so, Macnab would at all events have made them obedient pupils, for he was a physically large and powerful man—and might was unavoidably right in those regions!

Still, with all his energy and resources, the genial Highlander began, towards the end of winter, to feel an intense longing for a little intercourse with his equals.

Returning one night to the solitude of his little room, as was his wont, after a couple of hours' intercourse with his men in their own house, he sat down before his stove and addressed it thus:—

"It won't last long, I fear. My brain is gradually turning into something like mashed potatoes, and my heart into a tinder-box, ready enough to catch fire, but with neither flint nor steel to light it! The Indians won't be here for many weeks, and when they do come what good can I get from or do to them? Wow! wow! it's terribly slow work. Oh! Jessie, Jessie, my dear, what would I not give if I only had *you* here!"

Lest the reader should suppose Macnab to be a love-sick swain, I may remark here that Jessie was a sister whom he had left on the shores of Loch Ness, and with whom he kept up a vigorous biennial correspondence.

As the stove made no reply, he continued his address.

"If I only had a few books now, it wouldn't be so hard to bear. To be sure, the Bible is a great resource—a blessed resource; but you see I want something light now and then. A laugh, you know, seems to be absolutely needful at times. Why, now I think of it, we wouldn't have been given the power to laugh if it hadn't been necessary, and the last hearty laugh I had was, let me see—that time three months ago, when my long-nosed interpreter mistook a dead mouse in the soup—ha! ha!—for a bit of pemmican, and only found out his mistake when the tail got between his teeth!"

The solitary man burst into peals of laughter at the reminiscence, and then, becoming suddenly grave, looked slowly round the room.

"If I could only have an echo of that," he resumed, "from somebody else! Well, well, I'll just go and have another chat with Jessie."

So saying, Macnab rose, drew a small table near to the stove, laid upon it a very large desk made by himself of pine-wood, and, placing a sheet of paper thereon, began to write.

The sheet of paper merits notice. Like the man who wrote, it was extremely large, being several sizes bigger than foolscap, and very loosely ruled. As I have said, communication with the outer world being possible only twice in the year, our Highlander resolved, as usual, to make the most of his opportunities. Hence he not only used the largest paper which the company provided, but filled up several such sheets with the smallest possible writing, so that Jessie might ultimately get something worth having. It is but justice to add that Macnab wrote not only a very small but a remarkably clear and legible hand—a virtue which I earnestly commend to correspondents in general, to those of them at least who wish their epistles to meet with thorough appreciation.

It was late when our solitaire completed that evening's addition to his already voluminous letter, and he was thinking about going to bed when a stamping in the porch outside announced that a visitor was clearing the snow from his moccasins.

"One o' the men forgot something, I fancy," muttered Macnab to himself.

The latch was lifted, for locks were not deemed necessary in those regions, and the door opening slowly disclosed the copper-hued visage and tall bony figure of a very powerful and handsome native of the soil—perhaps I should rather say—of the snow!

"Hallo! hey! come in," shouted Macnab, giving way to a gush of his pent-up social feelings; "why it's good for sore eyes to see a new face, even a red one. What cheer? what cheer? Where d'ye hail from? Come in, come in, and welcome!"

The hearty Highlander spoke the Indian tongue fluently, but in the excitement of his feelings mingled it with a good deal of English and an occasional growl of expressive Gaelic.

The Indian, whose horned cap and person were well powdered with snow, stepped slowly over the threshold, extending his hand to the Highlander's grasp, and looking cautiously round with rolling black eyes, as if he half expected a dynamite explosion to follow his entrance. His garments bore evidence of rough usage. Holes in his moccasins permitted portions of the duffle socks underneath to wander out. Knots on his snow-shoe lines and netting told of a long rough journey, and the soiled, greasy condition of his leathern capote spoke of its having been much used not only as a garment by day but as a shirt by night.

Placing his gun and snow-shoes in a corner, after solemnly responding "watchee, watchee," to Macnab's "what cheer," the red-man seated himself on the floor beside the stove, with silent disregard of the chair that his host politely offered.

It is the custom of North American Indians—on arriving at an establishment—to withhold the most interesting portion of what they may have to communicate until after they have had a pipe, or a feed, and have answered the questions put on the less interesting objects of their visits. Being well aware of this trait of character, Macnab forebore to question too closely this fine-looking Indian until he had well thawed and smoked himself. Ultimately, however, he brought him to the point.

To the north-westward of Muskrat House, many long days' march, he said (of course in his native tongue) there was a grand country full of fine furs and fine people, who found it a very long journey indeed to come all the way to Muskrat House to trade their furs. Would his white father go and build a house there, near Lake Wichikagan, and shoot and fish, and trade?—waugh!

To which Macnab replied that he was glad to hear about the plenty of furs and the friendly natives and the fine country, and that he would take the matter into his consideration—waugh!

To this the red-man responded "ho!" and then "how!"—not interrogatively but interjectionally—with much gravity.

That night Macnab took the matter into consideration with his wonted vigour, and came to the conclusion that it was of sufficient importance to warrant a visit on his part to headquarters—Dunregan being headquarters to Muskrat House. Accordingly, he went to the men's house and introduced the stranger, whose name in the Indian tongue signified Big Otter. The men received him with as much joy as if he had been an angel of light.

"Get a sled and four of the best dogs ready to start by daybreak to-morrow," said Macnab to one of his men, "and have breakfast sharp," he added, turning to the cook. "You'll go with me to Dunregan, won't you, Big Otter?"

Big Otter was ready for anything at a moment's notice!

When daylight glimmered faintly in the east the following morning, Macnab sat at his table devouring venison steaks, pancakes, and tea. Big Otter sat opposite to him, having condescended to use a chair in order to be on a level with the table. The chair gave him much anxiety, however. He evidently feared to fall off or upset it, for, on rising to reach some food opposite, he had tilted it back, and received a tremendous though unacknowledged start from the crash that followed.

Half an hour later, Macnab, having left his interpreter in charge of the establishment, was beating the track on snow-shoes through the forest, his four wolfish-looking dogs following with a sled-load of provisions and bedding, and Big Otter bringing up the rear.

The day turned out to be bright calm, and frosty. It was in thorough unison with Macnab's feelings, for the near prospect of soon meeting with men somewhat like himself produced a calm and bright condition of mind which he had not experienced for many a day. It is true that the frost can scarcely be said to have represented the Highlander's temperament; but if there be truth in the saying that extremes meet, it may be admissible to say that intense cold, which had the effect of expanding water into ice so that it rent the very rocks, might be appropriately compared with that intense warmth of Macnab's feelings which had the effect of all but bursting his very bosom! There was not a breath of air stirring when the two men passed from the forest, and struck out upon the marble surface of the great lake which lay at the distance of about two miles from their establishment. The sun was rising at the time on the horizon of the ocean-like lake, gloriously bright and cheering, though with no appreciable warmth in its beams. Diamonds innumerable glittered on the frosted willow-boughs; the snow under the travellers' tread gave forth that peculiar squeak, or chirping sound, which is indicative of extreme Arctic frost, and the breath from their mouths came out like the white puffs of a locomotive, settling on their breasts in thick hoar-frost, and silvering such of their locks as straggled out beyond the margin of their caps. There was no life at first in the quiet scene, but, just as they passed through the last clump of bushes on the margin of the lake, a battalion of ptarmigan, seemingly a thousand strong, burst with startling whirr from under their very feet, and skimmed away like a snow-cloud close to the ground, while an Arctic fox, aroused from his lair by the noise, slank quietly off under the false belief that he had not been seen.

The rise of the ptarmigan had another effect, on which the travellers had not counted. The four wolfish dogs were so startled by the whirr, that their spirits were roused to the mischievous point. Up to that moment they had been toiling and panting through the soft snow in the woods. They had now emerged upon the hard, wind-beaten snow of the open ground and the lake. The sudden freedom in the action of their limbs, coupled with the impulse to their spirits, caused the team to bound forward with one accord. The sled swung round against Macnab's legs, and overturned him; and the tail-line was jerked out of Big Otter's grasp. In a vain effort to recover it, that solemn savage trod, with his right, on his own left snow-shoe, and plunged into a willow bush. Thus freed altogether, the dogs went away with railway speed over the hard snow, ever urged to more and more frantic exertions by the wild boundings of the comparatively light sled behind them.

"After them, lad!" shouted Macnab, as he cast off his snow-shoes and gave chase.

The Indian followed suit in desperate haste, for his receptive mind at once perceived the all but hopeless nature of a chase after four long-legged dogs, little removed from genuine wolves, over a hard level course that extended away to the very horizon.

Happily, there was a small island not far from the shore of the lake, on which grew a few willow bushes whose tops protruded above the overwhelming snow, and whose buds formed the food of the ptarmigan before mentioned. Towards this island the dogs headed in their blind race just as the white man and the red began to regret the comparative slowness of human legs.

"Good luck!" exclaimed Macnab.

"Waugh!" responded his companion.

There was ground for both remarks, for, a few minutes later, the dogs plunged into the bushes and the sled stuck fast and held them.

This was a trifling incident in itself, but it shook out of the travellers any remains of lethargy that might have clung to them from the slumbers of the previous night, and caused them to face the tramp that lay before them with energy.

"Oh, you *ras*cals!" growled Macnab, as he went down on his knees beside the leading dog to disentangle the traces which had been twisted up in the abrupt stoppage.

I know not whether those dogs, being intellectually as well as physically powerful beyond their fellows, understood the uncomplimentary term and lost their tempers, but certain it is that the words were no sooner uttered than the hindmost dog made an unprovoked assault on the dog in front of it. Of course the latter defended itself. The dog next to that, being probably pugnacious, could not resist the temptation to join in, and the leader, feeling no doubt that it was "better to be out of the world than out of the fashion," fell upon the rest with remarkable fury. Thus the sled, traces, and dogs, instantly became a tumultuous mass of yelling, gasping, heaving, and twisting confusion.

Big Otter carried a short, heavy whip. Without uttering a word, he quietly proceeded to flog the mass into subjection. It was a difficult duty to perform, but Big Otter was strong and persevering. He prevailed after some time. The mass was disentangled; the subdued dogs went humbly forward, and the journey, having been thus auspiciously begun, was continued until nightfall.

They had left the lake and Muskrat House some thirty miles behind them, and had got into a thick and profoundly still part of the great wilderness, when the waning light warned them to encamp.

* * * * *

CHAPTER FOUR.

The Winter Journey.

It was not long before our travellers had a large space cleared of snow, its floor spread with pine-branches, a roaring fire kindled, a couple of ptarmigan roasting and the tea-kettle bubbling, while the dogs in the background solaced themselves with raw birds to their heart's content.

Then the red-man and the white man smoked a friendly pipe. They would probably have smoked even if it had been an unfriendly pipe!

"I wonder," said Macnab, who was apt to become speculative and philosophical over his pipe after supper, "I wonder if dogs ever envy us our pipes? You look so comfortable, Big Otter, as you sit there with half-shut eyes letting the smoke trickle from your mouth and nose, that I can't help thinking they must feel envious. I'm sure that I should if I were not smoking!"

The Indian, who was neither a speculator nor a philosopher—though solemn enough for either or both—replied, "Waugh!"

"Very true," returned the Highlander, "I have no doubt your opinion is quite correct, though not as clearly put as might be wished. Have you ever been at Fort Dunregan?"

"Once when Big Otter was a little boy, he stood beside the Great River," answered the Indian, gravely; "but the white man had no tent there at that time."

"The white man has got some pretty big tents there now—made of wood most of 'em," returned Macnab. "In a few days you shall judge for yourself, if all goes well."

The red-man smoked over this remark in silence for a considerable time, evidently engaged in profound thought. He was one of those children of nature whose brains admit ideas slowly, and who, when they are admitted, turn them round and round and inside out without much apparent advantage.

At last he looked earnestly at his companion and asked—"Is there fire-water at Fort Dunregan?"

"Well, no—I believe not. At least there is none for red-men. Why do you ask? Did you ever taste fire-water?"

The Indian's dark eyes seem to gleam with unwonted light as he replied in tones more solemn than usual:—

"Yes. Once—only once—a white brother gave some fire-water to Big Otter."

"Humph!" ejaculated Macnab, "and what did you think of it!"

"Waugh!" exclaimed the red-man, sending a cloud out of his mouth with such energy that it seemed like a little cannon-shot, while he glared at his friend like a superannuated owl. "Big Otter thought that he was in the happy hunting-grounds with his fathers; his heart was so light and his limbs were so strong, but that was only a dream—he was still in this world. Then he took a little more fire-water, and the dream became a reality! He was away with his fathers on the shining plains; he chased the deer with the lightness of a boy and the strength of a bear. He fought, and his foes fell before his strong arm like snowflakes on the river, but he scalped them not. He could not find them—they were gone. Big Otter was so strong that he had knocked both their lives and bodies into the unknown! He saw his father and his mother—and—his wife and the little one who—died. But he could not speak to them, for the foes came back again, and he fought and took some more fire-water to make him fight better; then the world went on fire, the stars came down from the sky like snow when the wind is high. The Big Otter flew up into the air, and then—forgot—"

42

"Forgot what?" asked Macnab, much interested in his red friend's idea of intoxication.

"Forgot everything," replied the Indian, with a look of solemn perplexity.

"Well, I don't wonder; you must have had a good swig, apparently. How did ye feel next morning?"

If the Indian's looks were serious before, they became indescribably solemn now.

"Big Otter felt," he replied with bated breath, "like bags of shot—heavy like the great stones. He could scarcely move; all his joints were stiff. Food was no longer pleasant to his tongue. When he tried to swallow, it would not remain, but came forth again. He felt a wish to drink up the river. His head had an evil spirit inside which squeezed the brain and tried to burst open the skull. His eyes, also, were swelled up so that he could hardly see, and his nose was two times more big than the day before."

"That must have been an awful size, Big Otter, considering the size of it by nature! And what d'ye think was the cause of it all?"

As this question involved thought, the Indian smoked his pipe in silence for some time, staring for inspiration into the fire.

"It must have been," he at length replied, "hunting with his fathers before the right time had come. Big Otter was not dead, and he chased the deer too much, perhaps, or fought too much. It may be that, having only his earth-body, he ate too much."

"Don't ye think it's just possible," suggested Macnab, "that, having only your earth-body, you *drank* too much?"

"Waugh!" replied the red-man. Then, after a few minutes' devotion to the pipe, he added, "Big Otter would like very much to taste the fire-water again."

"It's well for you, my boy," returned the other, "that you can't get it in these regions, for if you could you'd soon be in the happy hunting-grounds (or the other place) without your earth-body."

At this point the Highlander became more earnest, and treated his companion to what would have passed in civilised lands for a fair temperance lecture, in which he sought to describe graphically the evils of strong drink. To this the Indian listened with the most intense attention and an owlish expression, making no audible comment whatever—with the exception, now and then, of an emphatic "Waugh!" but indicating his interest by the working of his features and the glittering of his great eyes. Whether the reasoning of Macnab had much influence at that time could not be ascertained, for he was yet in the middle of one of his most graphic anecdotes when the Indian's owlish eyes shut with a suddenness that was quite startling, and he roused himself just in time to prevent his chin from dropping on his chest.

"Waugh!" he exclaimed with a slightly-confused look.

"Just so," replied Macnab with a laugh, "and now, boy, we'll turn in, for it strikes me we're going to have warmish weather, and if so, we shall have to make the most of our time."

Soon the blankets were spread; the fire was replenished with mighty logs; the travellers lay down side by side and in a few minutes snored in concert; the flames leaped upwards, and the sparks, entangling themselves on the snow-encrusted branches of bush and tree, gleamed there for an instant, or, escaping, flew gaily away into the wintry sky.

While the two men were sleeping, a change came over the scene—a slow, gentle, scarce perceptible change, which, however, had a powerful influence on the prospects of the sleepers. The sky became overcast; the temperature, which had been down at arctic depth for many months, suddenly rose to that of temperate climes, and snow began to fall— not in the small sharp particles to which the fur-traders of the great northern wilderness are accustomed, but in the broad, heavy flakes that one often sees in England. Softly, silently, gently they fell, like the descent of a sweet influence—but steadily, persistently, continuously, until every object in nature became smothered in the soft white garment. Among other objects the two sleepers were buried.

The snow began by powdering them over. Had any one been there to observe the process, he would have seen by the bright light of the camp-fire that the green blankets in which they were wrapt became piebald first; then assumed a greyish-green colour, which speedily changed into a greenish-grey, and finally into a pure white. The two sleepers might thus have represented those figures in chiselled marble on the tombs of crusaders, had it not been that they lay doubled up, for warmth—perhaps also for comfort—with their knees at their chins, instead of flat on their backs with their hands pressed together. By degrees the correct outline of their forms became an incorrect outline, and gradually more and more rotund—suggesting the idea that the buried ones were fat.

As the night wore on the snow accumulated on them until it lay several inches deep. Still they moved not. Strong, tired and healthy men are not easily moved. The fire of course sank by degrees until it reached that point where it failed to melt the snow; then it was quickly smothered out and covered over. The entire camp was also buried; the tin kettle being capped with a knob peculiarly its own, and the snow-shoes and other implements having each their appropriate outline, while some hundredweights, if not tons, of the white drapery gathered on the branches overhead. It was altogether an overwhelming state of things, and the only evidence of life in all the scene was the little hole in front of each slumberer's nose, out of which issued intermittent pufflets of white vapour.

So the night passed by and the morning dawned, and the wintry sun arose like a red-hot cannon ball. Then Macnab awoke with a start and sat up with an effort.

"Hallo!" was his first exclamation, as he tried to clear his eyes, then he muttered something in Gaelic which, being incomprehensible, I cannot translate, although the worthy man has many a time since the day of which I write tried to explain it to me!

It may have been his action, or it may have been indignant northern fairies, I know not, but certain it is that the Gaelic was instantly followed by an avalanche of snow from the branch over the Highlander's head,

45

which knocked him down and reburied him. It also knocked Big Otter up and drew forth the inevitable "Waugh!"

"Humph!" said Macnab, on clearing himself a second time, "I was half afraid of this. We've got our work cut out for us."

The Indian replied not, but proceeded to light the fire and prepare breakfast, while his companion cleared the camp of some of its snow. The wolfish dogs took a lively interest in these proceedings, but lent no assistance beyond wagging their tails, either in approval or in anticipation of breakfast.

Of course breakfast was a repetition of the previous supper, and was soon disposed of both by men and dogs. Then the latter were harnessed to their sledge, the snow-shoes were put on, and the journey was resumed—Macnab manfully leading the way.

And let not the reader imagine that this leadership involved little or no manhood. Northern snow-shoes are about five feet long, and twelve or fifteen inches broad. The netting with which the frames are filled up—somewhat like the bottom of a cane chair—allows fine well-frozen snow to fall through it like dust and the traveller, sinking it may be only a few inches in old well-settled-down snow, progresses with ease. But when a heavy fall such as I have described takes place, especially in spring, and the weather grows comparatively warm, the traveller's circumstances change greatly for the worse. The new snow being light permits him to sink deep into it—perhaps eight or ten inches—at every step; being also soft, that which falls upon the shoes cannot pass through the netting, but sticks there, giving him many extra pounds weight to lift as he goes heavily along. Add to this that his thick winter garb becomes oppressive in mild weather, and you will perceive that Macnab's duties as beater of the track were severe.

At first their progress was very slow, for it was through the thick woods, where fallen trees and bushes obstructed them as well as deep snow, but towards noon they came out on a more open country—in summer a swamp; at that time a frozen plain—and the travelling improved, for a slight breeze had already begun to make an impression on the new snow in exposed places.

"Now, Big Otter," said Macnab, coming to a halt, "we'll have some grub here, and then you will take a turn in front."

The Indian was ready for anything. So were the dogs—especially for "grub." Indeed it was obvious that they understood the meaning of that word, for when Macnab uttered it they wagged their tails and cocked their ears.

It was a cold dinner, if I may describe the meal by that name. The work was too hard, and the daylight in which to do it too brief, to admit of needless delay. A frozen bird thrown to each of the dogs, and a junk of equally frozen pemmican cut out of the bag with a hatchet for the travellers, formed the repast. The latter ate it sitting on a snow-wreath. They, however, had the advantage of their canine friends in the matter of hard biscuits, of which they each consumed two as a sort of cold pudding. Then they resumed the march and plodded heavily on till near sunset, when they again selected a suitable spot in the woods, cleared away the snow, and encamped as before.

"It's hard work," exclaimed Macnab with a Celtic sigh, as he sipped his tea that night in the mellow light of the log fire.

"Waugh! Big Otter has seen harder work," returned the Indian.

"No doubt ye have, an' so have I," returned Macnab; "I mind, once, when away on a snow-shoe trip on the St. Lawrence gulf, bein' caught by a regular thaw when the snow turned into slush, an' liftin' the snow-shoes was like to tear one's legs out o' their sockets, not to mention the skinning of your toes wi' the snow-shoe lines, an' the wet turning your moccasins into something like tripe. Yes, it might be worse, as you say. Now, boy, I'll turn in."

The next day travelling was no better, and on the next again it became worse, for although the temperature was still below the freezing point, snow continued to fall all day as well as all night, so that our travellers and their dogs became like animated snowballs, and beating the track became an exhausting labour.

But difficulties cannot finally stop, though they may retard, a "Nor'-wester." On the sixth day, however, they met with a foe who had power to lay a temporary check on their advance. On the night of the fifth day out, another change of temperature took place. A thermometer, had they carried one, would probably have registered from ten to twenty below zero of Fahrenheit. This, however, was so familiar to them that they rather liked the change, and heaped up fresh logs on the roaring fire to counteract the cold; but when a breeze sprang up and began to blow hard, they did not enjoy it so much, and when the breeze increased to a gale, it became serious; for one cannot face intense cold during a gale without the risk of being frost-bitten. In the shelter of the woods it was all right, but when, towards noon, they came out on an extended plain where the wild winds were whirling the wilder snow in blinding drifts, they halted and looked inquiringly at each other.

"Shall we try it?" asked Macnab.

The Indian shook his head and looked solemn.

"It's a pity to give in without—"

A snow-drift caught the Highlander full in the mouth and literally shut him up! The effect was not to subdue, but to arouse.

"Yes," he said in a species of calm ferocity, when the gale allowed him the power of utterance, "we'll go on."

He went on, followed by the obedient native and the unhappy dogs, but he had not taken half a dozen steps when he tripped over a concealed rock and broke a snow-shoe. To walk with a broken snow-shoe is impossible. To repair one is somewhat difficult and takes time. They were compelled, therefore, to re-enter the sheltering woods and encamp.

"You're better at mending than I am," said Macnab to the Indian. "Set to work on the shoe when the camp is dug out, an' I'll go cut some firewood."

Cutting firewood is not only laborious, but attended with danger, and that day ill-fortune seemed to have beset the Highlander; for he had barely cut half a dozen logs, when his axe glanced off a knot and struck deep into the calf of his left leg.

A shout brought Big Otter to his side. The Indian was well used to such accidents. He bound up the wound securely, and carried his comrade into camp on his back. But now Macnab was helpless. He not only could not walk, but there was no hope of his being able to do so for weeks to come.

"Lucky for us we brought the dogs," he remarked when the operation was completed.

"Waugh!" exclaimed the Indian by way of assent, while he busied himself in preparing food.

It was indeed lucky, for if they had dragged the provision-sled themselves, as Macnab had once thought of doing, it would have fallen to Big Otter's lot to haul his comrade during the remainder of the journey. As it was, the dogs did it, and in the doing of it, despite the red-man's anxious and constant care, many a severe shake, and bump, and capsize in the snow did the unfortunate man receive before that journey came to a close. He bore it all, however, with the quiet stoicism characteristic of the race from which he sprang.

* * * * *

CHAPTER FIVE.

The Wounded Man.

It is needful now to return to Fort Dunregan.

The long winter is not yet past, but there are symptoms, as I have said, that it is coming to a close. Snow and ice are still indeed the prevailing characteristic of the region, but the air is no longer intensely cold. On the contrary, a genial warmth prevails, inducing the inhabitants to discard flannel-lined leathern capotes and fur caps for lighter garments. There is a honeycombed look about the snow-drifts, which gives them an aged appearance; and, above all, there is an occasional dropping of water—yes, actual water—from the points of huge icicles! This is such an ancient memory that we can scarce believe our senses. We sniff, too, as we walk about; for there are scents in the air—old familiar smells of earth and vegetation—which we had begun to fancy we had almost forgotten.

The excitement caused by the arrival of the winter packet had also by that time passed almost out of memory, and we had sunk back into that calm state of patient waiting which may probably be familiar to the convict who knows that some months of monotonous existence still lie before him; for, not until the snow and ice should completely clear away and the summer be pretty well advanced could we hope for the blessed sight of a new face and the cheering sound of a fresh human voice. Of course we had the agreeable prospect of hearing ere long the voices of wild-fowl in their noisy northern flight, but such a prospect was not sufficient to satisfy poor secluded humanity.

"Oh that I were a bird!" exclaimed Spooner, one morning as we were seated round the Carron stove in our hall.

"No need to wish that," said Lumley, "for you're a goose already!"

"Well, I'd even consent to be a real goose," continued Spooner, "if I could only thereby use my wings to fly away over the snowy wilderness and alight in my old home."

"What a surprise you'd give them if you did!" said Lumley, "especially if you came down with your ruffled feathers as clumsily as you tumbled into the saw-pit the other day when—"

He stopped, for at that moment I said "Hush!" and held up a finger.

"Sleigh-bells!" exclaimed Spooner, with a catch of his breath.

"Nothing new in that," said Lumley: "we hear them every day."

"Nothing new," I retorted, "to your unmusical ear, but these bells are not *our* bells—listen!"

I started up as I spoke, flung open the outer door, and we all listened intently.

Clear and pleasant they rang, like the music of a sweet new song. We all gave a shout, clapped on our caps, and ran out to the fort gate. There an almost new sensation thrilled us, for we beheld a team of dogs coming up weary and worn out of the wilderness, preceded by a gaunt yet majestic Indian, whose whole aspect—haggard expression of countenance, soiled and somewhat tattered garments, and weary gait—betokened severe exhaustion. On the sled, drawn by four lanky dogs, we could see the figure of a man wrapped in blankets and strapped to the conveyance.

"Who *can* it be?" exclaimed Lumley, as he hastened out to meet the new arrivals.

"A sick man from somewhere," suggested Spooner.

"Perhaps the governor," said I, "on an unexpected tour of inspection."

As we drew near we could see that the recumbent figure waved a hand and cheered.

51

"Macnab," said I, as the familiar voice struck my ear.

"Ill—dying!" gasped the anxious Spooner.

"No dying man ever cheered like that!" cried Lumley, "except a hero of romance in the hour of death and victory!"

A few seconds more and the matter was put at rest, while we warmly shook the hearty and genial Highlander by both hands.

"Help me out, boys," he said; "I'm tired o' this sled, and think I can do the little remaining bit o' the journey on foot with your help."

We disentangled him from the sledge and set him on his feet.

"Hold on, Lumley," he said, with a smile on his haggard and unshaven face, "I want to embrace you, like the Frenchmen. There—my arm round your neck—so. Now, Max, I want to embrace you likewise wi' the other arm. I've grown awful affectionate in my old age. You are rather short, Max, for a good crutch, but you're better than nothing. You see, I've only got one good leg."

"But what has happened to the other—when, how, and where?" we exclaimed in chorus.

Macnab answered the questions to our chief, who came forward at the moment with welcome in his visage and extended hands.

"It's only a cut, sir, stupidly done with my own hatchet when we had been but a few days out. But rest will soon put me to rights. My poor man, Big Otter, is more to be pitied than I. But for him I should have perished in the snow."

"What cheer? what cheer?" said our chief, grasping the Indian's hand on hearing this.

"What cheer?" we all exclaimed, following his example.

"Watchee! watchee!" echoed Big Otter, returning the hearty salutation as well as his tongue could manage it, and giving us each a powerful squeeze with his huge bony hand, which temporary exhaustion had not appreciably reduced in strength.

The native was obviously a sociable, well-disposed man, for his eyes glittered and his white teeth gleamed and his bronzed visage shone with pleasure when Macnab explained the cause of our sudden burst of affection for him.

Thus chatting and limping we got the Highlander slowly up to the hall, set him down in our only armchair—a wooden one without stuffing—and fetched him a basin of hot soup, that being a liquid which our cook had always more or less frequently on hand.

"Ha! boys!" cried Macnab, smacking his lips, "that's the thing to put life into a man! I've not had anything like it for many a day. You see, we had a small misfortune soon after my accident, which cost us our kettle, and rendered soup or tea impossible."

"How was that?" inquired our chief, sitting down, while we gathered round the stove to listen.

"Well, you see, sir, not long after my accident, there came a sharp frost which made the surface of the snow hard after the thaw, so the dogs could run on the top of the crust without breaking it, but Big Otter, bein' heavy, broke through—by the way, I hope he's bein' looked after."

"You may be sure of that," said Spooner. "I saw him safely placed in the men's house, and Salamander, who, it turns out, is a sort of relation of his, set to work to stuff him with the same sort of soup you think so much of. I only hope they've enough to keep him going, for before I left the house he had drunk off two bowls of it almost without taking breath, though it was scalding hot."

"Good. He'll do it ample justice," returned Macnab, taking another pull at his own bowl. "I hope you're well provisioned, for Big Otter's an awful consumer of victuals. Well, as I was saying, the surface of the snow got frozen thinly, and the work o' tramping after the sled and holding on to the tail-line was uncommonly hard, as I could see, for I lay with my head to the front, looping back on the poor man. But it was on the exposed places and going down the slopes that the greatest difficulty lay, for there the dogs were keen to run away. Once or twice they did fairly get off, and gave me some rough as well as long runs before my man could catch them up. At last we came one afternoon to an open plain

53

where the snow had felt the thaw and been frozen again pretty hard. The moment we got on it away went the dogs. Big Otter tried to run, but one of his shoes went through the crust and the other didn't, so down he came, and had to let go the line. I felt easy enough at first, for the plain was level, but after a time it became lumpy, and I got some ugly bumps. 'Never mind,' thought I, 'they'll be sure to come to some bushes, and that'll pull them up.' Just as I thought so, we came to a slope, and the team went slap over a bank. The sled and I threw a complete somersault. Fortunately we came down on the dogs, which broke our fall, though it half killed them!

"When Big Otter came and turned me right side up, I found that I had sustained no damage whatever, but, woe's me! our tin kettle was almost knocked flat. The worst of it was that in trying to put it right we drove a big hole in the bottom of it, so we had to bid farewell to hot food, except what we roasted. We could also melt snow by plastering up the hole so as to get enough to drink, but boiling water was quite out of the question."

"Well, Macnab," said our chief, rising, "since you have got the soup over at last, come along with me and let's hear about your Indian friend's proposals."

We assisted our visitor into the mess-room, which was also our principal council-chamber, and there left him to talk business with Mr Strang while we returned to Bachelors' Hall to let off our effervescing spirits by indulging in a running commentary on the unexpected visit, and a minute analysis of the characters of Macnab and Big Otter, which, I must add, was decidedly favourable.

"It seems to me a piece of good luck that he has got here at all," said Lumley, after we had finished the analysis.

"Why so?" asked Spooner.

"Because there are some unmistakable symptoms that winter is about over, and that snow-shoe and dog-sleigh travelling will soon be impossible."

That Lumley was right, the change of weather during the next few days clearly proved, for a thaw set in with steady power. The sun became at last warm enough to melt ice and snow visibly. We no longer listened with interest to the sounds of dropping water from eaves and trees, for these had become once more familiar, and soon our ears were greeted with the gurgling of rills away in mysterious depths beneath the snow. The gurgling ere long gave place to gushing, and it seemed as if all nature were dissolving into liquid.

While this pleasant change was going on we awoke with song and laugh and story the echoes of Bachelors' Hall—at no time very restful echoes, save perhaps in the dead hours of early morning; and even then they were more or less disturbed by snoring. For our sociable Highlander, besides having roused our spirits by his mere presence to the effervescing point, was himself much elated by the mighty change from prolonged solitude to joyous companionship.

"My spirit feels inclined," he remarked one day, "to jump clean out of my body."

"You'd better not let it then," said Lumley, "for you know it might catch cold or freeze."

"Not in this weather, surely," retorted Macnab, "and if I did feel coldish in the circumstances, couldn't I borrow Spooner's blanket-capote? it might fit me then, for I'd probably be a few sizes smaller."

"Come, Mac," said I, "give us a song. You know I'm wildly fond of music; and, most unfortunately, not one of us three can sing a note."

Our visitor was quite willing, and began at once to sing a wild ditty, in the wilder language of his native land.

He had a sweet, tuneful, sympathetic voice, which was at the same time powerful, so that we listened to him, sometimes with enthusiasm swelling our hearts, at other times with tears dimming our eyes. No one, save he who has been banished to a wilderness and long bereft of music, can understand the nature of our feelings—of mine, at least.

One evening, after our wounded man had charmed us with several songs, and we all of us had done what we could, despite our incapacity, to pay him back in kind, he pulled a sheet of crumpled paper out of his pocket.

"Come," said he, unfolding it, "I've got a poet among the men of Muskrat House, who has produced a song, which, if not marked by sublimity, is at least distinguished by much truth. He said he composed it at the rate of about one line a week during the winter, and his comrades said that it was quite a picture to see him agonising over the rhymes. Before they found out what was the matter with him they thought he was becoming subject to fits of some sort. Now, then, let's have a good chorus. It's to the tune of 'The British Grenadiers.'"

The World of Ice and Snow.

Come listen all good people who dwell at home at ease,
I'll tell you of the sorrows of them that cross the seas
And penetrate the wilderness,
Where arctic tempests blow—
   Where your toes are froze,
   An' the pint o' your nose,
      In the world of Ice and Snow.

You've eight long months of winter an' solitude profound,
The snow at your feet is ten feet deep and frozen hard the
    ground.
And all the lakes are solid cakes,
And the rivers all cease to flow—
   Where your toes are froze,
   An' the pint o' your nose,
      In the world of Ice and Snow.

No comrade to enliven; no friendly foe to fight;
No female near to love or cheer with pure domestic light;
No books to read; no cause to plead;
No music, fun, nor go—
    Ne'er a shillin', nor a stiver,
    Nor nothin' whatsomediver,
        In the world of Ice and Snow.

Your feelin's take to freezin', so likewise takes your brain;
You go about grump-and-wheezin', like a wretched dog in pain;
You long for wings, or some such things,
But they're not to be had—oh! no—
    For there you are,
    Like a *fixéd* star,
        In the world of Ice and Snow.

If you wished you could—you would not, for the very wish would
    die.
If you thought you would—you could not, for you wouldn't have
    heart to try.
Confusion worse confounded,
Would aggravate you so—
    That you'd tumble down
    On the frozen ground
        In the world of Ice and Snow.

But "never-give-in" our part is—let British pluck have sway
And "never-say-die," my hearties—it's that what wins the day.
To face our fate in every state,
Is what we've got to do,
    An' laugh at our trouble

Till we're all bent double—
In the world of Ice and Snow.

Now all ye sympathisers, and all ye tender souls;
Ye kind philanthropisers, who dwell between the poles,
Embrace in your affections
Those merry merry men who go—
Where your toes are froze,
An' the pint o' your nose,
In the world of Ice and Snow.

It almost seemed as though the world of ice and snow itself had taken umbrage at Macnab's song, for, while we were yet in the act of enthusiastically prolonging the last "sno–o–ow," there sounded in our ears a loud report, as if of heavy artillery close at hand.

We all leaped up in excitement, as if an enemy were at our doors.

"There it goes at last!" cried Lumley, rushing out of the house followed by Spooner.

I was about to follow when Macnab stopped me.

"Don't get excited, Max, there's no hurry!"

"It's the river going to break up," said I, looking back impatiently.

"Yes, I know that, but it won't break up to-night, depend on it."

I was too eager to wait for more, but ran to the banks of the river, which at that place was fully a mile wide. The moon was bright, and we could see the familiar sheet of ice as still and cold as we had seen it every day for many months past.

"Macnab's right," said I, "there will be no breakup to-night."

"Not so sure of that," returned Lumley; "the weather has been very warm of late; melting snow has been gushing into it in thousands of streams, and the strain on the ice—six feet thick though it is—must be tremendous."

He was checked by another crashing report; but again silence ensued, and we heard no more till next morning. Of course we were all up and away to the river bank long before breakfast, but it was not till after that meal that the final burst-up occurred. It was preceded by many reports— towards the end by what seemed quite a smart artillery fire. The whole sheet of ice on the great river seemed to be rising bodily upwards from the tremendous hydraulic pressure underneath. But though the thaws of spring had converted much snow into floods of water, they had not greatly affected the surface of the ice, which still lay hard and solid in all its wintry strength.

A greater Power, however, was present. If the ice had been made of cast-iron six feet in thickness, it must have succumbed sooner or later.

At last, as Macnab said, "She went!" but who shall describe *how* she went? It seemed as if the mighty cake had been suddenly struck from below and shattered. Then the turmoil that ensued was grand and terrible beyond conception. It was but an insignificant portion of God's waters at which we gazed, but how overwhelming it seemed to us! Mass rose upon mass of ice, the cold grey water bursting through and over all, hurling morsels as large as the side of a house violently on each other, till a mighty pile was raised which next moment fell with a crash into the boiling foam. Then, in one direction there was a rush which seemed about to carry all before it, but instead of being piled upwards, some of the masses were driven below, were thrust deep into the mud, and a jam took place. In a few minutes the ice burst upwards again, and the masses were swept on to join the battalions that were already on their way towards the distant lake amid noise and crash and devastation. It seemed as if ice and snow and water had combined to revive the picture if not the reality of ancient chaos!

Thus the drapery of winter was rudely swept away, and next morning we had the joy of seeing our river sweeping grandly on in all the liquid beauty of early and welcome spring.

* * * * *

CHAPTER SIX.

An Express and its Results.

Some weeks after the breaking up of the ice, as we were standing at the front gate of Fort Dunregan, we experienced a pleasant surprise at the sight of an Indian canoe sweeping round the point above the fort. Two men paddled the canoe, one in the bow and one in the stern.

It conveyed a message from headquarters directing that two of the clerks should be sent to establish an outpost in the regions of the far north, the very region from which Macnab's friend Big Otter had come. One of the two canoe-men was a clerk sent to undertake, at Dunregan, the work of those who should be selected for the expedition, and he said that another clerk was to follow in the spring-brigade of boats.

"That's marching orders for *you*, Lumley," said Macnab, who was beside us when the canoe arrived.

"You cannot tell that," returned Lumley. "It may be that our chief will select Max or Spooner. Did you hear any mention of names?" he asked of the new clerk, as we all walked up to the house.

"No, our governor does not tell us much of his intentions. Perhaps your chief may be the man."

"He's too useful where he is," suggested Macnab. "But we shall know when the letters are opened."

Having delivered his despatches, the new arrival returned to us in Batchelors' Hall, where we soon began to make the most of him, and were engaged in a brisk fire of question and reply, when a message came for Mr Lumley to go to the mess-room.

"I've sent for you, Lumley," said our chief, "to say that you have been appointed to fill an honourable and responsible post. It seems that the governor, with his wonted sagacity, has perceived that it would be advantageous to the service to have an outpost established in the lands lying to the westward of Muskrat House, on the borders of Lake Wichikagan. As you are aware, the Indian, Big Otter, has come from that very place, with a request from his people that such a post should be established, and you have been selected by the governor to conduct the expedition."

As our chief paused, Lumley, with a modest air, expressed his sense of the honour that the appointment conferred on him, and his willingness to do his best for the service.

"I know you will, Lumley," returned Mr Strang, "and I must do you the justice to say that I think the governor has shown his usual wisdom in the selection. Without wishing to flatter you, I think you are steady and self-reliant. You are also strong and big, qualities which are of some value among rough men and Indians, not because they enable you to rule with a strong hand, but because they enable you to rule without the necessity of showing the strength of your hand. Bullies, if you should meet with any, will recognise your ability to knock them down without requiring proof thereof. To say truth, if you were one of those fellows who are fond of ruling by the mere strength of their arms, I should not think you fit for the command of an expedition like this, which will require much tact in its leader. At the same time, a large and powerful frame—especially if united to a peaceable spirit—is exceedingly useful in a wild country. Without the peaceable spirit it only renders its possessor a bully and a nuisance. I am further directed to furnish you with the needful supplies and men. I will see to the former being prepared, and the latter you may select—of course within certain limits. Now go and make arrangements for a start. The lakes will soon be sufficiently free of ice, and you are aware that you will need all your time to reach your ground and get well established before next winter sets in."

"Excuse me, sir," said Lumley, turning back as he was about to depart. "Am I permitted to select the clerk who is to go with me as well as the men?"

"Certainly."

"Then I should like to have Mr Maxby."

Our chief smiled as he replied, "I thought so. I have observed your mutual friendship. Well, you may tell him of the prospect before him."

Need I say that I was overjoyed at this prospect? I have always felt something of that disposition which animates, I suppose, the breast of every explorer. To visit unknown lands has always been with me almost a passion, and this desire has extended even to trivial localities, insomuch that I was in the habit, while at fort Dunregan, of traversing all the surrounding country—on snow-shoes in winter and in my hunting canoe in summer—until I became familiar with all the out-of-the-way and the seldom-visited nooks and corners of that neighbourhood.

To be appointed, therefore, as second in command of an expedition to establish a new trading-post in a little-known region, was of itself a matter of much self-gratulation; but to have my friend and chum Jack Lumley as my chief, was a piece of good fortune so great that on hearing of it I executed an extravagant pirouette, knocked Spooner off his chair by accident—though he thought it was done on purpose—and spent five or ten minutes thereafter in running round the stove to escape his wrath.

As to my fitness for this appointment, I must turn aside for a few moments to pay a tribute of respect to my dear father, as well as to tell the youthful reader one or two things that have made a considerable impression on me.

"Punch," said my father to me one day—he called me Punch because in early life I had a squeaky voice and a jerky manner—"Punch, my boy, get into a habit of looking up, if you can, as you trot along through this world. If you keep your head down and your eyes on the ground, you'll see nothing of what's going on around you—consequently you'll know nothing; moreover, you'll get a bad habit of turning your eyes inward and always thinking only about yourself and your own affairs, which means being selfish. Besides, you'll run a chance of growing absent-minded, and won't see danger approaching; so that you'll tumble over things and damage your shins, and tumble into things and damage your clothes, and tumble off things and damage your carcase, and get run over by wheels, and poked in the back by carriage-poles, and killed by trains, and spiflicated in various ways—all of which evils are to be avoided by looking up and looking round and taking note of what you see as you go along the track of life—d'ye see?"

"Yes, father."

"And this," continued my father, "is the only mode that I know of getting near to that most blessed state of human felicity, self-oblivion. You won't be able to manage that altogether, Punch, but you'll come nearest to it by looking up. Of course there are times when it is good for a man to look inside and take stock—self-examination, you know—but looking *out* and *up* is more difficult, to my mind. And there is a kind of looking up, too, for guidance and blessing, which is the most important of all, but I'm not talking to you on that subject just now. I'm trying to warn you against that habit which so many people have of staring at the ground, and seeing and knowing nothing as they go along through life. I've suffered from it myself, Punch, more than I care to tell, and that's why I speak feelingly, and wish to warn you in time, my boy.

"Now, there's another thing," continued my father. "You're fond of rambling, Punch, and of reading books of travel and adventure, and I have no doubt you think it would be a grand thing to go some day and try to discover the North Pole, or the South Pole, or to explore the unknown interior of Australia."

"Yes, father," I replied, in a tone which made him laugh.

"Well, then, Punch, I won't discourage you. Go and discover these places by all means, if you can; but mark me, you'll never discover them if you get into the habit of keeping your eyes on the ground, and thinking about yourself and your own affairs. And I would further advise you to brush up your mathematics, and study navigation, and learn well how to take an observation for longitude and latitude, for if you don't know how to find out exactly where you are in unknown regions, you'll never be a discoverer. Also, Punch, get into a habit of taking notes, and learn to write a good hand, for editors and publishers won't care to be bothered with you if you don't, and maybe the time will come when you won't be able to make out your own writing. I've known men of that stamp, whose penmanship suggested the idea that a drunk fly had dipped its legs in the ink-pud an' straggled across his paper."

These weighty words of my dear father I laid to heart at the time, and, as a consequence I believe, have been selected on more than one occasion to accompany exploring parties in various parts of the world. One very important accomplishment which my father did not think of, but which, nevertheless, I have been so fortunate as to acquire, is, sketching from Nature, and marking the course of rivers and trend of coasts. I have thus been able not only to make accurate maps of the wild regions I have visited, but have brought home many sketches of interesting scenes of adventure, which words alone could not have sufficed to pourtray.

But to return from this long digression. I set about my preparations without delay, and was soon ready with a small but very select amount of baggage. You may be sure also that Lumley was active in his preparations, and the result was that, on a fine afternoon in the early spring, we—that is, Lumley, Macnab, Big Otter, and I—set out on our expedition in a strong new boat which was manned by two Indians, two Scotchmen, and a number of Canadian half-breeds—all picked men.

I must not however, drag my readers through the details of our arduous voyage, not because those details are devoid of interest or romance, far from it, but because I have other matters more interesting and romantic to relate. I will, therefore, pass them over in silence, and at once proceed to the remote region where our lot at that time was to be cast.

One beautiful evening we encamped on the margin of one of those innumerable lakelets which gleam like diamonds on the breast of the great wilderness through which for many weeks we had been voyaging. The vast solitudes into which we had penetrated, although nearly destitute of human inhabitants, were by no means devoid of life, for aquatic birds of varied form and voice made sweet music in the air as they swept over their grand domains on whirring wing, or chattered happily in their rich feeding-grounds.

Those pleasant sounds were augmented by the axes of our men as they busied themselves in cutting firewood, and preparing our encampment.

The spot chosen was a piece of level sward overhung by trees and surrounded by bushes, except on the side next the little lake where an opening permitted us to see the sheet of water gleaming like fire as the sun sank behind the opposite trees. By that time we had traversed hundreds of miles of wilderness, stemming many rivers and rivulets; crossing or skirting hundreds of lakes which varied from two hundred miles to two hundred yards in length; dragging our boat and carrying our baggage over innumerable portages, and making our beds each night, in fair weather and foul, under the trees of the primeval forest, until we had at last plunged into regions almost unknown—where, probably, the foot of a white man had never before rested. On the way we had passed Muskrat House. There, with feelings of profound regret, we parted from our genial Highlander, promising, however, to send him an unusually long account of all our doings by the packet, which we purposed sending to headquarters sometime during the winter.

The particular duty which Lumley and I undertook on the evening in question was the lighting of the fire, and putting on of the kettles for supper. We were aided by our guide, Big Otter, who cut down and cut up the nearest dead trees, and by Salamander, who carried them to the camp.

"Three days more, and we shall reach the scene of our operations," said Lumley to me, as we watched the slowly-rising flame which had just been kindled; "is it not so?" he asked of Big Otter, who came up at the moment with a stupendous log on his shoulders and flung it down.

"Waugh?" said the Indian, interrogatively.

"Ask him," said Lumley to Salamander, who was interpreter to the expedition, "if we are far now from the lodges of his people."

"Three times," replied the red-man, pointing to the sun, "will the great light go down, and then the smoke of Big Otter's wigwam shall be seen rising above the trees."

"Good; I shall be glad when I see it," returned Lumley, arranging a rustic tripod over the fire, "for I long to begin the building of our house, and getting a supply of fish and meat for winter use. Now then, Salamander, fetch the big kettle."

"Yis, sar," replied our little servant, with gleeful activity (he was only sixteen and an enthusiast) as he ran down to the lake for water.

"Cut the pemmican up small, Max. I've a notion it mixes better, though some fellows laugh at the idea and say that hungry men are not particular."

"That is true," said I, attacking the pemmican with a small hatchet; "yet have I seen these same scoffers at careful cookery doing ample and appreciative justice to the mess when cooked."

"Just so. I have observed the same thing—but, I say, what is Big Otter looking so earnestly at over there?"

"Perhaps he sees a bear," said I; "or a moose-deer."

"No, he never pays so much attention to the lower animals, except when he wants to shoot them. He shakes his head, too. Let's go see. Come, Salamander, and interpret."

"Big Otter sees something," said Lumley through Salamander as we approached.

"Yes, Big Otter sees signs," was the reply.

"And what may the signs be?"

"Signs of wind and rain and thunder."

"Well, I suppose you know best but no such signs are visible to me. Ask him, Salamander, if we may expect the storm soon."

To this the Indian replied that he could not tell, but advised that preparation should be made for the worst.

It may be well here to remark that although Lumley and I, as well as some of our men, had acquired a smattering of the Indian tongue, our chief deemed it expedient to give us a regular interpreter whose knowledge of both languages was sufficiently extensive. Such an interpreter had been found in the youth whom we had styled Salamander, and whose real name I have now forgotten. This lad's knowledge of Indian was perfect. He also understood French well, and spoke it badly, while his comprehension of English was quite equal to any emergency, though his power of speaking it was exceedingly limited. What he spoke could scarcely be styled a broken tongue; it was rather what we may call thoroughly smashed-up English! Such as it was, however, it served our purpose well enough, and as the lad was a willing, cheery, somewhat humorous fellow, he was justly deemed an acquisition to our party. While on this subject I may add that Blondin, who brought the winter packet to Dunregan, was one of our number—also, that both our Scotsmen were Highlanders, one being named Donald Bane, the other James Dougall. Why the first called the second Shames Tougall, and the second styled the first Tonal' Pane is a circumstance which I cannot explain.

Among the French-Canadian half-breeds our blacksmith, Marcelle Dumont and our carpenter, Henri Coppet, were the most noteworthy; the first being a short but herculean man with a jovial temperament, the latter a thin, lanky, lugubrious fellow, with a grave disposition. Both were first-rate workmen, but indeed the same may be said of nearly all our men, who had been chosen very much because of their readiness and ability to turn their hands to anything.

Soon the kettles boiled. In one we infused tea. In another we prepared that thick soup so familiar to the Nor'-wester, composed of pemmican and flour, which is known by the name of *robbiboo*. From a frying-pan the same substances, much thicker, sent up a savoury steam under the name of *richeau*.

There was not much conversation among us at the commencement of the meal, as we sat round the camp-fire, but when appetite was appeased muttered remarks were interchanged, and when tobacco-pipes came out, our tongues, set free from food, began to wag apace.

"Dere is noting like a good *souper*," remarked Marcelle Dumont, the blacksmith, extending his burly form on the grass the more thoroughly to enjoy his pipe.

"Shames Tougall," said Donald Bane, in an undertone, and with the deliberate slowness of his race, "what does he mean by soopy?"

"Tonal'," replied Dougall with equal deliberation, "ye'd petter ask his nainsel'."

"It be de French for *supper*," said Salamander, who overheard the question.

"Humph!" ejaculated Dougall and Bane in unison; but they vouchsafed no further indication of the state of their minds.

"You're a true prophet, Big Otter," said Lumley, as a low rumbling of distant thunder broke the silence of the night, which would have been profound but for our voices, the crackling of the fire, and the tinkle of a neighbouring rill.

Soon afterwards we observed a faint flash of lightning, which was followed by another and deeper rumble of heaven's artillery. Looking up through the branches we perceived that the sky had become overcast with heavy clouds.

Suddenly there came a blinding flash of lightning, as if the sun in noonday strength had burst through the black sky. It was followed instantly by thick, almost palpable darkness, and by a crash so tremendous that I sprang up with a sort of idea that the end of the world had come. The crash was prolonged in a series of rolling, bumping thunders, as though giants were playing bowls with worlds on the floor of heaven. Gradually the echoing peals subsided into sullen mutterings and finally died away.

* * * * *

CHAPTER SEVEN.

A Tremendous Storm and Other Experiences.

It need hardly be said that we all sprang up when the thunder-clap shook the earth, and began hastily to make preparation for the coming storm. The broad flat branches of a majestic pine formed a roof to our encampment. Dragging our provisions and blankets as near as possible to the stem of the tree, we covered them up with one of our oiled-cloths, which were somewhat similar in appearance and texture to the tarpaulings of seafaring men, though light in colour. Then we ran down to the lake, carried all our goods hastily to the same spot, covered them up in like manner, and finally dragged our boat as far up on the beach as possible.

Several blinding flashes and deafening peals saluted us while we were thus employed, but as yet not a drop of rain or sigh of wind disturbed us, and we were congratulating ourselves on having managed the matter so promptly, when several huge drops warned us to seek shelter.

"That will do, boys," cried Lumley, referring to the boat, "she's safe."

"*Voilà! vite!*" shouted Marcelle, our volatile son of Vulcan, as the first big drops of rain descended on him.

He sprang towards the sheltering tree with wild activity. So, indeed, did we all, but the rain was too quick for us. Down it came with the suddenness and fury of a shower-bath, and most of us were nearly drenched before we reached our pine. There was a good deal of shouting and laughter at first, but the tremendous forces of nature that had been let loose were too overwhelming to permit of continued levity. In a few minutes the ground near our tree became seamed with little glancing rivulets, while the rain continued to descend like straight heavy rods of crystal which beat on the earth with a dull persistent roar. Ere long the saturated soil refused to drink in the superabundance, and the crystal rods, descending into innumerable pools, changed the roar into the plash of many waters.

We stood close together for some time, gazing at this scene in silent solemnity, when a few trickling streams began to fall upon us, showing that our leafy canopy, thick though it was, could not protect us altogether from such a downpour.

"We'd better rig up one of the oiled-cloths, and get under it," I suggested.

"Do so," said our chief.

Scarcely had he spoken when a flash of lightning, brighter than any that had gone before, revealed to us the fact that the distant part of the hitherto placid lake was seething with foam.

"A squall! Look out!" shouted Lumley, grasping the oiled-cloth we were about to spread.

Every one shouted and seized hold of something under the strong conviction that action of some sort was necessary to avert danger. But all our voices were silenced in a dreadful roar of thunder which, as Donald Bane afterwards remarked, seemed to split the universe from stem to stern. This was instantly followed by a powerful whirlwind which caught our oiled-cloth, tore it out of our hands, and whisked it up into the tree-tops, where it stuck fast and flapped furiously, while some of our party were thrown down, and others seemed blown away altogether as they ran into the thick bush for shelter.

For myself, without any definite intentions, and scarce knowing what I was about, I seized and clung to the branches of a small tree with the tenacity of a drowning man—unable to open my eyes while sticks and

70

leaves, huge limbs of trees and deluges of water flew madly past, filling my mind with a vague impression that the besom of destruction had become a veritable reality, and that we were all about to be swept off the face of the earth together.

Strange to say, in this crisis I felt no fear. I suppose I had not time or power to think at all, and I have since that day thought that God perhaps thus mercifully sends relief to His creatures in their direst extremity—just as He sends relief to poor human beings, when suffering intolerable pain, by causing stupor.

The outburst was as short-lived as it was furious. Suddenly the wind ceased; the floods of rain changed to slight droppings, and finally stopped altogether, while the thunder growled itself into sullen repose in the far distance.

But what a scene of wreck was left behind! We could not of course, see the full extent of the mischief, for the night still remained intensely dark, but enough was revealed in the numerous uprooted trees which lay all round us within the light of our rekindled camp-fire. From most of these we had been protected by the great pine under which we had taken shelter, though one or two had fallen perilously near to us—in one case falling on and slightly damaging our baggage.

Our first anxiety, of course, was our boat, towards which we ran as if by one impulse, the instant the wind had subsided.

To our horror it was gone!

Only those who know what it is to traverse hundreds of leagues of an almost tenantless wilderness, and have tried to push a few miles through roadless forests that have grown and fallen age after age in undisturbed entanglement since the morning of creation, can imagine the state of our minds at this discovery.

"Search towards the woods, men," said Lumley, who, whatever he might have felt, was the only one amongst us who seemed unexcited. We could trace no sign of anxiety in the deep tones of his steady voice.

It was this quality—I may remark in passing—this calm, equable flow of self-possession in all circumstances, no matter how trying, that rendered our young leader so fit for the work with which he had been entrusted, and which caused us all to rely on him with unquestioning confidence. He never seemed uncertain how to act even in the most desperate circumstances, and he never gave way to discontent or depression. A gentle, good-humoured expression usually played on his countenance, yet he could look stern enough at times, and even fierce, as we all knew.

While we were stumbling in the dark in the direction indicated, we heard the voice of Salamander shouting:—

"Here it am! De bot—busted on de bank!"

And "busted" it certainly was, as we could feel, for it was too dark to see.

"Fetch a blazing stick, one of you," cried Lumley.

A light revealed the fact that our boat, in being rolled bodily up the bank by the gale, had got several of her planks damaged and two of her ribs broken.

"Let's be thankful," I said, on further examination, "that no damage has been done to keel or gun'le."

"Nor to stem or stern-post," added Lumley. "Come, we shan't be delayed more than a day after all."

He was right. The whole of the day that followed the storm we spent in repairing the boat, and drying such portions of the goods as had got wet, as well as our own garments. The weather turned out to be bright and warm, so that when we lay down to rest, everything was ready for a start at the earliest gleam of dawn.

"Lumley," said I, next day, as we rested after a good spell at the oars, "what would have become of us if our boat had been smashed to pieces, or bodily blown away?"

"Nothing very serious would have become of us, I think," he replied with an amused look.

"But consider," I said; "we are now hundreds of miles away from Muskrat House—our nearest neighbour—with a dense wilderness and no roads between. Without a boat we could neither advance nor retreat. We might, of course, try to crawl along river banks and lake shores, which would involve the wading or swimming of hundreds of rivulets and rivers, with provisions and blankets on our backs, and even then winter would be down on us, and we should all be frozen to death before the end of the journey. Besides, even if we were to escape, how could we ever show face after leaving all our supply of goods and stores to rot in the wilderness?"

"Truly," replied my friend with a short laugh, "the picture you paint is not a lively one, but it is I who ought to ask *you* to consider. There are many ways in which we might overcome our supposed difficulties. I will explain; and let me begin by pointing out that your first error lies in conceiving an improbability and an impossibility. In the first place it is improbable that our boat should get 'smashed to pieces.' Such an event seldom occurs in river navigation, except in the case of going over something like Niagara. In the second place it is impossible that a boat should be blown bodily away. But let us suppose that, for the sake of argument, something of the kind had happened, and that our boat was damaged beyond repair, or lost; could we not, think you, fabricate a couple of birch-bark canoes in a country where such splendid birch-trees grow, and with these proceed to our destination?"

"Very true," said I, "that did not occur to me; but," I continued, waxing argumentative, "what if there had been no birch-trees in this part of the country?"

"Why then, Max, there would be nothing to prevent our placing most of our goods *en cache*, construct a small portable raft for crossing streams, and start off each man with a small load for Big Otter's home, at which we should arrive in a week or two, and there set about the erection of huts to shelter us, begin a fishery, and remain until winter should set fast the lakes and rivers, cover the land with snow, and thus enable us to go back for our goods, and bring them forward on sledges, with aid, perhaps, from the red-men."

"True, true, Lumley, that might be done."

"Or," continued my friend, "we might stay where the disaster overtook us, remain till winter, and send Big Otter on to tell his people that we were coming. When one plan fails, you know, all you've got to do is to try another. There is only one sort of accident that might cause us a deal of trouble, and some loss—and that is, our boat getting smashed and upset in a rapid, and our goods scattered. Even in that case we might recover much of what could swim, but lead and iron would be lost, and powder damaged. However we won't anticipate evil. Look! there is a sight that ought to banish all forebodings from our minds."

He pointed as he spoke to an opening ahead of us, which revealed a beautiful little lake, whose unruffled surface was studded with picturesque bush-clad islets. Water-fowl of many kinds were swimming about on its surface, or skimming swiftly over it. It seemed so peaceful that I was led to think of it as a miniature paradise.

"Come, Henri, chante, sing," cried Lumley, with a touch of enthusiasm in eye and tone.

Our carpenter, Coppet, was by general consent our leading singer. He possessed a sweet tenor voice, and always responded to a call with a willingness that went far to counteract the lugubrious aspect of his visage. On this occasion he at once struck up the canoe-song, "*A la claire fontaine*," which, besides being plaintive and beautiful, seemed to me exceedingly appropriate, for we were at that time crossing a height of land, and the clear, crystal waters over which we skimmed formed indeed the fountain-head of some of the great northern rivers.

The sudden burst of song had a wonderful effect upon the denizens of Clear Lake, as we named the sheet of water; for, after a brief momentary pause in their chatter—as if of incredulity and blazing surprise—they all arose at once in such myriads that the noise of their wings was not unlike what I may style muffled thunder.

Before the song was well finished we had reached the other end of the lakelet, and found that a deep river ran out of it in a nor'easterly direction. The current of the river was powerful, and we had not proceeded many miles down its course when we came to a series of turbulent rapids.

As we entered them I could not help recalling Lumley's remarks about the risks we ran in descending rapids; but no thought of actual danger occurred to me until I saw Blondin, who was our bowman, draw in his oar, grasp a long pole with which he had provided himself, and stand up in the bow, the better to look out inquiringly ahead.

Now, it must be explained that the bowman's is the most important post in river navigation in the Nor'-west—equal, at all events, to that of steersman. In fact the two act in concert; the bowman, whose position commands the best view of rocks and dangers ahead, giving direction, and the watchful steersman acting sympathetically with his long oar or sweep, so that should the bowman with his pole thrust the head of the boat violently to the right the steersman sweeps its stern sharply to the left, thus causing the craft to spin round and shoot aside from the danger, whatever it may be. Of course the general flow and turmoil of a rapid indicates pretty clearly to skilled eyes where the deepest water lies; nevertheless, in spite of knowledge, skill, and experience, disasters will happen at times.

"Monsieur," said Blondin in French to Lumley, as we gained a smooth piece of water at the foot of a short rapid, "I know not the rocks ahead. It may be well to land and look."

"Do so, Blondin."

We ran the boat's head on shore, and while the bowman and our leader went to look at the rapids in advance, most of our men got out their pipes and began to chat quietly.

Our scouts quickly returned, saying that the rapids, though rough, were practicable. Soon we were among them, darting down with what would have seemed, to any inexperienced eye, perilous velocity. The river at the place was about a hundred yards wide, with an unusually rugged channel, but with a distinctly marked run—deep and tortuous—in the middle. On both sides of the run, sweeping and curling surges told of rocks close to the surface, and in many places these showed black edges above water, which broke the stream into dazzling foam.

"Have a care, Blondin," said our chief, in a warning voice, as the bowman made a sudden and desperate shove with his pole. A side current had swept us too far in the direction of a forbidding ledge, to touch on which might have been fatal. But Henri Coppet, who acted as steersman as well as carpenter, was equal to the occasion. He bent his lanky form almost double, took a magnificent sweep with the oar, and seconded Blondin's shove so ably that we passed the danger like an arrow, with nothing but a slight graze.

That danger past we were on the brink of another, almost before we had time to think. At the time I remember being deeply impressed, in a confused way, with the fact that, whatever might await us below, there was now no possibility of our returning up stream. We were emphatically "in for it," and our only hope lay in the judgment, boldness, and capacity of the two men who guided our frail bark—doubly frail, it seemed to me, when contrasted with the waters that surged around, and the solid rocks that appeared to bar our way in all directions. Even some of our men at the oars, whose only duty was to obey orders promptly, began to show symptoms of anxiety, if not of fear.

"Smooth water ahead," muttered Lumley, pointing to a small lake into which the turbulent river ran about a quarter of a mile further down.

"All right soon," I said, but just as I spoke the boat lightly touched a rock. Blondin saw that there was not sufficient depth in a passage which he had intended to traverse. With a shout to the steersman he thrust his pole over the side with all his might. The obedient craft turned as if on a pivot, and would have gone straight into a safe stream in another second, if Blondin's pole had not stuck fast either in mud or between two rocks.

In a moment our bowman was whisked over the side as if he had been a feather. Letting go the pole he caught the gunwale and held on. The boat was carried broadside on the rocks, and the gushing water raised her upper side so high that she was on the point of rolling over when all of us—I think instinctively—sprang to that side and bore her down.

"Over the side, some of you," cried Lumley, leaping into the water on the lower side, followed by six of us, including myself. Some of us were breast deep; others, on rocks, stood higher.

"Now—together—shove!—and hold on!"

There was no need to give us the latter caution.

Our boat shot into deep water and we all held on for life. Fortunately the more open part of the rapid had been gained. The steersman without aid could keep us in deep water, and, before we had fairly scrambled back into our places, we were floating safely on the quiet lake into which the river ran.

You may be sure that we had matter not only for gratulation but for conversation that night at supper; for, after discussing our recent adventure in all its phases, nearly every one of our party had numerous similar incidents to tell of—either as having occurred to himself, or to his friends. But the pleasure of that night's intercourse and repose was materially diminished by a pest with which for some time previously we had not been much afflicted.

Who has not heard of mosquitoes? We may inform those who have never seen or felt them that they are peculiarly virulent and numerous and vicious and bloodthirsty in the swampy lands of North America, and that night we had got into a region of swamps. It may also, perhaps, be unknown to some people that mosquitoes do not slumber—unless, indeed, they do it on a preconcerted plan of relieving guard. Either there is a "day and night shift" or they do not rest at all. As a consequence *we* did not rest. Groans and maledictions were the order of the night. We spent much time in slapping our own faces, and immolated hundreds of the foe at each slap, but thousands came on to refill the ranks. We buried our heads under our blankets, but could not sleep for suffocation. Some of the men left their faces exposed, went to sleep in desperate exhaustion, after hours of fruitless warfare, and awoke with eyes all but shut up, and cheeks like dumplings. Others lay down to leeward of the fire and spent the night in a compound experience of blood-sucking and choking. One ingenious man—I think it was Salamander—wrapped his visage in a kerchief, leaving nothing exposed save the point of his nose for breathing purposes. In the morning he arose with something like a huge strawberry on the end of his prominent feature.

Indeed, it was a wearing night to follow such a trying day!

* * * * *

CHAPTER EIGHT.

Deep in the Wilderness we find our Home which is Shared with the Wild Beast, the Wild Bird, and the Savage.

Availing myself now of that wonderful power which we possess of projecting the mind instantaneously through space and time, I will leave our adventurous fur-traders, and, conveying my reader still deeper into the heart of the great wilderness, set him down on the margin of one of those lesser sheets of water which lie some distance in a south-westerly direction from that mighty fresh-water ocean called Athabasca.

This lake, although small when compared with the vast reservoirs which stud those northern wilds, is, nevertheless, of goodly dimensions, being about six miles in diameter, and studded here and there with numerous islets, some of which are almost bare rocks of a few yards in extent, while others are not less than a quarter of a mile in circumference, and thickly wooded to the edge.

It is a somewhat peculiar lake. It does not lie, as many lakes do, in the bottom of a valley, from which the spectator lifts his eye to surrounding heights, but rests in a little hollow on a height of land from many points of which the eye looks down on the surrounding low country. It is true, that in one direction, westward, a line of distant blue hills is seen, which are obviously higher than our lake, for the land rises gently towards them; but when you ascend a wooded knoll close by, the summit of which is free from underwood, it is seen at a glance that on all other sides the land is below you, and your eye takes in at one grand sweep all round the compass a view of woodland and plain, mound and morass, lake, river, and rivulet, such as is probably unequalled—certainly unsurpassed—in any other part of the known world.

Solitude profound—as far as men and their works are concerned—marked this lovely region at the time of our arrival, though there was the most telling evidence of exuberant animal life everywhere, to the ear as well as to the eye; for the air was vocal with the plaintive cries and whistling wings of wild-fowl which sported about in blissful enjoyment of their existence, while occasional breaks in the glassy surface of the water, and numerous widening circles, told that fish were not less jovial in the realms below. This was at last the longed-for Lake Wichikagan.

Man, however, was not altogether absent, though less obviously present, at that time. At the extreme western end of the lake, where the view of the regions beyond was most extensive as well as most beautiful, there was a bright green patch of land, free from underwood as well as trees—a sort of natural lawn—which extended with a gentle slope towards the lake; ending in a pebbly beach on which the waters rested so calm and pure that it was difficult to distinguish the line where dry land and water met.

A little to the right of this beautiful spot there grew a small clump of bushes, and in the midst of these there crouched two Indians. One was middle-aged, the other was entering on the period of early manhood, and a strongly marked resemblance in feature and form indicated plainly that they stood to each other in the relation of father and son. Both were clothed in leather, with the usual ornamentation of beads, scalp-locks, and feathers. Their faces, however, were not disfigured with war-paint— a sign that at that time they were at peace with all mankind.

It might have struck an observer, however, that for men of peace they were in suspiciously warlike attitudes. The elder savage stooped low to conceal himself behind the foliage, and held a long single-barrelled gun in readiness for instant action, while the youth, also stooping low, held an arrow ready fitted to his short bow. The eyes of both glared with expressions that might have been indicative of joy, hope, hate, revenge, expectation, or anything else you please—for a glare is unquestionably an ambiguous expression at the best, needing a context to expound it.

"Let two die," muttered the elder redskin—of course in his own tongue. (I had the details from his own lips afterwards, and translate them as literally as may be.)

"Ho!" replied the son, without moving his glare from the direction from which the two doomed ones were expected to emerge.

Presently a flock of grey wild-geese came majestically along, close to the margin of the lake—flying low, as well as slow, and following the curvings of the shore as if in search of a suitable feeding-place at which to alight. The green of the natural lawn had evidently attracted these birds, for they skimmed over the bushes behind which our Indians crouched almost within pistol-shot.

Like statues the red-men stood until the geese were over them; then an arrow from the son's bow quivered in the heart of one bird, and brought it fluttering heavily to the ground. At the same instant the echoes around answered to the father's gun, and another goose lay dead upon the sward.

"Waugh!" exclaimed both Indians as they stepped forth and picked up their game.

These sons of the wilderness were not, however, very communicative, for they spake never a word more. Perhaps they were hungry, and it is well-known that hungry men are not sociable. At all events they maintained a profound silence while they cut down a small decayed tree, made a good fire, and prepared dinner, or—as the sun was beginning to decline at the time—I may call it supper.

The mode of preparation was simple. Of course they plucked the geese; an operation which revealed the fact that both birds were plump and fat. Next they split them open with their scalping-knives, and, going down to the lake, cleaned them out with the same weapons. Then, transfixing them on two pieces of stick, after the manner of red-men, they stuck them up before the fire to roast. The roasting did not take long, for they were either partial to underdone food or impatient, and began at once upon such portions of the birds as were first ready, by cutting them off and chewing away without removing the remainder of the roasts from the fire. By degrees the solid parts were devoured. Then the drumsticks and other extremities were picked; after that the merry-thoughts and smaller bones were cleaned, and not until every fragment of edible matter was consumed did father or son cease his toil or utter a word.

"Waugh!" exclaimed the father at last, regarding the skeleton of his meal with a sad look, as if grieved that all was over.

"Hough!" responded the son with a sigh of satisfaction, as he wiped his fingers on the grass and sheathed his scalping-knife. Then, searching in their little pouches, which contained flint steel, tinder, etcetera, they drew forth two little stone pipes with wooden stems, which they filled and began to smoke.

The first whiff seemed to break the magic spell which had hitherto kept them silent. With another emphatic "Waugh!" the elder savage declared that the goose was good; that it distended him pleasantly, and that it warmed the cockles of his heart—or words to that effect. To which the son replied with a not less emphatic "Hough!" that he was entirely of the same opinion. Thus, whiffing gently, letting the smoke slowly out of their mouths and trickling it through their nostrils, so as to get the full benefit—or or damage!—of the tobacco, those sons of the wilderness continued for some time to enjoy themselves, while the sun sank slowly towards the western horizon, converting every lake and pond, and every river and streamlet, into a sheet, or band, or thread of burnished gold. At last the elder savage removed his pipe and sent a final shot of smoke towards the sky with some vigour as he said, rather abruptly,—"Mozwa, my brother must be dead!"

"I hope not, father," returned the youth, whose name, Mozwa, signifies in the Cree language "moose-deer," and had been given to the lad because he possessed an unusual power of running great distances, and for long periods, at a sort of swinging trot that left all competitors of his tribe far behind.

"I also hope not," said his father, whose name was Maqua, or "bear," "but I am forced to think so, for when Big Otter promises he is sure to perform. He said to Waboose that he would be home before the berries were ripe. The berries are ripe and he is not home. Without doubt he is now chasing the deer in the happy hunting-grounds with his fathers."

Waboose, to whom this promise had been made, was a favourite niece of Big Otter, and had been named Waboose, or "rabbit," because she was pretty innocent, soft, and tender.

"My father," said Mozwa, rather solemnly, "Big Otter has not broken his word, for *all* the berries are not yet ripe."

He plucked a berry which chanced to be growing near his hand, as he spoke, and held it up to view.

"Waugh!" exclaimed the elder savage.

"Hough!" returned the younger.

What more might have been said at that time no one can tell, for the conversation was cut short by a sound which caused both Indians to listen with intense earnestness. Their eyes glittered like the eyes of serpents, and their nostrils dilated like those of the wild-horse, while each man gently moved his right hand towards his weapon.

And if the too inquisitive reader should ask me how I could possibly come to know all this, seeing that I was not there at the time, I reply that the whole matter was related to me with minute and dramatic power by young Mozwa himself not long afterwards.

There was indeed ground for the excitement and earnest attention of those red-men, for the sweet and distant notes of a Canadian canoe-song had at that moment, for the first time, awakened the echoes of that part of the Great Nor'-west.

The two men were not indeed ignorant of the fact that such songs were sung by Canadian voyageurs—Maqua had even heard some of them hummed once by the men of Muskrat House, when, a good while before, he had paid a visit to that remote trading-post—but never before had father or son listened to the songs sung in full chorus as they now heard them.

Spell-bound they waited until the sound of oars mingled with the gradually strengthening song. Then their fingers closed convulsively upon their weapons and they sprang up.

"What does my son think?"

"He thinks that the white man may be on the war-path, and it behoves the red-man like the serpent to creep into the grass and lie still."

The elder savage shook his head.

"No, Mozwa. The white man never goes on the war-path, except to track down murderers. When he goes through the land he travels as the red-man's friend. Nevertheless, it is well to be on our guard."

As he spoke, the song, which had been increasing in strength every moment, suddenly burst forth with great power in consequence of the boat which bore the singers rounding a rocky point and coming into full view.

To sink into the grass, imitate the serpent and vanish from the scene, was the work of a few seconds on the part of Maqua and his son.

Meanwhile the boat, which I need scarcely say was ours, came sweeping grandly on, for the fineness of the evening, the calmness of the lake, the splendour of the scene, and the prospect of a good supper, to be followed by a good night's rest lent fresh vigour to the arms as well as to the voices of our men.

"Hold on a bit, boys," cried Jack Lumley, standing up in the stern and looking shoreward, "this seems a pretty good place to camp."

"There is a better place a few yards further on," said Big Otter, who pulled the stroke oar. "I know every foot of the country here. It is a soft—"

"What does Big Otter see?" asked Lumley, for the Indian had come to a sudden stop, and was gazing earnestly ahead.

84

"He sees the smoke of a fire."

"Is it likely to be the fire of an enemy?"

"No—more like to be the camp of some of my people, but their wigwams are two days beyond this lake. Perhaps hunters are out in this direction."

"We shall soon see—give way, lads!" said Lumley, sitting down.

In a few minutes the boat was on the beach. We sprang ashore, and hastened to the spot where a thin wreath of smoke indicated the remains of a camp-fire.

Of course we carried our arms, not knowing whom we should meet with.

After examining the spot carefully, Big Otter stood up and was about to speak to our chief, when a slight peculiar chirp was heard in the bushes. It is probable that we should have deemed it that of some small bird and paid no attention to it if our Indian had not suddenly bent his head on one side as if to listen. At the same time he replied to the chirp. Again the sound was heard, and Big Otter, turning round quickly, without uttering a word, entered the bushes and disappeared.

"Stand ready, lads!" said Lumley in a quiet voice, bringing forward the muzzle of his gun, "there's no saying what may come of this."

Scarcely had he spoken when a rustling was heard in the bushes. Next moment they were thrust aside and Big Otter reissued from them, followed by two Indians, whom he introduced to us as his brother and nephew. At the same time he gave us the gratifying information that his tribe had moved up from the region in which they usually dwelt for the purpose of hunting and fishing in the neighbourhood of the lake, and that the camp was not more than six or seven miles distant from the spot on which we stood.

To this Lumley replied by expressing his gratification at the news, and shaking hands with the two Indians, who, however, received the shake with some distrust and much surprise, until Big Otter explained the nature and meaning of the white man's salutation. He also explained the meaning of

"What cheer." On hearing which Maqua, not to be outdone in politeness, extended his hand for another shake, and exclaimed "Watchee!" with profound gravity. Mozwa, with some hesitation, imitated his father's example.

While we were thus pleasantly engaged, a sonorous trumpet sound was heard behind the clump of small trees near us. A moment later and two magnificent wild swans sailed over the tree-tops and above our heads. They made a tumultuously wild swoop to one side on discovering the near proximity of their enemy man but were too late. Almost before any of the party had time to move a muscle, two sharp cracks were heard, and both swans fell stone dead, with a heavy splash, at the margin of the lake.

It was our chief, Jack Lumley, who had brought them down with his double-barrelled fowling-piece. I have omitted to mention that Lumley was one of the noted crack-shots of the country at that time—noted not only for the deadly precision, but also for the lightning-like rapidity of his aim.

The Indians, albeit themselves pretty fair marksmen, were deeply impressed with this evidence of skill, and it went far to strengthen the influence which our chief's manly proportions and genial countenance had already begun to exercise.

"That's a good beginning, Lumley," said I, "for it not only impresses our new friends favourably, but provides excellent fresh meat for supper."

"Yonder comes better meat for supper," he replied, pointing towards a neighbouring height, where we could see the forms of two men approaching, with the carcase of a deer between them.

It was Donald Bane and James Dougall who had been thus successful. These sons of the Scottish Highlands, being ardent sportsmen as well as good marksmen, had been appointed to the post of hunters to our party, and were frequently sent ashore to procure fresh meat.

"The country is swarmin' wi' game, Muster Lumley," said Bane, as they came up, and flung down the deer. "Not only teer an' rabbits, but tucks an' geese, an' all sorts o' pirds. Moreover, Tougall, she got into a bog after wan o' the peasts, an' I thought I wass goin' to lose him altogither. 'Shames Tougall,' says I, 'don't you go anither step till I come to you, or you're a lost man,' but Shames went on—he was always an obstinate loon—"

"Dat is true," remarked Salamander.

"Hold yer noise!" said Bane. "Well, sur, Tougall went on, an' sure enough the very next step down he went up to the neck—"

"No, Tonald," interrupted Dougall, "it wass not up to the neck; it wass only to the waist. The nixt after that it wass up to the neck, but *then* I wass soomin'."

"Ye would hey bin soomin' yet, Shames, if I had not pulled ye oot," said his friend.

"Oo ay, Tonald Pane. That iss true, but—"

"Well, Dougall," interrupted Lumley at this point, "it will be better to dry your garments than discuss the question just now. We will encamp here, so go to work, boys."

There was no need for more. During our long journey into these far-off wilds each man had fallen into his allotted place and work, and the force of habit had made us so like machines that I think if we had suddenly become a party of somnambulists we would have gone through the same actions each evening on landing.

Accordingly, Lumley and I gathered small branches and rekindled the Indians' fire, which had by that time almost gone out. Marcelle Dumont being professionally a forger of axes, and Henri Coppet, being an artificer in wood, went off to cut down trees for firewood; and Donald Bane with his friend set about cutting up and preparing the venison, while Blondin superintended and assisted Salamander and the others in landing the cargo, and hauling up the boat.

"Max," said Lumley to me that evening during an interval in our devotion to steaks and marrow-bones, "look around for a moment if

CHAPTER NINE.

A Bright Apparition—Followed by Rumours of War.

While we were thus feasting and chatting on the green sward of the region which seemed destined to be our future home, an object suddenly appeared among the bushes, near the edge of the circle of light cast by our camp-fire.

This object was by no means a frightful one, yet it caused a sensation in the camp which could hardly have been intensified if we had suddenly discovered a buffalo with the nose of an elephant and the tail of a rattlesnake. For one moment we were all struck dumb; then we all sprang to our feet, but we did not seize our firearms—oh no!—for there, half concealed by the bushes, and gazing at us in timid wonder, stood a pretty young girl, with a skin much fairer than usually falls to the lot of Indian women, and with light brown hair as well as bright blue eyes. In all other respects—in costume, and humble bearing—she resembled the women of the soil.

I would not willingly inflict on the reader too much of my private feelings and opinions, but perhaps I may be excused for saying that I fell over head and ears in love with this creature at once! I make no apology for being thus candid. On the contrary, I am prepared rather to plume myself on the quick perception which enabled me not only to observe the beauty of the girl's countenance, but, what is of far more importance, the inherent goodness which welled from her loving eyes.

Yes, reader, call me an ass if you will, but I unblushingly repeat that I fell—tumbled—plunged headlong in love with her. So did every other man in the camp! There is this to be said in excuse for us, that we had not seen any members of the fair sex for many months, and that the sight of this brilliant specimen naturally aroused many pleasant recollections of cousins, sisters, nieces, aunts, mothers, grandmothers—well, perhaps I am going too far; though, after all, the tender, loving-kindness in this girl's eyes might well have suggested grandmothers!

Before any of us could recover the use of our limbs, Big Otter had glided rapidly towards the girl. Grasping her by the hand, he led her towards Lumley, and introduced her as his sister's daughter, Waboose.

The red-man was evidently proud as well as fond of his fair niece, and equally clear did it become in a short time that the girl was as fond and proud of him.

"Your relative is very fair," said Lumley. "She might almost have been the daughter of a white man."

"She *is* the daughter of a white man."

"Indeed!"

"Yes; her father was a white hunter who left his people and came to dwell with us and married my sister. He was much loved and respected by us. He lived and hunted and went on the war-path with us for many years—then he was killed."

"In war?" I asked, beginning to feel sympathetic regard for the father of one who had stirred my heart to—but, I forget. It is not my intention to bore the reader with my personal feelings.

"No," answered the Indian. "He perished in attempting to save his wife from a dangerous rapid. He brought her to the bank close to the head of a great waterfall, and many hands were stretched out to grasp her. She was saved, but the strength of the brave pale-face was gone, and we knew it not. Before we could lay hold of his hand the current swept him away and carried him over the falls."

"How sad!" said Lumley. "What was the name of this white man?"

"He told us that his name was Weeum—but," said the Indian, turning abruptly to Waboose, whose countenance betrayed feelings which were obviously aroused by other matters than this reference to her lost father, "my child has news of some sort. Let her speak."

Thus permitted, Waboose opened her lips for the first time—disclosing a double row of bright little teeth in the act—and said that she had been sent by her mother in search of Maqua and his son, as she had reason to believe that the camp was in danger of being attacked by Dogrib Indians.

On hearing this, Maqua and Mozwa rose, picked up their weapons, and without a word of explanation entered the bushes swiftly and disappeared.

Big Otter looked after them for a moment or two in grave silence.

"You had better follow them," suggested Lumley. "If you should require help, send a swift messenger back and we will come to you."

The Indian received this with a quiet inclination of the head, but made no reply. Then, taking his niece by the hand, he led her into the bushes where his relatives had entered and, like them, disappeared.

"It seems like a dream," said I to Lumley, as we all sat down again to our steaks and marrow-bones.

"What seems like a dream, Max—the grub?"

"No, the girl."

"Truly, yes. And a very pleasant dream too. Almost as good as this bone."

"Oh! you unsentimental, unsympathetic monster. Does not the sight of a pretty young creature like that remind you of home, and all the sweet refining influences shed around it by woman?"

"I cannot say that it does—hand me another; no, not a little thing like that, a big one full of marrow, so—. You see, old boy, a band of beads round the head, a sky-blue cloth bodice, a skirt of green flannel reaching only to the knees, cloth leggings ornamented with porcupine quills and moccasined feet, do not naturally suggest my respected mother or sisters."

For the first time in our acquaintance I felt somewhat disgusted with my friend's levity, and made no rejoinder. He looked at me quickly, with slightly raised eyebrows, and gave a little laugh.

With a strong effort I crushed down my feelings, and said in a tone of forced gaiety:—

"Well, well, things strike people in strangely different lights. I thought not of the girl's costume but her countenance."

"Come, then, Max," returned my friend, with that considerate good nature which attracted men so powerfully to him, "I admit that the girl's face might well suggest the thought of dearer faces in distant lands—and especially her eyes, so different from the piercing black orbs of Indian squaws. Did you note the—the softness, I was going to say truthfulness, of her strangely blue eyes?"

Did I note them! The question seemed to me so ridiculous that I laughed, by way of reply.

I observed that Lumley cast on me for the second time a sharp inquiring glance, then he said:—

"But I say, Max, we must have our arms looked to, and be ready for a sudden call. You know that I don't love fighting. Especially at the commencement of our sojourn would I avoid mixing myself up with Indians' quarrels; but if our guide comes back saying that their camp is in danger, we must help him. It would never do, you know, to leave women and children to the mercy of ruthless savages."

"Leave woman and children!" I exclaimed vehemently, thinking of only one woman at the moment, "I should *think* not!"

The tone of indignation in which I said this caused my friend to laugh outright.

"Well, well," he said, in a low tone, "it's a curious complaint, and not easily cured."

What he meant was at the time a mystery to me. I have since come to understand.

"I suppose you'll all agree with me, lads," said Lumley to the men who sat eating their supper on the opposite side of the fire, and raising his voice, for we had hitherto been conversing in a low tone, "if Big Otter's friends need help we'll be ready to give it?"

Of course a hearty assent was given, and several of the men, having finished supper, rose to examine their weapons.

The guns used by travellers in the Great Nor'-west in those days were long single-barrels with flint-locks, the powder in which was very apt to get wet through priming-pans and touch-holes, so that frequent inspection was absolutely necessary.

As our party consisted of twelve men, including ourselves, and each was armed—Lumley and myself with double-barrelled fowling-pieces—we were able, if need be, to fire a volley of fourteen shots. Besides this, my chief and I carried revolvers, which weapons had only just been introduced into that part of the country. We were therefore prepared to lend effective aid to any whom we thought it right to succour.

Scarcely had our arrangements been made when the lithe agile form of Mozwa glided into the camp and stood before Lumley. The lad tried hard to look calm, grave, and collected, as became a young Indian brave, but the perspiration on his brow and his labouring chest told that he had been running far at the utmost speed, while a wild glitter in his dark eye betrayed strong emotion. Pointing in the direction whence he had come, he uttered the name—"Big Otter."

"All right. I understand you," said Lumley, springing up. "Now, boys, sharp's the word; we will go to the help of our guide. But two of you must stay behind to guard our camp. Do you, Donald Bane and James Dougall, remain and keep a bright look-out."

"Is it to stop here, we are?" asked Bane, with a mutinous look.

"Yes," exclaimed our leader so sharply that the mutinous look faded.

"An' are we to be left behind," growled Dougall, "when there's fightin' to be done?"

"I have no time for words, Dougall," said Lumley in a low voice, "but if you don't at once set about preparation to defend the camp, I'll give you some fighting to do that you won't relish."

Dougall had no difficulty in understanding his leader's meaning. He and his friend at once set about the required preparations.

"Now then, Mozwa," said Lumley.

The young Indian, who had remained erect and apparently unobservant, with his arms crossed on his still heaving chest, turned at once and went off at a swift trot, followed by all our party with the exception of the ill-pleased Highlanders, who, in their eagerness for the fray, did not perceive that theirs might be a post of the greatest danger, as it certainly was one of trust.

"Tonald," said Dougall, sitting down and lighting his pipe after we were gone, "I wass vera near givin' Muster Lumley a cood threshin'."

"Hum! it's well ye didn't try, Shames."

"An' what for no?"

"Because he's more nor a match for ye."

"I don't know that Tonald. I'm as stout a man as he is, whatever."

"Oo ay, so ye are, Shames; but ye're no a match for him. He's been to school among thae Englishers, an' can use his fists, let me tell you."

At this Dougall held up a clenched hand, hard and knuckly from honest toil, that was nearly as big as a small ham. Regarding it with much complacency he said, slowly:—

"An' don't you think, Tonald, that I could use my fist too?"

"Maybe you could, in a kind o' way," returned the other, also filling his pipe and sitting down; "but I'll tell ye what Muster Lumley would do to you, Shames, if ye offered to fight him. He would dance round you like a cooper round a cask; then, first of all, he would flatten your nose—which is flat enough already, whatever—wi' wan hand, an' he'd drive in your stummick wi' the other. Then he would give you one between the two eyes an' raise a bridge there to make up for the wan he'd destroyed on your nose, an' before you had time to sneeze he would put a rainbow under your left eye. Or ever you had time to wink he would put another under your right eye, and if that didn't settle you he would give you a finishin' dig in the ribs, Shames, trip up your heels, an' lay you on the ground, where I make no doubt you would lie an' meditate whether it wass worth while to rise up for more."

"All that would be verra unpleasant, Tonald," said Dougall, with a humorous glance from the corners of his small grey eyes, "but I duffer with ye in opeenion."

"You would duffer in opeenion with the Apostle Paul if he wass here," said the other, rising, as his pipe was by that time well alight, and resuming his work, "but we'll better obey Muster Lumley's orders than argufy about him."

"I'll agree with you there, Tonald, just to convince you that I don't always duffer," said the argumentative Highlander, rising to assist his not less argumentative friend.

The two men pursued their labour in silence, and in the course of an hour or so had piled all the baggage in a circle in the middle of the open lawn, so as to form a little fortress, into which they might spring and keep almost any number of savages at bay for some time; because savages, unlike most white men, have no belief in that "glory" which consists in rushing on certain death, in order to form a bridge of dead bodies over which comrades may march to victory. Each savage is, for the most part, keenly alive to the importance of guarding his own life, so that a band of savages seldom makes a rush where certain death awaits the leaders. Hence our two Highlanders felt quite confident of being able to hold their little fort with two guns each and a large supply of ammunition.

Meanwhile Mozwa continued his rapid trot through wood and brake; over swamp, and plain, and grassy mound. Being all of us by that time strong in wind and limb, we followed him without difficulty.

"Lads, be careful," said Lumley, as we went along, "that no shot is fired, whatever happens, until I give the word. You see, Max," he continued in a lower tone, "nothing but the sternest necessity will induce me to shed human blood. I am here to open up trade with the natives, not to fight them, or mix myself up in their quarrels. At the same time it would be bad policy to stand aloof while the tribes we have come to benefit, and of which our guide is a member, are assailed by enemies. We must try what we can do to make peace, and risk something in the attempt."

Arrived at the Indian camp, we found a band of braves just on the point of leaving it, although by that time it was quite dark. The tribe—or rather that portion of it which was encamped in leathern wigwams, on one of the grassy mounds with which the country abounded—consisted of some hundred families, and the women and children were moving about in great excitement, while the warriors were preparing to leave. I was struck, however, by the calm and dignified bearing of one white-haired patriarch, who stood in the opening of his wigwam, talking to a number of the elder men and women who crowded round him. He was the old chief of the tribe; and, being no longer able to go on the war-path, remained with the aged men and the youths, whose duty it was to guard the camp.

"My children," he said, as we came up, "fear not. The Great Spirit is with us, for our cause is just. He has sent Big Otter back to us in good time, and, see, has He not also sent white men to help us?"

The war-party was detained on our arrival until we should hold a palaver with the old chief and principal braves. We soon ascertained that the cause of disagreement between the two tribes, and of the declaration of war, was a mere trifle, strongly resembling in that respect the causes of most wars among civilised nations! A brave of the one tribe had insultingly remarked that a warrior of the other tribe had claimed the carcase of a moose-deer which had been mortally wounded, and tracked, and slain by him, the insulter. The insulted one vowed that he shot the deer dead—he would scorn to wound a deer at all—and had left it in hiding until he could obtain assistance to fetch the meat. Young hotheads on both sides fomented the quarrel until older heads were forced to take the matter up; they became sympathetically inflamed, and, finally, war to the knife was declared. No blood had yet been shed, but it was understood by Big Otter's friends—who were really the injured party—that their foes had sent away their women and children, preparatory to a descent on them.

"Now, Salamander," said Lumley, who, although he had considerably increased his knowledge of the Indian language by conversing with the guide during our voyage, preferred to speak through an interpreter when he had anything important to say, "tell the old chief that this war-party must not go forth. Tell him that the great white chief who guides the affairs of the traders, has sent me to trade furs in this region, and that I will not permit fighting."

This was such a bold—almost presumptuous, way of putting the matter that the old red chief looked at the young white chief in surprise; but as there was neither bluster nor presumption in the calm countenance of Lumley—only firmness coupled with extreme good humour—he felt somewhat disconcerted.

"How will my white brother prevent war?" asked the old chief, whose name was Muskrat.

"By packing up my goods, and going elsewhere," replied Lumley directly, without an instant's hesitation, in the Indian tongue.

At this, there was an elongation of the faces of the men who heard it, and something like a soft groan from the squaws who listened in the background.

"That would be a sad calamity," said old Muskrat, "and I have no wish to fight; but how will the young white chief prevent our foes from attacking us?"

"Tell him, Salamander, that I will do so by going to see them."

"My young braves will be happy to go out under the guidance of so strong a warrior," returned Muskrat, quite delighted with the proposal.

"Nay, old chief, you mistake me, I will take no braves with me."

"No matter," returned Muskrat; "doubtless the white men and their guns will be more than a match for our red foes."

"Still you misunderstand," said Lumley. "I am no warrior, but a man of peace. I shall go without guns or knives—and alone, except that I will ask young Mozwa to guide me."

"Alone! unarmed!" murmured the old man, in astonishment almost too great for expression. "What can one do against a hundred with weapons?"

"You shall see," said Lumley, with a light laugh as he turned to me.

"Now, Max, don't speak or remonstrate, like a good fellow; we have no time to discuss, only to act. I find that Muskrat's foes speak the same dialect as himself, so that an interpreter is needless. I carry two revolvers in the breast of my coat. You have a clasp-knife in your pocket; make me a present of it, will you? Thanks. Now, have our men in readiness for instant action. Don't let them go to rest, but let them eat as much, and as long, as they choose. Keep the old chief and his men amused with long yarns about what we mean to do in these regions, and don't let any one follow me. Keep your mind easy. If I don't return in three hours, you may set off to look for me, though it will I fear be of no use by that time; and, stay, if you should hear a pistol-shot, run out with all our men towards it. Now, Mozwa, lead on to the enemy's camp."

The young Indian, who was evidently proud of the trust reposed in him, and cared nothing for danger, stalked into the forest with the look and bearing of a dauntless warrior.

* * * * *

CHAPTER TEN.

Salamander Gives and Receives a Surprise, and War is Averted by Wise Diplomacy.

It has been already said that our interpreter, Salamander, possessed a spirit of humour slightly tinged with mischief, which, while it unquestionably added to the amusement of our sojourn in those lands, helped not a little to rouse our anxieties.

On returning to our men, after parting from Lumley, for the purpose of giving them their instructions, I found that Salamander was missing, and that no one could tell where he had gone. I caused a search to be made for him, which was unsuccessful, and would have persevered with it if there had not pressed upon me the necessity of obeying my chief's orders to keep the savages amused. This I set about doing without delay, and having, like my friend, been a diligent student of the language on the journey, found that I succeeded, more than I had ventured to hope for, in communicating my ideas.

As the disappearance of Salamander, however, was the subject which exercised my mind most severely at the time, and as he afterwards gave me a full account of the cause in detail, I shall set it down here.

Being possessed that evening, as he confessed, with a spirit of restlessness, and remembering that our two Highlanders had been left to guard the camp at Lake Wichikagan, he resolved to pay them a visit. The distance, as I have said elsewhere, was not much more than six miles—a mere trifle to one who was as fleet as a young deer and strong as an old bear. He soon traversed the ground and came up to the camp.

At first he meant merely to give the men a surprise, but the spirit to which I have already referred induced him to determine on giving them a fright. Approaching very cautiously, therefore, with this end in view, he found that things were admirably arranged for his purpose.

Donald Bane and James Dougall, having finished their fortress in the centre of the open lawn, as already described, returned to their fire, which, it may be remembered, was kindled close to the edge of the bushes. There they cooked some food and devoured it with the gusto of men who had well earned their supper. Thereafter, as a matter of course, they proceeded to enjoy a pipe.

The night, besides being fine and calm, was unusually warm, thereby inducing a feeling of drowsiness, which gradually checked the flow of conversation previously evoked by the pipes.

"It is not likely the redskins will come up here to give us a chance when there's such a lot of our lads gone to meet them," said Bane, with a yawn.

"I agree with you, Tonald," answered Dougall grumpily.

"It is quite new to hev you agreein' with me so much, Shames," returned Bane with another yawn.

"You are right. An' it is more lively to disagree, whatever," rejoined Dougall, with an irresistible, because sympathetic, yawn.

"Oo ay, that's true, Shames. Yie-a-ou!"

This yawn was so effusive that Dougall, refusing to be led even by sympathy, yawned internally with his lips closed and swallowed it.

The conversation dropped at this point, though the puffs went on languidly. As the men were extended at full-length, one on his side, the other on his back, it was not unnatural that, being fatigued, they should both pass from the meditative to the dreamy state, and from that to the unconscious.

It was in this condition that Salamander discovered them.

"Asleep at their posts!" he said mentally. "That deserves punishment."

He had crept on hands and knees to the edge of the bushes, and paused to contemplate the wide-open mouth of Bane, who lay on his back, and the prominent right ear of Dougall, whose head rested on his left arm. The débris of supper lay around them—scraps of pemmican, pannikins, spoons, knives, and the broken shells of teal-duck eggs which, having been picked up some time before, had gone bad.

Suddenly an inspiration—doubtless from the spirit of mischief—came over Salamander. There was one small unbroken egg on the ground near to Bane's elbow. Just over his head the branch of a bush extended. To genius everything comes handy and nothing amiss. Salamander tied the egg to a piece of small twine and suspended it to the twig in such fashion that the egg hung directly over Bane's wide-open mouth. At a glance he had seen that it was possible to lay a light hand on the inner end of the branch, and at the same time bend his mouth over Dougall's ear. He drew a long breath, for it was a somewhat delicate and difficult, being a duplicate, manoeuvre!

Pressing down the branch very slowly and with exceeding care, he guided the egg into Bane's mouth. He observed the precise moment when it touched the sleeper's tongue, and then exploded a yell into Dougall's ear that nearly burst the tympanum.

Bane's jaws shut with a snap instantly. Need we—no, we need not! Dougall leaped up with a cry that almost equalled that of Salamander. Both men rushed to the fortress and bounded into it, the one spurting out Gaelic expletives, the other rotten egg and bits of shell. They seized their guns and crouched, glaring through the various loopholes all round with finger on trigger, ready to sacrifice at a moment's notice anything with life that should appear. Indeed they found it difficult, in their excited condition, to refrain from blazing at nothing! Their friendly foe meanwhile had retired, highly delighted with his success. He had not done with them however. By no means! The spirit of mischief was still strong upon him, and he crept into the bushes to meditate.

"It wass an evil speerut, Shames," gasped Donald Bane, when he had nearly got rid of the egg. "Did you smell his preath?"

"No, Tonald, it wass not. Spirits are not corporeal, and cannot handle eggs, much less cram them down a man's throat. It wass the egg you did smell."

"That may be so, Shames, but it could not be a redskin, for he would be more likely to cram a scalpin' knife into my heart than an egg into my mouth."

"Iss it not dreamin' ye wass, an' tryin' to eat some more in your sleep? You wass always fond of overeatin' yourself—whativer—Tonald."

Before this question could be answered, another yell of the most appalling and complex nature rang out upon the night-air, struck them dumb, and seemed to crumple up their very hearts.

Salamander had been born with a natural gift for shrieking, and being of a sprightly disposition, had cultivated the gift in boyhood. Afterwards, being also a good mimic, he had made the subject a special study, with a view to attract geese and other game towards him. That he sometimes prostituted the talent was due to the touch of genius to which I have already referred.

When the crumpled-up organs began to recover, Bane said to Dougall, "Shames, this iss a bad business."

Dougall, having been caught twice that evening, was on his guard. He would not absolutely agree with his friend, but admitted that he was not far wrong.

Again the yell burst forth with intensified volume and complicated variation. Salamander was young; he did not yet know that it is possible to over-act.

"Shames!" whispered Bane, "I hev got a notion in my hid."

"I hope it's a coot w'an, Tonald, for the notions that usually git into it might stop there with advantage. They are not much to boast of."

"You shall see. Just you keep talkin' out now an' then as if I wass beside you, an' don't, whativer ye do, fire into the bushes."

"Ferry coot," answered Dougall.

Another moment, and Donald Bane glided over the parapet of their fort at the side nearest the lake; and, creeping serpent-fashion for a considerable distance round, gained the bushes, where he waited for a repetition of the cry. He had not long to wait. With that boldness, not to say presumption, which is the child of success, Salamander now began to make too many drafts on genius, and invented a series of howls so preposterously improbable that it was impossible for even the most credulous to believe them the natural cries of man, beast, demon, or monster.

Following up the sound, Donald Bane soon came to a little hollow where, in the dim light, he perceived Salamander's visage peering over a ridge in the direction of the fortress, his eyes glittering with glee and his mouth wide-open in the act of giving vent to the hideous cries. The Highlander had lived long in the wilderness, and was an adept in its ways. With the noiseless motion of a redskin he wormed his way through the underwood until close alongside of the nocturnal visitor, and then suddenly stopped a howl of more than demoniac ferocity by clapping a hand on Salamander's mouth.

With a convulsive wriggle the youth freed his mouth, and uttered a shriek of genuine alarm, but Bane's strong arm pinned him to the earth.

"Ye dirty loon," growled the man in great wrath, "wass you thinkin' to get the better of a Heelandman? Come along with ye. I'll give you a lesson that you'll not forget—whatever."

Despite his struggles, Bane held Salamander fast until he ceased to resist, when he grasped him by the collar, and led him towards the little fort.

At first, Salamander had been on the point of confessing the practical joke, but the darkness of the night induced him to hope for another escape from his position. He had not yet uttered a word; and, as he could not distinguish the features of the Highlander, it was possible, he thought, that the latter might have failed to recognise him. If he could give him the slip, he might afterwards deny having had anything to do with the affair. But it was not easy to give the slip to a man whose knuckly hand held him like a vice.

"Shames," said Bane as he came near the fortress, "I've cot the peast! come oot, man, an' fetch a stick wi' you. I'll ha'd 'im while you lay on."

Salamander, who understood well enough what he might expect, no sooner heard Dougall clambering over the barricade than he gathered himself up for a tremendous wriggle, but received such a fearful squeeze on the neck from the vice-like hand of his captor that he was nearly choked. At the moment a new idea flashed into his fertile brain. His head dropped suddenly to one side; his whole frame became limp, and he fell, as it were, in a heap on the ground, almost bringing the Highlander on the top of him.

"Oh! the miserable cratur," exclaimed Bane, relaxing his grasp with a feeling of self-reproach, for he had a strong suspicion that his captive really was Salamander. "I do believe I've killed him. Wow! Shames, man, lend a hand to carry him to the fire, and plow up a bit flame that we may see what we've gotten."

"Iss he tead, Tonald?" asked Dougall, in a pitiful tone, as he came forward.

"No, Shames, he's no tead yet. Take up his feet, man, an' I'll tak' his shouthers."

Dougall went to Salamander's feet, turned his back to them, and stooped to take them up as a man takes a wheelbarrow. He instantly received a kick, or rather a drive, from Salamander's soles that sent him sprawling on his hands and knees. Donald Bane, stooping to grasp the shoulder, received a buffet on the cheek, which, being unexpected, sent him staggering to the left, while the sly youth, springing to his feet bounded into the bushes on the right with a deep-toned roar ending in a laugh that threw all his previous efforts quite into the shade.

The Highlanders rose, but made no attempt to pursue.

"My friend," said Bane, softly, "if that wass not an evil speerut, I will be fery much surprised."

"No, Tonald, it wass *not* a speerut," replied the other, as they returned to their fortress. "Speeruts will not be kickin' an' slappin' like that; they are not corporeal."

While these scenes were enacting on the margin of Lake Wichikagan, Lumley and Mozwa arrived at the enemy's camp. It was a war-camp. All the women and children had been sent away, none but armed and painted braves remained.

They were holding a palaver at the time. The spot was the top of an open eminence which was so clear of underwood that the approach of a foe without being seen was an impossibility. Although the night was rather dark, Lumley and his guide had been observed the instant they came within the range of vision. No stir, however, took place in the camp, for it was instantly perceived that the strangers were alone. With the grave solemnity of redskin warriors, they silently awaited their coming. A small fire burned in their midst, for they made no attempt at concealment. They were prepared to fight at a moment's notice. The red flames gleamed on their dusky faces, and glittered in their glancing eyes, as Lumley and Mozwa strode boldly into the circle, and stood before the chief.

Intense surprise filled the hearts of the warriors at this unexpected apparition of a white man, but not an eye or muscle betrayed the smallest symptom of the feeling.

"The pale-face is welcome," said the chief, after a short pause.

"The pale-face is glad to meet with his dark-skinned brother, and thanks him," returned Lumley.

If the surprise at the sudden appearance of the pale-face was great, the astonishment to find that he spoke the Indian tongue was greater; but still the feeling was not betrayed.

After a few short complimentary speeches, our hero came at once to the point.

"My brothers," he said, looking round on the dusky warriors, who remained sitting all the time, "the white chief of the fur-traders has sent me into this country to trade with you."

This statement was received with a "waugh" of satisfaction from several of the warriors.

"And," continued Lumley, "I have brought men—strong men, who can work well—to help me to build a house, so that we may live among you and hunt together."

He paused here to let the statement have its full effect. Then he continued:—

"I have also brought plenty of guns, and powder, and lead."

Again he paused, and an emphatic "waugh" proved that the remark was fully appreciated.

"The white man knows," continued Lumley, in a more flowing style, "that his red brothers have need of many things which they do not possess, while the white man is in need of furs, and does not possess them. It is for the good of each that we should exchange. The Great Spirit, who is all-wise, as well as all-good, has seen fit to scatter His children over a wide world, and He has given some of them too much of one thing, some of them too much of another. Why has He done so? May we not think that it is for the purpose of causing His children to move about the world, and mingle, and help each other, and so increase Love? Some of the bad children prefer to move about and steal. But there is no need. It is easier to do good than to do evil. If all men would help and none would steal, there would be more than enough for all."

Again a pause. Some of the savages, who were thoughtful men, were greatly tickled in their minds by the arguments set forth. Others, who could not understand, were deeply impressed.

"Now," continued Lumley, coming to the marrow of his discourse, "the red-men have more than enough of furs."

"Waugh!" in a tone of emphasis, that implied "that's true."

"And the pale-faces have few furs, but want some very much."

"Waugh?" interrogatively, in a tone that implied "what then?"

"Well, but the pale-faces are not poor. They are rich, and have far too much of many things. They have far too much of those pleasant sweet things called sugar and molasses (the Indians involuntarily licked their lips). Too much cloth as bright as the sun at setting, and as blue as the sky at noon (the Indian eyes glistened). Too many guns, and too much powder and shot (the savage eyes glared). They have more beads, and blankets, and hatchets, and tobacco, than they know what to do with, so they have sent some of these things here to be given to you in exchange for furs, and food, and leather."

The waughs! and hows! and hos! with which these remarks were followed up were so hearty, that Lumley thought it best to make a considerable pause at this point; then he resumed:—

"But, my brothers,"—he stopped for a considerable time, and looked so grave, that the hearts of the red-men sank, lest the glorious vision which had been suddenly revealed to them, should be as suddenly withdrawn in some way.

"But," repeated Lumley, again, with a sort of awful emphasis, "the pale-faces detest war. They can fight—yes, and when they *must* fight, they *will* fight, but they do not love fighting, and if they are to stay here and open up trade with their guns, and their powder, and their blankets, and beads, and cloth (he wisely went all over it again for the sake of effect), there must be peace in the land. If there is war the pale-faces will take all their good things and go away—waugh!"

Finishing off in the true red-man style, Lumley sat down with decision, as though to say, "Now, the ball is at your own feet, kick it which way you please."

Then the chief of the savages rose with dignity, but with a tinge of eagerness which he could not altogether conceal, and said:—

"Let not my white brother talk of going away. War shall cease at his bidding. Let him and his pale-faced warriors fell trees, and build wigwams, and hunt. We have plenty furs—the black fox, the red fox, the beaver, the marten, the minks, the bear, and many other animals are plentiful. We will exchange them for the goods of the white man. We will bury the hatchet, and smoke the calumet of peace, and the sound of the war-whoop shall no more be heard in the land—waugh!"

"Are my brothers ready to go to the camp of Big Otter, and make friends at once?" asked Lumley.

This was a testing question, and for some time remained unanswered, while the chiefs and braves looked preposterously solemn. At last, however, they seemed to make up their minds, and the chief replied, "We are ready."

That night the hostile savages met on the shores of Lake Wichikagan, and encamped with the fur-traders. Fires were lighted, and kettles put on, a royal feast was prepared; and the reunited tribes of red-men finally buried the war-hatchet there, and smoked the pipe of peace.

* * * * *

CHAPTER ELEVEN.

Lumley on Duty—Fort Wichikagan begins to Grow.

The bold and prompt manner in which peace was established among the contending savages of Lake Wichikagan did more to raise my friend Jack Lumley in their estimation than if he had fought a hundred successful battles, and subdued a nation of foes. It seemed to be felt on all hands that he was a man who could be trusted, and his pointed reference to the Great Spirit conveyed an impression that truth and justice must be his guiding principles.

And on this point these children of nature read his character correctly, for, as I have had frequent occasion to observe, my friend was strictly truthful, and, I might almost say, sternly just. Duty indeed was his pole-star—duty to God and man.

"Max," he once said to me when we had got into a confidential chat beside our camp-fire, "let me advise you to take a sound view and a good grasp of what men call duty. There is a right and a wrong in everything that the mind or hand of man can be brought to bear upon. It is our duty to discover and do the right if we can—to recognise and avoid the wrong. True success in life depends upon this principle being acted on at all times, and in all things. Even what worldly men deem success—the acquisition of wealth, fame, etcetera—is largely dependent on strict regard to duty."

Of course I heartily agreed with him in this matter, but I am free to confess that I feel woefully far short of the standard to which he attained. Perhaps a soft and somewhat undecided nature had something to do with my failure. I say not this by way of excuse but explanation. Whatever the cause, I felt so very far below my friend that I looked up to him as a sort of demigod. Strange to say, his affection for me was also very strong. He never seemed to perceive my weak points—but, then, he was of a large-hearted, generous disposition, and he came to be loved not only by me and the Indians, but by the men of the expedition, some of whom, although good workers, were rather turbulent fellows.

All things having been satisfactorily arranged, as detailed in the last chapter, we now set about preparation for wintering. The first point to settle was the site for our establishment, and a council of the whole party was called to settle it on the lawn-like spot on the margin of our lake where the first fire had been kindled.

"No spot could be better, I think," said our chief, as we stood in a picturesque group around him, with Masqua, Mozwa, and several other Indians looking on. "The little rising ground and clump of wood at the back will shelter us from the north winds; the underwood on the east and west is sufficiently high to form a slight protection in those directions, and to the south the island-studded bosom of Lake Wichikagan lies spread out before us, to supply us with fish and water, and a cheering prospect."

"And to remind Donald Bane and James Dougall," said I, "of Loch Lomond or Loch Ness."

"I rather think," said Lumley, "that it strikes Dougall as having more resemblance to Loch Awe, if we may judge from the awesome expression of his face."

"Weel, Muster Lumley," returned Dougall with a slight smile, "not to spoil your choke, sir, it wass thinkin' o' the fush I wass, an' wonderin' if they wass goot fush."

"Big Otter says they are good," returned our chief, "and I think we may rely on his opinion. There's a little stretch of rock over there, jutting out from the shore, which could be made into a capital pier for our boats and canoes without much labour. What say you, Henri Coppet; could not a few trees and some planks be easily fitted to these rocks?"

"Oui, monsieur—yes, sir—very easily," answered the carpenter, in French.

"Ay, an' wan or two big stones on the other pint o' rocks there," observed Donald Bane, "would make a goot breakwater, an' a fine harbour, whatever."

"And I'm sure nothing could be finer than the view," said I, with feelings of enthusiasm.

"Well, then, since we all seem agreed on that point—here shall our house be raised," rejoined Lumley, driving the point of a stick he carried into the ground. "Come now, boys, go to work. Max, you will superintend the placing of the goods in a secure position and cover them with tarpaulin in the meantime. We'll soon have a hut ready. Dumont, set up your forge under yon pine-tree and get your tools ready. Overhaul your nets, Blondin, and take Salamander to help you—especially the seine-net; I'll try a sweep this afternoon or to-morrow. Come here, Max, I want to speak with you."

"Now, Max," he said, when we had gone aside some distance, "see that you arrange the goods so that they may be easily guarded, and don't let the redskins come too near. They may be honest enough, but we won't throw temptation in their way. We shall want one of them, by the bye, to keep house for us. What say you to hiring Waboose?"

"Out of the question," said I, quickly.

"Why so, Max?"

"Why, because—don't you see—she's far above that sort o' thing, she's quite a kind of princess in the tribe. Haven't you noticed how respectful they all are to her? And, besides, she is so—what one might almost call ladylike. I am convinced that her father must have been a gentleman."

111

"Perhaps so," returned Lumley, with a quiet laugh; "well, we won't insult her by asking her to fill such a position. Away to work now. I will sketch out the plan of our establishment. When the goods are all safe, send your men to fell heavy timber for the houses, and let them also cut some firewood. Off you go."

In a few minutes we were all at work, busy as bees—carrying, hauling, cutting, hammering and chopping; while some of the Indians looked on, intensely interested, others assisted under the direction of Big Otter, and the woods resounded with the noise of the new-born activity.

Soon Blondin had a net down, and before evening we had caught enough of that splendid staple of the North American lakes, the whitefish, to supply us with a good meal and leave something over for our red friends.

I observed during these operations that, after planning, sketching, and measuring, our chief took his axe into the wood and felled a tall pine, from which he proceeded to remove the branches and bark. Towards evening he took a spade, and dug a deep hole in the ground on the most prominent part of the lawn, in front of what was to be our future home.

"Come now, four of you," he said, "and help me to set up our flag-staff."

I ran with three others to assist, and in another minute or two the end of the tall taper stick was dropped into the hole and fixed there. A hole had been already bored in the top and a rope rove through it, to which Lumley soon attached the corners of a small red bundle.

"Ho! lads," he shouted, when all was ready, in a voice that rang out full and strong, "Fall in!"

We had previously been trained to obey this order with the utmost alacrity, by running towards our leader, carrying our loaded guns with us, and forming into line, so as to be ready for any emergency. It was a fancy of Lumley to drill us thus, and we fell in with his humour, most of us counting it a piece of fun to break off from what we chanced to be doing at the moment the order was given, and trying who should be first to reach the spot where he stood. As our guns were always loaded and primed, we never had to lose time in charging them.

On the occasion of which I write, we amazed and somewhat alarmed the Indians by our prompt action, for we stood together in a silent row in less than half a minute after the summons was shouted.

"I have called you up, lads," said Lumley, "to take part in a little ceremony. Through the goodness of the Almighty we have been brought in safety and health to our new home. It is already part of the Queen of England's dominions, and I now take possession of it in the name of the Hudson's Bay Company. May God prosper and bless us while we stay here!"

He hoisted, as he spoke, the small red bundle, which when shaken out proved to be a flag on which were the letters HBC in white.

"Now, boys, send a volley at the new moon up there. Ready—present—fire! Hoorah!"

The crash of the united volley and the wild huzza which followed caused many a redskin's heart to leap, and would doubtless have caused many a foot to run, but for the fact that their own redskin brother—Big Otter—was one of the firing party, and, perhaps, the wildest cheerer of the band!

The ceremony ended, orders were given to knock off work for the day, and set about the preparation oh supper.

The food was sweet that night, sweeter than usual, for we were very hungry; the stars were bright that night, brighter than usual, for we were very happy at the auspicious commencement of our sojourn; and our sleep was unusually sound, for we felt safer than ever under the guidance of a chief who had proved himself so capable of turning threatened war into peace. This being the condition of things, it was not surprising that we indulged in a longer rest than usual, and continued to slumber long after the sun had risen and converted Lake Wichikagan into a glorious sheet of silver.

It is true that our guide, with that sense of responsibility which seems to weigh heavy on guides even when asleep, had awakened at the usual hour of starting—daybreak—and, from the mere force of habit, had given forth his accustomed and sonorous "Lève! lève!"—rise, rise. From the mere force of habit, too, we all turned round to have a few seconds repose on our other sides before obeying the order, but suddenly light flashed into our minds, and various growls in varied keys saluted our guide.

"Go to sleep, men," said our chief, with a half laugh, which ended in a sigh of contentment.

French growls of doubtful meaning issued from the lips of Dumont and Coppet, but Blondin condescended on no remark at all, unless "Pooh!" may be considered such.

"Hoots! man—heigh-ho!" remonstrated Donald Bane, while his comrade Dougall merely said, "Wow!" and followed it with a prolonged snore.

For myself, I felt inclined to laugh, but, being much too lazy to do so, turned over, and was instantly lost again in oblivion. The whole camp was immediately in the same condition, and thus, as I have said, we remained till the sun was high.

Soon after daybreak, however, the Indians began to stir in their camp—which lay a little apart from ours—and, ascending a slight eminence, whence they could look down on our slumbering forms at their leisure, squatted there and continued to gaze—perhaps to wonder how long we meant to rest. They were soon joined by others—men, women, and children—from the neighbouring camp. Self-restraint, at least in some matters, is a characteristic of the red-men, and they remained very patiently and silently there; even the children spoke in whispers, and gazed in solemn earnestness at our slumbering camp.

When we rose and began active preparations for breakfast, the little ones melted away—influenced either by fear or by the orders of their parents. They returned, however, in greater force than ever when we began the labours of the day. Being all more or less naked, they resembled a band of brown monkeys without tails, whose great eyes were capable of expressing only one powerful sentiment—that of surprise!

Thus, watched with deep interest by a large portion of the tribe, we proceeded to the erection of the first house.

"The Hall will stand here, Max," said Lumley to me, as I approached him, bearing one end of a long squared log on my shoulder, the other end of which was carried by Big Otter, while Bane and one of the Canadians supported the centre of it. "Set it down there, lads—a little more this way—so."

We laid the timber on the green sward facing the lake, in such a way that it corresponded with the front line of a large square which had been traced on the turf by Lumley.

"Stay with me, Max, I want your help and advice." The men went back to the bush, from which, at the same moment, four others of our party issued, bearing a similar log.

It was laid at the other side of the square, parallel to the first one. In a few minutes the two end logs were carried up and deposited in their places. These logs had all been cut, squared, mortised at their ends, and fitted together in the woods before being brought to the lawn.

"Now, the question is," said Lumley, as he stood with coat off, shirt sleeves rolled up to the elbows, and pencil and plan in hand, "shall we turn the front of the house a little more to the south or a little more to the east? We must decide that now, before fixing the framework together."

"We should get more of the rising sun," said I, "if we turned it more towards the east. And you know we shall not have too much of its beams in winter to gladden our hearts and eyes."

"Right, Max, but then we might have too much of the east winds to trouble our toes and noses."

"Still the view eastward," said I, "is so extensive and varied—so full of sublimity."

115

"While that to the southward," urged Lumley, "is so soft and beautiful—so full of poetry and romance."

"Come, Jack, don't laugh at me. You know that I am not jesting; I mean what I say."

"I know it, Max, but though I may seem to be half jesting, is it not possible that I, too, may thoroughly mean what I say?"

He pointed as he spoke to the southward, where certain combinations of light and shade thrown on the numerous islets as well as on the clouds—all of which were reflected in the clear water—presented a scene which it is easier to imagine than describe.

I at once admitted the justice of his remark, and it was finally settled that the house should face due south.

"Fix the frame together now, Coppet," said Lumley to our carpenter, who came forward with a load of small timbers, "and let it face as it now lies. The ground is fortunately so flat that we won't require much levelling of foundations. Now, the next thing, Max," he added, turning to me and consulting the plan, "is this—have we made the best possible arrangement of our space? You see I am not much of an architect, but luckily we have not to contend with the civilised difficulties of lobbies and staircases."

"You intend our palace to have only one storey, I suppose?" said I.

"Just so, Max. Arctic gales, you see, might carry a top storey off. We shall have no lobby at all—only a front door and a back door entering direct upon our hall. Of course I shall have a porch and door outside of each, to keep wind and snow out. Now, see here. There, you observe, is the foundation frame now being laid down. Well, one-third of the space in the middle is to be the hall—our drawing-room, dining-room, library, snuggery, smokery, public-room, etcetera, all in one. It will extend from front to rear of the building; but at the back, you see, I have marked a little oblong space which is to be boarded off as a sort of larder, and gun-room, and place for rubbish in general. It will extend along the width of the hall, leaving only space for the back door."

116

"What a capital contrivance!" said I; "it will, besides being so useful, break in on the oblong shape of the hall and give variety of form."

"Just so, Max; then the space left on each side of the hall shall be partitioned off into four rooms—two on either side—with the doors opening into the hall. No passages, you see, anywhere, and no wasted space. One room for me, one for you, one for Salamander, who is to be our man-servant as well as interpreter, and one for Blondin, whom I intend to make a sort of overseer of the men. We shan't want a spare room, for we won't be troubled much, I fear, with guests; but if such a blessing should ever descend on us, we can turn Blondin or Salamander out. They will have to mess with the men at any rate; and, by the way, we must start the men's house and the store immediately, for I intend to carry on all three at the same time, so that we and the men and the goods may all get housed together."

"Are you to have attics?" I asked.

"No; but there will be a space under the sloping roof, which can be turned into a garret, and may be reached through a trap-door by a movable ladder. As to windows, the hall is to have two—one on each side of the door, which will give the house the lively aspect of appearing to have two eyes and a nose. The bedrooms will each have one window in its side, and you may take the one looking eastward if you choose, Max. In winter these windows shall have double frames and glass to keep the cold out. Go now, my boy, and see to the foundation of the men's house."

Need I say that we all toiled with hearty good-will; for, although the weather was pleasantly warm at the time, we knew that the short-lived autumn would quickly pass and render a good roof over our heads most desirable.

Soon a pit-saw which we had brought with us was set to work, and planks began to multiply. Henri Coppet and his men swung their great axes, and trees began to fall around, and to take unwonted shapes. The ring of Marcelle Dumont's anvil was heard from morn till eve, echoing through the wild-woods; and powerful bands, and nuts, and screws, of

117

varied size and form, were evolved from our bundle of iron bars. Thus the whole party wrought with untiring energy, and our future abode began to grow.

At all this our red friends gazed with countenances expressive of inconceivable surprise and profound admiration.

* * * * *

CHAPTER TWELVE.

A Narrow Escape—A Strange Meeting, and a Half-Revealed Mystery.

One afternoon, not very long after our arrival at Lake Wichikagan, Lumley and I found ourselves on the summit of a rising ground which was scantily clothed with trees, and from the top of which we could see the region all round like a map spread at our feet. We were out after a black bear whose footprints had led us to the spot.

"Bruin has escaped us this time," said Lumley, "and I don't feel disposed to go after him any further. You see, Max, I must be up early to-morrow to superintend Coppet at his water-mill, so I would advise resting here a bit to refresh ourselves at this spring, and then make tracks for home."

He descended as he spoke towards a small basin in the rocks, into which fell a rivulet formed by the spring referred to, and flung himself down beside it. Seating myself at his side I said:—

"Coppet needs superintendence, I suspect, for although he is an excellent carpenter and reliable workman, I'm not sure that he understands complicated or large works—except, indeed, the building of houses; but then he has been taught that since he was a boy."

"That's just it, Max," returned Lumley, filling the hollow of his hand with clear water for want of a better drinking-cup, "he can do anything which he has been taught, but I find that he cannot originate, and suspect that he has not a very deep knowledge of the strength of materials or the power of forces. The worst of it is that neither you nor I are very profound in such matters. However, we must do our best and make everything ten times stronger than there is any occasion for, and thus make up for the lack of engineering knowledge."

"Shall you want my help to-morrow earlier than usual?" I asked.

"No—not till after breakfast."

"Well then, as there is no necessity for my going to bed before my ordinary time, I'll let you return alone, for I don't feel at all disposed to give up this bear after tracking him so many hours. He's only a small one, to judge from his footprints, and I am a pretty sure shot, you know."

"Be it so, Max—but don't be late, else I'll have to send men to look for you!"

Lumley got up and left me—making a straight line for Fort Wichikagan, as we had named our outpost, and leaving me in a dreamy state of mind beside the spring.

It was a delightful afternoon in that most charming period of the American season which is styled the Indian summer; when mosquitoes, sand-flies, and all other insect-tormentors disappear, and the weather seems to take a last enjoyable fortnight of sunny repose before breaking into winter.

I fell into a pleasant reverie. The backwoods of the Great Nor'-west vanished from my mental view, and, with eyes half closed, I indulged in memories of home and all its sweet associations.

Bethinking me suddenly of my reason for remaining where I was, I sprang up, seized my gun, and began to follow the trail of the bear. Before descending from the eminence, however, I took a look round the landscape, and saw the figure of an Indian woman in the distance, proceeding towards our fort. Although too far-off to be distinguished by feature, I could clearly perceive the light-blue cotton kerchief which formed part of the dress of Waboose.

At once my interest in the bear vanished, and I began to follow the Indian girl instead. I had not seen her since the evening of our arrival at the lake, and I felt a strong desire to make further inquiries as to the circumstances of her father's life among the Indians and his unfortunate death.

Waboose had not seen me. By making a wide and rapid détour I got in front of her and sat down on a fallen tree at a spot where she was sure to pass.

As she drew near, I could not fail to observe how graceful her port was, and how different from that of the other girls with whom her lot had been cast.

"Assuredly," muttered I to myself, "her father was a gentleman!"

Leaving my gun on the bank on which I had been seated, I advanced to meet her. She showed a very slight symptom of surprise, and, I thought, of uneasiness, on seeing me, but made no remark until I had spoken. At first I was about to adopt the Indian style of address, and begin with "my red sister," but the phrase, besides being false, appeared to me ridiculous; still, the ice had to be broken somehow, so I made a bungling plunge.

"Blue-eyes wanders far to-day from the wigwams of her—her—people?"

A gleam of surprise mingled with pleasure rippled over her pretty face when she found that I could speak to her in the native tongue.

"Yes," she replied in the same language. "I have wandered far. I was the bearer of a message."

As she volunteered no more I continued:

"If Waboose goes to her wigwam, will she object to the pale-face bearing her company?"

With something like a graceful inclination of the head, the Indian girl gave me to understand that she had no objection.

"An *Indian*!" thought I, "she's a *lady* in disguise, as sure as I am a fur-trader!"

Of course I was careful not to give her, either by tone or look, the slightest hint of what was passing in my mind, and was about to continue my remarks, when a rustling in the bushes caused us both to look round quickly. The foliage parted next moment close to us, and before I had time to think a large brown bear bounded into the open space. It seemed to be taken as much by surprise as we were, and I have no doubt would have turned and fled if it had not been so near. It rose on its hind legs, however, to attack us, and then I perceived that it was not the small bear which Lumley and I had been tracking.

The blood rushed to my head when I remembered that the monster stood between me and the bank on which my gun was lying! Then the feeling that the helpless Indian girl was at its mercy filled me with feelings which are indescribable. Thought is swifter than the lightning-flash. Much more than I have written flashed through my brain during those two or three seconds, but one overmastering idea filled me—I would save *her*, or perish!

I glanced sharply round. To my surprise she had fled! So much the better. I could at least keep the creature engaged till she had got well away.

Drawing the small hatchet which like all Nor'westers I carried in my belt, I rushed at the bear and made a cut at its head with all the force that lay in my arm. Where the blow fell I know not, but apparently it was ineffective, for, with a quick vicious turn of its paw, the bear struck my weapon from my hand with such violence that it flew over the tree-tops as if shot from a catapult, and I stood unarmed—helpless—at the creature's mercy!

The terrible feeling that death was so near almost unnerved me, but the thought of Waboose caused me to utter a roar of mingled rage and despair as I doubled my fist and launched it full against the monster's nose!

At that moment a loud report at my ear deafened and almost stunned me. Next instant the bear lay dead at my feet. I looked round and beheld Waboose standing close to me with my gun in her hands!

"Noble heroine!" I exclaimed, but as I exclaimed it in English she did not understand. She had, indeed, a very slight smattering of that

122

language—of which more hereafter—but "Noble heroine" was not at that time in her vocabulary!

Instead of trembling or looking pale, as I might have expected to see her, Waboose looked at me in the most composed manner, and with something on her lip that seemed to me like a smile of amusement. In some confusion, I thanked her for having saved my life.

She did not object to the thanks, but replied by asking me if it was the usual practice of white men to attack bears with their fists.

I could not help laughing at this.

"No, Waboose," I replied, as I recharged my gun, "it is by no means usual; but when a man has no other weapon at hand, he is compelled to use his fists. And let me tell you," I added, for I was somewhat nettled by the obvious laugh that nestled in the girl's blue eyes,—"let me tell you that we English are pretty good at using our fists."

"I know that," she replied, becoming suddenly very grave as we walked on.

"You know that?" I repeated in surprise; "how came you to know that?"

"My dear father was English," she answered in a low sad tone that smote me to the heart for having felt nettled—though I believe I did not show the feeling on my face or in my tone.

"Ah! Big Otter told me that," said I, in an earnest tone of sympathy. "If it does not hurt her feelings too much to recall the past, I should like Waboose to tell me about her father."

The girl looked at me in surprise. I had a fancy, at the time, that this was the result of the novel sensation of a man having any consideration for her feelings, for Indian braves are not, as a rule, much given to think about the feelings of their women. Indeed, from the way in which many of them behave, it is probable that some red-men think their women have no feelings at all.

In a low, melodious voice, and with some of that poetic imagery which marks the language, more or less, of all North American Indians, the girl began to speak—raising her eyes wistfully the while to the sky, as if she were communing with her own thoughts rather than speaking to me.

"My father was good—oh! *so* good and kind," she said. "When I was small, like the foolish rabbit when it is a baby, he used to take me on his shoulders and run with me over the prairie like the wild mustang. Sometimes he put me in his bark canoe and skimmed with me over Lake Wichikagan till I fancied I was a grey-goose or a swan. Ah! those were happy days! No one can ever understand how much my father loved me. My mother loves me much, but she is not like my father. Perhaps it is the nature of the pale-faces to love more deeply than the red-men."

Waboose uttered this last sentence as if she were questioning the sky on the point. I felt at the time that there was at least one pale-face who loved her better than all the red-men or women on earth, but a sense of justice caused me to repudiate the general idea.

"No, Waboose," said I, firmly, "that is a mistake. Rough surroundings and a harsh life will indeed modify the heart's affections, but the mere colour of the skin has nothing to do with it. The heart of the redskin can love as deeply as that of the white man—both were made by the same Great Master of Life."

The girl cast her eyes meditatively on the ground and murmured simply, "It may be so."

The reader must not suppose that I expressed my meaning in the Indian tongue during this conversation as clearly as I have set it down in English. No doubt I mangled the sentences and confused the ideas sadly, nevertheless Waboose seemed to have no difficulty in understanding me. I had certainly none in comprehending her.

I was about to ask Waboose to relate the circumstances of her father's death while in the act of rescuing her mother, but feeling that it might cause her needless pain, and that I could get the details as easily from some of the Indians, I asked her instead where her father came from. She looked at me sadly as she replied—

"I cannot tell. My dear father had nothing to conceal from me but that. On all other things his heart was open. He spoke to me of all the wonders of this world, and of other places that my people know nothing of, and of the great Master of Life, and of His Son Jesus, who came to save us from evil, and of the countries where his white brothers live; but when I asked him where he came from, he used to pat my head and smile, and say that he would perhaps tell me one day, but not just then. I shall never know it now."

"At all events you must know his name, Waboose?"

"His name was Weeum," replied the girl quickly.

"Was that all?"

"All," she replied with a quick look, "was not that enough?"

"Well, perhaps it was," I replied, scarce knowing what to say. "And why did he give you the name of Waboose?" I asked.

"Because when I was small I was round and soft," replied the girl, with a slight smile, "like the little animal of that name. He told me that in his own language the animal is called rubbit."

"Rabbit, not rubbit," said I, with a laugh.

"My father taught me rubbit," returned Waboose, with a simple look, "and he was *always* right."

I felt that it would be useless to press my correction, and therefore changed the subject by asking if her father had never tried to teach her English. Immediately she answered, with a somewhat bashful air—

"Yes, a leetil."

"Why, you can *speak* English, Waboose," I exclaimed, stopping and looking down at her with increasing interest.

"No—note mush, but me un'erstan' good—deal," she returned, with a hearty laugh at my expression.

I found on trial, however, that the girl's knowledge of English was so slight that we could not readily converse in it. We therefore fell back on the Indian tongue.

"I wish I had known your father, Waboose," I said earnestly. "He must have been a very good man."

She looked at me gratefully.

"Yes," she returned, "he was *very* good."

As she said this Waboose cast on me a look which I could not understand; it was so intense, as if she were trying to read my thoughts, and at the same time seemed mingled with doubt. Then, with some hesitation, she said—

"My father left a secret with me. He told me never to show it to my tribe, as they could not understand it—not even to my mother."

"What is the secret, Waboose?" I asked, seeing that she hesitated again and looked at me with another of her searching glances.

"I do not know," she replied.

"It must indeed be a secret, if none of your people know it, and you don't know it yourself," I returned with a peculiar smile.

"It is a written secret, I believe, but I—I—do not know. He told me never to show it to any but a white man—to one whom I felt that I could trust. May I trust *you?*" she asked, looking me full in the face.

The question naturally surprised as well as flattered me.

"You may trust me, Waboose," I said earnestly, laying my hand involuntarily on my heart, "I would die rather than deceive or injure you."

She seemed satisfied and resumed in a low tone—

"Not long before my dear father died he took me into the woods to walk in a place that we were both fond of. We had long sweet talks in that wood; sometimes walking under the trees, sometimes sitting on the hill-tops, and always happy—very happy! One day he looked sad. He took my hand as we sat together on a bank. He said, 'I have sometimes longed to open up all my heart to you, my rubbit,' (he was fond of calling me by the English name), 'but I cannot do so yet.'"

"'Why not, my father?' I asked.

"'Because—because—' he answered, 'it could do no good, and it might do harm. No, my rubbit, the time may come, but not now—not

126

yet. Listen; for your mother's sake I left the home of the pale-faces and came to live with your tribe. For her sake I shall remain. But you know that life is uncertain. We cannot tell when the Great Master of Life may call us away. Sometimes he calls us suddenly and we are forced to leave our works unfinished. I may be called away thus, before the time comes when I may tell you what I want you to know. If so, you will find it all here.'

"My father took from the breast of his coat a small bundle wrapped in birch-bark and placed it in my hands.

"'Do not open it,' he said. 'Do not show it to man or woman in the tribe. They could not understand, but if ever a white man comes here, *whom you feel that you can trust*, show it to him.'

"My father rose as he said this, and as he seemed to wish not to speak more about it, I did not trouble him, but I went and hid the parcel with care. It was almost immediately afterwards that my dear father was taken from me."

We were suddenly interrupted at this point by the appearance of a man in the distance walking smartly towards us. I could perceive, as he drew near, that it was James Dougall.

"Well, well, Muster Maxby," he said on coming up, "it's gled I am to find you. I've been seekin' you far an' near."

"Nothing wrong, I hope, Dougall," said I with some anxiety, on observing that the man was perspiring and panting vehemently.

"No, no, nothin' wrong, Muster Maxby, only it's runnin' aboot the wuds I've been, lookin' for ye an' skirlin' like a pair o' pipes. We're aboot to draw the seine-net, ye see, an' Tonald Pane said it would be a peety, says he, to begin when ye wur awa', an' Muster Lumley agreet wi' um, an' sent me oot to seek for 'ee—that's a'."

"Come along then, Dougall, we won't keep them waiting."

Nodding adieu to Waboose, I hurried away towards Fort Wichikagan, followed by the sturdy Highlander.

* * * * *

CHAPTER THIRTEEN.

Fishing and its Results—Engineering and its Consequences.

I found on reaching Wichikagan that the fun was about to begin. Blondin, who was our chief fisherman, had let down a long seine-net, which was being drawn slowly in by a band of natives, whose interest in a process which they had never before seen was deepening into excitement, as they observed here and there a symptom of something shooting below the surface of the still water, or beheld a large fish leap frantically into the air.

At first, when the net was being prepared, those children of the forest had merely stood by and looked on with curiosity. When Blondin and his men rowed out from the shore, letting the net drop off the stern of our boat as they went, they indulged in a few guesses and undertoned remarks. When the boat gradually swept round and turned shoreward again, having left a long line of floats in its wake, they perceived that a large sheet of water had been enclosed, and a feeling of wonder, combined with a half guess as to what all this portended caused their black orbs to enlarge, and the whites thereof to glisten. But when they were requested to lay hold of a rope attached to the other end of the net and haul, the true state of the case burst upon their awakened minds and proportionate excitement followed.

As the circle of the net diminished and the evidences, above referred to, of life in the water became more frequent, gleeful expectation took the place of wonder, and a disposition to chatter manifested itself, especially among the women and children, who by that time had eagerly laid hold of the drag-rope.

Soon it became apparent that a mighty mass of fish had been enclosed, and the creatures seemed themselves to become suddenly alive to their danger, for the crowded condition of their element—which, no doubt, caused only surprise at first—became so inconvenient that with one accord they made a terrified rush to the right. Failing to obtain relief they turned and rushed to the left. Discomfited again, they dashed lakeward. Each rush was followed by a howl of anxiety from the natives; each failure was hailed with a yell of joy. Three birch-bark canoes followed the net to send the more obstreperous of the fish shoreward. Finding that they could not escape, the finny prisoners seemed to lose their wits and took to rushing skyward, with splashing consequences that almost drove the red-men mad!

"Hold on! not so hard! You'll break it!" shouted Lumley to the men and women at the rope.

"What a tremendous haul!" said I, as I joined my friend, who stood at the outer end of our little wharf, enjoying the scene.

"I hope the net won't break," he replied. "If it does we shall lose them all, and the disappointment to the Indians might be almost too much to bear. See, they prepare for action!"

This was very obvious. The men of the tribe, who might be described as glaring maniacs, had dropped their robes, and, almost naked, ran waist-deep into the water in a vain attempt to catch some of the larger fish as they were slowly forced towards the beach. Even some of the women lost self-control and, regardless of petticoats, floundered after the men. As for the children, big and little, they developed into imps of darkness gone deranged.

Suddenly a very wave of fish was sent upon the shore, where, of course, they began to leap about wildly. Not less wildly did the Indians leap among them, throttling the big ones and hurling armfuls of the lesser ones high up on the sward.

By that time the net was close in shore. The whole of the enclosed space became a sweltering mass. Treading on the fish at last, many of both men and boys slipped in the water, and fell down over head and ears, so that the spectacle was presented of human beings bounding out of the water in apparent emulation of their prey. The excitement was almost too much for them. Several of the boys were seen to rush up into the woods and dash back again, with no apparent reason except the desire to get rid of superabundant energy. One brave, in particular, so far forgot the characteristic dignity of the red-man, that he rushed up on the bank, bent forward, clapped a hand on each knee, threw back his head, shut his eyes, opened wide his mouth, and sought to relieve his feelings in one stupendous roar. But it would not do. He became suddenly solemn, glared again, and went at the fish more furiously than ever.

Our men in the canoes landed, and rendered assistance. Salamander was in one of the canoes which ran alongside of the wharf. The only other occupant was Donald Bane, who sat in the stern and steered. Salamander was greatly excited. As the canoe ran up to the wharf, the bow was thrust over the net-rope, and he gazed at the struggling creatures below with intense delight on his brown visage.

"You had petter take care," said Donald Bane, as he grasped the edge of the wharf, and cautiously rose up, "for canoes are easily overturned." But Salamander was too much engrossed to hear or reply. The Highlander, who had not forgotten the trick formerly played on him and his countryman by the interpreter, stepped carefully out on the wharf. As he did so, he gave the canoe a little tilt with his foot, and Salamander went head-foremost down among the fish!

A simulated cry of consternation broke from Donald Bane.

"Wow—wow!" he exclaimed, as Salamander's head appeared with a number of little fish struggling in his hair, and a pike or jack-fish holding on to the lobe of his left ear, "the poor cratur! Tak a grup o' my hand, man. Here! wow! but it seems a fery frundly jack-fush that—whatever."

Amid much spluttering, Salamander was hauled out, and, regardless of his mishap, both he and Donald immediately joined the others in securing their prey.

"It wass a grand haul, man, Tonald," said Dougall that night at supper.

"Oo ay, Shames. It was no that paad," replied Donald.

And, truly, it *was* a grand haul; for, not only did we obtain enough of every species of fish that swarmed in Lake Wichikagan, to provide a right royal feast to ourselves and our red friends, but a good many were left over and above to form the commencement of a store for the future.

By that time we had fairly commenced the fishery with a view to a winter supply. The weather was still delicious, and had begun to grow cool at nights, but as there was yet no frost, all the fish we took had to be hung up by the tail, and thus partially dried. Afterwards, when the frost fairly set in, this hanging process was dispensed with, for fish, once frozen in those regions, remain perfectly fresh during the entire winter, so that those eaten in spring are quite as good as those consumed in autumn.

Lumley now set me to superintend the digging and constructing of an ice-house, which should be ready to receive in spring the ice that would be required to keep our provisions fresh during the following summer. It consisted merely of a shallow square pit or hole in the ground, over which a log hut was constructed. The pit we intended to floor with solid cubes of ice measuring about a yard on each side. This lowest foundation, in those northern ice-houses, never melts, but a fresh stratum is laid above it which is cleared out and renewed every spring, and it is amongst this that the meat or fish to be preserved is laid in summer.

Another piece of work that Lumley gave me to superintend at this time was the construction of a water-wheel and dam to drive our pit-saw. You see, I had a turn for mechanics, and was under the impression that my powers in that way were greater than they afterwards turned out to be. We were sitting at tea alone in our hall at the time the subject was mooted.

"Where have you sent the carpenter?" I asked, as I pushed in my pannikin for more of the refreshing beverage.

I must interrupt the thread of my narrative here for a moment to say that we took no crockery with us on that expedition. Our cups were tin pannikins, our plates were made of tin; our pots and kettles were either tin or copper. We had no sugar basins, or butter-dishes, or table-cloths, or any of the other amenities of civilised life. But everything we had was strong and serviceable, and the same may be said of the things we constructed. The deal tables and chairs made for us by Coppet were very strong if not elegant, and the plank walls and ceiling of our rooms were cheerful, though neither papered nor whitewashed. It has often struck me, while sojourning in the great Nor'-west, that civilised man surrounds himself with a great many needless luxuries which do not by any means add to his comfort, though the removal of them might add considerably to his distress.

But to return.

"Coppet is off," said Lumley in reply to my question, "to get some timber for oars, as well as birch-bark to make a canoe or two; we must also set about making a new boat some day or other."

"Lumley," said I, "it has often occurred to me that it takes a terrible deal of time to cut trees into planks with our pit-saws, and occupies far too much of the time of two men who might be much more profitably employed."

"True, Max—what then?"

"Why then," said I, "what would you say if I were to construct a saw-mill!"

"I'd say you were a clever fellow," replied my friend, with one of his knowing looks.

"But what say you to my making the attempt?"

"Do so, by all means, my boy—only don't use up too many pit-saws in the attempt!"

I saw that he did not believe in my powers, and became all the more determined to succeed.

Accordingly, I went next day with Coppet and Dumont, on whom of course I depended for the carrying out of my designs, to examine the ground where the mill-dam was to be made.

"You see," I explained, "we have a superabundance of water in the rivulet at the back of the fort, and by collecting it we may get any amount of power we please, which is of importance, because it will enable us to simplify the machinery."

"Oui, oui, monsieur," said Coppet, who either was, or wished to appear, very knowing on such matters.

"Now," continued I, "here is a natural basin formed by rocks, which only wants a small dam at its lower end to enable us to collect water enough to drive the biggest mill in the world. By making our opening at the very bottom of the basin, the pressure of water, when it is full, will be so great that a very small water-wheel, without any multiplying gear, will suffice to drive our saw—don't you see?"

"Oui, monsieur, oui," answered Dumont, whose knitted brows showed that the worthy blacksmith was at least doing his best to understand me.

"Well, then," I continued, "you see that we shall have no difficulty as to the dam. Then, as to the wheel, it will be a simple one of not more than four feet diameter, presented vertically to what I may term the water-spout, so that its axle, which will have a crank in it, will work the saw direct; thus, avoiding toothed wheels and cogs, we shall avoid friction, and, if need be, increase the speed easily, d'you see?"

"Bon, monsieur—good, good," exclaimed Coppet, becoming quite enthusiastic in his appreciation of my plans.

"Of course," I continued, "the saw can easily be fitted to a frame, and a very simple contrivance can be made to drive along the larger frame that will carry the logs to be sawn; but these are trifling matters of detail which you and I will work out at our leisure, Dumont."

"Oui, monsieur, oui," replied the blacksmith, with tighter knitted brows, and with a readiness of assent which I do believe the good fellow would have accorded if I had proposed to fit a new axis to the world.

"There is only one thing that troubles me," said I: "how are we to gauge or estimate the force of our water-spout so as to regulate our mill when made? Do you understand such matters—the measurement of force—Coppet?"

The carpenter shook his head.

"That's unfortunate. Do you, Dumont?"

"Non, Monsieur."

"H'm! I'm sadly ignorant on the point myself," I continued. "Of course I know that so many cubic feet of water will exert a certain pressure, but then I don't know what that certain pressure is, nor how to find out how many cubic feet our somewhat irregular dam will contain. Nor do I know precisely the strength of the material required in the dam to resist the water."

Dumont humbly suggested here that we could at all events act on the principle that guided Adam and Eve in the formation of their first water-mill, and find out by experiment. And Coppet said that we could get over the difficulty about the strength of materials by making everything ten times stronger than was required.

"You are right lads," said I, much amused with the earnest manner in which they gave the advice. "Now let us go at it without delay, so that we may get into working order before the frost stops us."

We set to with enthusiasm, and progressed with our labour much faster than I had expected. The natural basin to which I have referred lay just below a ledge of rock over which the rivulet flowed into it, forming a pretty deep pool about ten feet in diameter. Flowing out of this pool, it ran about twelve feet further through a narrow gorge, where it dropped over another ledge. Now, all that we had to do was to shut up the outlet of the narrow gorge with a strong dam, and so cause the pool to swell and rise into a small but very deep pond.

Our first step was to divert the channel of the brook so as to leave us free to construct the dam. The nature of the ground rendered this easy enough. Then, before going further, we made the trough which was to conduct the water out of the dam. It was made of four strong planks about ten feet long and eight inches wide, forming, so to speak, a square pipe. This we laid firmly in the bottom of the basin with its end projecting over the lower ledge. To the inner end we attached a perpendicular piece of wooden piping which rose several feet from the ground. This was meant to prevent mud and stones from getting into, and choking, the pipe.

This done, we laid some very large timbers over the pipe and across the opening of the gorge, above and between which we put heavy stones and large quantities of gravel—also turf and twigs, and all sorts of rubbish. Thus was the dam begun, and we continued the process until we raised it to a height of some twenty feet or so.

"What a magnificent pool it will be to dive in!" said Lumley, one day, when he came to see us at work.

"Won't it," said I; "especially in winter!"

"Whatever happens to your works, the dam, I think, will never give way," continued Lumley; "it seems to me unnecessarily strong."

Not to try the reader's patience, I may say at once that we advanced with our labour without a hitch until it was nearly finished. To the opening in the pipe or spout we attached a powerful sluice by which to stop the flow desired, and, all being ready, broke down the dyke that had turned aside our stream, and let the water in. Of course we had constructed an overflow part of the basin by which to conduct the surplus water back to its proper channel below our works.

It was a trying moment when we first let the water in. Would it leak?—would it break down?—was in everyone's mind. I had no fear as to the latter point, but felt uncertain as to the former. We had much longer to

135

wait, however, for the filling than I had expected; but when at last it was full up to the brim, and the trees around were reflected on its surface, and no leak appeared anywhere, I could not resist giving a cheer, which was heartily taken up and echoed by our whole party—for we had all assembled to watch the result.

"Now, Coppet, lend a hand at the winch. We'll open the sluice and observe the force."

After a few turns our winch refused to move, and only a small part of the opening had been uncovered, from which the water was squirting furiously.

"Something wrong," said I, looking down at the men below. "Just take a look, Salamander, and see what it is."

Our lively interpreter went down on hands and knees and made an earnest examination, despite the squirting water.

"Oh! I sees. All right now," he shouted, "heave away!"

"Get out of the way, then," we cried, as we once more applied all our force to the winch. It turned with unexpected suddenness, the sluice flew up, and out came a straight column of water with extreme violence. It hit Salamander full in the stomach, lifted him off his legs, and swept him right down the gully, pitching him headlong over another ledge, where he fell with such force that his mortal career had certainly been ended then and there but for a thick juniper bush, which fortunately broke his fall. As it was, he was little the worse of his adventure, but he had learned a lesson of prompt obedience to orders which he did not soon forget.

I now planned a sort of movable buffer by which the force of the water-spout could be diminished or even turned aside altogether. It acted very well, and, under its protection, we set up the saw and started it. We were all assembled again, of course, at the first starting of the saw, along with a good many of our red friends, whose curiosity in our various proceedings knew no bounds.

Opening the sluice slowly, and fixing the buffer so as to turn at least three-quarters of the furious water-spout aside, I had the extreme satisfaction of seeing the saw begin to rip up a large log. It went on splendidly, though still with somewhat greater force than I desired. But, alas! my want of critical knowledge of engineering told heavily against us, for, all of a sudden, the sluice broke. The buffer still acted, however, and being needlessly strong, was, I thought, safe, but the hinges of the thing were far too weak. They gave way. The violent spout thus set free dashed against the wheel with its full force, turning it round with a whirr–r–r! that sent the saw up and down so fast as to render it almost invisible.

We stood aghast! What fearful termination to the machine impended we could not guess. A moment later and the crank broke, entangled itself with the wheel and stopped it. As if maddened by this additional resistance, the water-spout then swept the whole concern away, after which, like a wild-horse set free, it took a leap of full thirty feet—a straight column of solid water—before it burst itself on the ground, and rushed wildly down to the lake! It was a humiliating termination—and showed how terrible it is to create a power which one cannot control.

I draw a veil over the story here. My feelings forbid me to write more!

* * * * *

CHAPTER FOURTEEN.

Arrival of Strange Indians.

About this time a band of strange Indians came in with a large supply of valuable furs. They had heard, they said, of the establishment of the new post, and had gladly come to trade there, instead of making their customary long journey to Muskrat House.

The change to these Indians was, in truth, of the utmost importance, for so distant were some of their hunting-grounds from Macnab's establishment, that nearly all the ammunition obtained there—the procuring of which was one of the chief desires of their hearts—was expended in shooting for mere subsistence on the way back to their hunting-grounds. It will be easily understood, then, that they received us with open arms.

By this time we were quite prepared for their visit. The two dwelling-houses for ourselves and the men were completed, so also was the store for our goods. There only remained unfinished one or two outhouses and our back kitchen, the latter a detached building, afterwards to be connected with the main dwelling by a passage. The store was an unusually strong log-house of one storey with a very solid door. It was attached to the side of our dwelling, with which it was connected by an inner door, so that we could, if necessary, enter it without having to go outside—a matter of some importance in case we should ever be forced to defend the fort.

I had just returned, much dispirited, from a visit to the camp of our own Indians, when this band of strangers arrived.

Remembering my last conversation with Waboose, and being very curious to know what were the contents of the mysterious packet she had mentioned, I had gone to the camp to visit her, but, to my extreme regret, found that Big Otter and several of the Indians had struck their tents and gone off on a long hunting expedition, taking their families with them—Waboose among the rest.

On finding, however, that strange Indians had arrived with a goodly supply of furs to trade, thoughts of all other matters were driven out of my mind, the depression of spirits fled, and a burst of enthusiasm supervened as the thought occurred to me that now, at last, the great object of our expedition was about to begin in earnest. I verily believe that the same spirit of enthusiasm, or satisfaction—call it what you will—animated more or less every man at the fort. Indeed, I believe that it is always so in every condition of life; that men who lay claim to even the smallest amount of spirit or self-respect, experience a thrill of justifiable pride in performing their duty well, and earning the approval of their official superiors. My own thoughts, if defined, would probably have amounted to this—

"Now then, here's a chance at last of driving a good trade, and we will soon show the Governor and Council of the Fur-traders that they were well advised when they selected John Lumley as the chief of this trading expedition into the remote wilderness!"

"Come, Max," cried my friend, whom I met hastening to the store as I arrived, "you're just in time. Here's a big band of redskins with splendid packs of furs. I fear, however, that what is our gain will to some extent be poor Macnab's loss, for they say they used to take their furs to him in former years."

"But, then," said I, "will not the company gain the furs which used to be damaged, and therefore lost, on the long voyage to Muskrat? Besides, the Indians will now be enabled to devote the time thus saved to hunting and trapping, and that will also be clear gain."

We reached the store as I said this, followed by a dozen Indians with large packs on their shoulders. These were the chief men of the tribe, who were to be attended to first. The others, who had to await their turn with what patience they could command, followed behind in a body to gaze at least upon the outside of the store—that mysterious temple of unknown wealth of which all of them had heard, though many of them had never seen or entered one.

Putting a large key into the lock, Lumley turned it with all due solemnity, for it was his plan among savages to make all acts of importance as impressive as possible in their eyes. And this act of visiting for the first time the stores—the palace of wealth—the abode of bliss—the red-man's haven of rest—was a very important act. It may not seem so to the reader, but it was so to the savage. The very smell of the place was to him delicious—and no wonder, for even to more cultivated nostrils there is an odour about the contents of a miscellaneous store—such as tea, molasses, grindstones, coffee, brown paper, woollen cloths, sugar, fish-hooks, raisins, scalping-knives, and soap—which is pleasantly suggestive.

Entering, then, with the dozen Indians, this important place, of which I was the chief and only clerk, Lumley salesman and trader, and Salamander warehouseman, the door was shut. Becoming instantly aware of a sudden diminution in the light, I looked at the windows and observed a flattened brown nose, a painted face and glaring eyes in the centre of nearly every pane!

When I looked at this band of powerful, lithe, wiry, covetous savages, and thought of the hundreds of others whom they could summon by a single war-whoop to their side, and of the smallness of our own party, I could not help feeling that moral influence was a powerful factor in the affairs of man. No doubt they were restrained to some extent by the certain knowledge that, if they attacked and killed us, and appropriated our goods without the preliminary ceremony of barter, the white men would not only decline to send them goods in future, but would organise a force to hunt down and slay the murderers: nevertheless, savages are not much given to prudential reasoning when their cupidity or passions are roused, and I cannot help thinking that we owed our safety, under God, to the belief in the savage mind that men who put themselves so completely in their power, as we did, and who looked so unsuspicious of evil, *must* somehow be invulnerable.

Be that as it may, we calmly acted as if there could be no question at all about our being their masters. Lumley conveyed that impression, however, without the slightest assumption of dignity. He was all kindness, gentleness, and urbanity, yet treated them with that unassertive firmness which a father exercises—or ought to exercise—towards a child.

"Now then, Salamander," said Lumley, when he was inside the counter, and the Indians stood in a group on the other side, "tell the principal chief to open his pack."

Lumley, I may remark, made use of Salamander as an interpreter, until he found that the dialect of those Indians was not very different from that to which he had been accustomed. Then he dispensed with his services, and took up the conversation himself, to the obvious astonishment as well as respect of the Indians, who seemed to think the white chief had actually picked up a new language after listening to it for only half an hour!

The principal chief opened his pack slowly and spread its contents on the counter with care. He did not hurry himself, being a very dignified man. There were beavers, martens, otters, silver-foxes, and many other valuable furs, for which large sums are given in the European markets. To obtain these, however, the Company of Traders had to expend very large sums in transporting goods into those northern wilds, and still larger sums would have to be paid to voyageurs, clerks, and employés generally, as well as risks run and time spent before these furs could be conveyed to market and turned into gold—hence our red chief had to content himself with moderate prices. These prices, moreover, he did not himself put on his furs. Lumley did that for him, according to the tariff used by the fur-traders all over the country, every article being rated at a standard unit of value, styled a "made-beaver" in some parts of the country—a "castore" in other parts. On the counter was marked, with a piece of chalk, the value of each fur—a beaver was valued at so many castores, according to its quality, a fox at so many—and when the sum was added up, the total was made known by a number of goose-quills being presented to the chief, each quill representing a castore. The Indians, being acquainted with this process, did not require to have it explained.

Profoundly did that chief gaze at his bundle of quills on receiving them from Lumley after Salamander had swept his furs into a corner. He was studying, as it were, the credit balance of his bank-account before investing.

"Now then, chief," asked Lumley, with an urbane expression of countenance, "what shall I give you?"

The chief gazed solemnly round the store with his piercing black eyes, while all the other piercing black eyes around gazed at him expectantly! At last his gaze became riveted on a particular spot. The surrounding black eyes turned to that spot intently, and the chief said:

"*Baskisigan.*"

"Ah, I thought so—a gun?" said Lumley; "hand one over, Salamander."

The interpreter went to a box which contained half a dozen of the common cheap articles which were supplied for the trade. Long, single-barrelled affairs they were, the barrels of blue metal, stocks extending to the muzzles and stained red, brass mountings of toy-like flimsiness, and flint-locks; the entire gun being worth something less than a pound sterling. These weapons were capable, nevertheless, of shooting pretty straight, though uncomfortably apt to burst.

One having been handed to the chief he received it with a grasp of almost reverential affection, while Lumley extracted from his funds the requisite number of quills in payment.

"What next?" asked Salamander, and again the solemn gaze went slowly round the store, on the shelves of which our goods were displayed most temptingly. Black eyes riveted once more! What is it?

"A green blanket."

"Just so. Fetch a four-point one, Max, he's a big man."

I took up one of our largest-sized thick green blankets, handed it to the chief, and Lumley abstracted a few more quills from the bundle.

At this point the red-man seemed to get into the swing of the thing, for a white blanket of medium size, and another of very small dimensions, were demanded. These represented wife and infant. After this a tin kettle and a roll of tobacco were purchased. The chief paused here, however, to ponder and count his quills.

"Do you observe," said Lumley to me, in a low voice, "what a well-balanced mind he has?"

"I can't say that I do, Lumley."

"No? Don't you see; first a gun—self-and-family-preservation being the first law of nature; then, after thus providing for war and hunting, comes repose, d'you see? a big blanket, which immediately suggests similar comfort to the squaw, a smaller blanket; then comes comfort to the baby, a miniature blanket; then, how naturally the squaw and the squawker conduct his mind to food—a tin kettle! after which he feels justified in refreshing himself with a slight luxury—tobacco! But you'll see that he will soon repress self, with Indian stoicism, and return to essentials."

Lumley was right for he had barely ceased to speak, when the chief turned and demanded an axe; then fish-hooks; then twine for lines; then awls for boring holes in the bark with which he made his canoes; then powder and shot and pipes. After this, another fit of tenderness came over him, and he bought some bright scarlet and blue cloth—doubtless for the squaw or the baby—and some brilliantly coloured silk thread with needles and variegated beads to ornament the same. Soon his quills dwindled away till at last they disappeared; yet his wants were not fully supplied—would the pale-face chief advance him some goods on credit?

Oh yes—he seemed a good and trustworthy brave—the pale-face chief had no objection to do that!

Accordingly I opened a ledger and inserted the man's name. It was almost Welsh-like in difficulty of pronunciation, but, unlike a Welshman, I spelt it as pronounced, and set down in order the additional goods he required. When Lumley thought he had given him enough on credit, he firmly closed the account, gave the man a small gratuity of tobacco, powder and shot, etcetera, and bade another chief come forward.

It was slow but interesting work, for, as the Indians grew familiar with the place and our ways, those of them who were loquacious, or possessed of humour, began to chat and comment on the goods, and on the white man's doings in a way that was very diverting.

After the chief men had traded their furs, the rank and file of the band came on, and, as is the case with all rank and file, there were some indifferent, and a few bad characters among them. It was now that I observed and admired the tact, combined with firmness, of Lumley. He spoke to these Indians with exactly the same respect and suavity that had characterised him when trading with the chiefs. When he saw any one become puzzled or undecided, he suggested or quietly advised. If a man's eye appeared to twinkle he cut a mild joke with him. If one became too familiar, or seemed disposed to be insolent he took no notice, but turned aside and busied himself in arranging the goods.

At last, however, an incident occurred which called for different treatment. There was among the Indians a long-legged, wiry fellow who had been named Attick, or Reindeer, because he was a celebrated runner. Those who disliked him—and they were numerous—said he was good at running away from his foes. However that might be, he was undoubtedly

144

dexterous in the use of his fingers—and it was through this propensity that we were first introduced to him. It happened thus:

Lumley, whose powers of observation often surprised me, had noticed that Attick looked often and with longing eyes at a very small roll of tobacco which belonged to one of his comrades, and lay on the counter temptingly near at hand. Slowly, and, as it were, inadvertently, he advanced his hand until it touched the tobacco, then, laying hold on it, when the owner was busy with something else, he carried it towards the bosom of his leather hunting-shirt. Before it reached that place of concealment, however, Lumley quickly, yet so quietly that the act was scarce perceived, seized the elbow of the chief and gave him a look. Attick promptly put the tobacco down and looked at Lumley with a scowl, but the pale-face chief was smilingly giving some advice to the man with whom he was trading.

He thought that the man would not attempt anything more of a similar kind, at least at that time, but he was mistaken. He under-estimated the force of covetousness and the power of temptation in a savage. Soon afterwards he saw Attick deftly pass a packet of bright beads, belonging to another comrade, from the counter to his breast, where he let it remain, grasped in his hand. Immediately afterwards the owner of the beads missed them. He turned over his goods hastily, but could not find the packet and looked suspiciously at Salamander, who had been standing near all the time, besides fingering the things occasionally.

"A comrade has stolen it," said Lumley, in a quiet voice and without looking at any one save the robbed man.

This was received with scowls and strong marks of disapprobation.

"Not so! The interpreter, the pale-face, has stolen it," returned the Indian fiercely.

Instead of replying, Lumley vaulted lightly over the counter, stood before the astonished Attick, thrust his hand into the bosom of that savage, and, by main force, dragged forth the thieving fist still closed over the missing packet. The Indians were too much taken by surprise at the promptness of the act to speak—they could only glare.

"My friends," said Lumley, still maintaining, however, something of kindliness in his look of stern gravity, "the Great Master of Life does not love thieving, and no thief will be permitted to enter this store."

What more he would have said I know not for, swift as lightning, Attick drew his knife and made a plunge at my friend's heart. Expecting a scuffle, I had also leaped the counter. Lumley caught the wrist of the savage; at the same time he exclaimed, "Open the door, Max."

I obeyed, expecting to see the Indian kicked out, but I was wrong, for my friend, with a sharp twist turned Attick's back to his own breast, then, seizing him by both elbows, he lifted him off his feet as if he had been a mere infant, carried him forward a few paces, and set him gently down outside. Then, stepping back, he shut the door.

A roar of laughter from those without showed the light in which they viewed the incident, and the amused looks of some of those in the store told that at least they did not disapprove of the act.

Without paying any regard to these things, however, Lumley returned to his place, and with his usual air of good humour continued to barter with the red-men.

Thus the work of trading went on for three days, and, during that time, there was much fraternising of what I may call our home—Indians with the newcomers, and a great deal, I regret to say, of gambling. We found that this evil prevailed to a great extent among them, insomuch that one or two of them gambled away all that they possessed, and came to us with very penitent looks, asking for a small quantity of goods on credit to enable them to face the winter!

I need scarcely say that our amiable chief complied with these requests, but only on the solemn promise that the goods so advanced should not be risked in gambling, and I have reason to believe that these men were faithful to their promises. This gambling was of the simplest kind, consisting of the method which is known by the name of "odd or even?"

In the evenings the chiefs were encouraged to come into our hall and palaver. They availed themselves of the invitation to come, and sometimes palavered, but more frequently smoked, with owlish solemnity, squatting on the floor with their backs against the wall.

Nevertheless, on these occasions we gained a good deal of information, and Lumley availed himself of the opportunities sometimes to lecture them on the sin of gambling. He always, I observed, laid much more stress on the idea that the Great Master of Life was grieved with His children when they did evil, than that He visited the sin with disagreeable consequences. On one of these occasions an elderly chief surprised us by suddenly putting the question, "Do the pale-faces trade fire-water?"

Every pipe was removed from every lip, and the glittering eyes of expectancy, coupled with the all but total cessation of breathing, told of the intense interest with which they awaited the answer.

"No," replied Lumley, "we sell none. We do not love fire-water."

A deep but quiet sigh followed, and the pipes were resumed in silent resignation. And, I must add, I felt devoutly thankful that we did *not* sell fire-water, when I looked at the strong features and powerful frames of the red-men around me.

* * * * *

CHAPTER FIFTEEN.

A Catastrophe, a Letter, and a Surprise.

Autumn at length gradually drew to a close, and we began to make preparations for the long winter that lay before us.

Our saw-mill, having been repaired and improved, had worked so well that we had cut a considerable quantity of planks, as well for the boats which we intended to build as for the houses. It was fortunate that this had been accomplished before the occurrence of an event which put an effectual stop to that branch of our industries. It happened thus:

One afternoon the fine weather which we had been enjoying so long gave place to boisterous winds and deluges of rain, confining us all to the fort and making us feel slightly miserable.

"But we mustn't grumble, Max," said Lumley to me, as we looked out of our small windows. "We must take the evil with the good as it comes, and be thankful."

"Please, I wasn't grumbling," said I, sharply.

"No? I thought you were."

"No, I was not. It must have been internal grumbling by yourself that you heard," I retorted, sauntering back to the fire, which by that time we had begun to light daily.

"I daresay you're right, Max; it has often struck me as a curious fact that, when one is cross or grumpy, he is apt to think all the rest of the world is also cross or grumpy. By the way, that reminds me—though I don't see why it should remind me, seeing that the two things have no connection—that Coppet came to me last night saying he had discovered a slight leak in the dam. We'd better look to it now, as the rain seems to have moderated a little."

We went out forthwith, and found Coppet already on the spot, gazing at a small rill of water which bubbled up from behind a mass of rock that jutted out from the cliff and formed a support for the beams of our dam.

"Something wrong there, Coppet," said Lumley, inspecting the place carefully.

"Oui, monsieur—it is true."

"Can you guess where it comes through?" I asked.

"Vraiment, monsieur, I know not, but surely the dam it is quite strong."

"Strong!—of course it is, unnecessarily strong," said I, looking up at its edge, over which the water, rendered muddy by the rains, flowed in a considerable volume. "What think you, Lumley?"

I asked my friend's opinion somewhat anxiously, because I observed that he seemed to examine the place with unusually grave looks.

"Max," he said at last, "your engineering is defective. It is true that the beams and stuffs of which the dam is composed could resist all the weight or force of water that can be brought to bear on them—even an untrained eye like mine can see that—but you had not observed that this mass of rock, against which the whole affair rests, has got a crack in it, so that it is partially, if not altogether, detached from the cliff. No doubt it is a large heavy mass, but the strain upon it must be very severe, and its stability depends on its foundations."

"The foundations seem secure enough," said I, looking down.

"True, but natural foundations are sometimes deceptive, and that bubbling spring may be quietly washing these away. We must use a little art here. Go, Coppet," he added, turning to the carpenter, "fetch all the men, and your tools, and as many heavy timbers as you can readily lay hands on. Come, Max, help me to lift this one."

149

The decision of Lumley's manner and the energetic way in which he threw off his coat and set to work, convinced me that he thought danger of some sort was impending. I therefore followed his example, and set to with a will.

We fixed a heavy log in front of the suspected mass of rock, placing its end against the centre of the mass, and sinking the other end into the ground—having previously, however, sunk a strong crossbeam into the ground to bear the pressure of that end.

"This of itself," said my chief, "will go far to avert evil, but we will adopt your tactics, Max, and, by giving it superabundance of strength, make assurance doubly sure."

In pursuance of this plan, he ordered the men to plant several ponderous logs in the same position as the first beam, over which other logs were thrown crosswise, and the whole was weighted with heavy stones.

During our operations, which occupied us all till evening, the rain increased tenfold, and at last came down in absolute sheets, flooding our dam to such an extent that it overflowed nearly all round the brim in pretty solid cataracts of dirty water, which brought down branches and leaves and other débris from the higher parts of the stream.

I was gratified to see, however, that our embankment showed no symptoms of weakness, and felt assured that the powerful structure we had just set up was more than sufficient to prevent any rupture in the rock itself. Comforted by these thoughts, Lumley and I returned to the hall in a burst of thunder, lightning, and rain—thoroughly saturated, and in a condition to do ample justice to the sea-biscuit, fried salt-pork, hung whitefish and tea, which Salamander had prepared for supper.

Blondin, being a polite, intelligent fellow as well as our foreman, was privileged to take his meals with us, besides occupying one of our four rooms. In consequence of this we conversed chiefly in the patois French of the country, for the worthy man was not deeply learned in English.

Salamander messed with the men in their own house, after preparing and spreading our meals.

"What say you to a game of chess?" said Lumley to me, after the tea-things had been carried away by Blondin.

"By all means," I replied, going to a corner cupboard, in which we kept miscellaneous articles, and bringing out the chess-board.

This board and its men, by the way, merit passing remark, for they were fashioned by our chief entirely, and very neatly, out of the pith of a bush, the name of which I forget; and, on the voyage, many an hour that might otherwise have been tedious we whiled away with this interesting game. I knew nothing of it when we began, but Lumley taught me the moves, and I soon picked up enough of the game to enable me to fight a fairish battle before being beaten. At first Lumley always won, and was wont to signalise his victory by the expression of a modest hope that the tables would be turned ere long. That hope—whether genuine or pretended—was not long of being gratified, for as my mind by degrees began to grasp the mysteries of chess, I succeeded in winning a game now and then.

On this particular night, however, the tables were turned literally, and in a way that we little expected.

Blondin, being left to himself, had sought the companionship of his pipe, and was dozing over the fire, more than half asleep—at least not more awake than was consistent with the keeping of his pipe between his lips. Ever and anon he was startled into a more wakeful condition by the tremendous blasts which frequently shook the house; but these did not disturb him much, for he had helped to build the house, and knew that it was strong.

We were all indeed pretty well tired by our recent exertions, and rather sleepy, so that the game languished a little. Salamander, having obtained permission to retire, was in bed in his own corner-room, entertaining us with a duet through the nose—if I may call that a duet in which both nostrils played the same air.

151

"Check!" said Lumley, rousing himself a little, and placing a knight in such a position as to endanger my king.

"Mate!" I exclaimed ruefully.

"Hallo!" cried Blondin, waking up at the familiar word.

"No—not that sort of mate," said I, with a laugh, "but the—"

I stopped abruptly, for at that moment we heard a sound that sent a thrill to our hearts. It was something between a rend and a crash. We looked at each other in consternation.

"The dam's going," exclaimed Lumley.

Another crash, that there was no misunderstanding, proved that it was gone.

We ran towards the back door, but before reaching it, we had an additional proof that was even more convincing than the last. A rush of tumultuous water was heard outside. Next moment the back door was burst inward, and a deluge of water met us. Lumley, who was nearest the door, was swept off his legs, and came against me with such violence that I fell over him. Blondin, who was furthest off, tried to stop us, but also went down, and all three were swept into the lower side of the hall amid a jumble of tables, chairs, billets of wood, stray garments, and chessmen.

The fire had been put out; so had the candle, and we were thus in nearly pitch darkness, when we heard a yell from Salamander. It was followed by a great splash, and we dimly perceived something like a half-naked ghost floundering towards us.

It was Salamander!

"Hold on!" shouted Lumley.

"Dere's noting to hold on to, monsieur," cried the interpreter in desperation, as he tripped over something and rose again—gasping.

The rush was over in half a minute, but the great weight of water that had entered held the front door, which opened inwards, so tight, that our hall was converted into a water-tank about three feet deep, while a huge mass of logs and débris outside blocked the opening of the back door.

"Stay, don't move till I get a light," cried Lumley, wading to the corner cupboard, where, on an upper shelf, we kept our candles, with flint, steel, and tinder.

While he was striking a light we all stood silent and shivering, but when a candle was with difficulty lighted, I burst into an irresistible fit of laughter for the scene we presented was ludicrous in the extreme. It was not our woe-begone looks which tickled me, so much as the helpless, drowned-rat-like aspect we had all assumed—all except our chief, whose tall, strong figure holding a candle over his dishevelled head looked like the spirit of destruction presiding over a scene of desolation.

A rapping at the front door was the first thing that recalled us to the necessity for action.

"Is it drownded ye all are, Muster Lumley?"

It was the voice of Donald Bane.

"Not quite," cried Lumley, with a laugh and a shiver. "Come in, Donald."

"Ay, ay, sur, I would come in if I could, but the door won't open."

"Shove hard, Donald."

"I wull, sur. Here, Shames, lend a hand."

We heard both the Highlanders put their broad backs against the door and groan in Gaelic as they heaved, but they might as well have tried to lift the house. They caused the door to crack, however.

"Wheesht! What's that Shames?"

"We've splut the toor, 'Tonald."

"Never mind; heave again, boys," cried Lumley.

At that moment poor Salamander, who was groping about with nothing but his shirt on, stumbled over something, and, in trying to recover himself, pitched head first against the door with considerable violence.

This was a climax. The door, although it had withstood the pressure from without, could not resist this additional pressure within. It collapsed and burst outwards suddenly. The great mass of water went forth with

153

the gushing hilarity of a prisoner set free, and, with something like a roar of triumph, carried Salamander like a chip on its crest. He was launched into the bosom of the amazed James Dougall, who incontinently went with the stream, laying hold of and carrying off Donald Bane as he passed.

After a few turns over on the lawn, the three men regained their footing, and made their way back to the house, while the stream, subsiding almost immediately, left us in peace to make the best of what James Dougall called a paad chob!

What had actually occurred was this: the rock that held the main supports of our dam, being detached from the cliff as Lumley had surmised, had been undermined by the unusual floods of the previous week. Even in that condition it might have remained fast, so strong was our artificial buttress, but as the foundation wore away the rock heeled over to one side a little; this deranged the direct action of the buttresses, and in an instant they flew aside. The rock was hurled over, and the whole of our dam was dashed in dire confusion into the bed of the stream. It was this choking of the natural channel which sent the great flood over our lawn, and, as we have seen, created such a hubbub in the hall.

Of course all danger was now past. The roaring torrent soon forced its way into its own bed again, and all we had to do was to repair damages as well as we could, and make ourselves as comfortable for the night as circumstances would admit of.

Fortunately the next day was fine and warm, with brilliant sunshine. Being Sunday we let everything remain just as it was, for Lumley and I were of the same mind in regard to the Sabbath-day, and, from the commencement of our expedition, had as far as possible rested from all week-day labour on that day. Both of us had been trained to do so from infancy.

Well do I remember my dear old father's last advice to me on this subject. "Punch," said he, "wherever you go, my boy, 'remember the Sabbath-day to keep it holy.' You'll be tempted to do ordinary work, and to go in for ordinary amusement on that day, but don't do it, my boy—don't do it. Depend upon it, a blessing always attends the respecter of the Sabbath."

"But, father," said I, venturing for the first time in my life to echo what I had often heard said, "is it true, as some people assert, that the Sabbath is a Jewish institution, and no longer binding on Christians? Pardon my venturing to repeat this objection—"

"Objection!" interrupted my father, "why, dear boy, there's nothing I like better than to hear fair, honest objections, because then I can meet them. How can the Sabbath be a Jewish institution when the commandment begins with 'remember'? The day to be remembered was instituted at Creation, given to man as a blessed day of rest from toil, and recognised as binding by our Saviour, when He sanctioned works of necessity and mercy on that day."

I never forgot my father's advice on this subject, and have experienced mental, physical, and spiritual benefit as the result.

Owing to our belief in the Sabbath, then, we invariably, while travelling, remained in camp on that clay, and found that we not only did not lose, but actually had gained in speed at the end of each week—comparing our rate of progress with that of those who did not rest on Sundays. And I now recall to mind a certain bishop of the Church of England who, while travelling in the great Nor'-west between two well-known stations, made the fastest journey on record, although he regularly remained in camp on the Sabbath-day. On that day, also, after our arrival at Lake Wichikagan, and all through the winter, Lumley made a regular practice of assembling the men and reading a sermon from a book which he had brought for the purpose. And he did not neglect instruction of another kind, to which I shall refer as well as to our winter amusements, in the proper place.

During all this time our larder had been well supplied by Blondin with fresh fish from the lake, and by the Indians with haunches of reindeer and moose, or elk, venison. They also brought us beaver-meat, the tails of which were considered the best portions. Bear's-meat was offered us, but we did not relish it much, possibly from prejudice; but we would have been glad of it, doubtless, if reduced to short allowance. Of course wild-fowl of all kinds were plentiful, and many of these were shot by Lumley and myself, as well as by our men.

Some of the geese we had at first salted, but, the frost having come, we were by that time able to preserve fish and meat quite fresh for winter use—so that both net and gun were in constant occupation.

One day, while Lumley and I were sitting at dinner—which we usually took about noon—we were agreeably surprised by the appearance of a strange Indian, and still more agreeably surprised by his entering the hall and holding out a packet to Lumley. Having delivered it, the man, who looked wayworn, strode to the fire, sat quietly down and began to smoke a pipe which I had handed to him ready charged.

"Why, what's this?" exclaimed Lumley, unwrapping the covering of the packet, "not a letter, surely!—yes, I declare it is—and from Macnab too. Come, this *is* an unlooked-for treat."

I was quite excited—indeed we both were—for a letter in those regions was about as rare as snow in July.

Lumley opened it hastily and read as follows:—

"My dear Lumley, you will be surprised to get a letter from me, and dated, too, from an unknown post. Yes, my boy, like yourself, I have been transferred from my old home, to this region, which is not more than two hundred miles from your present residence. The governor sent me to establish it soon after you left. I have named it the *Mountain House*, because there's a thing the shape and size of a sugar-loaf behind it. So, I'll hope to look you up during the winter. Before going further let me give you a piece of news—I've got my sister out here to stay with me! Just think of that!"

At this point Lumley laid down the letter and stared at me.

"Why, Max, such a thing was never heard of before! If he had got a wife, now, I could have understood it, but a sister!"

156

"Well, whatever she is to him, she's a civilised white woman, and that's a sight worth seeing in those regions. I wonder what she's like?" said I.

"Like himself, of course. Tall, raw-boned, square-shouldered, red-haired (you know he told us she was red-haired), square-jawed, Roman-nosed—a Macnab female could be nothing else."

"Come," said I, "don't be impolite to Highland females, but go on with the letter."

Lumley obeyed, but the letter contained little more of interest. We cared not for that, however. We had now a subject capable of keeping us in speculative talk for a week—the mere fact that there was actually a civilised woman—a *lady* perhaps—at all events a Macnab—within two hundred miles of us!

"No doubt she's a rugged specimen of the sex," said Lumley, as we sat beside the fire that night, "no other kind of white female would venture to face this wilderness for the sake of a brother; but she *is* a white woman, and she *is* only two hundred miles off—unless our friend is joking—and she's Macnab's sister—Jessie, if I remember rightly—

"'Stalwart young Jessie,
The flower of—'"

"Come, Lumley, that will do—good-night!"

* * * * *

CHAPTER SIXTEEN.

The Joys of Camping Out—Important Additions to the Establishment—Serious Matters and Winter Amusements.

At last winter came upon us in earnest. It had been threatening for a considerable time. Sharp frosts had occurred during the nights, and more than once we had on rising found thin ice forming on the lake, though the motion of the running water had as yet prevented our stream from freezing; but towards the end of October there came a day which completely changed the condition and appearance of things.

Every one knows the peculiar, I may say the exhilarating, sensations that are experienced when one looks out from one's window and beholds the landscape covered completely with the first snows of winter.

Well, those sensations were experienced on the occasion of which I write in somewhat peculiar circumstances. Lumley and I were out hunting at the time: we had been successful; and, having wandered far from the fort, resolved to encamp in the woods, and return home early in the morning.

"I do love to bivouac in the forest," I said, as we busied ourselves spreading brush-wood on the ground, preparing the kettle, plucking our game, and kindling the fire, "especially at this season of the year, when the sharp nights render the fire so agreeable."

"Yes," said Lumley, "and the sharp appetites render food so delightful."

"To say nothing," I added, "of the sharp wits that render intercourse so pleasant."

"Ah, and not to mention," retorted Lumley, "the dull wits, stirred into unwonted activity, which tone down that intercourse with flashes of weakly humour. Now then, Max, clap on more wood. Don't spare the firing—there's plenty of it, so—isn't it grand to see the thick smoke towering upwards straight and solid like a pillar!"

"Seldom that one experiences a calm so perfect," said I, glancing upward at the slowly-rising smoke. "Don't you think it is the proverbial calm before the storm?"

"Don't know, Max. I'm not weather-wise. Can't say that I understand much about calms or storms, proverbial or otherwise, and don't much care."

"That's not like your usual philosophical character, Lumley," said I— "see, the column is still quite perpendicular—"

"Come, Max," interrupted my friend, "don't get sentimental till after supper. Go to work, and pluck that bird while I fill the kettle."

"If anything can drive away sentiment," I replied, taking up one of the birds which we had shot that day, "the plucking and cleaning of this will do it."

"On the contrary, man," returned Lumley, taking up the tin kettle as he spoke, "true sentiment, if you had it, would induce you to moralise on that bird as you plucked it—on the romantic commencement of its career amid the reeds and sedges of the swamps in the great Nor'-west; on the bold flights of its maturer years over the northern wilderness into those mysterious regions round the pole, which man, with all his vaunted power and wisdom, has failed to fathom, and on the sad—I may even say inglorious—termination of its course in a hunter's pot, to say nothing of a hunter's stom—"

"Lumley," said I, interrupting, "do try to hold your tongue, if you can, and go fill your kettle."

With a laugh he swung off to a spring that bubbled at the foot of a rock hard by, and when he returned I had my bird plucked, singed, split open, and cleaned out. You must understand, reader, that we were not particular. We were wont to grasp the feathers in large handfuls, and such as would not come off easily we singed off.

"You see, Lumley," said I, when he came back, "I don't intend that this bird shall end his career in the pot. I'll roast him."

"'Tis well, most noble Max, for I wouldn't let you pot him, even if you wished to. We have only one kettle, and that must be devoted to tea."

It was not long before the supper was ready. While it was preparing Lumley and I sat chatting by the fire, and gazing in a sort of dreamy delight at the glorious view of land and water which we could see through an opening among the trees in front of us; for, not only was there the rich colouring of autumn everywhere—the greens, yellows, browns, and reds of mosses, grasses, and variegated foliage—but there was a bright golden glow cast over all by the beams of the setting sun.

Ere long all this was forgotten as we lay under the starry sky in profound slumber.

While we slept, the Creator was preparing that wonderful and beautiful change to which I have referred. Clouds gradually overspread the sky—I observed this when, in a half-sleeping state I rose to mend our fire, but thought nothing of it. I did not, however, observe what followed, for sleep had overpowered me again the instant I lay down.

Softly, silently, persistently, and in large flakes, the snow must have fallen during the entire night, for, when we awoke it lay half a foot deep upon us, and when we shook ourselves free and looked forth we found that the whole landscape, far and near, was covered with the same pure white drapery. The uniformity of the scene was broken by the knolls of trees and shrubs and belts of forest which showed powerfully against the white ground, and by the water of the numerous ponds and lakes and streams which, where calm, reflected the bright blue sky, and, where rough, sparkled in the rising sun; while every twig and leaf of bush and tree bore its little fringe or patch of snow, so that we were surrounded by the most beautiful and complicated forms of lacework conceivable of Nature's own making.

"It is glorious to look at," said Lumley, after our first burst of enthusiasm, "but it will be troublesome to walk through, I fear."

We did not, however, find it as troublesome as we had expected; for, although nearly a foot deep, the snow was quite dry, owing to the frost which had set in, and we could drive it aside with comparative ease when we started on our journey homeward.

Arrived at the fort we found our men and the few Indians who had not left us for their hunting-grounds, busy at the nets, or finishing the buildings that were yet incomplete.

We also found that Big Otter had come in, bringing with him his wife, and his niece Waboose, with her mother. The health of the latter had broken down, and Big Otter had brought her to the fort in the hope that the white chief could do something for her.

"I'll do what I can," said Lumley, on hearing her case stated, "though I make no pretence to being a medicine-man, but I will do this for you and her:—I will engage you, if you choose, to help Blondin at his fishery, and your wife to make moccasins for us. I'll also let you have that little hut beside our kitchen to live in. You'll find it better and warmer than a wigwam, and as there are two rooms in it you won't be overcrowded."

Big Otter was delighted with this arrangement, and I took him away at once to show him the hut he was to occupy.

As this was the first time I had met with the unknown Englishman's widow, and the mother of Waboose, it was with no little interest and curiosity that I regarded her.

She was evidently in very bad health, but I could easily see that when young she must have been a very handsome woman. Besides being tall and well-formed, she had a most expressive countenance and a dignified air, coupled with a look of tender kindness in it, which drew me to her at once. She seemed in many respects much superior—in manners and

161

habits—to the other Indian women of the tribe, though still far below her daughter in that respect, and I could easily perceive that the latter owed her great superiority and refinement of manner to her father, though she might well have derived her gentleness from her mother.

What the illness was that broke that mother down I cannot tell. It resembled consumption in some respects, though without the cough, but she improved in health decidedly at first on getting into her new house, and set to work with zeal to assist in the making of moccasins and other garments. Of course Waboose helped her; and, very soon after this arrival, I began to give her lessons in the English language.

Lumley quizzed me a good deal about this at first, but afterwards he became more serious.

"Now, Max, my boy," he said to me, one evening when we were alone, in that kindly-serious manner which seemed to come over him whenever he had occasion to find fault with any one, "it is all very well your giving lessons in English to that Indian girl, but what I want to know is, what do you expect to be the upshot of it?"

"Marriage," said I with prompt decision, "if—if she will have me," I added with a more modest air.

My friend did not laugh or banter me, as I had expected, but in an earnest tone said:—

"But think, Max, you are only just entering on manhood; you can't be said to know your own mind yet. Suppose, now, that you were to express an intention to marry Waboose, the Hudson's Bay Company might object till you had at least finished your apprenticeship."

"But I would not think of it before that," said I.

"And then," continued Lumley, not noticing the interruption, "if you do marry her you can never more return to the civilised world, for she is utterly ignorant of its ways, and would feel so ill at ease there, and look so much out of place, that you would be obliged to take to the woods again, and live and die there—and—what would your father say to that?"

I confess that this reference to my dear father shook me.

162

"But, Lumley," said I, "she is *not* a mere Indian girl, and would *not* look out of place anywhere. Her father was obviously a gentleman, and has tried, with much success I find, to cultivate a naturally gentle and delicate mind and disposition in his child. Surely, very little is required to make a lady of her—I mean in the sense that society understands by that term—and even if that were not possible, is mere polish to be weighed in the balance against gentleness, sweetness, unselfishness, tenderness, truthfulness, modesty, loving-kindness—to say nothing of beauty—"

A hearty laugh interrupted me here.

"Oh! Max, I admit that polish must go down before such a splendid array of virtues. But," added my friend, becoming grave again, "is Waboose a Christian?"

"Yes," I replied, stoutly, "a far, far better Christian than I am, for I find that her father has taught her the truths of the Bible—and you—you see that *fruit* in her which I fear you don't see much of in me."

"Well, we have not had much time to see the fruit yet, but now I must speak to you as your chief. You say you have no thought of marriage till your apprenticeship is up. That is a good while yet. You may change your mind."

"Never!" said I, with emphasis.

"Well, I respect your honourable feelings, my boy, but it is just possible that even if she were willing (which has yet to be proved) she may change *her* mind, therefore you must promise me faithfully that in all this teaching of English there shall be no lovemaking. You are bound *in honour*, Max, to avoid trying to win her affections, or in any way to influence her till—till time, a considerable time—shall have passed."

"I promise you, Lumley, with all my heart. I think it is ennobling to a man to love a girl because of her pure and sterling qualities irrespective of her looks, and I would count it foul disgrace to do anything to win her unless I saw my way quite clearly to wed her."

"Which you do not at present, Max?"

"Which I do not at present, Lumley, so I will continue the lessons with the air and manner of a heartless pedagogue!"

This having been arranged between us, the subject was dropped, and not again referred to for many months.

Meanwhile winter advanced with rapid strides. One night an intense frost set in and covered the entire lake, as far at least as we could see, with a sheet of pure ice. It had set fast in a profound calm, and the surface was so smooth that every tree and bush on the outlying islets was reflected as if in water. Indeed, it could scarcely be told that the ice was not water except by going on it.

Being a somewhat expert skater, and having brought my skates with me, I put them on, resolved to enjoy a few hours of what used to be a favourite amusement when I was a boy. Lumley could not skate, to my regret; besides, he had no skates, and none of the men had ever learned the art, so that I was forced to skate alone. And at this time I learned a lesson about solitary amusement which I never afterwards forgot.

"Max," said Lumley, as I went down to the lake, skates in hand, "while you're off amusing yourself I'll go finish the track on the hillside—that will afford amusement enough for me and the men. I'll give them a holiday, as it is such a splendid day."

"That's a new kind of holiday," said I with a laugh, as I fixed on my skates, "to set them to the finishing of a track!"

The track referred to was a straight wide cutting up the face of the hill at the side of the fort. Lumley had ordered the men to clear it of trees and shrubs, from the hill-top—which extended far behind as well as high above the fort—down to the edge of the lake. It had remained in this unfinished state for some time, and now, being covered with snow, formed a long white-floored avenue to the hill-top.

"I'm sorry you can't join me," said I, making a few circles before starting. "It feels *so* selfish to go off alone."

"Never mind, old boy, off you go, and see that you don't get upon weak ice."

164

Lumley waved his hand as he spoke, and I shot swiftly away over the glassy lake.

Oh! it was a glorious burst, that first dash over an apparently illimitable sheet of water, for, although small for an American lake, the opposite shore of Wichikagan was so far-off as to appear dim and low, while, in one direction, the sky and water met at the horizon, so that I enjoyed the romantic feeling of, as it were, skating out to sea! The strength of youth thrilled in every nerve and muscle; the vigour of health and life coursed in every vein. I felt, just then, as if exhaustion were impossible. The ice was so smooth that there was no sensation of roughness under foot to tell of a solid support. The swift gliding motion was more like the skimming of the swallow than the skating of a man. The smallest impulse sent me shooting ahead with an ease that almost surprised me. In sensation, as well as in appearance, I was rushing over a surface of water in which the sun was reflected with a brilliancy that quite dazzled me. I became almost wild with delight. Indeed I grew reckless, and gave a sort of leap—with what intent I know not—which caused the back of my head to smite the ice and my body to proceed fifty yards or more on its back, with the legs in the air and a starry constellation corruscating in the brain!

Considerably sobered by this, I arose and cut the figure of eight thoughtfully for five minutes. After this I resumed my rapid pace, which I kept up until the necessity of pausing to recover breath impressed me. Making a wide circle outwards with my left leg in the air and my right hand pointed to the sky in the most approved manner, I gradually caused the circle to diminish until I came to a stand.

Looking back, I saw Fort Wichikagan like a mere speck on the horizon. In the opposite direction the lake still presented a limitless horizon. On either side the distant shores marked, but could hardly be said to bound, the view, while, closer at hand, the islets were reflected in the ice as clearly as if it had been water. I felt as if standing on a liquid ocean. Once more a bounding sense of joyous freedom and strength filled me. The starry corruscations had vanished. The bump on the back of my head had ceased to grieve me. Away I went again like—but words fail me. Imagery and description avail nothing when the indescribable is reached!

After an hour of this enjoyment I took to circling, and, in the exuberance of my feelings, attempted some quite new and complex performances, which resulted in a few more corruscations and bumps. But these were trifles. I heeded them not.

At last, however, I stood still and became thoughtful. We must all become thoughtful sooner or later. A sense of loneliness began to oppress me, and I longed for companionship in my joy. Knowing that this was a useless longing, I cast it aside and resumed my evolutions, rushes, bumps, and corruscations. But it would not do. The longing returned with redoubled violence. After another hour I turned to skate homeward, very much toned down in spirits, and deeply convinced of the truth—in more senses than one—of the words, "It is not good that man should be alone."

Before leaving this subject I may add that I tried skating again the next day, but again grew weary of it in less than an hour for want of companionship; that I made up my mind, in disgust to try no more; and that, on the day following, sympathetic Nature aided me in my resolve by covering the entire lake with eighteen inches of snow—thus rendering my once favourite exercise impossible.

But, to return. When I drew near to the fort, I observed that several black specks were gliding with lightning speed down the white track on the hillside which Lumley had undertaken to finish. These specks, after descending the steep hill, slid over the level shore and shot far out upon the lake, where some of them seemed to roll over and over. Wondering what this could be, I put on a spurt. Suddenly the truth dawned upon me. My friend Lumley had cleared the slope for the purpose of sledging down it!

"Max," he had remarked to me, long before, when talking about our men and our plans, "'All work and no play,' you know, 'makes Jack a dull boy;' so I'll get up some kind of winter amusement for the lads which will keep them in health and spirits."

Need I say that my recent cogitations and experience led me to join this riotous crew with redoubled ardour? Taking off my skates hurriedly and climbing up the hill, I leaped on the tail of Big Otter's toboggan, without invitation, just as he was starting at the top of the snow-slope to follow Lumley. I gave the sled such an impetus that we overtook our chief, and upset him just as he reached the lake, causing him to collide with Donald Bane and James Dougall, who, seated on the same toboggan, were anxiously striving to keep their balance. The result was, that we all resolved ourselves into a conglomerate of toboggans and men, which went shooting and struggling over the smooth lake for fifty yards or upwards at the rate of twelve miles an hour, if not more. This, of course, afforded unutterable delight to the rest of our men, and to Waboose and her mother; as well as to several Indians, who had just arrived. Among these last were Attick and Maqua with his son Mozwa.

It was rough but health-giving, as well as enjoyable, work, and sent us to our respective beds that night in a condition of readiness to fall promptly into a state of absolute oblivion.

* * * * *

CHAPTER SEVENTEEN.

Describes a Tremendous Visitation—A Feast—A Surprise—And an Attempt at Murder.

I must beg the reader now to leap with me into the middle of winter.

It is New Year's Day. That festive season of the year is not less marked and honoured in the Great Nor'-west than it is in civilised lands, though there are comparatively few to honour it, and their resources are somewhat meagre. These facts do not however, diminish the hearty zeal of the few—perchance they tend rather to increase it.

Be that as it may, I now convey the reader to an ice-bound forest. Deep snow has buried the frozen ground. Masses of snow weigh down the branches of the leafless trees; and evergreens, which are not leafless, are literally overwhelmed, almost obliterated, by the universal covering. But the scene is by no means dismal. A blue sky overhead and a bright sun and calm frosty air render it pre-eminently cheerful. The ground is undulating, and among these undulations you may see two men and a couple of sledges slowly making their way along.

The sledge in rear is the ordinary provision-sled used by winter travellers in that land; it is hauled by an Indian. The one in front is styled a cariole. It resembles a slipper-bath in form, is covered with yellow parchment, gaily painted, and drawn by four fine wolf-like dogs. The rider in that cariole is so whelmed in furs as to be absolutely invisible. The man who beats the track has a straight, stalwart frame, and from what of his countenance is left exposed by his fur cap and whiskers, one may judge that he is a white man.

Slowly and silently they plod along through the deep snow—the sleigh-bells on the dog's harness tinkling pleasantly. Ere long they come out upon a lake, where, the snow being beaten pretty hard, they proceed rapidly—the dogs trotting, and the leader, having changed to the rear, holding on to the cariole-line to restrain them.

Towards the afternoon the travellers draw towards the end of the lake, and then a spirit of mischief seems to enter into the wolf-like dogs, for, on turning round a point which reveals a wide reach of hard snow stretching away towards a distant group of buildings more than half buried in drift, they make a sudden bound, overturn the stalwart white man, jerk the tail-line from his grasp, and career away joyously over the ice, causing their bells to send up an exceeding merry and melodious peal.

From certain incomprehensible growls that escape the stalwart white man as he picks himself up, it might be conjectured that he had taken to the Chipewyan tongue; perhaps a Scotsman might have been led by them to recall the regions that lie north of the Grampians.

Lumley and I were sitting in the hall of Fort Wichikagan, awaiting the advent of dinner, when the sound of the sleigh-bells just referred to broke upon our ears. We bounded from our seats as if galvanised, seized our caps and rushed out.

"A cariole!" shouted Lumley.

"Run away!" said I.

As I spoke, the figure of a man was seen rushing round the point in pursuit.

"Macnab!" cried Lumley, with blazing eyes, "I'd know his figure at twenty miles off. I say, Max, the runaway cariole must certainly contain the sister—the carroty-haired Jessie! Hurrah! We must stop it, my boy, else the dogs will run slap into the fort, and dash the fair six-footer against one o' the houses. Look out, man!"

But Lumley was wrong. Either the dogs had run as much as they desired, or the decided manner in which we faced them caused them to swerve aside, and stop when they came close to us. The swerve had the effect of overturning the cariole gently, and emptying its contents at our feet, and out from the mass of wraps and furs there arose—not a red-headed six-footer, but a young and sprightly girl, with clear dark complexion, a neat, rounded little figure, and a pair of magnificent black eyes, which, at the moment, were opened to their utmost with an expression of intense amazement.

Lumley gazed at this apparition open-mouthed, with a look of blank surprise. I believe that my own visage must also have worn some remarkable expression, for suddenly the girl's gorgeous eyes half closed, and she burst into a hearty fit of laughter.

"Well, this *is* a surprise!" exclaimed Lumley, on recovering some of his usual self-possession.

"So it would seem," replied the apparition, still laughing, "for it has robbed you of common politeness. Why don't you introduce yourself and welcome me? No doubt you are my brother's friend, Mr Lumley!"

She drew a very small white hand from a very large leather mitten, and held it out.

"Forgive me, Miss Macnab—for of course you can be no other," said Lumley, advancing promptly and grasping the hand, "but your—your— sudden, and I may almost say magical, appearance has so taken me by surprise, that—that—"

"Yes, yes, I understand, Mr Lumley—that you find it difficult to recover yourself,—why, your friend Mr Maxby has not yet recovered," said the fair Jessie, turning and holding out her hand to me.

She was right. I had not recovered, but stood there open-mouthed and eyed, bereft of speech, until the necessity for action was thrust upon me. My apologies were, however, cut short by the coming up of her brother, who, while yet a long way off, began to shout in his stentorian tones:—

"Hallo! Lumley, my boy, how are ye? Here we are at last. A happy New Year, Max. Glad to see you once more—all alive and hearty? Eh? More than I expected to find *you*, Jess, after such a run with these rascally dogs—absolute wolves! But it might have been worse. Give us a shake o' your fists, my boys, on this happy New Year's Day."

By this time our hearty friend was beside us, shaking us both vigorously by the hands, wishing us all manner of good luck, and compliments of the season, and otherwise letting off the steam of his exuberant feelings.

"You've introduced yourselves, I see," he continued; "come, Lumley, give your arm to Jessie, and show us the way to the fort."

"If Miss Macnab," began Lumley, advancing, but his speech was here cut short.

"Miss Macnab!" echoed the explosive Peter in a sarcastic shout, "call her Jessie, man! who ever heard of a '*Miss* Macnab' in the backwoods? When men take to living in the wilderness, it's time to cast off all the humbuggin' politenesses o' civilised life."

"Pardon me, Macnab," returned my friend, with more than his usual urbanity, "I differ from you there."

"Oh, ay, I daresay ye do," interrupted the other. "It's been said of Scotsmen that 'they can aye objec',' and I think it's equally true of Englishmen that they can always differ!"

"Men who live in the wilderness," continued Lumley, merely answering the interruption with a smile, "ought to be unusually particular about keeping up all the politenesses of civilised life, instead of dropping them, and ought to be inexpressibly thankful when a soft and civilising influence, like Miss Macnab, condescends to visit them with a ray of sunshine from the old country."

"Bravo, Lumley," cried Macnab, with a boisterous laugh, "that speech was worthy of an Irishman! Call her what you like, my good fellow, so long as you never call her too late for meals; but come along now and let's have something to eat, for I'm famishing."

By this time the Indian with the sled had joined us, so we all went off to the fort in a state of boisterous joy, of which those unfortunates who have never been banished from their fellows for months—or for years—can form no conception. As dinner was opportunely smoking on the table when we entered the hall, our visitor's hilarity was, if possible, increased. Moreover, we had company that New Year's Day, for a knife and fork had been laid in the hall for every man at the fort. You see, Lumley was a strict disciplinarian, and, therefore, could afford at special times to relax without loss of dignity and with a great increase of good-will on the part of all under him. At all other times we and the men—excepting our guide—messed apart; but on Christmas and New Year's Days all distinctions were laid aside, discipline was relaxed, and we acted on the principle of that brotherhood which is based upon the assumption that all men have the same objects in life and the same hopes after death. That morning we had all played football on the ice together, had slidden and tumbled down the snow-slope together, and now we were about to mess together in the hall. Still further, our company was to be increased, and our festive board to be graced, by the presence of Waboose and her mother. Little had we imagined, when all this was planned, that we were to have the addition of our old friend Macnab, and that glorious beam from the sun of civilisation, his sister Jessie!

I will, however, make but brief reference to this festive occasion, and proceed to tell of an event which created an unexpected sensation in our little community, and might have closed our New Year's Day amusements with a terrible tragedy.

After dinner we circled round the blazing fire and enjoyed ourselves listening to Macnab, who had a happy facility in giving a graphic account of his sledge journey from the Mountain Fort—his recently built trading-post—to Fort Wichikagan, and I observed particularly that the presence of a lady among us had a most wonderful and irresistible influence in softening the tones and the manners of all.

As the evening advanced tea was introduced—we had nothing stronger, and did not, indeed, feel any desire for fire-water. Under the inspiriting influence of this beverage, several of our men were induced to tell stories, which were more or less humorous.

During the meal—at which Lumley insisted that "Miss Macnab" should preside, to the immense disgust of Salamander—I observed that the dark-haired white girl and the fair-haired Indian, drew very closely together. It appeared to me that they had fallen in love with each other at first sight, a fact which afforded me lively satisfaction, though I had no very clear perception as to why it should do so.

Songs naturally followed the cheering cup, and at this point Lumley became unusually bold.

"I wonder," he said, with a peculiar air of modesty which somewhat puzzled me, "if I may venture to ask Miss Macnab for a song."

"Ha! ha!" shouted her brother, before she could reply, "you *may* venture to ask, my boy, but you'll find it difficult to draw a song out of Jessie. Why, she never could sing a note!"

"I've a good mind to sing now, Peter," said the girl with a laugh, "just to prove that you are a false man."

"No, no, Jessie, spare me," returned the Highlander, "but get out your accordion, and—"

"Accordion!" almost shouted Lumley, "do you play the accordion? Have you really got one here?"

It is but right to say, in justification of Lumley's enthusiasm, that music of any kind was so seldom heard in those wilds, that the mere prospect of hearing good music excited us, for of course our natural thought was that a girl like Jessie Macnab could not perform anything but good music.

As she rose to go for the instrument to Salamander's room—which had been made over to her—a growling Gaelic exclamation made me aware of the fact that the faces of Donald Bane and James Dougall were beaming with hope, mingled with admiration of their countrywoman. She had naturally paid these men a good deal of attention, and, in addition to her other good qualities, spoke their native tongue fluently. As Dougall afterwards said, "She hes the Gaelic!"

On returning to the hall with the once familiar and well-remembered instrument, I believe every man there felt a tendency to worship her. But who shall describe the effect produced when she began to play, with the utmost facility and with deep feeling, one of the most beautiful of the plaintive Scottish melodies? Bane and Dougall shaded their rugged faces with their rugged hands to hide the tears that could not be restrained. Lumley, whose mind, although untouched by associations, was peculiarly susceptible to sweet sounds, sat entranced. So did Big Otter, who could only glare; because instrument, tune, and performer, were alike new and magical to him. Even Salamander forgot his jealousy and almost collapsed with wonder. As for Dumont, Coppet, and the others—they clasped their hands, opened their eyes and mouths, and simply drank it in.

There was no applause when the air ceased, but a deep sigh from every one seemed to be the indication of a return to ordinary consciousness. Waboose and her mother did not sigh, however. They sat still and gazed in silent wonder. Jessie Macnab, with a slight blush at the unexpected effect, ran her fingers lightly over the keys of her instrument, and then suddenly began to play a Highland reel with tremendous vigour!

If an electric shock had traversed the marrow or our backbones, the result could not have been more surprising.

"Wow! Tougall, man!" exclaimed Bane, starting up and flinging away his chair.

Dougall said nothing, but he uttered a Celtic yell suggestive of war and all its horrors to Big Otter, and, starting up, began the Highland fling opposite to his friend in the most violent manner. As I was not a bad dancer of Scots' reels myself, and the music had caused me also to boil over, I started up likewise and faced Macnab, who, being equally affected, stood up to me in a moment, and away we went, hammer and tongs, with stamp and whoop and snap of finger—oh! the scene is indescribable.

Indeed, I may say that to an ordinary civilised man who never saw it, the scene is inconceivable, so—we will pass on.

While these stirring events were taking place inside the hall, a black-faced, red-painted savage was flattening his ugly nose against a pane of glass outside one of the windows. It was Attick, whom our chief had convicted of stealing about the time of our arrival. That unpleasant savage had never forgiven Lumley, and, being exceedingly vindictive, had resolved to murder him! With this end in view, he had been prowling about the place for several days, having arrived with a band of his tribe who had assembled at Christmas-time to enjoy some of the good cheer which they understood to be going at that season among the pale-faces.

On New Year's night unknown to his comrades—for it was his intention to do the deed secretly, and leave the imputation upon all—he watched his opportunity, and thought he had found it when, after the dance was over and the guests had retired, he saw Lumley seated by the fire in conversation with the newly-arrived pale-face girl. Macnab and I had gone with the men to their house for some purpose—I forget what—so that the two were left alone.

Attick might easily have opened the door and shot his victim, but the report, he knew, would have roused every one; besides, his absence at the moment and his dirty gun would have betrayed him to his comrades; so, being a strong man, he preferred the scalping-knife, with the use of which he was of course familiar.

Now, it chanced that there hung a small looking-glass over the hall fireplace. In that glass Lumley could see not only himself, but the door and windows of the room behind him, as he sat chatting with Jessie Macnab. Happening to glance into the glass, he observed the flattened nose of Attick on the window-pane with the glaring eyes above it. A *tête-à-tête* with the fair Jessie was too pleasant, however, to be interrupted by such a trifle; he therefore continued the conversation, though he kept a sharp look-out behind him. Presently he saw the door open—open so gently that it gave forth no sound. Immediately after, a blackened and savage head appeared with a diabolical expression on the countenance. It was followed slowly by a hand in which a gleaming knife was clutched. Lumley now fully understood what was meditated, for he recognised Attick through his war-paint. He did not move, however, for he felt that if he sprang up too soon the savage could easily leap back through the doorway and escape into the dark woods. He therefore laid strong constraint on himself and waited.

Miss Macnab's back was turned to the savage, but not having the advantage of the glass, she could not see him, and continued her pleasant prattle. Like a dark, noiseless shadow, the Indian advanced, and raised his knife.

"Then you like this wilderness life?" asked Jessie, at that moment.

"Yes, I confess, Miss Macnab, that it has its charms as well as its disagreeables—the utter want of society being the worst of the latter."

"I should have thought," said the girl, looking up, "that you—but—but—why do you gaze and frown so fiercely at that—"

She was promptly answered, for Lumley sprang up at the moment with panther-like agility, wheeled round, seized the uplifted arm, and, with a wrench so violent as to break it, he hurled the savage to the ground.

Jessie Macnab sprang up in consternation, but did not give way to that supposed female-in-alarm necessity—a scream. At the same moment Macnab and I entered.

"Hallo! Lumley. What's all this?" cried Macnab. "Nobody hurt, I hope?"

"I fear the Indian is hurt somewhat," said our chief, looking down at his enemy, who lay stunned upon the floor. "Go, Max, assemble our men and fetch all the Indians."

In a few minutes all were assembled in the hall, when Lumley, in a low, stern voice, related what had occurred, appealing to Jessie to corroborate what he said.

"Now," he added in conclusion, turning to the Indians, "I have no quarrel with you. There lies your comrade. He has forfeited his life to me, but I forgive him. Take him away."

Lumley said no more, as, in solemn surprise and silence, the Indians lifted up their comrade and bore him out of the hall; but he took good care to make no reference whatever to the looking-glass, and I verily believe that to this day it is believed by the red-men of that region that Lumley has eyes in the back of his head.

* * * * *

CHAPTER EIGHTEEN.

The Mysterious Packet—Friends depart, and Lumley is caught singing.

The uncertainty of all sublunary things is a truism so trite that I do not mean to insult the reader's understanding by attempting to prove it. I merely refer to it in order to say that the great Nor'-west is not exempt from that general rule of uncertainty.

At first peace and prosperity attended us, at least in all the main lines of life, with only trivial variations, and we felt disposed to believe that the sunshine would continue to gladden us throughout the whole winter. But such was not to be the case. Soon after the events narrated in the last chapter, clouds began to gather, the peaceful flow of our life was interrupted, and at last a storm burst which filled the inhabitants of our little fort with consternation.

After the attempted murder by Attick on New Year's Day, the Indians left the fort, taking their wounded friend along with them. No doubt they felt that it would be scarcely reasonable in them to expect to be entertained with the good things of the pale-faces after the dastardly attempt that had been made on our chief's life. But Attick, who had been wounded more deeply in his feelings than in his body, resolved to be revenged. He was the more urged to this because his savage affections had been fixed on, and no doubt he had been sharp enough to perceive my own regard for the girl, and was jealous enough to believe that I would take advantage of my position and of her residence at the fort to supplant him.

Bad men invariably find like-minded spirits ready to help them in their dark designs. Among the redskins of his tribe Attick found no difficulty in securing the allegiance of one or two men, who were in the habit of looking up to him as their leader, and it was not very long before he found his opportunity—as shall soon be told. When the Macnabs had spent three weeks with us, they set off on the return journey to the Mountain Fort, taking Waboose along with them—for Jessie Macnab had taken so strong a fancy to the fair-haired half-caste that she had prevailed on her to agree to visit the Mountain Fort in company with her mother, from whom she refused to be separated even for a few days.

Before their departure, however, I had a conversation with Waboose, in which I reminded her of the packet about which she had spoken to me on a memorable occasion in the woods. I may remark here in passing that I had conscientiously held to my promise to Lumley, and had carefully abstained from making the slightest effort to gain the girl's affections, or to show her the state of my own feelings. Indeed, I had rather avoided her as much as possible without appearing rude or unkind. Of course I could not however, help showing my pity for, and sympathy with, her poor invalid mother, and as I was the only one in our little community who possessed the smallest knowledge of medicine or surgery I was forced to visit their hut daily in the capacity of doctor.

"Waboose," said I, during the conversation above referred to, "you need not be anxious about your mother. I feel assured that her complaint is of such a nature that her general health will be benefited by a trip over the snow—provided she is kept warm and does not travel too far each day. Of course there is no fear of that, with you and Miss Macnab to look after her, and I have given careful directions to Mr Macnab how to treat her."

"You are very kind," replied the girl with much earnestness of tone and manner.

"And now, Waboose," I continued, "you remember saying long ago you would show me the packet that—"

"Yes, it is here," she said, quickly, taking it out of the folds of a light shawl which covered her shoulders—the gift of Jessie—and handing it to me.

"Thank you. Well, I will examine it carefully this afternoon and give it back to you to-morrow before you start."

"No, keep it. I can trust you," she said, with a simple look that somehow depressed me, for it was almost too simple and sisterly to my mind. "Besides," she added, "it is safer in your hands than mine, and when I come again you will explain to me what it contains."

Next day the party left us. It consisted of Macnab, who, with his wonted energy of nature, was leader and beater of the track; the sprightly Jessie in a cariole drawn by four dogs; Waboose's mother in a similar cariole, and the fair Waboose herself, on snow-shoes, for she preferred the mode of travelling to which she had been most accustomed. Two Indians dragging provision-sleds brought up the rear.

It had been arranged that I should convoy the party to their first bivouac in the snow, spend the night with them, and continue to journey with them the second day as far as was consistent with the possibility of returning to the fort that night. Jack Lumley accompanied us at first, but another small party of Indians had come in to stay at the fort at that time, and although he had, I am certain, a very strong desire to go further, with his usual self-sacrificing spirit when duty pointed another way, he turned and left us at the end of a few miles.

I spent the night in the snow-bivouac as arranged, and continued to journey onward with the party next day, until Macnab refused to let me go another step.

"Now, Max," he said, laughingly, "you must turn here. Why, man, it will be midnight before you get in, good walker though you be. Come, good-bye."

"Well, well, I suppose it's better to turn since you seem tired of my company," said I, turning to Jessie, who stood up in her sleigh to shake hands. "Good-bye, Miss Macnab."

180

"Jessie, man, Jessie—none of your Miss Macnabs here, else I'll tumble you into the snow by way of farewell," shouted the irrepressible Highlander.

"Very well, good-bye, Jessie," said I, with a laugh, though my heart was heavy enough. "Good-bye, Waboose—farewell all."

With a wave of his hand Macnab tramped on ahead, the sleigh-bells rang out merrily and the rest of the party followed.

After they had gone a few yards Waboose turned and waved her hand again. As I looked on her fair face, glowing with health and exercise, her upright, graceful figure in its picturesque costume and her modest mien, I felt that two beams of light had shot from her bright blue eyes and pierced my heart right through and through. It was a double shot—both barrels, if I may say so—well aimed at the centre of the bull's-eye!

Next moment she was gone—the whole party having dipped over the brow of a snow-drift.

"An Indian! a half-caste!" I exclaimed in a burst of contempt, going off over the plain at five miles an hour, "nothing of the sort. A lady—one of Nature's ladies—born and br——no, not bred; no need for breeding where genuine purity, gentleness, tenderness, simplicity, modesty—"

I stuck at this point partly for want of words and partly because my snow-shoes, catching on a twig, sent my feet into the air and stuck my head and shoulders deep into a drift of snow. Though my words were stopped, however, the gush of my enthusiasm flowed steadily on.

"And what can be more worthy of man's admiration and respectful affection?" I argued, as I recovered my perpendicular, coughed the snow out of my mouth and nose, and rubbed it out of my eyes; "what more worthy of true-hearted devotion than this—this—creature of—of light; this noble child of nature—this *Queen of the Wilderness?*"

I repeated "This Queen of the Wilderness" for a considerable time afterwards. It seemed to me a happy expression, and I dwelt upon it with much satisfaction as I sped along, sending the fine snow in clouds of white dust from my snow-shoes, and striding over the ground at such a pace that I reached Fort Wichikagan considerably before midnight in spite of Macnab's prophecy.

I am not naturally prone thus to lay bare the secret workings of my spirit. You will, therefore, I trust, good reader, regard the revelation of these things as a special mark of confidence.

On reaching the fort I observed that a bright light streamed from the hall windows, casting a ruddy glow on the snow-heaps which had been shovelled up on each side of the footpath in front, and giving, if possible, a paler and more ghostly aspect to the surrounding scenery.

I went to one of the windows and, imitating Attick, flattened my nose against a pane. A pain was the immediate result, for, the glass being intensely cold, I was obliged to draw back promptly.

Lumley was seated alone at one side of the fire, in the familiar attitude of a man who meditates profoundly—or sleepily; namely, with his legs stretched straight out in front of him, his hands deep in his trousers-pockets, and his chin sunk on his breast, while his eyes stared fixedly at the flames.

I was about to quit my post of observation when a sudden action of my friend arrested me.

Drawing up his legs, grasping his knees with his hands, turning his eyes to the ceiling with that gaze which implies that planks and roof count for nothing in the way of intercepting the flight of Mind to the realms of Inspiration, Lumley opened his handsome mouth and broke forth into song. He had a magnificently harsh voice. I could distinguish both air and words through the double windows. The song was that which I have already quoted elsewhere—"Lovely young Jessie, the flower of Dunblane." The deep pathos of his tone was thrilling! It flashed a new thought into my brain. Then I became amazed at my own blind stupidity. I now understood the meaning of that restless activity which had struck me recently as being so uncharacteristic of my sedate friend; that anxiety to have all our food well cooked and nicely served, in one who habitually took food just as it came, and cared nothing for quality or appearance; that unusual effort to keep our hall neat and in order; those sharp reproofs to the astonished Salamander for failure in punctuality at meal-hours; that very slight indication of a more frequent use of the brush and comb, in one whose crisp curls required little aid from such implements.

Under the excitement of my discovery I burst into the room with, "Oh! Lumley, you deceiver!" cutting him short in the very middle of those repeated "lovely young Jessies" which constitute the very pith and marrow of the song.

"Why, Max! back already?" cried my friend, starting up with a slightly-confused look, which confirmed my suspicion, and rattling on at a pace which was plainly meant to carry me past the subject. "How you must have walked, to be sure, unless, indeed, you convoyed them only a short part of the way; but that could not have been the case. It would have been so unlike your gallant nature, Max—eh? Well, and how did they get on? Snow not too soft, I hope? Encampment comfortable? But no fear of that of course, with Peter Macnab as leader. No capsizes?"

"None," said I, seizing advantage of a slight pause; "everything went as well as possible, and the carioles went admirably—especially Jessie's."

I looked at him pointedly as I said this, but he coolly stooped to lift a billet and put it on the fire as he rattled on again.

"Yes? That's just what I hoped for, though I could not be quite sure of it for she has the old one which I had patched up as well as possible. You see, as Macnab said—and of course I agreed with him—it was only fair that the invalid should have the strongest and easiest-going conveyance. By the way, Max, I've heard some news. Do you know that that scoundrel Attick is stirring up the tribes against us?"

"No—is he?" said I, quite forgetting the fair Jessie, at this piece of information.

"Yes, and the rascal, I fear, may do us irreparable damage before we can tame him, for he has considerable influence with the young and fiery spirits among the savages—so Big Otter says. Fortunately his power lies only in the tongue, at present, for it seems I broke his arm the night he tried to murder me; but that will mend in time."

"Very unfortunate," said I, "that this should happen at the beginning of our career in this region. We must thwart his plans if we can."

"Moreover," continued Lumley, with a sly look, "I am told that he has the presumption to aspire to the hand of Waboose!"

"Indeed!" I exclaimed, as a flame of indignation seemed to shoot through my whole frame; "we must thwart his plans in *that* direction emphatically."

"Of course, of course," said my friend, gravely; "it would never do to let such a sweet girl throw herself away on a savage; besides, she's such a favourite with Jessie Macnab, you know. It would never do—never."

I looked at him quickly, but he was gazing abstractedly at the fire. I felt that I was no match for my friend at badinage, and gave it up!

"But what do you think he could do!" I asked with some anxiety, after a few minutes' thought. "You know that Waboose would as soon think of marrying that bloodthirsty savage as she would think of marrying a—a—"

"A pine-tree or a grizzly bear. Yes, I know," interrupted Lumley, "he will never get her with her own consent; but you know that savages have a knack of marrying women without their consent and then there is the possibility of his attempting to carry her off—and various other possibilities."

I saw that my friend was jestingly attempting to test my feelings, but I made no reply at first, though I felt strongly on the subject.

"Well, Lumley," said I, at length, "your first suggestion I meet with the reply that the consent of parents is not ignored among Indians, and that Waboose's mother is an Indian of so high-minded and refined a nature— partly acquired, no doubt, from her husband—that *she* will never consent to give her daughter to such a man; such a brute, I might say, considering what he attempted. As to Waboose herself, her father's gentle nature in her secures her from such a misfortune; and as to her being carried

184

off—well, I don't think any savages would be bold enough to try to carry off anything from the grip of Peter Macnab, and when we get her back here we will know how to look after her."

"It may be so," said Lumley, with a sigh; "and now, my boy, to change the subject, we must buckle to our winter's work in right good earnest; I mean what may be styled our philanthropic work; for the other work— firewood-cutting, hunting, store arranging, preparation for the return of Indians in spring, with their furs, and all the other odds and ends of duty—is going along swimmingly; but our classes must be resumed, now that the holidays are over, for we have higher interests to consider than the mere eating that we may live, and living that we may eat."

"All right," said I heartily, for I was very glad to help in a species of work which, I felt gave dignity to all our other labours. "I'll get the slates out and start the men at arithmetic to-morrow evening, from the place where we left off. What will you do? Give them 'Robinson Crusoe' over again?"

"No, Max, I won't do that, not just now at all events. I'll only finish the story and then begin the 'Pilgrim's Progress.' You observed, no doubt that I had been extending my commentaries on 'Robinson,' especially towards the last chapters."

"Yes—what of that?"

"Well, I am free to confess that that was intentionally done. It was a dodge, my boy, to get them into the habit of expecting, and submitting to, commentary, for I intend to come out strong in that line in my exposition of the Pilgrim—as you shall see. I brought the book with this very end, and the long winter nights, in view. And I mean to take it easy too—spin it out. I won't bore them with too much at a time."

"Good, but don't spin it out too long, Lumley," said I; "you know when men set their hearts on some magnificent plan or scheme they are apt to become prosy. I suppose you'll also take the writing class, as before?"

"I suppose I must," returned my friend, with a sigh, "though it goes against the grain, for I was never very good at penmanship, and we have lost our best scholars too, now that Waboose and her mother are gone."

"By the way, that reminds me," said I, "that Waboose gave me the packet which she received from her father not long before he was drowned. Here it is."

I drew it from my breast-pocket and held it up. "She told me her father had said it was no use her opening it, as she could not read it, but that she was to give it to the first white man whom she could trust; you remember my mentioning that to you? she gave it to me only yesterday, and I have not yet found time to read it."

"Did she say she could trust *you*, Max!"

"Of course she did. Why not?"

"Oh, certainly, why not?" repeated my friend, with a peculiar look. "Did she say you might communicate its contents to *me*?"

"Well, no, she did not," I replied, feeling rather perplexed. "But I am quite sure that, if she meant to trust me at all, she meant to trust to my discretion in the whole matter; and—Jack Lumley," I added, getting up and grasping my friend's hand, "if I cannot trust *you* I can trust nobody."

"That will do," he said, returning the squeeze. "You are safe. Go ahead."

The packet was wrapped in a piece of birch-bark, and tied with a bit of fibrous root. This covering removed, I found a white cambric handkerchief, inside of which was something hard. It turned out to be the miniature of a handsome man, somewhere between forty and fifty. Beside it was a manuscript in English. On one corner of the kerchief was marked in faded ink the name "Eve."

Holding out the portrait I said,—"You see. I knew he was a gentleman. This must be her father."

"No doubt," replied Lumley—"but what says this letter?"

Unfolding the manuscript I spread it carefully on my knee and began to read.

* * * * *

CHAPTER NINETEEN.

Opening of the Mysterious Packet.

The manuscript was without date or preface, and its contents interested as well as surprised us not a little. It began at once as follows:—

"Whoever receives this packet and letter from my daughter receives a sacred trust which he dare not shake off, and which I solemnly charge him in the sight of God to take up and fulfil. At the moment while I write I am well and strong, and not old. It is my firm intention, if God spares me, to pursue the course which is herein detailed, but I know too well the risk and dangers of the wilderness to feel assured that I shall live to act out my part. I therefore write down here, as briefly as I can, my story and my wishes, and shall give the letter with my miniature to my darling Waboose—whose Christian name is Eve, though she knows it not—with directions not to open it, or let it out of her hands, until she meets with a white man *whom she can trust*, for well assured am I that the man whom my innocent and wise-hearted Eve can *trust*—be he old or young—will be a man who cannot and will not refuse the responsibility laid on him. Why I prefer to leave this packet with my daughter, instead of my dear wife, is a matter with which strangers have nothing to do.

"I begin by saying that I have been a great sinner, but thank God, I have found Jesus a great Saviour. Let this suffice. I was never given to open up my mind much, and I won't begin now—at least, not more than I can help. It is right to say, at the outset, that I have been regularly married by a travelling Wesleyan minister to my dear wife, by whom also Eve and her mother were baptized.

"My fall began in disobedience to my mother. Probably this is the case with most ne'er-do-wells. My name is William Liston. My father was a farmer in a wild part of Colorado. He died when I was a little boy, leaving my beloved mother to carry on the farm. I am their only child. My mother loved and served the Lord Christ. And well do I know that my salvation from an ungovernable temper and persistent self-will is the direct answer to her unceasing prayers.

"I left home, against her will, with a party of backwoodsmen, my heart being set on what I once thought would be the free and jolly life of a hunter in the great American wilderness. I have lived to find the truth of that proverb, 'All is not gold that glitters,' and of that word, 'There is no rest, saith my God, to the wicked.'

"I was eighteen when I left home. Since then I have been a homeless wanderer—unless a shifting tent may be considered home! Long after my quitting home, and while staying with a tribe of Indians at the head waters of the Saskatchewan river, I met an Indian girl, whose gentle, loving nature, and pretty face, were so attractive to me that I married her and joined her tribe. The marriage ceremony was, as I have said, confirmed by a Wesleyan minister, whose faithful words made such an impression on me that I resolved to give up my wild life, and return with my wife and child to my old home. My character, however—which is extremely resolute and decided when following the bent of my inclinations, and exceedingly weak and vacillating when running counter to the same—interfered with my good intentions. The removal of the tribe to a more distant part of the land also tended to delay me, and a still more potent hindrance lay in the objection of my wife—who has been faithful and true to me throughout; God bless her! She could not for a long time, see her way to forsake her people.

"Ever since my meeting with the Wesleyan, my mind has been running more or less on the subject of religion, and I have tried to explain it as far

188

as I could to my wife and child, but have found myself woefully ignorant as well as sinful. At last, not long ago, I procured a New Testament from a trapper, and God in mercy opened my eyes to see and my heart to receive the truth as it is in Jesus. Since then I have had less difficulty in speaking to my wife and child, and have been attempting to teach the latter to read English. The former, whose mother and father died lately, has now no objection to go with me to the land of the pale-faces, and it is my present intention to go to my old home on the return of spring. I have not heard of my poor mother since I left her, though at various times I have written to her. It may be that she is dead. I hope not—I even think not, for she was very young when she married my father, and her constitution was strong. But her hair was beginning to silver even before I forsook her—with sorrow, I fear, on my account. Oh! mother! mother! How unavailing is my bitter regret! What would I not give to kneel once more at your feet and confess my sin! This may perhaps be permitted—but come weal, come woe, blessed be God we shall meet again.

"If my prayer is granted, this paper will never be seen by human eyes. If God sees fit to deny me this, and I should die in the wilderness, then I charge the man to whom my packet is given, to take my wife and daughter to Colorado; and if my mother—Mrs William Liston, of Sunny Creek—be still alive, to present them to her with this written paper and miniature. If, on the other hand, she be dead, then let him buy for them an annuity, or otherwise invest four thousand pounds for their benefit, according to the best of his judgment. How to come by the four thousand pounds I will now explain.

"Away in the beautiful and sequestered valley at the head of Lake Wichikagan there stands a stunted pine, near a rock fallen from the cliff above. The spot is not easily found, but my Eve knows it well. It was a favourite resort of ours when we went picnicking together. There is a small hole or dry cave in the cliff just behind the fallen rock. Two feet underneath the soil there will be found a bag containing a set of diamonds worth the sum I have named, with a smaller bag containing five hundred pounds in gold. It may not be amiss to say that both jewels and money have been honestly come by. The money I dug out of the Californian mines, and bought the jewels in a drunken frolic when in Canada—'for my future wife,' as I then boasted. My dear wife has never seen them, nor has Eve. They do not know of their existence. The five hundred pounds in gold is to be retained for himself by the man who accepts this trust to enable him to pay his way and carry it out.

"William Liston."

It is difficult to express the conflict of feelings that assailed me when I had finished reading this remarkable manuscript. For some time Lumley and I gazed at each other in silence.

"You accept the trust, I suppose?" said my friend at last.

"Of course. How could I do otherwise?"

"But you cannot remain in the service of the Hudson's Bay Company if you do. They would never give you leave of absence for such a purpose."

"No matter. I will not ask leave of absence. I will resign. My time was up, you know, this year. I will write to the governor by the spring-brigade, and start away for Colorado in summer."

"But this poor man may have been slightly deranged," suggested Lumley. "He says that at one time he led a wild life. It is possible that his brain may have been affected, and he only dreams of these jewels and the gold."

"I think not," said I, decidedly; "the letter is so calm and simple in style that the idea is absurd; besides, we can soon test it by visiting the valley and the spot referred to. Moreover, even if there were no money, and the poor man were really deranged, he could never have imagined or invented all that about his mother and Colorado if it were not true. Even if we fail to find the jewels and cash I will accept the trust and fulfil it."

"What! without money?"

"Ay, without money," said I firmly, though I am bound to confess that I did not at the moment see clearly how the thing was in that case

190

to be done. But I was—and, indeed, still am—of an ardent disposition, and felt sanguine that I should manage to fulfil the obligations of this remarkable trust somehow.

"Well, Max, you and I will visit this valley to-morrow," said Lumley, rising; "meanwhile we will go to bed."

Accordingly, next morning, after breakfast Lumley and I slung our snow-shoes over our shoulders on the barrels of our guns,—for the lake was as hard as a sheet of white marble,—and started off to pay a visit to the spot indicated in what I may style poor Liston's will.

It was a bright bracing day—quite calm, but with keen frost, which tended to increase the feelings of excitement already roused by the object we had in view. As we passed through the lake's fringe of willows, the tops of which just rose a foot or two above the drifted snow, a great covey of ptarmigan rose with a mighty whirr, and swept along the shore; but we took no heed of these—our minds being bent on other game!

The distance to the upper end of the lake was considerable, and the day was far advanced when we reached it. As we took to the land the covey of ptarmigan, which had preceded us to the place, again rose. This time, however, we were prepared for them. Lumley shot a brace right and left, taking the two last that rose with sportsman-like precision. I confess that I am not a particularly good shot—never was—and have not much of the sportsman's pride about me. I fired straight into the centre of the dense mass of birds, six of which immediately fell upon the snow.

"What a lot of flukes!" exclaimed my companion, with a laugh, as he recharged.

"Luck before precision, any day!" said I, following his example.

"Ay, Max, but there is this difference, that luck is rather uncertain, whereas precision is always sure."

"Well, be that as it may," said I putting on my snow-shoes, for the snow in the wood we were about to enter was deep and soft, "we have enough for a good supper at all events."

"True, and we shall need a good supper, for we must camp out. There is no chance of our finding this treasure—even if it exists—until we have had a good search, and then it will be too late to return home with comfort, or even safety, for it is difficult on a dark night to distinguish tracks on the hard snow of a lake, as I've sometimes found to my cost."

We set up several other coveys of ptarmigan as we traversed the belt of willows lying between the lake and the woods, and when we entered the latter, several grouse, of a species that takes to trees, fluttered away from us; but we did not molest them, having already more than we could consume swinging at our belts.

We went straight up the valley to what we deemed the most sequestered part of it, and then paused.

"This looks somewhat like the spot, doesn't it?" said Lumley, glancing round. "Yonder is a cliff with rocks at the base of it."

"Yes, but too many rocks," said I; "the paper mentions only one; besides, it refers to a stunted pine, and I see nothing of that sort here."

"True, it must be higher up the valley. Come along."

On we plodded, hour after hour, halting often, and examining with care many a secluded spot that seemed to answer more or less the description of the spot for which we searched, but all in vain. Sunset found us as far from our object as ever, and as hungry as hawks. Darkness of course put an end to the search, and, with a feeling of disappointment and weariness that I had not experienced since arriving in that region, I set to work to fell and cut up a tree for fire wood, while Lumley shovelled a hole in the snow at the foot of a pine, and otherwise prepared our encampment.

But youth is remarkably elastic in spirit! No sooner was the fire crackling, the kettle singing, and the delicious odour of roasted ptarmigan tickling our nostrils, than disappointment gave way to hope and weariness to jollity.

"Come, we shall have at it again to-morrow," said Lumley.

"So we shall," said I—"mind that kettle. You have an unfortunate capacity for kicking things over."

192

"One of the disadvantages of long legs, Max. They're always in the way. Get out the biscuit now. My ptarmigan is ready. At least, if it isn't, I can't wait."

"Neither can I, Jack. I sometimes wish that it were natural to us to eat things raw. It would be so very convenient and save sh——a—lot—of—time."

Hunger and a wrenched-off drumstick checked further utterance!

That night we lay in our snow camp, gazing up at the stars, with our feet to the fire, talking of gold and diamonds with all the eagerness of veritable misers—though it is but justice to myself to add that Eve's blue eyes outshone, in my imagination, all the diamonds that ever decked the brow of Wealth or Beauty! When at last we slept, our dreams partook of the same glittering ideas—coupled, of course, with much of the monstrous absurdity to which dreams are liable. I had just discovered a gem which was so large that I experienced the utmost difficulty in thrusting it into my coat-pocket, and was busy shovelling small diamonds of the purest water into a wheelbarrow, when a tremendous whack on my nose awoke me.

Starting up with an indignant gasp I found that it was a lump of snow, which had been detached by the heat of our fire from a branch overhead.

"What's wrong, Max?" growled my companion, who lay curled up in his buffalo robe, like a huge Newfoundland dog. "Bin dreamin'?"

"Yes," said I, with a loud yawn, "I was dreaming of shovelling up diamonds by the thousand when a lump of snow fell and hit my nose!"

"Str'nge," sighed Lumley, in the sleepiest voice I ever heard, "so's I—dr'm'n 'f g'ld'n sass–gs an' dm'nd rupple-ply."

"What nonsense are you talking, man? What were you dreaming of?"

"'F gold'n saus'ges an' dim'nd rolly-p'ly. I say—'s fire out?"

"Nearly."

"'S very cold. G't up—mend it, l'ke good f'llow. I'll help you, d'rectly."

He finished off with a prolonged snore, so I rose with a slight laugh, mended the fire, warmed myself well, observed in a sleepy way that the night was still bright and calm, and then lay down in a state of semi-consciousness to drop at once into a nest made of golden filigree filled with diamond eggs!

Next morning we rose at daybreak, relighted the fire and had breakfast, after which we resumed our search, but still—without success.

"I fear that my surmise as to the state of poor Liston's mind is correct," said Lumley. "We have searched the whole valley, I believe."

"Nay, not quite," I returned, "it is much varied in form, and full of out-o'-the-way nooks. Besides, we have not yet discovered the stunted pine, and you know the paper says the spot is difficult to find. As to Liston's mind I feel quite sure that it was all right, and that the man was a good and true one. The father of Waboose could not have been otherwise."

I said this somewhat decidedly, for I felt sorely disappointed at our failure, and slightly annoyed at my friend's unbelief in one whose last writing proved him—at least to my mind—to be genuine and sincere.

"Well, Max," returned Lumley, with his wonted pleasant look and tone, "it may be that you are right. We will continue our search as long as there seems any chance of success."

Accordingly, we ranged the valley round, high and low, until we had visited, as we thought, every nook and cranny in it and then, much dispirited, returned home.

One morning, about three months after these events, Lumley came into my bedroom where I was drawing a plan for a new store.

"Max," said he, sitting down on the bed beside me, "I mean to start this afternoon on a visit to the mountain fort. You know I promised Macnab that I would look him up about this time and fetch Waboose and her mother back."

194

"Indeed. When do you start!"

"This afternoon."

I was not surprised at the suddenness of this announcement. Our chief was eminently a man of action. He seldom talked much about plans, but thought them well out, and when his mind was made up acted without delay.

"You'll take my letter to the governor and tell Mac to forward it with his spring packet?" said I.

"Yes, that is just what I came to see you about. Is it ready—and are you quite decided about retiring?"

"Quite decided. See, here is the letter. And don't forget your promise to say nothing to Waboose or anyone else about Liston's packet."

"Not a word, my boy."

That afternoon my friend set off on snow-shoes accompanied by two men.

"Any message, Max?" he said, at parting.

"Of course. My kind regards to everybody."

"Nothing warmer to *anybody*?"

"Oh, yes," I returned quickly, "I forgot you may, if you choose, say something a little more affectionate to Miss Macnab!"

"I will, Max, I will," he replied, with a loud ringing laugh and a cheery good-bye.

Some time after that an Indian came to the fort bearing a letter from Lumley. It was written, he said, merely because the Indian chanced to be travelling towards Wichikagan, and contained nothing of importance. To my surprise and disappointment it contained no reference whatever to Waboose. On turning over the last page, however, I found a postscript. It ran thus:

"P.S.—By the way, I had almost omitted to mention Eve. My dear boy, I believe you are right. She is one of Nature's ladies. Jessie has prevailed on her to put on one of her dresses and be her companion, and when they are walking together with their backs towards me, upon my word

195

I have difficulty in deciding which is the more ladylike of the two! And that you will admit, is no small compliment from me. Jessie has been giving her lessons in English, and music and drawing too. Just think of that! She says she is doing it with an end in view. I wonder what that end can be! Jessie is sometimes difficult to understand. She is also remarkably wise and far-sighted. I expect to be home soon—farewell."

* * * * *

CHAPTER TWENTY.

I come out in a New Light, and have a very Narrow Escape.

During the absence of my friend everything went on at the fort in the usual quiet way, with this difference, that part of our educational course had to be given up, and I had to read the Pilgrim's Progress instead of my friend, for the men had become so deeply interested in the adventures of Christian that they begged of me to continue the readings.

This I agreed to do, but confined myself simply to reading. I observed, however, that my audience did not seem to appreciate the story as much as before, and was getting somewhat disheartened about it, when one evening, as I was about to begin, Donald Bane said to me—

"If ye please, sur, the other laads an' me's been talking over this matter, an' they want me to say that they would pe fery much obleeged if ye would expound the story as you go along, the same as Muster Lumley did."

This speech both surprised and embarrassed me, for I had never before attempted anything in the way of exposition. I felt, however, that it would never do for a man in charge of an outpost in the Great Nor'-West to exhibit weakness on any point, whatever he might feel; I therefore resolved to comply.

"Well, Donald Bane," I said, "it had been my intention to leave the exposition of the allegory to Mr Lumley, but as you all wish me to carry on that part of the reading I will do my best."

So saying, I plunged at once into the story, and got on much more easily than I had expected; ideas and words flowing into my mind copiously, insomuch that I found it difficult to stop, and on more than one occasion was awakened by a snore from one of the audience, to the fact that I had sent some of them to sleep.

In the midst of this pleasant, and I hope not unprofitable, work, an event occurred which had well-nigh stopped my commentaries on the Pilgrim's Progress, and put an end to my career altogether.

I had gone out one morning with my gun to procure a few fresh ptarmigan, accompanied by Big Otter. Our trusty Indian was beginning by that time to understand the English language, but he would not condescend to speak it. This, however, was of slight importance, as I had learned to jabber fluently in the native tongue.

We speedily half-filled the large game-bag which the Indian carried.

"I think we'll go into the thicker woods now," said I, "and try for some tree grouse by way of variety."

Big Otter gave a mild grunt of assent. He was not naturally given to much talking, and, being amiable, was always ready to conform to any plan without discussion, unless expressly asked. Indeed, even when expressly asked, it was not always possible to get a satisfactory answer out of him.

"Do you think we should go up the Dark Valley, or over the Rocky Knoll," said I, referring to two well-known spots a considerable distance from the fort.

"The pale-face chief knows best."

"Yes, but the pale-face asks what the red-face thinks," said I, somewhat amused by the answer.

"He thinks that there are grouse in the Dark Valley, and also in the lands towards the setting sun over the Rocky Knoll."

"If I were to ask you, Big Otter, which of the two directions you would like to take, what would you reply?"

"I would reply, 'The direction that best pleases the pale-face chief.'"

"Now, Big Otter," said I, firmly, for I was determined to get an answer out of him, "in which of the two paths are we most likely to find the greatest number of birds?"

"Assuredly in the path which shall be chosen by the pale-face. Is he not a great hunter? Does he not know the land?"

I gave in with a short laugh, and, turning, led the way over the Rocky Knoll into the dense forest at the back of the fort. Passing through a belt of this, we came upon more open ground, where the trees grew in clumps, with willow-covered spaces between. Beyond that we re-entered the thick woods, and at once set up a covey of the birds we were in search of. There were six of them, and they all perched on a neighbouring tree.

Now it is sometimes the case that the birds of which I write are so tame that they will sit still on a tree till they are all shot, one by one, if only the hunter is careful to fire at the lowest bird first, and so proceed upwards. If he should kill the top bird first, its fluttering fall disturbs the rest, causing them to take wing. Fully aware of this fact, Big Otter and I fired alternate shots, and in a few seconds brought down the whole covey. This quite filled one of our bags.

"You may take it home, Big Otter," said I, "and tell them not to be alarmed if I don't return till to-morrow. Perhaps I shall camp out."

With his usual quiet grunt of acquiescence my red-skinned companion shouldered the full bag, and left me. I then struck into the thick woods, with the general bearings of which I was well acquainted, and soon after came across the fresh tracks of a deer, which I followed up hotly.

I am naturally a keen sportsman, and apt to forget both time and distance when pursuing game. As to distance, however, a backwoods hunter who intends to encamp on the spot where night finds him, does not need to concern himself much about that. I therefore plodded on, hour after hour, until the waning light told of the approach of darkness, and convinced me that further pursuit would be useless.

Looking round me then, for a suitable spot on which to make my encampment, I experienced almost a shock of surprise, not unmingled with alarm, on making the discovery that I had forgotten to bring my fire-bag!

To some people the serious nature of this may not at first be apparent. But they may appreciate the situation in some degree when I tell them that on that occasion I suddenly found myself about twenty miles from home, fatigued, hungry, with the night descending over the wilderness, the thermometer about thirty-five below zero, of Fahrenheit's scale, with the snow for my bed, and without that all important flint, steel and tinder, wherewith to procure fire for the cooking of my food and the warming of my frame!

It is true I had my gun, which was a flint one, so that by rubbing some slightly moistened gunpowder on a piece of rag, which I tore from my shirt for the purpose, and snapping the lock over it there was a possibility of a spark catching, but unfortunately the flint was a much worn one which I had chipped away to such an extent during the day, to improve its fire-producing powers, that only the merest glimmer of a spark was evolved after many snappings, and it was so feeble as to be quite unable to catch hold of my extemporised tinder. After prolonged and fruitless efforts the intense cold began to chill me, and being well aware of the great danger of getting benumbed, or of falling into that torpid state of indifference to life, coupled with intense desire for rest which precedes death from cold, I made up my mind at once, tired and hungry though I was, to turn round and walk straight back to the fort.

I knew myself to be quite capable of walking forty miles on snow-shoes in ordinary circumstances. My being tired and the darkness of night, were against me, but what of that? it would only require me to brace myself to a severer task than usual!

I had not gone many miles, however, on the return journey, when a doubt occurred as to whether I was taking the right direction. In the confidence of my knowledge of the country I had carelessly left my old track, which was indeed rather a devious one, and had struck what I believed to be a straight line for the fort. It was by that time too late to retrace my steps and too dark to distinguish the features of the landscape. I stopped for a minute to think, and as I did so the profound oppressive silence of the night, the weird pallid aspect of the scarce visible snow, and the dark pines around me, which were only a shade or two darker than the black sky above, together with the ever-increasing cold, made such an impression on my mind that the prayer, "God help me!" burst almost involuntarily from my lips.

Feeling that delay surely meant death, I started off again with redoubled energy, and this impulse of determination, along with the exercise, increased my temperature somewhat, so that hope became strong again, and with it muscular energy.

Suddenly I came upon a snow-shoe track. I went down on my knees to examine it, but the light was insufficient to make it out clearly. What would I not have given for a match at that moment! However, as the size of the shoe-print seemed to my *feeling* the same with that of the shoe I wore, I concluded that it must certainly be my own track out from home—all the more that it ran almost parallel with the line I was following.

Getting upon it then, I stepped out with much greater ease and with a lighter heart.

After a time the track led me to a slightly open space where the light was better. I thought that objects seemed familiar to me as I looked round. Advancing, I came on a spot where the snow was much trodden down. There was a bank of snow near. I went towards it while a terrible suspicion flashed into my mind. Yes, it was the very spot on which I had been sitting hours before, while I was making fruitless efforts to obtain a light from the flint of my gun! I had been doing that of which I had often read and heard, walking unwittingly in a circle, and had actually come back to the spot from which I set out.

What my feelings were on making this discovery it is scarcely possible to describe. My first act was to look up and exclaim as before, "God help me!" But there was nothing impulsive or involuntary in the prayer this time. I fully realised the extent of my danger, and, believing that the hour had come when nothing could save my life but the direct interposition of my Creator, I turned to Him with all the fervour of my heart.

At the same time I am bound to confess that my faith was very weak, and my soul felt that solemn alarm which probably the bravest feel at the approach of death, when that approach is sudden and very unexpected.

Nevertheless, I am thankful to say that my powers of judgment and of action did not forsake me. I knew that it would be folly to attempt to follow my track back again through the intricacies of the forest in so dark a night, especially now that the track was partly mingled and confused with that which I had made in joining it. I also knew that to give way to despair, and lie down without a fire or food, would be to seal my own doom. Only one course remained, and that was to keep constantly moving until the return of day should enable me to distinguish surrounding objects more clearly.

I went to work therefore without delay, but before doing so once again solemnly and earnestly committed my soul and body to the care of God. And, truly, the circumstances of my case intensified that prayer. I felt as if I had never really prayed in earnest in my life before that night.

Then, laying aside my gun, blanket and cooking utensils, so as to commence my task as light as possible, I went to the most open space of ground I could find, and there described a large circle with my snow-shoes on. This was the track on which I resolved to perform a feat of endurance. To walk all night without intermission, without rest, so as to keep up my animal heat was the effort on the success of which depended the issue of life or death.

I began with that vigour which is born of hopeful determination to succeed or die. But, as time wore on, the increasing weakness and exhaustion began to render me less capable of enduring the intense cold. Having my wallet on my back I took out some biscuit and pemmican and ate it as I walked. This revived me a good deal, nevertheless I restrained myself, feeling convinced that nothing but steady, quiet perseverance would carry me through. Soon thirst began to torment me, yet I did not dare to eat snow, as that would have merely injured the inside of my mouth, and frozen the skin of my lips. This feeling did not however last long. It was followed by a powerful sense of drowsiness.

This I knew to be the fatal premonitory symptom, and strove against it with all my power. The better to resist it I began to talk aloud to myself.

"Come now, my boy, you mustn't give way to *that*. It is death, you know. Hold up! Be a man! Act as Lumley would have acted in similar circumstances. Dear Lumley! How he would run to help me if he only knew!"

Suddenly the words, "In Me is thy help," seemed to sound in my very ears. I stopped to listen, and was partly roused, but soon hurried on again.

"Yes, yes," I exclaimed aloud, "I know the text well," but the words had scarcely left my lips when I stumbled and fell. Owing to my sinking powers I had failed to keep the centre of the track; my right snow-shoe had caught on the edge of it and tumbled me into the soft snow.

How shall I describe the delicious feeling of profound rest that ensued when I found myself prone and motionless? Equally impossible is it to describe the agonising struggles that I made to induce my unwilling spirit to rouse my listless body. Those who have striven in semi-consciousness to throw off the awful lethargy of nightmare may have some conception of my feelings. I knew, even then, that it was the critical moment—the beginning of the end. In a burst of anxiety I began to pray—to shout with all my strength—for deliverance. The effort and the strange sound of my own voice roused me.

I staggered to my feet and was able to continue my walk. Being somewhat brighter than I had been before the tumble, I perceived that the circular track was by that time beaten hard enough to bear me up without snow-shoes, so I put them off and walked with much more ease.

From this point however my mind became so confused that I can give no reliable account of what followed. I was conscious at various periods during that dreadful night of becoming alive to several incidents and states of mind. I recollect falling more than once, as I had fallen before, and of experiencing, more than once, that painful struggle against what I may style mental and physical inertia. I remember breaking out frequently into loud importunate prayer, and being impressed with a feeling of reviving energy at such times. Sometimes a text of Scripture seemed to flash before my eyes and disappear. On these occasions I made terrible efforts to grasp the text, and have an indistinct sensation of increased strength resulting from the mere efforts, but most of the texts faded as quickly as they came, with the exception of one—"God is our Hope." Somehow I seemed to lay firm hold of that, and to feel conscious of holding it, even when sense was slipping away, but of the blanks between those conditions I know nothing. They may have been long or they may have been short—I cannot tell. All remains on my memory now like the unsubstantial fragments of a hideous dream.

The first thing after that which impressed itself on me with anything like the distinctness of reality was the sound of a crackling fire, accompanied with the sensation of warmth in my throat. Slowly opening my eyes I became aware of the fact that I was lying in front of a blazing fire, surrounded by Big Otter, Blondin, and Dougall, who stood gazing at me with anxious looks, while Henri Coppet knelt at my side, attempting to pour some warm tea down my throat.

"Dere now, monsieur," said Coppet, who was rather fond of airing his English, especially when excited, "Yoos kom too ver queek. Ony drink. Ha! dere be noting like tea."

"Wow! man, mind what yer aboot. Ye'll scald him," said Dougall, anxiously.

"You hole yoos tongue," replied the carpenter contemptuously, "me knows w'at mees do. Don' wants no Scoshmans for tell me. *Voilà!* Monsieur have swaller *un peu!*"

This was true. I had not only swallowed, but nearly choked with a tendency to laugh at the lugubrious expression of my friends' faces.

"Where am I?" said I, on recovering a little, "What has happened?"

"Oo ay, Muster Maxby," answered Dougall, with his wonted nasal drawl; "somethin' *hess* happened, but it's no sae pad as what *might* hev happened, whatever."

As this did not tend to clear my mind much, and as I knew from experience that the worthy Celt refused to be hurried in his communications, I turned an inquiring look on Blondin, who at once said in French—

"Monsieur has been lost and nearly frozen, and Monsieur would surely have been quite frozen if James Dougall had not discovered that Monsieur had left his fire-bag at home, by mistake no doubt; we at once set out to search for Monsieur, and we found him with his head in the snow and his feet in the air. At first we thought that Monsieur was dead, but happily he was not, so we kindled a fire and rubbed Monsieur, and gave him hot tea, which has revived him. *Voilà!* Perhaps Monsieur will take a little more hot tea?"

While Blondin was speaking, the whole scene of the previous day and of the terrible night rushed in upon my brain like a flood, and I thanked God fervently for my deliverance, while I complied with the man's suggestion and sipped some more tea.

It revived me much, but on attempting to rise I found myself so weak that I fell back helplessly with a deep sigh.

"Ye've no need to trouble yoursel', Muster Maxby," said Dougall, "we've brought the new dowg-sleigh for 'ee."

Looking in the direction in which he pointed, I observed not far-off the splendid new dog-sleigh which we had spent much time in making and painting that winter. Our fine team of four semi-wolf dogs, gay with embroidered harness as they lay curled up on the snow, were attached to it.

"I suspect I should have died but for your thoughtful care, Dougall," I said, gratefully, as the good fellow assisted to place me in the vehicle and wrap the buffalo robes around me.

"Hoots! Muster Maxby," was the remonstrative reply.

Big Otter placed himself in front of the *cortège* to beat the track. The dogs followed him with the sleigh-bells ringing merrily. Blondin took hold of the tail-line, and the others brought up the rear.

Thus comfortably, with a bright sun shining in the blue sky, I returned to Fort Wichikagan.

* * * * *

CHAPTER TWENTY ONE.

A Buffalo Hunt Followed by a Palaver, an Arrival, and a Traitor-Chase.

We must turn away now, for a short time, to another, though not far distant, part of the Great Nor'-West.

It is a more open country than that immediately around Fort Wichikagan, and lies to the south of it. Here and there long stretches of prairie cut up the wilderness, giving to the landscape a soft and park-like appearance. The scenery is further diversified by various lakelets which swarm with water-fowl, for the season has changed, early spring having already swept away the white mantle of winter, and spread the green robes of Nature over the land. It is such a region as a millionaire might select in which to build a palace, but no millionaire has yet beheld the lovely spot. With unlimited wealth at his command he still confines himself to the smoke and dust of civilisation, leaving the free air and the brilliant beauty of the wilderness to the wild-fowl and the penniless hunter, and the wandering savage!

In the midst of one of the stretches of rolling prairie-land, great herds of buffalo are scattered in groups, browsing with all the air of security peculiar to domestic cattle. Happily their memories are short. They seem prone to enjoy the present, forgetful of the past and regardless of the future—happily, I say, for those humpy and hairy creatures are not unacquainted with man's devices—the sudden surprise, the twang of the red-man's bow and the crack of the hunter's rifle.

It was the forenoon of a splendid day, when this peaceful scene was broken in upon by obstreperous, fighting, peace-destroying man. A little cloud of dust on the horizon was the first indication of his approach, and a very antique buffalo-bull was first among the thousands of innocents to observe the cloud. It stirred the memory of other days, no doubt within his capacious bosom, and probably sent a thrill through his huge frame, which, terminating naturally in his tail, caused that appendage to vibrate and curl slightly upwards. At the same time he emitted softly a low rumble, which might have served for the bass of a cathedral organ.

Most of the cows near the patriarch looked up in evident surprise, as though to say, "What in all the world do you mean by *that?*" But the patriarch took no notice of them. He kept his wicked little eyes fixed intently on the cloud of dust, twitching his tail nervously, and rumbling cathedral-organically. If I might venture to guess at the mental operations of that patriarch, I should say that he was growling to himself, "Is that you again, you galloping, spitfiring, two-legged, yelling monsters?" or some such bovine expression.

By degrees the cloud came nearer and enlarged. Simultaneously the groups of buffaloes drew together and began to gaze—perchance to remember! The patriarch became excited, wriggled his tail, which was ridiculously small for his body, pawed the ground, trotted hither and thither, and commenced playing on all the deeper notes of his organ.

At last there could be no doubt. The two-legged monsters came on, mounted on four-legged brutes, which began to trot as the distance between them diminished. This was enough. The patriarch tossed his haunches to the sky, all but wriggled off his tail, gave utterance to a bursting bellow, and went scouring over the plains like a gigantic wild pig. The entire buffalo host performing a similar toss and wriggle, followed close on his heels.

At this the redskins put their steeds to the gallop, but did not at once overtake their prey. Clumsy though their gait was, the buffaloes were swift and strong, causing the whole plain to resound under their mighty tread. Indian steeds, however, are wiry and enduring. By slow degrees they lessened the distance between them—both pursued and pursuers lengthening out their ranks as the "fittest" came to the front. Thundering on, they approached one of the large clumps of woodland with which the plain was covered, as with islets. The patriarch led to the left of it. The savages, sweeping aside, took to the right.

The sudden disappearance of the pursuers seemed to surprise the patriarch, who slackened his pace a little, and, lifting his shaggy head, looked right and left inquiringly. "Was it all a dream!" he thought—no doubt.

If he thought it was, he received in a few minutes a rude awakening, for the redskins came sweeping round the other end of the clump of trees, yelling like fiends, brandishing their weapons and urging their steeds to the uttermost.

To snort, bellow, turn off at a tangent, and scurry along faster than ever, was the work of a moment, but it was too late! The savages were in the midst of the snorting host. Bows were bent and guns were levelled. The latter were smooth-bores, cheap, and more or less inaccurate, but that mattered not.

Where the range was only two or three yards, guns and bows were true enough for the end in view. At such work even bad shots met their reward. Arrows sank to the feathers; bullets penetrated to the heart or shattered the bones. Ere long numerous black lumps on the prairie told of death to the quadrupeds and success to the bipeds.

But I do not drag the reader here merely to tell of savage sport and butchery. The Indian was only following his vocation—working for his food.

That same evening two of the Indians stood on a hillock, a little apart from their camp where smoking fires and roasting meat and marrow-bones, and ravenously-feeding men and women, and gorging little boys and girls, formed a scene that was interesting though not refined. One of the Indians referred to was Big Otter. The other was Muskrat, the old chief of his tribe.

"Does my father not know?" said Big Otter, deferentially, "that Attick plans mischief against the pale-faces of Wichikagan?"

"No, Big Otter," returned the old chief with a scowl; "Muskrat does not know that, but he hears, and if it is true he will have Attick flayed alive, and his skin dressed to make moccasins for our young squaws."

"It is true," rejoined Big Otter, sternly. "His plan is to attack the fort by night, kill the pale-faces, and carry off the goods."

"Attick is a fool!" said Muskrat, contemptuously. "Does he not know that no more goods would evermore be sent into our lands if we did that, and also that the pale-faces always hunt murderers to death? No; if that had been possible, or wise, Muskrat would have done it himself long ago."

After this candid statement he stared solemnly at his companion, as though to say, "What think ye of that, my brave?"

Apparently my brave did not think much of it one way or other, for he only looked indifferent and said, "Waugh!"

"Big Otter's ears are sharp," continued Muskrat. "How did he come to hear of Attick's intentions?"

The younger Indian paused thoughtfully before replying.

"Waboose told me," he said.

"Does the daughter of Weeum the Good hold communion with evil spirits?" asked the old chief, with a slight elevation of the eyebrows.

"Not willingly, but evil spirits force themselves upon the daughter of Weeum the Good. My father knows that Attick is presumptuous. He wishes to mate Waboose."

"Yes, I knew he was presumptuous, but I did not know he was so great a fool," replied the old chief scornfully.

"My father knows," continued Big Otter, "that when the pale-face chief went and brought Waboose back to Fort Wichikagan, Attick was staying there in his wigwam by the lake. The big chief of the pale-faces, who fears nothing, had forgiven him. Attick went to Waboose, and offered to take her to his wigwam; but the daughter of Weeum the Good turned away from him. Attick is proud, and he is fierce. He told Waboose that he would kill all the pale-faces. Although a fool, he does not boast. Waboose knew that he was in earnest. She went to the pale-face Muxbee (by which name Big Otter styled my humble self), and told him all, for she has set her heart on Muxbee."

"Did she tell you so?" asked Muskrat, sharply.

"No; but the blue eyes of Waboose tell tales. They are like a kettle with holes in the bottom—they cannot hold secrets. They spoke to Attick as well as to me, and he became jealous. He swore he would take the scalp of Muxbee. One day, soon after the lake opened, Muxbee asked Waboose to go with him in a canoe to the valley at the head of lake Wichikagan. Attick followed in another canoe, but kept far behind. They did not know it was Attick. Waboose found it out afterwards. Muxbee did not talk to Waboose of love. The ways of the pale-faces are strange. Once I thought that Muxbee liked Waboose, and that, perhaps, he might wed with her, and stay with us as the Good Weeum did, but I doubt it now. He only asked her to take him to the stunted pine where her father was so fond of going with her. When there he went looking here and there about the rocks, and found a splendid thing—I know not what—but Waboose told me it shone and sparkled like the stars. Beside it was a bag of the yellow round things that the pale-faces love so much. He told her he had expected to find these things, but she must not ask him questions just then—he would tell her afterwards. I suppose he is a great medicine-man, and holds intercourse with the spirit-world." Big Otter paused thoughtfully a few seconds, and then continued:—

"When he was putting these things in his breast, Waboose caught sight of Attick among the bushes, and pointed him out. Muxbee sprang up and levelled his gun with the two pipes at him, but did not fire. Attick fled and they saw him no more."

"Did Waboose tell Big Otter all this?" asked the old chief.

"Yes. Waboose has no secrets from her mother's brother."

"And why has Big Otter left the pale-faces, and brought Waboose away from them?" asked Muskrat.

"Because he fears for the pale-faces, that Attick will kill them and carry off Waboose. By bringing Waboose here with us we draw Attick along with us away from the pale-faces, and as long as Waboose is in our camp she is safe. Attick dare not harm her."

A gleam of intelligence lit up the swarthy features of the old chief as he said "Waugh!" with much satisfaction.

But both he and Big Otter were wrong in their calculations. So far, indeed, the latter was right. The presence of Waboose in the camp effectually drew Attick after them, and thus removed danger from the inhabitants of Fort Wichikagan, but they were wrong when they thought their camp a place of safety for the poor girl.

"Did Muxbee not care when Big Otter carried Waboose away?" asked the old man.

"He did not know she was going, and I did not tell her she was not to return. I took her away with her mother when Muxbee was out hunting. I told the big pale-face chief that I must go with my tribe to hunt the buffalo in the south, and that they must go with me. He was very unwilling to let them go at first but I was resolved, and Waboose is a good obedient girl."

That night two events occurred in the redskin camp which caused a good deal of surprise and commotion.

The first was the sudden disappearance of Waboose and her mother. They had been gone some time, of course, before any one thought of suspecting flight. The moment that suspicion was aroused, however, Big Otter went straight to the wigwam of Attick. It was deserted! He knew well the bad and weak men of the tribe who were led or swayed by Attick. Hurrying to their tents he found that these also had fled. This was enough.

212

"Masqua," he said to the first Indian he chanced to meet at the moment of quitting the last wigwam, "Attick has carried off Waboose. Assemble some of the young men. Choose only the strong, and those whose horses are swift. Go yourself with your son Mozwa—gallop round the camp till you find in which direction they have gone—then return to me at the council tent and wait."

Masqua understood the value of prompt obedience. Without a word of reply he turned and bounded away.

Big Otter hurried to the council tent, where old Muskrat was already surrounded by his chiefs. There was less than usual of the grave deliberation of North American Indians in that meeting, for the case was urgent. Nevertheless, there was no bustle, for each bronzed warrior knew that the young men would require a little time to hunt up the trail of the fugitives, mingled as it must be with the innumerable footprints of man and beast in the neighbourhood of a camp; and, until that trail was found, they might as well deliberate calmly—especially as all the men met at the council armed, and ready to vault on the steeds which were already pawing the earth outside. These horses were restrained by youths who longed for the time when they too might be styled braves, and meet in council.

"Is all prepared?" asked the old chief, as Big Otter entered the tent.

"The young men are out," was the curt reply.

"Good. The night is dark, but my warriors have sharp eyes, and the moon will rise soon. No effort must be spared. The daughter of Weeum the Good must be brought back. It is not necessary to bring back Attick or his men. Their scalps will do as well."

"Waugh!" pronounced with much emphasis showed that the old man's words were not only understood, but thoroughly appreciated.

At this moment occurred the second event which I have said was the cause of surprise in the camp that night, if not of commotion. While the old chief was yet speaking, his words were checked by the sound of horses' hoofs beating heavily on the prairie.

"The young men," said Muskrat; "they have been swift to find the trail."

"Young men in haste bringing news do not trot," said Big Otter.

"Waugh!" assented the council.

"There are but two riders," murmured the chief, listening intently to the pattering sounds, which rapidly grew louder.

He was right, for, a few seconds later, two horsemen were seen to trot into the camp, and make straight for the council fire. Some of the Indians had turned out with arms ready as they approached, but on hearing a word or two from one of the riders, they quietly let them pass.

Pulling up sharply, one of the strangers leaped to the ground, flung his reins to the other, and entered the council tent where he was received with looks of surprise, and with the ejaculation from Big Otter of the single word "Muxbee!"

Yes, good reader, that stranger was none other than myself, and my companion was Salamander. To account for our sudden appearance I must explain.

On returning to Fort Wichikagan four days after Big Otter had left, and hearing what had occurred, I told Lumley I would follow in pursuit and fetch Waboose back. He remonstrated, of course, but in vain.

"You know that a sacred trust has been imposed upon me," said I, earnestly, "and I have resolved to fulfil it. The manner in which I should set about it has perplexed me sorely, I confess, but this sudden departure relieves me, at all events, from uncertainty as to my present course of duty. If Waboose goes off with the tribe to no one knows where, she may never be found again. You are aware that she is still ignorant of the contents of the packet, and the value of the found treasure. I have kept her so, temporarily, by your advice. If I had told her and her kindred, she would not probably have gone away, but it is too late to regret that, now. By going off at once I may overtake the tribe. Three days' journey on foot will bring me to Indians who are rich in horses. Once well mounted I can push on, and will easily overtake them if you will lend me Salamander to aid in following up the trail."

"But what of the service?" asked Lumley, with a sad smile, for he saw I was resolved. "You are not yet free."

"True, but you know that Spooner is already on his way here to replace me, my resignation having been accepted. In a week, or two at farthest, he will arrive, when I shall be absolutely free to go where I please. Meanwhile, to prevent even a shadow of impropriety, I ask your majesty for a fortnight's leave of absence to go a-hunting. Surely you won't refuse so small a favour? I will be sure to find Waboose, and bring her back by that time."

"Well, Max, my boy, I won't refuse. Go, and God go with you. I shall expect to see you again in two weeks, if not sooner."

"Unless, of course, circumstances render my return so soon impossible."

"Of course, of course," said Lumley.

Thus we parted, and thus it was that Salamander and I found ourselves at last in the Indian camp. The pursuit, however, had been much longer than I had expected. More than the stipulated fortnight had already passed.

But to return from this digression. After we had looked at each other silently for a few seconds in the council tent, as already described, I advanced to Big Otter and held out my hand. I then shook hands with the old chief, sat down beside him, and expressed a hope that I did not intrude.

"We palaver about the disappearance of Waboose," said the old chief.

"Disappearance! Waboose!" I exclaimed, turning abruptly to Big Otter.

"Attick has fled," said the Indian, sternly, "carrying Waboose and her mother along with him."

"And you sit here idly talking," I exclaimed, almost fiercely, as I sprang up.

Before I could take action of any kind, the young Indian, Mozwa, entered the tent abruptly, and said a few words to Muskrat. At the same moment the councillors rose.

"We go in pursuit," whispered Big Otter in my ear. "Mount, and join us."

Almost bewildered, but feeling perfect confidence in my Indian friend, I ran out, and vaulted into the saddle. Eager and quick though I was, the redskins were mounted as soon as myself. No one seemed to give orders, but with one accord they put their horses to the gallop, and swept out of the camp. The last words of the old chief as we darted off, were—

"Bring her back, my braves, and don't forget the scalps of Attick and his men!"

* * * * *

216

CHAPTER TWENTY TWO.

The Chase, the Capture, and the Revelation.

A stern chase is usually a long one. There are not many proverbs the truth of which comes more powerfully home than this—at least to those who have had the misfortune to engage in many such chases. To make a slant at a fugitive, so as to cut him off, or to make a short cut and head him, is pleasant if you be strong in wind and limb, but to creep up right astern, inch by inch, foot by foot, yard by yard, and to overcome him at last by sheer superiority and perseverance, is a disheartening task.

That was the task we undertook the night we left the Indian camp, and went off at full gallop over the rolling prairie in pursuit of the scoundrel Attick and his crew.

But Indians are by nature persevering, and, for myself, I was roused to the highest pitch of indignation and anxiety. Salamander and I had ridden far and fast that day, besides which we had eaten only a mouthful of pemmican and biscuit since breakfast; nevertheless, under the excitement of the moment our weariness vanished, our hunger fled, and we engaged in the pursuit with all the ardour of the youngest brave among them.

Fortunately I had secured two exceptionally fine horses, so that they were quite able to compete with the inferior, though fresher, horses of the Indians.

"How long is it since you discovered that they were gone?" said I, as I galloped alongside of Big Otter.

"Not more than an hour," he replied.

"Do you think they had a long start before that?"

"I cannot tell. Perhaps two hours, perhaps four. Certainly not five, for they were seen in camp when the sun was high."

I was greatly relieved to learn that they had not got a longer start of us, and very thankful that I had come up in time to join the pursuers. I was calming down somewhat under the influence of these thoughts, when I had a sudden feeling of being shot from a cannon into the air. This was succeeded by a sensation of having my nose converted into a ploughshare, and that was instantly followed by oblivion!

In the uncertain light my steed had put his foot in a badger hole—that was all, but it sufficed to check the pace of the whole party!

On recovering I found my head on Salamander's knee. I felt dreamy and indifferent. "What has happened?" I asked, in English.

Our interpreter, who had a tendency to answer in whatever language he was addressed—whether English, French, or Indian—replied—

"Yoos bin a-most busted, sar!"

Suddenly the true state of the case flashed upon me. Langour fled. I leaped up, and scrambled somehow into the saddle.

"Have I been long insensible, Salamander?" I asked, as we resumed our headlong pace.

"On'y what time I kin count twinty, sar."

Rejoiced to find that no longer time had been lost, I galloped along contentedly, and in silence, though with a rather confused feeling in my brain, and a sensation of being possessed of six noses rolled into one.

Although no one, as I have said, seemed to lead the party when we started, I soon found that Big Otter was really our chief. He rode ahead of us, and more than once pulled up to dismount and examine the trail. On these occasions the rest of the party halted without orders, and awaited his decision. Once we were completely thrown off the scent. The fugitives had taken to a wooded tract of country, and it required our utmost caution not to lose the trail.

Presently we came to a small stream and crossed it, but the trail ended abruptly here. We were not surprised, being well aware of the common Indian device of wading in a stream, which holds no footprints, so as to throw pursuers out. Dividing our force, one party went up stream, the other down, but although eager, sharp, and practised eyes examined the banks, they could not discover the spot where the fugitives had again taken to dry land. Returning to the place where we had divided, Big Otter again examined the trail with minute care, going down on his knees to turn over the blades of grass and examine the footprints.

"Strange," said I, impatiently, "that so simple a device should baffle us."

As I spoke, the chief arose, and, dark though it was, I could see a gleam of intelligence on his swarthy visage.

"Attick thinks he is wise," he said, in a low voice, "but he has no more brains than a rabbit. He was from childhood an idiot."

Having paid his tribesman this compliment, he remounted, and, to my surprise, went straight back the way we had come.

"What means this!" I asked, unable to restrain my impatience.

"Attick has doubled back, that is all. If there had been more light we should easily have seen that. We shall soon find the place where the trail breaks off again."

The Indian was right. On clearing the wooded land we found that the moon was up, and we followed the trail easily. Coming to a hillock in the open ground, the top of which was covered with thick and stunted bushes, we rode into them and there experienced much difficulty in picking our way.

Suddenly Big Otter turned at a right angle from the line we had been hitherto pursuing, and, putting his horse to the gallop, held on with the decision of one who knows he is on the right road.

As the prairie was open, and the moon growing brighter, we had now no difficulty in following up the fugitives, and pressed on as fast as our horses could go.

219

Daylight came and found us still galloping; but as there was no sign of those whom we pursued, and as our horses were getting tired, we halted at a small stream for a short rest and breakfast.

"They must be well mounted," said I, as we sat on the banks of the stream appeasing our hunger with masses of dried buffalo meat, while the horses munched the grass near us.

"Attick is always well mounted," replied Big Otter; "but his men may not be so well off, and women are difficult to urge on when they are unwilling."

"Then you have no doubt that we shall overtake them?" I asked.

"We *must* overtake them," was the laconic reply. I felt somewhat comforted by the decision of the Indian's tone, and a good deal more so by his ordering his warriors to remount before half an hour had passed. He did not however, press on as hard as before, fearing, no doubt that the horses would break down.

I felt assured that Attick would not dare to halt until he believed himself almost beyond pursuit; and, as the chase therefore bade fair to be a very long one, it seemed wise thus to spare the horses.

About noon, however, we passed through a strip of woodland, and, on coming out at the other side, observed a party of horsemen on the distant horizon.

"Waugh!" exclaimed Big Otter, shaking the reins of his steed and going off at racing speed. We soon began to overhaul the cavalcade, and then perceived that they were doing their utmost to get away from us.

"It is Attick and his party—is it not?" I asked, excitedly.

"It is Attick," was the brief reply.

Another belt of woodland lay a little to the right on the horizon. The fugitives headed for it. We urged our horses to their utmost speed and soon dashed through the belt of wood, expecting to see the fugitives on the plain beyond. What was our surprise, then, to find them assembled in a group, calmly tying up their horses, and kindling a fire as if for the purpose of cooking their mid-day meal. As most of the men had laid

220

aside their guns, and we outnumbered them by two to one, we checked our headlong course, and trotted quietly up to them.

To my great joy I saw, as we approached, that the girl who stooped to kindle the fire was Waboose. Her mother sat on a bank near her, looking very pale and worn.

Attick, who still carried his gun in the hollow of his left arm, expressed well-feigned surprise at seeing us.

"Big Otter seems to be on the war-path," he said, "but I have seen no enemies."

"Big Otter's enemy stands before him," returned our leader, sternly. "Attick has been very foolish. Why did he run away with the daughter of Weeum the Good?"

"Attick scorns to run away with a squaw. Waboose agreed to go with him on the hunt. There she is: ask her."

This was a bold stroke of the wily savage. Instead of flying from us, he pretended to have been merely hurrying after a band of buffalo, which was said to be moving southward, and that he had halted in the chase for a short rest and food. This plan he had hastily adopted, on perceiving that it was impossible to escape us, having previously warned Waboose that he would shoot her dead if she did not corroborate what he said. But Attick was incapable of believing that fearless heroism could dwell in the breast of a woman, and little knew the courage of the daughter of Weeum the Good. He mistook her silence and her downcast eyes for indications of submission, and did not doubt that the delicate-looking and shrinking girl was of much the same spirit as the other women of his tribe.

Great, then, was his astonishment when he saw the Saxon blood in her veins rush to her fair brow, while she gazed at him steadily with her large blue eyes, and said—

"The tongue of Attick is forked. He lies when he says that the daughter of Weeum agreed to follow him. He knows that he carried her from the camp by force against her will."

221

Attick had thrown forward and cocked his gun, but happily the unexpected nature of the girl's reply, and the indignant gaze of her eyes, caused an involuntary hesitation. This did not afford time for any one to seize the intending murderer, but it enabled me hastily to point my rifle at the villain's head and fire. I have elsewhere said that my shooting powers were not remarkable; I missed the man altogether, but fortunately the bullet which was meant for his brain found its billet in the stock of his gun, and blew the lock to atoms, thus rendering the weapon useless.

With a fierce shout he dropped the gun, drew his scalping-knife, and sprang towards Waboose, or—as I had by that time found a pleasure in mentally styling her—Eve Liston.

Of course every man of our party sprang forward, but it fell to Salamander to effect the rescue, for that light-hearted and light-limbed individual chanced to be nearest to the savage when I fired at him, and, ere the knife was well drawn, had leaped upon his back with the agility of a panther. At the same moment Big Otter flung his tomahawk at him. The weapon was well, though hastily, aimed. It struck the savage full on the forehead, and felled him to the earth.

The rest of Attick's party made no attempt to rescue him. Like all bad men, they were false to each other in the hour of need. They quietly submitted to be disarmed and led away.

We had to encamp early that evening, because the unwonted and severe exercise to which Waboose's mother had been exposed had rendered her quite unfit to travel further without rest. Attick, who had soon recovered sufficiently to be able to walk, was bound, along with his men, and put under a guard. Then the encampment was made and the fires kindled. While this was being done I led Waboose aside to a little knoll, from which we could see a beautiful country of mingled woodland and prairie, stretching far away to the westward, where the sun had just descended amid clouds of amber and crimson.

"Is it not glorious!" I exclaimed. "Should we not be grateful to the Great Spirit who has given us such a splendid home?"

Waboose looked at me. "Yes, it is glorious," she said—"and I am grateful; but it is strange that you should use the very same words that were so often on the lips of my father just before he—"

She stopped abruptly.

"Just before he went home, Eve," I interposed; "no need to say died. Your father is not dead, but sleepeth. You shall meet him again. But it is not very strange that men should use the same words when they are animated by the same love to the Great Spirit."

The girl raised her large eyes with a perplexed, inquiring look.

"What troubles you, Eve?" I asked.

"Eve!" she repeated, almost anxiously. "Twice you have called me by a name that father sometimes used, though not often, and when he used it he always spoke low and *very* tenderly."

I felt somewhat perplexed as to how I should reply, and finally took refuge in another question.

"Tell me, Waboose," said I, "did your father ever tell you his own name?"

"Of course he did," she answered, with a look of surprise—"you know well it was Weeum."

"Yes, William," said I; "but—"

"No—Weeum," she said, correcting me. "Once or twice I have heard him say Willum, but all our people call him Weeum."

"Had he no other name?" I asked.

"No. Why should he have another? Is not one enough?"

"You never heard of Liston?"

"Liston?—No, never."

"Waboose," said I, with sudden earnestness, "I am going to tell you something that will probably surprise you, and I will show you something that may give you pleasure—or pain—I know not which. You remember, that when I found the curious ornaments near to the stunted pine-tree, I asked you not to question me at that time about the packet you gave to me long ago. Well, the time has come when I ought to tell you all about it. But, first, look at this."

I had taken from my pocket, while speaking to her, the miniature of her father, which I now handed to her. She fixed her eyes on it with a startled look, then sprang up with an exclamation, at the same time drawing one hand across her eyes, as if to clear away some mists that dimmed them. Eagerly she gazed again, with parted lips and heaving bosom, then burst into a passionate flood of tears, pressing the miniature alternately to her lips and to her heart.

I stood helplessly gazing at her—anxious to comfort but unable.

"Oh! why, why," she cried, suddenly dropping the miniature, "why do you mock me with this? It is so little, yet so like. It looks alive, but it is dead. It is nothing—a mockery!"

The poor girl caught it up, however, and began to kiss and caress it again.

Some time elapsed before her passionate grief was sufficiently subdued to permit of her listening to me. When it was nearly exhausted, and found vent only in an occasional sob, I took her hand gently and said—

"Give me the picture now, Waboose. I will wrap it up again, for I have much to say."

Then, unfolding the last writing of the poor fellow whom the Indians had styled Weeum the Good, I slowly translated it into the Indian language. It was not an easy task; for, besides feeling that it stirred the heart of the listener with powerful emotions, I had great difficulty in taking my eyes off her changeful face, so as to read the manuscript.

"Now, Eve Liston—for that is your real name," said I, when I had finished, "what do you think ought to be done?"

The girl did not reply at once, but sat so long with her hands clasped tightly on her lap, and her eyes fixed wistfully on the ground, that I had to repeat the question.

"What is to be done?" she replied, simply; "of course, what father wished to be done."

"And are you ready to go with me to the far south to see your father's mother? Can you trust me to protect you?"

"Oh, yes," she replied, with a straightforward look that almost disconcerted me; "have you not protected me well already?"

"And are you willing, Eve, to leave your tribe and go off alone with me?"

"Alone!" she repeated, with a look of surprise; "oh! no—not alone. Mother must go too, and also Big Otter."

Once more I felt somewhat confused, for, to say truth, I had totally forgotten her mother and Big Otter for the moment.

"Well now, Eve—for I intend to call you by that name in future, except when in the presence of your people—I must talk this matter over with your mother and Big Otter. I have some fear that the latter may object to go with us."

"He will not object," said Waboose, quietly. "He loved my father, and always obeyed him."

"Very good. So much the better. Now, as to the valuable jewels—the ornaments, I mean."

"Have you got them here!" asked Eve.

"Yes. Knowing the risk I shall run of losing them or having them stolen from me, I have had a belt made which fits round my waist under my clothes, in which the jewels and the money are placed. If I can manage to get them and you safely conveyed to Colorado, all will be well, but it is a long, long journey, Eve, and—"

I was interrupted at this point by Big Otter, who came to tell us that supper was ready, and that, as the region in which they were encamped was sometimes visited by hostile Indians, as well as by white trappers— many of whom were great scoundrels—it would be prudent to keep within the circle of sentinels after dark.

* * * * *

225

CHAPTER TWENTY THREE.

Attacked by Bandits—A Sad Death and a Sudden Rescue.

It was well that we had been warned not to go beyond the camp, for there happened at that time to be abroad on the prairies a band of miscreants who would certainly have shot whoever they had caught straying. The band was composed of white men—that class of white men who, throwing off all moral and social restraints, give themselves up to the practice of every species of iniquity, fearing neither God nor man. They were, in short, a band of robbers and cut-throats, whose special business at that time was hunting buffalo, but who were not averse to sell their services to any nation that chanced to be at war, or to practice simple robbery when opportunity offered.

These men held the opinion that Indians were "vermin," to exterminate which was commendable. When, therefore, they discovered our camp by the light of the fires, they rode towards it with the utmost caution, taking advantage of every bush and knoll until our sentinels observed them. Then they rushed upon us like a hurricane, sending a volley of bullets before them.

Several of our men fell, mortally wounded. Our sentinels ran in, and a wild attempt at defence was made; but it was in vain, we had been taken completely by surprise, and, as the only chance of safety, our party scattered in all directions, each man making for the nearest woods.

Only Big Otter, Salamander, and I remained beside the camp-fires, resolved to defend our helpless females or die with them. This brought about a most unexpected turn of affairs, for the villains were so eager to hunt and kill the flying Indians, that every man went in hot pursuit of a fugitive, leaving us for the moment absolutely alone!

We were not slow in taking advantage of this. Although at the onset some of our terrified horses broke their fastenings and galloped away, others remained quiet. Among these last I observed, were my own horse and that of Salamander, which I have already said were splendid animals.

Scarcely believing our good fortune, we all bounded towards these. In a moment I had mounted. Eve seized my hand, put her foot on my toe, and, with a light spring, seated herself behind me. Big Otter, vaulting on Salamander's steed, swung Eve's mother up behind him.

"Catch another horse—there are plenty good enough for a light weight like you, Salamander," said I, as I put my horse to its utmost speed.

Salamander was not slow to obey, but had scarcely mounted when a loud halloo told that our action had been observed. I did not look back. One consuming idea filled my mind, and that was to save Eve Liston. That the miscreants who now thundered after us would show us no mercy I felt well assured, and plied the heavy thong I carried with all my might. The noble steed did not require that. It strained every muscle to the uttermost.

I felt cheered to observe that Big Otter kept well up with me, and could hear that Salamander was not far behind.

We now felt that our only hope, under God, lay in the superiority of our horses, and for some time we listened to the pattering of the hoofs behind us with intense anxiety. Soon I began to fancy that we were distancing them, and ere long we became sure of this, at least as to the most of our pursuers, but there was one who kept drawing closer and closer.

Presently a shot was fired and a bullet whizzed close past my head.

At that moment Big Otter reined up so violently as to throw his horse almost on its haunches. I checked my speed but did not rein up. Looking back, I saw my Indian friend wheel round, raise his gun to his shoulder and fire. The moon was bright, and I could see that the man who had been closing with us dropped to the ground. Whether he was killed or only wounded we did not wait to ascertain, but dashed on again as fast as ever. We soon drew rein, however, on observing that the fall of our pursuer had checked his companions. On reaching him they halted, dismounted, and finally gave up the chase. We soon left them out of sight behind us, but still we held on at a hand-gallop, resolved to put as much distance as possible between us before encamping.

During all this exciting chase Waboose's mother had clung to her stalwart support with the uncomplaining patience of Indian women; but we were deeply concerned to find on halting that she was too much exhausted to dismount and that blood was trickling from her lips. Indeed, she would have fallen to the ground if Big Otter had not caught her in his arms.

"Are you wounded, mother?" exclaimed Eve, going down on her knees, seizing one of the poor woman's hands and kissing it tenderly.

"No, Waboose, but I think there is something wrong here." She pressed her breast gently and coughed up some blood.

"She is quite worn out," said I. "Come, Big Otter, let us carry her to a more comfortable place, and make a fire. A cup of tea will soon revive her."

I spoke cheerily, with a view to comfort Eve, but I confess that great anxiety filled me when I looked at the poor woman's wan face and emaciated frame. The blood, too, appeared to me a fatal symptom, though I had but a hazy idea of everything relating to disease.

The place we had selected for our encampment was a dense mass of forest which covered the prairie in that part to an extent of about two square miles. Near the outer margin of this patch there was a curious steep mound which rose so high that from the top of it one could see over the surrounding trees. It rose somewhat in the form of a cone with a flat space at the apex of not more than twenty feet in diameter. On the outer rim of this apex was a fringe of rocks and low bushes. It was, in fact, a natural fortress, which seemed so suitable for us in our circumstances that we at once set about making our camp on the top of it. We took care, however, to kindle our fire in the lowest-lying and densest thicket we could find at the foot of the mound. We also made the fire as small and free from smoke as possible, for fear of attracting any one to the spot.

While I was busy down in the dell preparing the tea, Salamander having been left to take care of the camp on the mound, Big Otter came to me. I was alarmed by the solemn expression of his face.

"Nothing wrong, I hope?" said I, anxiously.

"The wife of Weeum the Good is dying," said the Indian, mournfully.

"Oh! say not so," I exclaimed, "how dreadful to poor Waboose if this were to happen just now! You must be mistaken."

"Big Otter may be mistaken. He is not a medicine-man, but he saw a young girl of his tribe with the same look and the same flow of blood from the mouth, and she died."

"God forbid!" I exclaimed, as I took up the kettle in which the tea was being made. "See, it is ready, I will take it to her. It may at least revive her."

I hurried to the top of the mound, where poor Eve sat by the couch of brush we had spread, holding her mother's hand and gazing into her face with painful anxiety. She looked up hastily as I approached, and held up a finger.

"Does she sleep?" I asked, in a low voice, as I seated myself beside the couch and set down the kettle.

"Yes—I think so—but—"

She stopped, for at the moment her mother opened her eyes, and looked wistfully round.

"Weeum!" she murmured, in a faint voice. "I thought I heard him speak."

"No, dear mother," said Eve, beginning to weep silently. "Your spirit was in the land of dreams."

"See," said I, pouring some hot tea into a cup and stirring it. "I have brought you some of the pale-faces' sweet-water. I always carry a little of it about with me when I go hunting, and had some in my wallet when we started on this wild race. Was it not fortunate? Come, take a little, it will strengthen you, mother."

It was the first time I had called her mother, and I did so from a feeling of tenderness, for she seemed to me at the time certainly to be dying; but she misunderstood my meaning, for she looked at me with pleased surprise, and then laughed very softly as she glanced at Eve. I perceived, however, from the innocent look of inquiry returned by the latter, that she did not understand her.

After taking some of the tea, the poor woman revived, and I whispered to her daughter,—"Don't you think it might please her to see the little picture?"

"Perhaps. I am not sure. Yes, give it to me. I will show it, but say nothing about my father's writing or wishes. I have not yet been able to speak to her."

To our disappointment she could make nothing of the portrait. Perhaps the moonlight was insufficient, though very bright, but it is more probable that her sight was even then failing.

"What is that?" said Eve, with a startled look, pointing at something behind me.

I turned sharply round, and beheld a column of bright flame shooting high up into the night-air. An exclamation of bitter chagrin escaped me, for I knew well what it was. After I had got the fire kindled down in the thicket on our arrival, I had noticed that I had laid it close to the roots of a dead fir-tree, the branches of which were covered to the top with a species of dried moss. At the time I knew that there was danger in this, but as our fire was to be very small, and to be extinguished the moment we were done with it, I had allowed it to remain rather than be at the trouble of shifting and rekindling it. I afterwards found that Big Otter had left the fire in charge of Salamander, and gone to shift the position of the horses; and Salamander had left it to fetch water from a neighbouring spring. Thus left to itself, the fire took advantage of the chance to blaze up; the moss on the dead tree had caught fire, and the instantaneous result was a blaze that told of our whereabouts to whoever might be on the look-out within ten or fifteen miles of us in every direction.

Immediately afterwards Big Otter and Salamander came leaping into our fortress.

"What is to be done now?" I asked, in a tone of deep mortification.

"I would say mount and fly," replied the Indian, "if it were not for *her*." He pointed to the dying woman as he spoke.

"It is quite out of the question," said I. "She cannot be moved."

"The pale-face talks wisdom," said Big Otter. "We must put the place in a state of defence, and watch instead of sleep."

A deep sigh from Salamander told that the proposed mode of spending the night was most unsatisfactory.

Having no other resource left, however, we at once set about our task.

A number of large loose stones lay about on the little plateau that crowned our mound. These we rolled close to the edge of it, and ranging them in line with those that were already there, formed a sort of breastwork all round. Our three guns we had of course brought with us, as well as ammunition, and as mine was a double-barrelled fowling-piece we had thus four shots at command at any moment. The weapons being already charged, we placed ourselves at three points of our circle and prepared for a weary watch.

The blaze of the burning fir-tree soon went out, and there were fortunately no other dead trees at hand to be kindled by it. The moon had also become obscured with clouds, so that we were left in comparative darkness. The dead silence which it was needful to maintain, and the occasional murmur of the dying woman rendered our position eerie and sad in the extreme.

At such times, when danger threatens and everything that is calculated to solemnise surrounds one, thought is apt to be very busy; and often, in such circumstances, the mind is more prone to be occupied with distant scenes and persons than with those near at hand. Ere long the sick woman appeared to have fallen asleep, and her daughter was seated in perfect silence by her side. No sound whatever fell upon my listening ear, for the night was intensely calm, and in spite of my efforts to resist it, my thoughts strayed away to the home in "the old country"; to scenes of boyhood, and to the kind old father, who used, as a term of endearment, to call me "Punch."

A slight motion on the part of Salamander recalled me, and, by way of rousing myself to the necessity of present watchfulness, I examined the priming of my gun. Then it occurred to me that a bullet, if fired at a foe in the dark, would be very unlikely to hit; I, therefore, drew both charges, and loaded with buckshot instead. You see, thought I, there is no absolute necessity to kill any one. All I can possibly wish to do is to disable, and big shot is more likely to do that without killing, than bullets.

While thus engaged the clouds rolled off the moon, and I saw my companions clearly, sitting like statues at their posts. In a few minutes I heard the sweet, low voice of Eve. She was speaking to her mother. As I sat there and observed her fair hair and skin, and recalled (for I could not just then see) her blue eyes, I found it difficult to believe that there was even a drop of Indian blood in her veins. "Not that I object to Indian blood," I said to myself, mentally, in self-justification, "by no means. Indians are God's creatures as well as white men, and many of them are a great deal better creatures than many white men, but—"

At this point my mental remarks ceased, for I observed, to my surprise, that Eve opened a small book, and from the continuous tone of her voice, I knew that she was reading.

"It must be the Testament," thought I, "which poor Liston mentioned in his manuscript as having been obtained from a hunter."

The voice became more distinct as she proceeded, and I could make out that she read the English slowly and with great difficulty, and then translated it into Indian to her mother.

"God so loved the world," she read with peculiar emphasis, and paused, as if wishing to impress the blessed truth, "that He gave his only-begotten Son, that whosoever believeth in him should not perish but have everlasting life."

She closed the book at this point and I observed that she bent over the sick woman a long time.

Suddenly there arose on the still night-air a low wail, so deep—so suggestive of a breaking heart, that I sprang up and leaped to the girl's side.

There was no occasion to ask what had occurred. The mother lay there dead, with the jaw dropped and the glazing eyes staring at the sky. Kneeling down I gently closed the eyes, and with a napkin bound up the face. Big Otter glided towards us, followed by Salamander. One glance sufficed. They cast a look of pity at the orphan, who, with her face on her knees, sobbed as if her heart would break. Then, without a word, they glided back to their posts. I turned to Eve and took her hand.

"Dear girl," I began—but she checked me.

"Go," she said, "danger may be near; your post is unguarded."

Raising her hand to my lips I left her without a word, and resumed my watch. Again profound silence reigned around, broken only now and then by an irrepressible sob from Eve.

Some hours afterwards—I knew not how many, for I had been half asleep—Big Otter came to me.

"We may not stay here," he said. "Come, I need your help."

Without reply I rose and followed. It was still very dark. He went to where the body of the Indian woman lay. It was cold and stiff by that time. In passing I noticed that poor Eve acted as sentinel for Big Otter—occupied his post and held his gun.

I found that a shallow grave had been hollowed out close to where the corpse lay.

Understanding at once the purpose for which I had been called, I kneeled at the head while the Indian kneeled at the feet. Grasping the shoulders carefully I waited for a word or look from Big Otter, but instead he turned his head to one side and uttered the single word,—"Come!"

Eve glided instantly towards us, went down on her knees, and printed a long passionate kiss on the cold forehead. Then the Indian looked at me, and we lifted the body into the grave. Eve spread a blanket carefully over it, and at once left us to resume her post at the breastwork, while we covered in the grave with earth and dead leaves.

We had barely accomplished this duty when a loud report rudely broke the silence of the night, and a rushing of feet was heard at the foot of the mound. Leaping to my post, I instantly fired one of the barrels of my gun. Several fierce cries followed, showing that the buckshot had taken effect, and from the nature of the cries we at once perceived that our assailants were white men. I purposely reserved my second barrel, for my comrades, having also fired, were swiftly reloading, and, therefore, defenceless.

It was well that I did so, for two men, who had not been in the first rush, now came up the mound at a run. Aiming right between them, I fired and shot them both. They fell with hideous cries, and, rolling head over heels down the steep ascent, went crashing into the bushes.

"They are the men from whom we have just escaped," said I to Big Otter; but my Indian friend was so elated by the success of my shot and withal so excited by the fray, that instead of answering, he gave vent to a terrific war-whoop in true Indian style.

The attacking party had come on in front from the direction of the plains. To my consternation, Big Otter's war cry was replied to in our rear. Turning quickly, I saw the dark forms of several savages running up the slope of our fortress. These, like the white men, had been attracted to us by our column of fire. I was going to send a charge of buckshot amongst them, when my Indian friend stopped me.

"Let them come," he said, quickly. "They and the white men are sworn foes. Be ready to follow me."

This last was said to all of us, for we had instinctively drawn to the centre of our plateau with the idea of fighting back to back with the foes who surrounded us. Again we heard the white men charging up the front of our little hill, but, before they reached the top, a dozen savages had leaped into our enclosure.

"Help! against the pale-face dogs," cried Big Otter, pointing his gun, and firing at them as they came up.

A wild war-whoop rang out from the Indians, who were only too ready to accept the invitation to fight the pale-faces. A defiant cheer burst in reply from the white men, who were equally eager for the fray.

"Come!" whispered Big Otter at this point.

We had no difficulty in slipping away at the rear unperceived amid the din and smoke, and ran to where our horses had been tied. Mounting, like squirrels, we went off like the wind in the direction of the open prairie, and soon left our little fortress far behind us, with the redskins and the pale-faces fighting on the top of it like wild cats!

* * * * *

CHAPTER TWENTY FOUR.

The Power of Sleep—Plans discussed and a Far Journey resolved on.

It was broad daylight when we once again drew rein, and then we were all so overcome with sleep and exhaustion, after the prolonged watching and excitement of the night, that we could scarcely sit on our horses.

Eve, who sat behind me, grasping my waist with both arms, swayed so heavily once or twice, as nearly to throw me down.

"We *must* stop," said I to Big Otter, who was close beside me.

"Yes," replied the Indian; but his tone told that he was barely awake.

"If you doosn't me *drop*," said Salamander. The worthy interpreter seemed to think English the easiest language in the circumstances.

"Oh! I'm *so* sleepy," said poor Eve, whose grief helped to increase her exhaustion.

"Come, we will camp in this thicket!" said Big Otter, turning his horse in the direction of a long strip of bush that lay a few hundred yards to our right.

On reaching it, we penetrated, almost mechanically, to the thickest part of it, dismounted, and fastened our horses to the trees. Turning instantly, to assist Eve in making a couch of leaves, I found that she had lain down where she had dismounted, and was already fast asleep.

"Here, Salamander, lend a hand to lift her," I said, looking round; but Salamander was also in the land of Nod, flat on his back, with his eyes shut, and his mouth open.

Turning to Big Otter, I found that he was standing staring at me with an expression of such awful solemnity that I was partially roused with a feeling of alarm.

"Hallo!" I exclaimed, "what has happened?—speak, man!"

But Big Otter only gazed more intensely than ever, swayed slightly to and fro, and gave a sort of wink, or rather a slap together of both eyes. Then I understood that the wretched man was only glaring like an owl in the sunshine, in his tremendous efforts to keep awake. He assisted me, however, to lift Eve to a more comfortable position, and while he was in the act of laying her fair head gently on a pillow of moss, I observed that he sank down and instantly fell into a profound slumber; but even in that hour of mingled danger and exhaustion, the Indian did not neglect to hold his gun to his breast with a firm grasp. I also had enough wit left to keep my double-barrel in my hand, and was in the act of examining the locks, seated at Eve's feet, where my own senses forsook me.

We lay there, perfectly silent and motionless, during the whole of that day, for it was not until the sun was descending towards the western horizon that we awoke. I happened to be the first to move. Rising softly, so as not to disturb the others, I went to search for water, and was fortunate enough to find a small pool, which, though not very clear, was nevertheless sufficiently good to slake our thirst. Sitting down beside the pool, I lifted my heart and voice in thanksgiving to God for having thus far delivered and guided us.

While thus engaged a slight rustling in the bushes caused me to spring up. It was caused by Big Otter, who had followed me.

"What does the pale-face think?" he asked, sitting down beside me.

"He thinks that the Great Master of Life has delivered us from our enemies. He is good," said I, being still influenced by the devotional feeling which had been broken in upon.

For a few moments the Indian did not reply, but continued to look thoughtfully at the ground. At length he spoke.

"Was the Great Master of Life good when He let Waboose's mother die in the midst of war and weakness? Was He good to Waboose when He left her fatherless and motherless?"

"Yes, He was good," I answered, confidently. "He took the mother of Waboose home to dwell with Himself and with her father Weeum. And men and women, you know, cannot be taken to the happy land without leaving their children behind them—fatherless and motherless."

Big Otter did not reply, but I saw by his grave look that he was not satisfied. After a brief pause he resumed,—"Was the Great Master of Life good to the wicked pale-faces, when He allowed the red-men to slay them in their sins?"

"Yes," I returned, "He was good, because the Great Master of Life cannot be otherwise than good. He has made our brains capable of understanding that, and our hearts capable of resting on it. But He is our Father. Children do not understand all that a father does. Big Otter has touched on a great mystery. But what we know not now we shall know hereafter. Only let the red-man be sure of this, that whatever we come to know in the hereafter will tend more and more to prove that the Great Master of Life is good."

For a long time the Indian remained silent, and I could not tell by the expression of his grave face whether my reasoning weighed with him or not; I therefore offered up a brief prayer that the Spirit of God might open his eyes—as well as my own—to see, and our hearts to receive, the *truth*, whatever that might be. Then I said,—"The thoughts of Big Otter are deep, what do they lead to?"

"No," he replied, "his thoughts are not deep, but they are confused, for he has heard his pale-face brother call Waboose, Eve. How did he come to know that name? It was only used by Weeum, and seldom by him—never by any one else."

It struck me that now was as suitable a time as might present itself to let the Indian know about the contents of the packet, so I said,—"Listen, Big Otter, I have something important to tell."

238

From this point I went on, and, in as few words as possible, related all that the reader knows about the packet, and the wishes of poor William Liston. I also showed him the miniature, at which he gazed with visible but suppressed emotion.

"Now," said I, in conclusion, "what do you think we should do?"

"What Weeum wished must be done," he replied simply but firmly.

"You were fond of Weeum?" I said.

"Yes, Big Otter loved him like a brother."

"Don't you think," said I, after some minutes' thought, "that it is our duty first to return to the camp of your tribe, and also that I should send Salamander back to Fort Wichikagan to tell where I have gone, and for what purpose? For Salamander is not free like myself. He is still a servant of the fur-traders."

"No, that is not your duty," said the Indian decidedly. "Your duty is to obey the commands of Weeum! My tribe will not die of grief because Waboose does not return. As for Salamander—send him where you please. He is nobody—nothing!"

Although not quite agreeing with Big Otter in his contemptuous estimate of the value of Salamander, I believed that I could get along quite well without him; and therefore resolved to send him back—first to the Indian camp to tell of our safety and intentions, and then to the fort with an explanatory letter to Lumley, who, I knew full well, would be filled with great anxiety on my account, as well as with uncertainty as to how he should act, destitute as he was of the slightest clue to my fate or my whereabouts.

"And you, my friend," I said, "what will your movements be?"

"Big Otter will go and help you to obey the commands of Weeum," he replied. "There is no wife, no child, waiting for him to return. He must be a father to Waboose. Muxbee will *be* her brother. The trail to Colorado is long. Big Otter has been there. He has been a solitary wanderer all his life, and knows the wilderness well. He has crossed the great mountains where

239

the snow lies deep even in summer. He can be a guide, and knows many of the mountain tribes as well as the tribes of the prairie—Waugh!"

"Well, my friend," said I, grasping the Indian's strong hand, "I need not tell you that your decision gives me joy, and I shall be only too glad to travel with you in the capacity of a son; for, you know, if you are to be a father to Waboose, and I am to be her brother, that makes you my father—don't you see?"

The grave Indian smiled faintly at this touch of pleasantry, and then rose.

"We have nothing to eat," he said, as we returned to the place where we had slept, "and we cannot hunt in the night. Is your bag empty?"

"No," said I, glancing at the contents of my wallet, "there is enough of biscuit and pemmican to give us a light meal."

"That will do," he returned; "we need rest more than food just now."

This was indeed true; for, notwithstanding that I had slept so soundly during that day, I still felt a strong disinclination to rouse myself to action, and an intense desire to lie down again. These feelings being shared by my companions, it was resolved to spend the night where we were, but we took good care to kindle no fire to betray us a second time. We roused Eve and Salamander to take some food, after which we all lay down, and, ere long, were again sound asleep.

This double allowance of rest had the most beneficial effect upon our frames. We did not awake till an early hour the following morning, and felt so much refreshed as to be ready and anxious to set off on our journey, without the delay of breakfasting. This was fortunate, for the scraps that remained in my wallet would only have sufficed for one meal to a man of ordinary appetite; and, as it was important to expedite Salamander on his return journey, these had to be given to him. Poor fellow! he was much cast down on hearing of my decision in regard to him.

"But, sar," he said, with a sorrowful countenance, "w'at for I no go vith you?"

"Because you are still a servant of the Fur Company, and not entitled to break your engagement. Besides, it is desirable that Big Otter's people should know why he and Waboose have left them, and where they have gone; and if you explain matters correctly they will be quite satisfied, for they all respect the memory of Weeum the Good. Moreover, it is important that Mr Lumley should know what has prevented my return, both to relieve his mind, and prevent his sending out to search for me."

"But sar," objected Salamander, "w'at if me meets vid de vite scoundrils?"

"You must fight them, or run away from them."

"Vell, me kin fight but me kin more joyfulerly run avay. But," he continued, still objecting, "me got no grub."

"Here is enough for one day," I said, giving him all I possessed, "if you spin it out. To-morrow you can roast and eat your moccasins, and the third day you can starve. Surely that's not hard on a strong young fellow like you; and if you push on fast enough you'll reach the camp of the redskins early on the third day."

Salamander sighed, but made no further objection, and half an hour later he left us.

As we now possessed only two horses, it naturally fell to my lot, being a light weight compared with Big Otter, to take Eve up behind me.

"We must get a horse for Waboose," said the Indian, as we galloped over the prairie that day. "There is a tribe of Blackfoot Indians not far from here who have good horses, and understand the value of gold, for some of them have been to the settlements of the pale-faces. You tell me that you have gold?"

"Yes, I found a bag of five hundred gold pieces with the diamonds in Weeum's packet."

Big Otter looked at me inquiringly, but did not speak, yet I guessed his thoughts; for, though I had shown him Liston's letter and the miniature, I had not shown him the gold or the jewels, and he must have wondered where I carried them; for he knew, of course, that they were necessarily somewhat bulky and were not in my wallet, which I had emptied more than once in his presence. I therefore explained to him:—

"You know, perhaps, that gold is heavy, and five hundred pieces are bulky and troublesome to carry; so I have had a piece of cloth made with a hole in the middle of it for my head to go through; one end of it hangs over my breast under my shirt, like a breastplate, and one end hangs over my back, and on each of these plates there are rows of little pockets, each pocket the size of a gold piece. Thus, you see, the gold does not feel heavy, being equally distributed, and it does not show, as it would if carried in a heap—besides, it forms a sort of armour—though I fear it would not resist a rifle-bullet!"

"Waugh!" exclaimed Big Otter, with an intelligent look.

"As to the diamonds, they are not bulky. I have concealed them in an under-belt round my waist."

As Big Otter had predicted, we came to a large village of Blackfoot Indians two days afterwards, and were received with cordial friendship by the inhabitants, who knew my Indian well. He had visited them during his wanderings many a time, and once, at a very critical period in their history, had rendered important service to the tribe, besides saving the life of their chief.

A new tent was set aside for our use, and a small one pitched close to it for Waboose, whose dignified yet modest bearing made a profound impression on those children of the wilderness. They recognised, no doubt that Indian blood flowed in her veins, but that rather increased their respect for her, as it gave them, so to speak, a right to claim kinship with a girl who was obviously one of Nature's aristocracy, besides possessing much of that refinement which the red-men had come to recognise as a characteristic of some of the best of the pale-faces.

Indeed, I myself found, now that I had frequent opportunities of conversing with Eve Liston, that the man who had been affectionately styled Weeum the Good by the Indians, had stored his child's mind with much varied secular knowledge, such as Indians never possess, besides instilling into her the elevating and refining precepts of Christianity. Being of a poetical turn of mind, he had also repeated to Eve many long and beautiful pieces from our best poets, so that on more than one occasion the girl had aptly quoted several well-known passages—to my inexpressible amazement.

"I wonder," said I, when we three were seated in our tent that night, refreshing ourselves with a choice morsel of baked buffalo-hump, with which the hospitable Blackfeet had supplied us, "how it comes to pass that Indians, who are usually rather fond of gifts, absolutely refuse to accept anything for the fine horse they have given to Waboose?"

"Perhaps," said Eve, with a little smile, in which the extreme corners of her pretty mouth had the peculiar tendency to turn down instead of up—"perhaps it is because they are grateful. Indians are not altogether destitute of that feeling."

"True, Eve, true; it must be that. Will you tell us, Big Otter, how you managed to make these fellows so grateful?"

"I saved the chief's life," returned the Indian, curtly.

"Yes; but how, and when?"

"Four summers have passed since then. I was returning from a trip to the Rocky Mountains when it happened. Many bad pale-faces were in the mountains at that time. They were idle bad men from many lands, who hated work and loved to fight. One of them had been killed by a Sioux Indian. They all banded together and swore that they would shoot every Indian they came across. They killed many—some even who were friendly to the white men. They did not ask to what tribe they belonged. They were 'redskin varmints,' that was enough!

"The Strong Elk, whose hospitality we enjoy to-night, was chief of the Blackfeet. I was on my way to visit him, when, one evening, I came upon the camp of the pale-faces. I knew that sometimes they were not friendly to the red-man, so I waited till dark, and then crept forward and listened. Their chief was loud-voiced and boastful. He boasted of how many Indians he had killed. I could have shot him where I lay and then escaped easily, but I spared him, for I wished to listen. They talked much of the Strong Elk. I understood very little. The language of the pale-face is difficult to understand, but I came to know that in two hours, when the moon should sink, they would attack him.

"I waited to hear no more. I ran like the hunted buffalo. I came to Strong Elk and told him. It was too late to move the camp, but we put it in a state of defence. When the pale-faces came, we were ready. Arrows, thick as the snowflakes in winter, met them when they came on, and many of them bit the dust. Some ran away. Some, who were brave, still came on and leaped our barricades. They fought like fiends. Their boastful chief saw Strong Elk and rushed at him. They grappled and fell. The pale-face had a keen knife. It was raised to strike. One moment more, and the Blackfoot chief had been in the happy hunting-grounds with his fathers, when the gun of Big Otter came down on the skull of the boastful one. It was enough. Strong Elk was saved—and he is grateful; waugh!"

"Well, he has reason to be!" said I, much impressed by the modest way in which the story was told. "And now," I added, "since we have got a capital horse, and the journey before us is long, don't you think we should start to-morrow!"

"Yes, to-morrow—and it is time for Waboose to rest. She is strong, but she has had much to weary her, and her grief is deep."

With a kindly acknowledgment of the Indian's thoughtful care of her, Eve rose and went to her tent. Big Otter lighted his pipe, and I lay down to meditate; but almost before I had time to think, my head drooped and I was in the land of forgetfulness.

It is not my purpose, good reader, to carry you step by step over the long, varied, and somewhat painful journey that intervened between us and Colorado at that time. It was interesting—deeply so—for we passed through some of the most beautiful as well as wildest scenery of the North American wilderness. We kept far to the westward, near the base of the Rocky Mountains, so as to avoid the haunts of civilised men.

But space will not permit of more than a brief reference to this long journey.

I can only say that on arriving at a village belonging to a remote tribe of Indians, who were well-known to my guide, it was arranged that Big Otter and Waboose should stay with them, while I should go to the cities of the pale-faces and endeavour to convert my diamonds into cash. Happening to have a friend in Chicago I went there, and through his agency effected the sale of the diamonds, which produced a little over the sum mentioned by William Liston in his paper. This I took with me in the convenient form of bills on well-known mercantile firms in the region to which I was bound, and, having wrapped them in a piece of oiled silk and sewed them inside of the breastplate that contained my gold, I set off with a light heart, though somewhat weighted shoulders, to return to my friends in the Far West.

* * * * *

CHAPTER TWENTY FIVE.

Tells of a Wonderful Meeting and a Frustrated Foe.

I must change the scene now, and advance the courteous reader considerably in regard to time as well as place on the journey which we have pursued so long together.

It is one of those scenes of romantic beauty on the extreme frontiers of civilisation, where the rifle has not even yet given place to the plough; where the pioneer husbandman and the painted warrior often meet—the one to look with patronising superiority on the savage, whom he means to benefit; the other to gaze curiously at the pale-face, and to wonder, somewhat indignantly, when and where his encroachments are to cease.

Woodlands and prairies, breezy uplands and grassy bottoms, alternate in such picturesque confusion, and such lovely colours co-mingle, that a painter—had one been there—must have deemed the place at all events the vestibule of paradise.

There is a small hamlet on the slope of a hill, with a broad river winding in front, a few hundred yards from the hamlet, which opens out into a lake. On the margin of this lake lie a few boats. On the surface of it float a few more boats, with one or two birch-bark canoes. Some of these are moving to and fro; the occupants of others, which appear to be stationary, are engaged in fishing. There is the sound of an anvil somewhere, and the lowing of cattle, and the voices of children, and the barking of dogs at play, and the occasional crack of a gun. It is an eminently peaceful as well as beautiful backwood scene.

To a particular spot in this landscape we would direct attention. It is a frame-house, or cottage, which, if not built according to the most approved rules of architecture, is at least neat, clean, comfortable-looking, and what one might style pretty. It is a "clap-boarded" house, painted white, with an edging of brown which harmonises well with the green shrubbery around. There is a verandah in front, a door in the middle, two windows on either side, and no upper storey; but there are attics with dormer windows, which are suggestive of snug sleeping-rooms of irregular shape, with low ceilings and hat-crushing doorways.

This cottage stands on the apex of a little hill which overlooks the hamlet, commands the river and the lake, as well as an extensive view of a sparsely settled district beyond, where the frontier farmer and the primeval forest are evidently having a lively time of it together. In short the cottage on the hill has a decidedly comfortable come-up-quick-and-enjoy-yourself air which is quite charming.

On a certain fine afternoon in autumn Eve Liston, *alias* Waboose, Big Otter and I, rode slowly up the winding path which led to this cottage. We had been directed to it by the postmaster of the hamlet,—a man who, if he had been condemned to subsist solely on the proceeds of the village post-office, would have been compelled to give up the ghost, or the post, in a week.

"We must be careful, Eve, how we break it to her," said I, as we neared the top.

Arrived at the summit of the hill we found a rustic table, also a rustic seat on which was seated a comely matron engaged in the very commonplace work of darning socks. She cast on us a sharp and remarkably penetrating glance as we approached. Doubtless our appearance was peculiar, for a pretty maiden in savage costume, a somewhat ragged white man, and a gigantic savage, all mounted on magnificent steeds and looking travel-stained and worn after a journey of many weeks, was not probably an everyday sight, even in those regions.

Dismounting and advancing to act as spokesman, while my companions sat motionless and silent in their saddles, I pulled off my cap.

"I have been directed to this house as the abode of Mrs Liston," said I with a tremor of anxiety, for I knew that the comely matron before me could not be she whom I sought, and feared there might be some mistake.

"You have been directed aright, sir. May I ask who it is that desires to see her?"

"My name is Maxby," said I, quickly, for I was becoming nervously impatient. "I am quite a stranger to Mrs Liston, but I would see her, because I bring her news—news of importance—in fact a message from her long-lost son."

"From Willie Liston?" exclaimed the lady, starting up, and seizing my arm, while she gazed into my face with a look of wild surprise. "Is he—but it cannot be—impossible—he must be—"

"He is dead," said I, in a low, sad voice, as she hesitated.

"Yes," she returned, clasping her hands but without any of the wild look in her eyes now. "We have mourned him as dead for many, many years. Stay, I will call his—but—perhaps—sometimes it is kindness to conceal. If there is anything sad to tell, might it not be well to leave his poor mother in ignorance? She is old and—"

"No, madam," I interrupted, "that may not be. I have a message from him to his mother."

"A message! Then you knew him?"

"No; I never saw him."

"Strange! You have a message from him, yet never saw him. Can you not give me the message, to convey it to her? She is getting frail and a shock might be serious. I am William Liston's cousin, and have come to take care of my aunt, and manage her farm."

248

"The message, by Mr Liston's wish," said I, "was to be delivered by me to his mother. I will be very careful to deliver it gently."

"Well, I will bring her to you. She usually comes out about this time to enjoy the sunset. I will trust to your discretion; but bear in remembrance that she is not strong. Forgive me," she added, turning to my companions, "this surprise has made me forget my duty. Will your friends dismount?"

Eve at once dismounted, and shook the hand which the lady extended; but Big Otter sat quite still, like a grand equestrian statue, while the lady entered the house.

I saw that the poor girl was much agitated, but, true to her Indian training, she laid powerful constraint on herself.

In a few minutes an old lady with the sweetest face and most benignant aspect I ever saw, came out of the cottage and advanced to the rustic seat. Before sitting down she looked at us with a pleasant smile, and said,—"You are heartily welcome. We are always glad to see strangers in these distant parts."

While speaking she tremblingly pulled out, and put on, a pair of spectacles to enable her to have a clearer view of her visitors. The scene that immediately followed took me very much by surprise, and completely frustrated all my wise plans of caution.

She looked at me first and nodded pleasantly. Then she looked at Eve, who was gazing at her with an intense and indescribable expression. Suddenly the old lady's eyes opened to their widest. A death-like pallor overspread her old face. She opened her arms wide, bent forward a little towards Eve, and gasped,—"Come to me—Willie!"

Never was invitation more swiftly accepted. Eve bounded towards her and caught her in her arms just in time to prevent her falling.

The poor old mother! For years she had prayed and longed for her lost Willie, though she never once regarded him as "lost." "Is not the promise *sure?*" she was wont to say, "Ask and ye shall receive." Even when she believed that the erring son was dead she did not cease to pray for him—because he *might* be alive. Latterly, however, her tone of resignation proved that she had nearly, if not quite, given up all hope of seeing him again in this life, yet she never ceased to think of him as "not lost, but gone before." And now, when at last his very image came back to her in the form of a woman, she had no more doubt as to who stood before her than she had of her own identity. She knew it was Willie's child—one glance sufficed to convince her of that—but it was only Willie—the long-lost Willie—that she thought of, as she pressed the weeping girl with feeble fervour to her old and loving heart.

During the time that this scene was enacting, Big Otter remained still motionless on his horse, without moving a muscle of his grave countenance. Was he heartless, or was his heart a stone? An observer might readily have thought so, but his conduct when the old lady at last relaxed her hold of Eve, proved that, Indian like, he was only putting stern restraint on himself.

Dismounting with something of the deliberate and stately air of one who is resolved not to commit himself, the Indian strode towards Mrs Liston, and, tenderly grasping one of her hands in both of his, said,— "Weeum!"

Truly there is but a step from the sublime to the ridiculous, and in some cases that step is an exceeding short one. It seemed so to me now, as I beheld the tall Indian stooping to gaze with intense earnestness into the tear-besprinkled face of the little old lady, who gazed with equally intense amazement into his huge, dark visage.

"What *does* he mean by Weeum?" she asked, with an appealing look at me.

"Weeum," I replied, "is the Indian way of pronouncing William. Your late son, dear madam, was much beloved and respected by the tribe of Indians with whom he dwelt, and was known to them only by the name of William, or Weeum. This man was his most intimate and loving friend and brother-in-law."

The poor old lady was deeply affected while I spoke, for of course my words confirmed at last, her long resisted fear that Willie was indeed no longer of this world.

Big Otter waited a few seconds, still holding her hand, and then, turning to me, said in his native tongue,—"Tell the pale-face mother that the sister of Big Otter was the wife of Weeum; that Big Otter loved Weeum better than a brother, and that Weeum loved Big Otter more than any man of his tribe. Every one loved Weeum the Good. He was so kind, and so brave! At first he was very fierce, but afterwards that passed away, and when Waboose began to grow tall and wise, Weeum turned soft like a woman. He spoke often to the red-men about the Great Master of Life, and he taught Big Otter to love the Great Master of Life and the name of Jesus. Often Weeum talked of going to the far south to see one whom he called a *dear old one*. We did not understand him then. Big Otter understands him now. So shall it be in the great hereafter—things that are dark now shall be light then. But Weeum could not leave his wife and child, and we would not let him take them away. Sometimes Weeum spoke mysteries. One day he said to me, 'Brother, I *must* go to the far south to see the dear old one. I will take my wife and child, and will return to you again—if the great Master of Life allows. If, however, I die or am killed, Waboose will reveal all that is in Weeum's heart. She cannot reveal it now. She will not even understand until a *good* pale-face visits your tribe.' Weeum said no more. He left the mind of Big Otter dark. It is no longer dark. It is now clear as the sun at noon. The 'good pale-face' is here (pointing to me as he spoke), and the 'dear old one' is before me."

He paused a moment at this point, and then, with an evident effort to suppress emotion, added,—"Weeum was drowned, soon after the day he spoke to me, while trying to save life. Since then there has been no sun in the sky for Big Otter."

The poor old mother listened to this speech with intense interest and deepening emotion, but I could see that the tears which flowed over the wrinkled cheeks were tears of gladness rather than of sorrow. It could scarcely at that time come as news to her that her son was dead, but it did come as a gladsome surprise that her wilful Willie had not only found the Saviour himself—or, rather, been found of Him—but that he had spent his latter days in striving to bring others to that great Source of blessedness.

Being too much overcome to speak, she submitted to be led away into the cottage by the comely matron, who had been a keen and sympathetic observer of all that passed. Of course Eve accompanied them, for Weeum's mother refused to let go her hand, even for a moment, and Big Otter and I were left outside alone.

"Come," said I, vaulting into my saddle, "you and I will go and have a gallop, my friend, and see the land, for I mean to dwell here and would strongly advise you to do the same."

"Waugh!" exclaimed the Indian, as he leaped on the back of his steed, and followed me.

"You see," said I, as we rode along, followed by the admiring gaze of the village children—for, accustomed though they were to savages, they had never seen so grand an Indian as Big Otter on so magnificent a horse—"you see, they will require some time to clear up matters in the cottage, for Eve's English, good though it be, is not perfect, and all their minds will naturally be a little confused at first. You did me good service to-day, my friend."

"How? The speech of Muxbee is mysterious."

"Don't you see," I replied, "that the speech you made to old Mrs Liston, broke the ice as it were, and told her nearly all that I had to tell. And if you knew how many anxious hours I have spent in thinking how I should best break the sad news to the poor old mother, you would better understand how grateful I am to you."

"The speech of Muxbee is still full of mystery. What does he mean by breaking news? When Big Otter has got news to tell, he tells it. When people have got something to hear, why should they not hear it at once?"

I felt that there are some things which some minds cannot understand; so, instead of answering, changed the subject.

"See," said I, pointing to a part of the uncleared bush into which we had ridden, "there are two redskins. One is about to let fly an arrow. Hold on—we may disturb his aim!"

My companion looked, and with a start threw forward the muzzle of his gun.

Little did I think, riding as we then were in a semi-civilised region—what the aim was that I was so anxious not to disturb.

I was suddenly and rudely enlightened when I heard the twang of the bow, and saw the arrow flying straight towards me. It was too late to leap aside, or dodge it. Full on the centre of my chest the shaft struck me. I experienced something of the shock that one feels when death is suddenly and very unexpectedly brought near. I have a distinct recollection of the solemn impression made by the belief that my last hour had come, yet I did not fall. I saw that the savage was hastily fitting another arrow to the bow, but was so stunned by surprise that I made no effort to save myself. Happily Big Otter had his wits about him. He fired before the arrow winged its flight, and shot the Indian dead.

The other savage at once turned and fled, but my companion gave chase and overtook him in a few seconds. Seeing that he could not escape he turned round, flung down his weapons in token of submission, and stood sullenly before his captor.

Big Otter at once leaped off his steed, seized the man, bound his arms behind him with a thong, and led him to the spot where the dead man was lying on his face.

Meanwhile, I had discovered that the arrow which should have pierced my heart had been stopped by one of the gold pieces which formed my breastplate! It had, indeed, pierced the coin, but had only entered my flesh about a quarter of an inch! Thanking God for the wonderful deliverance, I plucked it out, and, casting it away, rode up to the place where the dead man lay. My companion had turned him over, and to my great surprise, revealed the face of my old foe, Attick!

"Waugh!" exclaimed Big Otter, turning to the captured savage. "Are there not deer enough in the woods, and buffalo enough on the plains, that the red-man should take to testing his arrows on pale-faces?"

"I did not shoot," was the stern reply.

"True, but you were the companion, perhaps the friend, of the dead man."

"I was *not* his friend," replied the savage, more sullenly than ever.

"Then how came you to be with him when making this cowardly attack?" I asked, in a tone which was meant to conciliate.

The tone had the desired effect. The savage explained that about three weeks previously he had, while in danger of being killed by a grizzly bear which he had wounded, been rescued by Attick, who told him that he was in pursuit of a foe who had injured him deeply, and whom he meant to hunt to death. Out of gratitude the Indian had consented to follow him—believing his story to be true. Attick explained that he had followed his foe from the far north, day by day, week by week, month by month, seeking an opportunity to slay him; but so careful a watch had been kept by his foe and the Indian and woman who travelled with him that he had not up to that time found an opportunity. Attick and his new ally had then dogged us to Sunny Creek—the village at which we had arrived—and, finding that we no longer feared danger from hostile Indians, and had relaxed our vigilance, they had made up their minds to stay there patiently till the deed could be accomplished. That day, while consulting about the matter in the woods, we had suddenly and unexpectedly appeared before them, and Attick had discharged his arrow.

"But" concluded the savage, with a perplexed look, "the pale-face cannot be killed. Arrows cannot pierce him."

"You are right," said I, suddenly coming to a decision in regard to the man. "Neither bullet nor arrow can kill me till my work is done, and the

Great Master of Life permits me to die. Go—and be more careful whom you follow in future."

I cut the thong that bound him, as I spoke, and set him free.

Without a word, though with an irresistible look of surprise, the savage turned, picked up his weapons and strode majestically into the bush.

"My brother is not wise," remarked Big Otter.

"That may be so," said I, "but it grieves me that the blood of one Indian has been shed on my account, and I don't want to let the authorities here have the chance of shedding that of another. Come, we must let them know what has happened."

So saying I turned and rode off. We went direct to the authorities above-mentioned, told who we were and what we had done, guided a party of men to the scene of the intended murder; and then, while the stars were beginning to twinkle in the darkening sky, returned to see what was going on in the little cottage on the hill at Sunny Creek.

* * * * *

CHAPTER TWENTY SIX.

One of the Difficulties of Correspondence enlarged on—Coming Events, etcetera.

About six weeks after the events narrated in the last chapter, I seated myself before a desk in a charming attic-room in the cottage—no need to say what cottage—and began to pen a letter.

I was in an exceedingly happy frame of mind. The weather was agreeable; neither too hot nor too cold; circumstances around me were conducive to quiet contemplation, and my brain was quite clear, nevertheless I experienced unusual difficulty in the composition of that letter. I began it at least half-a-dozen times, and as many times threw my pen down, tore it up and began another. At last I received a summons to dinner, and had then got only half-way through my letter.

Our dinner-party consisted of old Mrs Liston, her comely niece, Mrs Temple, who by the way was a widow, Eve Liston, and myself. Big Otter, unable to endure the restraints of civilisation, had gone on a hunting expedition for a few days, by way of relief!

"You is very stupid, surely, to take three hours to write one letter," remarked Eve, with that peculiar smile to which I have before referred.

"Eve," said I, somewhat sternly, "you will never learn English properly if you do not attend to my instructions. *You* is plural, though *I* am singular, and if you address me thus you must say you *are* not you *is*."

"You *are* right in saying you are singular," interposed Aunt Temple, who was rather sharp witted, and had intensely black eyes. Eve had called her "aunt" by mistake at first, and now stuck to it.

"I don't think there is another man in the district," continued the matron, "who would take so long to write a short letter. You said it was going to be short didn't you?"

"Yes—short and sweet; though I doubt if the dear old man will think it so at first. But he'll change his mind when he gets here."

"No doubt we will convert him," said Aunt Temple.

"Eve will, at all events," said I.

There was not much more said at that dinner which calls for record. I will therefore return to the attic-room and the letter.

After at least another hour of effort, I succeeded in finishing my task, though not entirely to my satisfaction. As the letter was of considerable importance and interest—at least to those concerned—I now lay it before the reader. It ran thus:—

"My Dear Father,

"I scarcely know how to tell you—or how to begin, for I fear that you will not only be very much surprised, but perhaps, displeased by what I have to write. But let me assure you, dear father, that I cannot help it! It almost seems as if the thing had been arranged for me, and as if I had had no say in the matter. The fact is that I have left the service of the Fur-Traders, and am engaged to be married to a dear beautiful half-caste girl (quite a lady, however, I assure you), and have made up my mind to become a farmer in one of the wildest parts of Colorado! There—I've made a clean breast of it, and if that does not take away your breath, nothing will! But I write in all humility, dearest father. Do not fancy that, having taken the bit in my teeth, I tell you all this defiantly. Very far from it. Had it been possible, nothing would have gratified me more than to have consulted you, and asked your approval and blessing, but with three thousand miles of ocean, and I know not how many hundred miles of land between us, that you know, was out of the question; besides, it could not have altered matters, for the thing is fixed.

"My Eve's mother was an Indian. A very superior woman, indeed, let me hasten to say, and an exceptionally amiable one. Her father was an English gentleman named William Liston—son of a clergyman, and a highly educated man. He was wild and wilful in his youth, and married an Indian, but afterwards became a really good man, and, being naturally refined and with amiable feelings, spent his life in doing good to the people with whom he had cast his lot, and perished in saving the life of his wife. Eve evidently takes after him.

"As to my Eve herself—"

I will spare the reader what I said about Eve herself! Suffice it to say that after an enthusiastic account of her mental and physical qualities, in which, however, I carefully refrained from exaggeration, and giving a brief outline of my recent experiences, I wound up with,—"And now, dear father, forgive me if I have done wrong in all this, and make up your mind to come out here and live with us, or take a farm of your own near to us. You know there is nothing to tie you to the old country; you were always fond of the idea of emigrating to the backwoods; your small income will go twice as far here as there, if properly laid out, and you'll live twice as long. Come, dear dad, if you love me. I can't get married till you come. Ever believe me, your affectionate son—George Maxby."

Reader, shall we visit the dear old man in his dingy little house in old England while he peruses the foregoing letter? Yes, let us go. It is worth while travelling between four and five thousand miles to see him read it. Perhaps, if you are a critical reader, you may ask, "But how came *you* to know how the old gentleman received the letter?" Well, although the question is impertinent, I will answer it.

I have a small cousin of about ten years of age. She dwells with my father, and is an exceedingly sharp and precocious little girl. She chanced to be in the parlour waiting for my father—who was rather given to being late for breakfast—when my letter arrived. The familiar domestic cat was also waiting for him. It had mounted the table and sat glaring at the butter and cream, but, being aware that stealing was wrong, or that the presence of Cousin Maggie was prohibitive, it practised self-denial. Finding a story-book, my cousin sat down on the window seat behind the curtain and became absorbed—so much absorbed that she failed to notice the entrance of my father; failed to hear his—"Ha! a letter from Punch at last!"—and was only roused to outward events by the crash which ensued when my father smote the table with his fist and exclaimed, "im-possible!" The cups and saucers almost sprang into the air. The cat did so completely, and retired in horror to the furthest corner of the room. Recovering itself, however, it soon returned to its familiar post of observation on the table. Not so Cousin Maggie, who, observing that she was unperceived, and feeling somewhat shocked as well as curious, sat quite still, with her mouth, eyes, and especially her ears, wide-open.

From Maggie then—long afterwards—I learned the details.

My father sat down after smiting the table, gasped once or twice; pulled off and wiped his spectacles; put them on again, and, laying strong constraint on himself, read the whole through, aloud, and without a word of comment till he reached the end, when he ejaculated—"in-con-ceivable!" laid the letter down, and, looking up, glared at the cat. As that creature took no notice of him he incontinently flung his napkin at it, and swept it off the table. Then he gave vent to a prolonged "wh–sh!" burst into a fiendish laugh, and gave a slap to his thigh that shattered the cat's peace of mind for the remainder of that morning, after which he re-opened the letter, spread it carefully out on the table, and, in the most intensely cynical tones, began a disjointed commentary on it as follows:—

"Your 'dear father,' indeed! That's the first piece of humbug in your precious letter. Very 'dear' I am to you, no doubt. And *you*—you—a chit—a mere boy (he forgot that several years had elapsed since I left him). Oh! no—I'm neither surprised nor displeased—not at all. The state of my mind is not to be expressed by such phraseology—by no means! And you were always such a smooth-faced, quiet little beggar that—well—no matter. 'Couldn't help it!' indeed. H'm. 'Quite a lady!' Oh! of *course*. Necessarily so, when you condescended to fall in love with her! 'Humility!' well! 'Given up the service,' too! 'Colorado!' 'One of the wildest parts'—as if a tame part wouldn't have done just as well! A 'farmer!' Much *you* know about farming! You don't tell all this 'defiantly.' Oh! no, certainly not, but if you don't *do* it defiantly, I have misunderstood the meaning of the word self-will till I am bald. Why didn't you 'consult' me, then? Much *you* care for my blessing—and 'the thing is fixed!'"

Exasperation was too much developed at this point to permit of blowing off steam in the form of sarcastic remark. My poor father hit the table with such force that the cream spurted out of its pot over the cloth—and my father didn't care! The cat cared, however, when, at a later period, it had the cleaning up of that little matter all to itself! This last explosion caused so much noise—my cousin told me—as to attract the attention of my father's only domestic, who bounced into the room and asked, "did 'e ring." To which my father returned such a thundering "No!" that the domestic fled precipitately, followed by the cat—rampant.

"*Your* 'Eve!' indeed," said my father, resuming the sarcastic vein. "'Mother an Indian'—a Hottentot, I suppose, or something of that sort—short skirt of peacock feathers; no upper part worth mentioning, flat nose and lips, and smeared all over with fat, I dare say. Charming mother-in-law. Calculated to create some impression on English society. No wonder you've chosen the *wilds* of Colorado! Ah, now, as to 'my Eve herself'—just let us have it strong, my boy—h'm, 'sweet'—yes, yes—

260

'amiable,' exactly, 'fair hair and blue eyes'—ha, you expect me to swallow *that*! oh, 'graceful,' ha! 'perfection,' undoubtedly. 'Forgive' you! No—boy, I'll *never* forgive you. You're the most arrant ass—idiot—but this caps all—'come out here and live with us!' They'll give me one quarter of the wigwam, I suppose—curtained off with birch-bark, *perhaps*, or deerskin. 'Your affectionate'—dolt! wh–why—what do you glare like *that* for?"

This last question was put to my small cousin, who, in the horror of her belief that my father had gone mad, had agitated the window-curtain and revealed herself!

My poor dear father! I can imagine the scene well, and would not have detailed it so minutely here if—but enough. I must not forecast.

The afternoon on which this letter was despatched Big Otter returned to Sunny Creek cottage with a haunch of fat venison on his lusty shoulders.

He found us all grouped round the rustic table in front of the door, enjoying a cup of fragrant tea, and admiring the view. Eve was sitting on a low stool at the feet of Mrs Liston, engaged in ornamenting a bright blue fire-bag with bead and quill work of the most gorgeous colouring and elegant design. The design, of course, was her own. Mrs Liston was knitting small squares of open cotton-work, of a stitch so large that wooden needles about the size of a goose-quill were necessary. It was the only work that the poor old lady's weak eyesight and trembling hands could accomplish, and the simple stitch required little exercise of mind or muscle. When Mrs Liston completed a square she rolled it away. When sixteen squares were finished, she sewed them together and formed a strip about eight feet long and six inches broad. When sixteen such strips were completed, she sewed them all together and thus produced a bed-quilt. Quilts of this sort she presented periodically, with much ceremony and demonstration of regard, to her most intimate friends. In that region the old lady had not many intimate friends, but then it luckily took much time to produce a quilt.

The quilt then in hand—at that time near its completion—was for Eve.

"Thank you *so* much for your venison," said Mrs Liston, as the hunter, with an air of native dignity, laid the haunch at her feet. "Take it to the kitchen, dear," she added to Mrs Temple, who was pouring out the tea.

"It has just come in time," said Mrs Temple, with a pleasant nod to Big Otter; "we had quite run out of fresh meat, and your friend Muxbee is such a lazy boy that he never touches a gun. In fact I don't know how to get him out of the house even for an hour."

As this was said in English, Big Otter did not understand it, but when he saw the speaker stoop to pick up the venison, he stepped quickly forward and anticipated her. "Thank you, carry it this way," said Aunt Temple (as I had begun to style her), leading the Indian to the pantry in rear of the cottage.

"Well, Big Otter," said I, when they returned, "now do you find the country round here in regard to game?"

"There is much game," he answered.

"Then you'll make up your mind to pitch your wigwam here, I hope, and make it your home."

"No, Big Otter's heart is in his own land in the far north. He will go back to it."

"What! and forsake Waboose?" said Eve, looking up from her work with an expression of real concern.

With a gratified air the Indian replied, "Big Otter will return."

"Soon!" I asked.

"Not very long."

"When do you start?"

"Before yon sun rises again," said Big Otter, pointing to the westward, where the heavens above, and the heavens reflected in the lake below, were suffused with a golden glow.

"Then I shall have to spend the most of the night writing," said I, "for I cannot let you go without a long letter to my friend Lumley, and a

262

shorter one to Macnab. I have set my heart on getting them both to leave the service, and come here to settle alongside of me."

"You see, your friend Muxbee," said Aunt Temple, using the Indian's pronunciation of my name, "is like the fox which lost his tail. He wishes all other foxes to cut off *their* tails so as to resemble him."

"Am I to translate that?" I asked.

"If you can and will."

Having done so, I continued,—"But seriously, Big Otter, I hope you will try to persuade them to come here. Give them a glowing account of the country and the climate, and say I'll not marry till they come to dance at my wedding. I would not wait for that however, if it were not that Eve thinks she is a little too young yet, and besides, she has set her heart on my father being present. I'll explain all that in my letters, of course, but do you press it on them."

"And be sure you tell the dark-haired pale-face," said Eve, "that Waboose expects her to come. Give these from her friend Fairhair—she was fond of calling me Fairhair."

Eve rose as she spoke, and produced a pair of beautiful moccasins, which had been made and richly ornamented by her own hands. At the same time she presented the fire-bag to the Indian, adding that she was glad to have had it so nearly ready when he arrived.

"For whom are these pretty things, my dear?" asked Mrs Liston.

"The fire-bag, mother, is for Big Otter, and the moccasins is—"

"Are, Eve—are—plural you know."

"*Is,*" replied Eve, with emphasis, "for my dear friend, Jessie, the black-haired pale-face."

"Well done, Waboose!" exclaimed Aunt Temple. "I'm glad to see that you improve under my tuition."

"You *can't* spoil her," I retorted, quietly.

"Well, my dear," said Mrs Liston, "send a message from me to your dark-haired pale-face that I shall begin a quilt for her next week."

"I hope she will come to receive it," said Aunt Temple. "Tell her that, Muxbee, with my love, and add that I hope we shall be good friends when we meet. Though I doubt it, for I can't bear Highlanders—they're so dreadfully enthusiastic."

"How much of that message am I to send?" I asked.

"As much as you please. I can trust to your discretion."

That evening I retired to my snug little attic-room earlier than usual, and, spreading out a large sheet of narrow-ruled foolscap paper before me, began a letter to my old chum on the banks of lake Wichikagan. I had much to relate, for much had happened since I had sent off the brief note by Salamander, and I found it difficult to check my pen when once it had got into the flow of description and the rush of reminiscence and the gush of reiterative affection. I had covered the whole of the first sheet of narrow-ruled foolscap, and got well into the second sheet—which I had selected unruled, that I might write still more narrowly—when I heard a gentle tap at the door.

I knew the tap well—sprang up and opened the door. Eve stood there, looking as modest and beautiful and elegant as ever—which is saying a good deal, for, in deference to Mrs Liston's prejudices, she had exchanged her old graceful tunic reaching to a little below the knee, and her pretty bead-wrought leggings, and other picturesque accompaniments of Indian life, for the long dress of civilisation. However, I consoled myself with the fact that *nothing* could spoil her, and recalled with satisfaction the words (I don't quite remember them), which refer to a rose smelling equally sweet under any other name.

"Prayers," said Eve.

Lest any one should feel perplexed by the brevity of her announcement, I may mention that dear old Mrs Liston's habit was to recognise her "Best Benefactor" night and morning by having worship in the household, and invariably conducted it herself in her soft, slightly tremulous, but still musical voice.

As we descended the stairs, Eve said,—"You must sit beside me to-night, Geo'ge. When you sit opposite you gaze too much and make me uncomfortable."

"Certainly, dear one," said I. "But pray don't call me Geo'ge—say Geo–r–ge. There's an r in it, you know."

"Yes, Geo–o–o–r–r–r–r–ge!"

"Eve," I whispered, as we sat on the sofa together, while Mrs Liston was wiping her spectacles, "I've been earnestly considering that last attempt of yours, and I think upon the whole, that 'Geo'ge' is better."

* * * * *

CHAPTER TWENTY SEVEN.

A Peculiar Wedding and a Wonderful Walk.

Turn we once again to the great wilderness, and if we do so with half the zest felt by Big Otter when he set forth on his journey, we will certainly enjoy the trip, you and I, whoever you be.

But we must take the journey at a bound.

It is Christmas-time once more. Lake Wichikagan has put on its top-coat of the purest Carrara marble. The roof of the little fort once again resembles a French cake overloaded with creamy sugar. The pines are black by contrast. The willows are smothered, all save the tops where the snow-flakey ptarmigan find food and shelter. Smoke rises from the various chimneys, showing that the dwellers in that remote outpost are enjoying themselves as of old. The volumes of smoke also suggest Christmas puddings.

Let us look in upon our old friends. In the men's house great preparation for something or other is going on, for each man is doing his best with soap, water, razor, brush, and garments, to make himself spruce. Salamander is there, before a circular looking-glass three inches in diameter in the lid of a soap-box, making a complicated mess of a neck-tie in futile attempts to produce the sailor's knot. Blondin is there, before a similar glass, carefully scraping the bristles round a frostbite on his chin with a blunt razor. Henri Coppet, having already dressed, is smoking his pipe and quizzing Marcelle Dumont—who is also shaving—one of his chief jokes being an offer to give Dumont's razor a turn on the grindstone. Donald Bane is stooping over a tin basin on a chair, with his hair and face soap-sudded and his eyes tight shut, which fact being observed by his friend Dougall, induces that worthy to cry,—"Tonal', man—look here. Did iver man or wuman see the likes o' *that*!"

The invitation is so irresistible to Donald that he half involuntarily exclaims, "Wow, man, Shames—what is't?" and opens his eyes to find that Shames is laughing at him, and that soap does not improve sight. The old chief, Muskrat, is also there, having been invited along with Masqua and his son Mozwa, with their respective squaws, to the great event that is pending, and, to judge from the intense gravity—not to say owlish solemnity—of these redskins, they are much edified by the proceedings of the men.

In the hall preparations are also being carried on for something of some sort. Macnab is there, with his coat off, mounted on a chair, which he had previously set upon a rickety table, hammering away at a festoon of pine-branches with which one end of the room is being decorated. Spooner is also there, weaving boughs into rude garlands of gigantic size. The dark-haired pale-face, Jessie, is there too, helping Spooner—who might almost be called Spooney, he looks so imbecile and sweet. Jack Lumley is likewise there. He is calm, collected, suave, as usual, and is aiding Macnab.

It was a doubly auspicious day, for it was not only Christmas, but, a wedding-day.

"It seems like a dream," cried Macnab, stopping his noisy hammer in order to look round and comment with his noisy voice, "to think, Jessie, that you should refuse at least a dozen sturdy Highlanders north o' the Grampians, and come out to the backwoods at last to marry an Englishman."

"I wish you would attend to what you are doing, brother," said Jessie, blushing very much.

"She might have done worse," remarked Spooner, who happened to be an Englishman.

267

Lumley said nothing, but a pleased smile flickered for a minute on his lips, while Macnab resumed his hammering with redoubled zest to a chuckling accompaniment.

"It would be nothing," he resumed, turning round again and lowering his hammer, "if you hadn't always protested that you would *never* marry, but—oh, Jessie, I wonder at a girl who has always been so firm in sticking to her resolves, turning out so fickle. I really never thought that the family of Macnab could be brought so low through one of its female members."

"I know one of its male members," said Lumley, in a warning voice, "who will be brought still lower if he keeps dancing about so on that rickety—there—I told you so!"

As he spoke, Peter Macnab missed his footing and came down on the table with a crash so tremendous that the crazy article of furniture became something like what Easterns style a split-camel—its feeble legs spread outwards, and its body came flat to the ground.

Sprawling for a moment Macnab rose dishevelled from a mass of pine-branches and looked surprised.

"Not hurt, I hope," said Lumley, laughing, while Jessie looked anxious for a moment.

"I—I think not. No—evidently not. Yes, Jessie, my dear, you may regard this as a sort of practical illustration of the value of submission. If that table had resisted me I had been hurt, probably. Giving way as it did—I'm all right."

"Your illustration is not a happy one," said Lumley, "for your own safety was purchased at the cost of the table. If you had taken the lesson home, and said that 'pride goes before a fall,' it would have been more to the purpose."

"Perhaps so," returned Macnab, assisting to clear away the split table: "my pride is at its lowest ebb now, anyhow, for not only does Jessie Macnab become Mrs Lumley within an hour, but I am constrained to perform the marriage ceremony myself, as well as give her away."

The Highlander here referred to the fact that, for the convenience of those numerous individuals whose lives were spent in the Great Nor'-west, far removed at that time from clergymen, churches, and other civilised institutions, the commissioned gentlemen in the service of the Hudson's Bay Company were legally empowered to perform the marriage ceremony.

Of course Jessie regretted much the impossibility of procuring a minister of any denomination to officiate in that remote corner of the earth, and had pleaded for delay in order that they might go home and get married there; but Lumley pointed out firstly, that there was not the remotest chance of his obtaining leave of absence for years to come; secondly, that the marriage tie, as tied by her brothers would be as legally binding as if managed by an Archbishop of Canterbury or a moderator of the Scottish General Assembly; and thirdly, that as he was filled with as deep a reverence for the Church as herself, he would have the rite re-performed, ("*ceremonially*, observe, Jessie, not *really*, for that will be done to-day,") on the first possible opportunity.

If Jessie had been hard to convince, Lumley would not have ended that little discourse with "thirdly." As it was, Jessie gave in, and the marriage was celebrated in the decorated hall, with voyageurs, and hunters, and fur-traders as witnesses. Macnab proved himself a worthy minister, for he read the marriage-service from the Church of England prayer-book with an earnest and slightly tremulous tone which betrayed the emotion of his heart. And if ever a true prayer, by churchman or layman, mounted to the Throne, that prayer was the fervent, "God bless you, Jessie!" to which the Highlander gave vent, as he pressed the bride to his heart when the ceremony was over.

There were some peculiarities about this wedding in the wilderness which call for special notice. In the first place, the wedding-feast, though held shortly after mid-day, was regarded as a dinner—not as a breakfast. It was rather more real, too, than civilised feasts of the kind. Those who sat down to it were hungry. They meant feeding, as was remarked by Salamander when more "venison steaks" were called for. Then there was no champagne or strong drink of any kind. Teetotalism—with or without principle—was the order of the day, but they had gallons of tea, and they consumed them, too; and these stalwart Nor'westers afterwards became as uproarious on that inspiring beverage as if they had all been drunk. There was this peculiarity, however, in their uproar, that it was reasonable, hearty, good-humoured; did not degenerate into shameful imbecility, or shameless impropriety, nor did it end in stupid incapacity. It subsided gradually into pleasant exhaustion, and terminated in profound refreshing slumber.

Before that point was reached, however, much had to be done. Games had to be undertaken as long as the daylight lasted—chief among which were tobogganing down the snow-slope, and football on the ice. Then, after dark, the Hall was lighted up with an extra supply of candles round the room—though the powerful blaze of the mighty wood fire in the open chimney rendered these almost unnecessary, and another feast was instituted under the name of supper, though it commenced at the early hour of six o'clock.

At this feast there was some speechifying—partly humorous and partly touching—and it remains a disputed point to this day whether the touching was more humorous or the humorous more touching. I therefore refrain from perplexing the reader with the speeches in detail. Only part of one speech will I refer to, as it may be said to have had a sort of prophetic bearing on our tale. It fell from the lips of Lumley.

"My friends," he said, with that grave yet pleasant urbanity which I have before said was so natural to him, "there is only one regret which I will venture to express on this happy day, and it is this, that some of those who were wont to enliven us with their presence at Fort Wichikagan, are not with us to-night. I really do not think there would be a single element wanting in the joy which it has pleased a loving God to send me, if I could only have had my dear young friend, George Maxby, to be my best man—"

270

He had to pause a few moments at this point, because of noisy demonstrations of assent.

"And I am quite sure," he continued, "that it would have afforded as much satisfaction to you as it would to my dear wife and me, if we could only have had our sedate friend, Big Otter—"

Again he had to pause, for the shouting with which this name was received not only made the rafters ring, but caused the very candles on the walls to wink.

"If we could only have had Big Otter," repeated Lumley, "to dance at our wedding. But it is of no use to sigh after the impossible. The days of miracles are over, and—"

As he spoke the hall door slowly opened, and a sight appeared which not only bereft the speaker of speech, but for a few minutes absolutely petrified all the rest of the company. It was the face and figure of a man—tall, gaunt and worn.

Now, good reader, as Lumley said (without very good authority!) the days of miracles are over, yet I venture to think that many events in this life do so much resemble miracles that we could not distinguish them from such unless the keys to their solution were given to us.

I give you the key to the supposed miracle now in hand, by asking you to accompany me deep into the wild-woods, and backward in time to about an hour before noon of the day preceding Christmas. It is a tangled shady spot to which I draw attention, the snow-floor of which is over-arched by dark pine-branches and surrounded by walls of willows and other shrubs. There is a somewhat open circular space in the centre of the spot, into which an Indian on snow-shoes strode at the hour mentioned. Even his most intimate friends might have failed at a first glance to recognise Big Otter, for he was at the time very near the close of a long, hard, wearisome journey, during the course of which he had experienced both danger and privation. Latterly he had conceived an idea, which he had striven with all his powers—and they were not small—to carry out. It was neither more nor less than to arrive in time to spend Christmas Day with his friends at Fort Wichikagan.

But to accomplish this feat, commencing at the time he conceived it, required that the Indian should travel without fail upwards of forty miles every day. This, on snow-shoes, could only be done by a very Hercules, and that only for a few days at a stretch. Big Otter knew his powers of endurance, and had carried out his resolve nearly to completion, when a storm arose so fierce, with temperature so bitterly cold, that he could not force against it, and thus lost the greater part of a day. Still, the thing was not impossible, and, as the difficulties multiplied, our Indian's resolve to conquer increased.

In this state of mind, and much worn and fagged in body, with soiled and rent garments that told of weeks upon weeks of toil, he entered the circle, or open space before referred to, and, coming to a stand, rested the butt of his gun on one of his snowshoes, heaved a deep sigh, and looked round, as if undecided how to act.

But Big Otter's periods of indecision never lasted long. Being naturally of a sociable turn of mind he partially revealed his mental condition by low mutterings which I take leave to translate.

"Yes, I can do it. The pale-faces are pleasant men; pleasanter at Christmas-time than at other times. They love song, and Big Otter loves to hear song, though he does not love to do it. Men do not love to try what they cannot do. The pale-faces have much food, too, on Christmas Day, and much good-will. Big Otter loves both the good-will and the food, especially that round thing they are so fond of—plum-puddinn they call it. They dance much also. Dancing gives not much joy, though Big Otter can do some of it—but plum-puddinn is glorious! Waugh! I will do it!"

Having communed with himself thus far, the Indian leaned his gun against a tree, flung down his provision-bag, took off his snow-shoes, cleared away the snow, kindled a fire, spread his bed of pine-brush and his blanket above it—and, in short went through the usual process of encamping. It was early in the day to encamp, but there was only one way in which our Indian could hope to partake of the plum-puddinn, and that was to walk a little over fifty miles at one stretch. That distance still lay between him and Fort Wichikagan, and it had to be traversed within fourteen and fifteen hours—including rests and food.

To prepare himself for the feat Big Otter drew from his wallet an enormous mass of venison which he roasted and consumed. Then he filled a small portable kettle with snow, which, with the aid of a fierce fire, he soon converted into tea. You see our Indian was becoming civilised by intercourse with pale-faces, and rather luxurious, for he carried tea and sugar on this journey. He did not deem butter a necessity, but could afford to dispense with that, because of having the remains of a rogan, or birch basket, of bear's grease (unscented, of course!) which he had reserved at the end of his fall hunt.

The meal, or rather the gorging, over, Big Otter rolled himself head and feet in a blanket, pillowed his head on the provision-wallet, and suddenly went to sleep.

Hour after hour passed, but not the slightest motion was perceptible in that recumbent figure save the slow regular rise and fall of the deep chest. The short-lived sun of winter soon passed its zenith and began to decline towards its early couch in the west, but still the sleeper lay motionless like a log. At last the shades of early evening began to fall, and then Big Otter awoke. He rose at once, stretched himself with a sort of awful energy, rolled up his blanket, put on his snow-shoes, caught up wallet and gun, and set off on his journey.

To see a strong man stride over the land on snowshoes is a grand sight at any time, but to see Big Otter do it on this occasion would have been worth a long journey. With his huge and weighty frame and his mighty stride he made nothing of small obstacles, and was but little affected by things that might have retarded ordinary mortals. Small bushes went down before him like grass, larger ones he turned aside, and thick ones he went crashing through like an African elephant through jungle, while the fine frosted snow went flying from his snow-shoes right and left. There was no hesitancy or wavering as to direction or pace. The land he was acquainted with, every inch. Reserve force, he knew, lay stored in every muscle, and he was prepared to draw it all out when fatigue should tell him that revenue was expended and only capital remained.

As the sun went down the moon rose up. He had counted on this and on the fact that the land was comparatively open. Yet it was not monotonous. Now he was crossing a stretch of prairie at top speed, anon driving through a patch of woodland. Here he went striding over the surface of a frozen river, or breasting the slope of a small hill. As the night wore on he tightened his belt but did not halt to do so. Once or twice he came to a good-sized lake where all impediments vanished. Off went the snowshoes and away he went over the marble surface at a slow trot—slow in appearance, though in reality quicker than the fastest walk.

Then the moon went down and the grey light of morning—Christmas morning—dawned. Still the red-man held on his way unchanged—apparently unchangeable. When the sun was high, he stopped suddenly beside a fallen tree, cleared the snow off it, and sat down to eat. He did not sit long, and the breakfast was a cold one.

In a few minutes the journey was resumed. The Indian was drawing largely on his capital now, but, looking at him, you could not have told it. By a little after six o'clock that evening the feat was accomplished, and, as I have said, Big Otter presented himself at a critical moment to the wonder-stricken eyes of the wedding guests.

"Did they make much of him?" you ask. I should think they did! "Did they feed him?" Of course they did—stuffed him to repletion—set him down before the massive ruins of the plum-puddinn, and would not let him rise till the last morsel was gone! Moreover, when Big Otter discovered that he had arrived at Fort Wichikagan, not only on Christmas Day, but on Chief Lumley's wedding-day, his spirit was so rejoiced that his strength came back again unimpaired, like Sampson's, and he danced

274

that night with the pale-faces, till the small hours of the morning, to the strains of a pig-in-its-agonies fiddle, during which process he consumed several buckets of hot tea. He went to rest at last on a buffalo robe in a corner of the hall in a state of complete exhaustion and perfect felicity.

* * * * *

CHAPTER TWENTY EIGHT.

The Wilderness again—New Plans mooted—
Treacherous Ice, and a Brave Rescue.

The well-known disinclination of time and tide to wait for any man holds good in the wilderness of the Great Nor'-west, as elsewhere.

Notwithstanding the momentous events which took place at Fort Wichikagan and in Colorado, as detailed in preceding chapters, the winter passed away as usual, spring returned, and the voice of the grey-goose and plover began once more to gladden the heart of exiled man.

Jack Lumley sat on a rustic chair in front of the Hall, gazing with wistful eyes at the still ice-covered lake, and occasionally consulting an open letter in his hand with frowning looks of meditation. The sweet voice of Jessie Lumley came from the interior of the Hall, trilling a tuneful Highland air, which, sweeping over the lawn and lake, mingled with the discords of the plover and geese, thus producing a species of wild-wood harmony.

Peter Macnab—who, since the memorable day when the table became a split-camel under his weight, had been to the Mountain Fort and got back again to Wichikagan—came up, sat down on a bench beside his brother-in-law, and said,—"Shall I become a prophet?"

"Perhaps you'd better not, Macnab. It is not safe to sail under false colours, or pretend to powers which one does not possess."

"But what if I feel a sort of inspiration which convinces me that I do possess prophetic powers, at least to some extent?"

"Then explode and relieve yourself by all means," said Lumley.

"You have read that letter," resumed Macnab, "at least fifty times, if you have read it once."

"If you had said that I had read it a hundred and fifty times," returned Lumley, "you would have been still under the mark."

"Just so. And you have meditated over it, and dreamed about it, and talked it over with your wife at least as many times—if not more."

"Your claim to rank among the prophets is indisputable, Macnab—at least as regards the past. What have you got to say about the future?"

"The future is as clear to me, my boy, as yonder sun, which gleams in the pools that stud the ice on Lake Wichikagan."

"I am afraid, brother-in-law," returned Lumley, with a pitiful smile, "that your intellects are sinking to a par with those of the geese which fly over the pools referred to."

"Listen!" resumed the Highlander, with a serious air that was unusual in him. "I read the future thus. You have already, as I am aware, sent in your resignation. Well, you will not only quit the service of the HBC, but you will go and join your friend Maxby in Colorado; you will become a farmer; and, worst of all, you will take my dear sister with you."

"In some respects," said Lumley, also becoming serious, "you are right. I have made up my mind that, God willing, I shall quit the service—not that I find fault with it, very much the reverse; but it is too much of a life of exile and solitude to my dear Jessie. I will also go to Colorado and join Maxby, but I won't take your sister from you. I will take you with me, brother-in-law, if you will consent to go, and we shall all live together. What say you?"

Macnab shook his head, sadly.

"You forget my boy, that your case is very different from mine. You have only just reached the end of your second term of service, and are still a youth. Whereas, I am a commissioned officer of the Fur Trade, with a fairish income, besides being an elderly man, and not very keen to throw all up and begin life over again."

There was much in what Macnab said, yet not so much but that Lumley set himself, with all his powers of suasion and suavity, to induce his brother-in-law to change his mind. But Lumley had yet to learn that no power of Saxon logic, or personal influence, can move the will of a man from beyond the Grampian range who has once made up his mind.

When all was said, Macnab still shook his head, and smiled regretfully.

"It's of no use wasting your breath, my boy,—but tell me, is Jessie anxious for this change?"

"She is anxious. She naturally pines for female society—though she did not say so until I urged her solemnly to tell me all her mind. And she is right. It is not good for woman, any more than for man, to be alone, and when I am away on these long expeditions—taking the furs to the depot, searching out the Indians, hunting, etcetera,—she is left unavoidably alone. I have felt this very strongly, and that was why, as you know, I had made up my mind during the winter, and written to the governor and council that, as my time had expired, I meant to retire this spring."

"Yes, boy, I know," returned Macnab. "I foresaw all this even long before you began to move in the matter, and I also took steps with a view to contingencies. You know that I am entitled to a year's furlough this spring. Well, I wrote during the winter to say that I intended to avail myself of it. Now, then, this is what I intend to do. When you retire, and go off to the States, I will go with you on leave of absence. We won't lose time by the way, for you may depend on it that Maxby will not delay his wedding longer than he can help. Fortunately, his old father won't be able to wind up his affairs in England, and set off to Colorado quite as quickly as the son expects, so that will help to delay matters; and thus, though we can hardly expect to be in time for the wedding, we will at least be time enough to claim a revival and extension of the festivities. Then, you know, Big Otter—"

"Aye, what of him?" asked Lumley, seeing that Macnab paused.

278

"Well, I think we may prevail on him to go with us, as our guide, till we reach the civilised world, after which, we can take him in charge—turn the tables as it were—and guide him to Sunny Creek."

"Yes—or send him on in advance of us, through the wood in a straight line, like the swallow, to announce our approach."

At this point, Jessie, who had been busy with the household bread, came to the door with a face radiant from the combined effect of hard work and happiness.

"What is the subject of all this earnest conversation, Jack?" she asked, pulling down the sleeves that had been tucked up above her elbows.

"Ask your brother, Jess," said Lumley, rising. "I shall have time before supper to pay a visit to Big Otter on a matter of some importance."

He passed into the house to take up his gun and powder-horn, while Jessie sat down on the rustic chair, and her brother returned to the subject that had been interrupted.

Now there occurred that afternoon an event which might have put a final and fatal termination to the plans which had just been so eagerly discussed.

I have said that spring was so far advanced at that time, that pools of water were formed on the ice of Lake Wichikagan. The heat which caused these had also the effect of softening the snow in the woods, so as to render walking in snow-shoes very laborious. As walking without them, however, was impossible, Lumley had no other course left than to put them on and plod away heavily through the deep and pasty snow.

Big Otter at that time occupied the important position of hunter to the establishment. He supplied it with fresh meat and dwelt in a small wigwam, about six miles distant from the fort, on the borders of a little lake—little at least for that region, but measuring somewhat over three miles in diameter. He also, for his own advantage and recreation, carried on the business of a trapper, and had that winter supplied many a silver fox and marten to the fur-stores at Wichikagan.

When Lumley set out to visit the chief he knew that there was a possibility of his being out after deer, but in that case he meant to await his arrival, at least until nightfall, and then he could leave a hieroglyphic message, which the Indian would understand, requiring his immediate presence at the fort. In any case Lumley thought nothing of a twelve-mile walk, even though the snow *was* soft and deep.

Nothing worthy of notice occurred until he reached the lake above-mentioned, on the borders of which he halted. Looking across the bay, on the other side of which the hunter's wigwam stood, he could discern among the pines and willows the orange-coloured birch-bark of which it was made, but no wreath of blue smoke told of the presence of the hunter.

"H'm! not at home!" muttered Lumley, who then proceeded to debate with himself the propriety of venturing to cross the bay on the ice.

Now, it must be told that ice on the North American lakes becomes exceedingly dangerous at a certain period of spring, for, retaining much of its winter solidity of appearance, and, indeed, much of its winter thickness, it tempts men to venture on it when, in reality, it has become honeycombed and "rotten." Ice of this kind—no matter how thick it be,—is prone to give way without any of those friendly cracks and rends and other warnings peculiar to the new ice of autumn, and, instead of giving way in angular cakes, it suddenly slides down, letting a man through to the water, by opening a hole not much larger than himself. Of course Lumley was well aware of this danger—hence the debate with himself, or rather with his judgment.

"It looks solid enough," said Lumley.

"Looks are deceptive," said his judgment.

"Then, it's rather early yet for the ice to have become quite rotten," said Lumley.

"So everyone goes on saying, every spring, till some unfortunate loses his life, and teaches others wisdom," said judgment; "besides, you're a heavy man."

"And it is a tremendous long way round by the shore—nearly four times the distance," murmured Lumley.

"What of that in comparison with the risk you run," remarked judgment, growing impatient.

"I'll venture it!" said the man, sternly.

"You're a fool!" cried the other, getting angry.

It is surprising with what equanimity a man will stand insulting language from himself! With something like a contemptuous smile on his lips, Lumley took off his snow-shoes and set off to cross the bay.

As he had anticipated, he found it as firm as a rock. The surface, indeed, had a dark wet look about it, and there were various pools here and there which he carefully avoided; but there was no other indication of danger until he had got three-quarters of the way across. Then, without an instant's warning, the mass of ice on which he stood dropped below him like a trap-door and left him struggling in a compound of ice and water!

The first shock of the cold water on his robust frame was to give it a feeling of unusual strength. With a sharp shout, caused by the cold rather than alarm, he laid both hands on the edge of the ice, and, springing like an acrobat out of the water to his waist, fell with his chest on the still sound ice; but it was not long sound. His convulsive grip and heavy weight broke it off, and down he sank again, over head and ears.

It is not easy to convince a very powerful man that he may become helpless. Lumley rose, and, with another Herculean grip, laid hold of the edge of the ice. His mind had not yet fully admitted that he was in absolute danger. He had only been recklessly vigorous at the first attempt to get out—that was all—now, he would exercise caution.

With the coolness that was natural to him—increased, perhaps, by the coolness of the water—he again laid his hands on the edge of the ice, but he did not try to scramble upon it. He had been a practised gymnast at school. Many a time had he got into a boat from deep water while bathing, and he knew that in such an effort one is hampered by the tendency one's legs have to get under the boat and prevent action—even as, at that moment, his legs were attempting to go under the ice. Adopting, therefore, his old plan and keeping his hands on the edge of the ice, he first of all paddled backwards with his legs until he got himself into a quite perpendicular position, so that when he should make the spring there would be no fear of retarding his action by scraping against the ice with his chest. While in this position he let himself sink to the very lips—nay, even lower—and then, acting with arms and legs at the same moment, he shot himself full half his length out of the water.

The whole process was well calculated, for, by sinking so deeply before the spring, he thus made use of the buoyancy of water, and rendered less pressure with his hands on the ice needful. But, although he thus avoided breaking the ice at first he could not by any device lessen the weight of his fall upon it. Again the treacherous mass gave way, and once more he sank into the cold lake.

Cold, far more than exertion, tells on a man in such circumstances. A feeling of exhaustion, such as poor Lumley had never felt before, came over him.

"God help me!" he gasped, with the fervour that comes over men when in the hour of their extremity.

Death seemed at last evidently to confront him, and with the energy of a brave man he grappled and fought him. Again and again he tried the faithless ice, each time trying to recall some device in athletics which might help him, but always with the same result. Then, still clinging to life convulsively, he prayed fervently and tried to meet his fate like a man. This effort is probably more easy on the battle-field, with the vital powers unexhausted, and the passions strong. It was not so easy in the lone wilderness, with no comrade's voice to cheer, with the cold gradually benumbing all the vital powers, and with life slipping slowly away like an unbelievable dream!

The desire to live came over him so strongly at times, that again and yet again, he struggled back from the gates of the dark valley by the mere power of his will and renewed his fruitless efforts; and when at last despair took possession of him, from the depths of his capacious chest he gave vent to that:—

"Bubbling cry
Of some strong swimmer in his agony!"

Sleeping soundly in his wigwam, Big Otter heard the cry.

Our Indian was not the man to start up and stare, and wonder, and wait for a repetition of any cry. Like the deer which he had so often roused, he leaped up, bounded through the doorway of his tent, and grasped gun and snow-shoes. One glance sufficed to show him the not far distant hole in the ice. Dropping the gun he thrust his feet into the snowshoes, and went off over the ice at racing speed. The snow-shoes did not impede him much, and they rendered the run over the ice less dangerous. Probably Lumley would not have broken through if he had used his snow-shoes, because of the larger surface of ice which they would have covered.

To come within a few yards of the hole, slide to the edge of it on his chest, with both snow-shoes spread out under that, by way of diffusing his weight over as much surface as possible, was the work of only a few minutes. But by that time the perishing man was almost incapable of helping himself. The great difficulty that the rescuer experienced was to rouse Lumley once more to action, for the torpor that precedes death had already set in, and to get on his knees on the edge of the ice, so as to have power to raise his friend, would only have resulted in the loss of his own life as well. To make sure that he should not let go his hold and slip, Big Otter tied the end of his long worsted belt round his friend's right wrist.

"Now," he said, earnestly, "try once more."

"Too late—too late! God bless you, Big—" He stopped, and his eyes closed!

"No!" cried the Indian, vehemently, giving the perishing man's head a violent shake—then, putting his mouth close to his ear, added in a deep tone—"Not too late for the Master of Life to save. Think! The dark-haired pale-face waits for you."

This was a judicious touch. The energy which could not be aroused by any consideration of self was electrified by the thought of the waiting wife. Lumley made one more desperate effort and once again cried to God for help. Both acts contributed to the desired end, and were themselves an answer to the prayer of faith. Mysterious connection! Hope revived, and the vital fluid received a fresh impulse. In the strength of it Lumley raised himself so far out of the water that the Indian was able to drag half his body on the ice, but the legs still hung down. Creeping back a few feet, the Indian, still lying flat on his face, cut a hole in the ice with his hatchet into which he stuck his toe, and seized hold of the end of his worsted belt.

"That's right," said his friend, faintly—"wait."

Big Otter knew that full consciousness had returned. He waited while Lumley, gently paddling with his legs, got them into a horizontal position.

"Now!" cried Lumley.

The Indian pulled—softly at first, then vigorously, and Lumley slid fairly on the ice. The rest, though still dangerous, was easy. In a few minutes more the red-man had the pale-face stripped beside a rousing fire in the wigwam—and thus he brought him back to life from the very gates of death.

"You have saved me, my good friend," said Lumley, when he began to recover.

"The Great Master of Life saved you," returned the Indian. "He made use of me—for which I thank him."

It was not until late on the following day that Lumley felt strong enough to return to the fort, and relate what had occurred. Then the

284

plans for the future were laid before Big Otter, and, to the satisfaction of all parties, he agreed at once to fall in with them.

"But," said he, "Big Otter will not stay. He loves the great wilderness too well to be content to live among the wooden wigwams of the pale-faces."

"Well, we won't bother ourselves on that point just now," said Macnab, "and so, as that's comfortably settled, I'll pack up and away back to my mountain fort to get ready for a trip, with you and Lumley and Jessie, to Colorado."

* * * * *

CHAPTER TWENTY NINE.

The Last.

Once more I change the scene, from the wild regions of the north to the little less wild lands of Colorado.

On a certain bright forenoon in Autumn I stood in the doorway of Sunny Creek Cottage watching a clumsy vehicle as it laboured slowly up the hill. I was alone that day, old Mrs Liston, Eve, and "Aunt Temple" having gone off in the waggon for a long drive to visit a relative with hunting proclivities, who had built himself a log-hut in a ravine of the neighbouring mountains, that he might be in closer proximity to the bears and deer.

With some curiosity I approached the lumbering machine to assist the occupant, who seemed unable, or too impatient, to open the door. It was a stiff door, and swung open with a jerk which caused the occupant's hat to fall off, and reveal a bald head.

"Father!" I gasped.

"Punch, my boy!"

The dear old man tripped in his haste to get down, plunged into my bosom, threw his arms round my neck to save himself, and almost bore me to the ground. Neither of us being demonstrative in our affections, this unpremeditated, not to say unintentional, embrace I felt to be quite touching. My father obviously resolved to make the most of his opportunities, for he gave me a thoroughly exhaustive hug before releasing me.

"I—I—didn't m–mean," said my father, blazing with excitement, and gasping with a mingled tendency to laugh and weep, "didn't mean to come it quite so strong, P–Punch, my boy, b–but you'll make allowance for a momentary weakness. I'm getting an old man, Punch. What makes you grin so, you backwoods koonisquat?"

The last sentence, with its opprobrious epithet (coined on the spot), was addressed with sudden asperity to the driver of the clumsy vehicle, who was seated on his box, with mouth expanded from ear to ear.

"Wall, stranger, if you will insist on knowin'," said he, "It's sympathy that makes me grin. I *do* like to see human natur' out of its go-to-meetin' togs, with its saddle off, an' no bridal on, spurtin' around in gushin' simplicity. But you're wrong, stranger," continued the driver, with a grave look, "quite wrong in callin' me a koonisquat. I *have* dropt in the social scale, but I ain't got quite so low as that, I guess, by a long chalk."

"Well, you compound of Welshman and Yankee, be off and refresh yourself," returned my father, putting an extra dollar, over and above his fare, into the man's hand, "but don't consume it on your filthy fire-water cock-tails, or gin-slings, or any other kind of sling-tails. If you must drink, take it out in strong hot coffee."

The man drove off, still grinning, and I hurried my father into the cottage where, while I set before him a good luncheon, he gave me a wildly rambling and interjectional account of his proceedings since the date of his last letter to me.

"But why did you take me by surprise in this way, dear daddy; why didn't you let me know you were coming?"

"Because I like to take people by surprise, especially ill-doing scapegraces like—by the way," said my father, suddenly laying down his knife and fork, "where is she?"

"Where is who?"

"She—her, of course; the—the girl, the Hottentot, the savage. Oh! George, what an ass you are!"

"If you mean Eve, sir," said I, "she is away from home—and everybody else along with her. That comes of your taking people by surprise, you see. Nobody prepared to receive you; nothing ready. No sheets aired even."

"Well, well, Punch, my boy, don't be sharp with your old father. I won't offend again. By the way," he added, quickly, "you're not married *yet*? eh?"

"No, not yet."

"Ah!" said my father with a sigh of relief, as he resumed his knife and fork, "then there's the barest chance of a possibility that if—but you've asked her to marry you, eh?"

"Yes, I have asked her."

"And she has accepted you?"

"Yes, she has accepted me. I wrote all that to you long ago."

"Ah!" said my father, with a profound sigh of resignation, "then there is *no* chance of a possibility, for if a man tries to win the affections of a girl and succeeds, he is bound in honour to marry her—even though he were the Emperor of China, and she a—a Hottentot. Now, Punch, I have made up my mind to like the girl, even though she painted scarlet circles round her eyes, and smeared her nose with sky-blue—but you *must* let your poor old father blow off the steam, for you have been such a—a donkey!—such a hasty, impatient, sentimental, romantic idiot, that—another glass of that milk, my boy. Thank'ee, where do you get it? Beats English milk hollow."

"Got it from one of our numerous cows, daddy," said I, with a short laugh at this violent change of the subject, "and my Eve made the butter."

"Did she, indeed? Well, I'm glad she's fit for even that small amount of civilised labour; but you have not told me yet when I shall see her?"

"That is a question I cannot exactly answer," said I, "but you will at all events be introduced to-night to her father's mother, and her cousin (whom we call aunt), as well as to a young lady—a Miss Waboose—who

288

is staying with us at present. And now, father," I added, "come, and we'll have a stroll round the farm. I don't expect the ladies back till evening. Meanwhile, I want you to do me a favour; to humour what I may call a whim."

"If it's not a very silly one, Punch, I'll do it, though I have not much confidence in your wisdom *now*."

"It is simply that you should agree, for this night only, to pass yourself off for a very old friend of mine. You need not tell fibs, or give a false name. You are a namesake, you know. There are lots of Maxbys in the world!"

"Weak, my boy; decidedly weak. They'll be sure to see through it and I won't be able to recollect not to call you Punch."

"No matter. Call me Punch. I'll tell them you are a very familiar old friend—a sort of relation, too, which will account for the name."

"Well, well," said my father, with a smile of pity, "I'll not object to humour your whim, but it's weak—worthy of a man who could engage himself to a miserable red-Indian Hottentot!"

This being finally settled, and my father having been pretty well exhausted by his ramble round the farm, I set him down on the rustic chair with a newspaper and left him, saying that I should be back in an hour or so.

I knew the road by which the waggon was to return, walked along it several miles, and then waited. Soon it drove up to the spot where I stood. They were surprised to see me, but more surprised when I ordered the ladies to get out, and walk with me, while the coachman drove on slowly in advance.

Then I hurriedly told of my father's arrival, and explained more fully than I had yet ventured to do his misconceptions and prejudices as to Eve. "Now, I want you all," said I, "to help me to remove these prejudices and misconceptions as quickly as possible by falling in with my little plans."

Hereupon I explained that my father was to be introduced as an old friend and namesake, while Eve was to be presented to him as a visitor at the cottage named Miss Waboose. I had feared that old Mrs Liston would not enter into my plan, but found that, on the contrary, having a strong sense of humour, she quite enjoyed the notion of it. So did Aunt Temple, but Eve herself felt doubtful of her ability to act out her part. I had no doubt on that point, for she had undertaken it, and well did I know that whatever Eve undertook she could, and would, accomplish.

It might be tedious to recount in detail the scenes that followed. The dear old man was charmed with Miss Waboose—as I had fully expected— and Miss Waboose was more than charmed with the dear old man! So that when we bade the ladies good-night, he kissed her fair forehead with quite fatherly tenderness.

When I conducted the old man to his room I was struck, and made quite anxious, by the disconsolate expression of his face, and asked earnestly what was wrong.

"Wrong!" he exclaimed, almost petulantly. "Everything's wrong. More particularly, *you* are wrong. Oh, George, I *can't* get over it. To think that you are tied hard and fast—*irrevocably*—to—a red-Indian—a painted savage—a Hottentot. It is too—too bad!"

He kicked off one of his shoes so viciously at this point, that it went straight into, and smashed, a looking-glass; but he didn't seem to care a straw for that. He did not even condescend to notice it.

"And to think, too," he continued, "that you might have had that adorable young lady, Miss Waboose, who—in spite of her heathenish name—is the most charming, artless, modest young creature I ever saw. Oh! Punch, Punch, what a consummate idiot you have been."

It was impossible to help laughing at my poor father's comical expression of chagrin, as he sat on the edge of his bed, slapped his hands down on both knees and looked up in my face.

"Excuse me, daddy, but what ground have you for supposing that Miss Waboose would accept me, even if I were free to ask her hand?"

"Ground? Why the ground that she is fond of you. Any man with half an eye could see that, by the way she looks at and speaks to you.

Of course you have not observed that. I trust, my boy, you are too honourable to have encouraged it. Nevertheless, it is a fact—a miserable, tantalising, exasperating fact—a maddening fact, now that that hideous red-Indian—Hottentot stands in the way."

"That red-Indian—Hottentot," said I, unable any longer to cause my dear father so much pain, "does *not* stand in the way, for I am happy to tell you that Miss Waboose and Eve are one and the same person."

"Come, come, Punch," returned my parent, testily, "I'm in no humour for jesting. Go away, and let me get to bed and pillow my head on oblivion if possible."

I do assure you, reader, that I had no slight difficulty in persuading my father that Eve Liston and Waboose were really the same person.

"But the girl's *fair*," objected my father, when the truth began to force an entrance.

"Yes—'passing fair,'" said I.

"And with blue eyes and golden hair!" said he.

"Even so," said I.

"No more like a savage than I am?" said my father.

"Much less so," said I.

When at length he did take in the fact, he flung his arms round my neck for the second time that day, and did his best to strangle me. Then, under a sudden impulse, he thrust me out into the passage and shut and locked the door.

"You won't pillow your head on oblivion now, will you, daddy?" I asked through the keyhole.

"Get away, you deceiver!" was the curt reply.

But surprises did not come singly at that time. Call it a miracle, or a coincidence, or what you will, it is a singular fact that, on the very next day, there arrived at Sunny Creek cottage four travellers—namely, Jack Lumley, the black-haired pale-face, Peter Macnab, and Big Otter.

On beholding each other, Jessie Lumley and Eve Liston, uttering each a little shriek, rushed into each other's arms, and straightway, for the space of five minutes, became a human amalgam.

"Not too late, I hope?" said Lumley, after the first excitement of meeting was over.

"Too late for what?" said I.

"For the wedding, of course," said he.

"By no means. It is fixed for this day three weeks."

"Good—Jessie and I will have the knot tightened a little on the same day by the same man."

"Wind and weather permitting," said Macnab, with his wonted irreverence. "Now, Maxby, my boy, take us into the house, and introduce us to old Mrs Liston. But what splendid creature is this coming towards us?"

"Why that's Aunt Temple," I whispered, as she came forward. "Let me introduce you, aunt, to Mr Macnab—the jolly fur-trader of whom you have heard me speak so often and so much."

Macnab made a profound obeisance, and Aunt Temple returned a dignified bow, expressing herself, "much pleased to make the acquaintance," etcetera, and saying that Mrs Liston, being unable to come out to greet them, was anxious that we should enter. "Particularly Big Otter," said Aunt Temple, turning to the grave chief, "for whom she has a very great regard."

Thus invited and specially complimented, our tall Indian stooped to enter the cottage door, but not being accustomed to the wooden wigwams of the pale-faces, he did not stoop low enough, struck his head against the top, and rather damaged an eagle's feather with which his hair was decorated.

Nothing, almost, could upset the dignity and imperturbable gravity of Big Otter. He stooped lower to conquer the difficulty, and when inside drew himself up to his full height, so that the eagle's feather touched the ceiling, and tickled up some flies that were reposing in fancied security there.

Glancing round till his black eyes caught sight of old Mrs Liston in a darkish corner on a sofa, he stepped forward, and, stooping to grasp one of her small hands in both of his, said tenderly—"Watchee."

"What cheer—what cheer?" said the accommodating old lady, responding to the salutation in kind. "Tell him, George, that I'm *so* happy to see once again the friend of my beloved William."

"Big Otter rejoices to meet again the mother of Weeum," replied the Indian.

"And tell him," said Mrs Listen, "that I hope he has now come to stay with us altogether."

The Indian smiled gravely, and shook his head, intimating that the question required consideration.

When the other members of the party were introduced—Jessie and Eve having been separated for the purpose—we all adjourned to the verandah to interchange news.

Need it be said that we had much to hear and tell? I think not. Neither need the fact be enlarged on that we all retired late that night, in a state of supreme felicity and mental exhaustion.

There was one exception, however, as regards the felicity, for Mrs Liston, out of regard for the friend of her darling William, insisted that Big Otter should occupy the best bedroom on the ground floor. The result was eminently unsatisfactory, for Big Otter was not accustomed to best bedrooms. Eve conducted the Indian to his room. He cared nothing for his comfort, and was prepared humbly to do whatever he was bid. He silently followed her and looked round the room with open-mouthed wonder as she pointed to his bed and, with a pleasant nod, left him.

Resting his gun in a corner—for he never parted with that weapon night or day—and laying his powder-horn and shot-pouch on the ground, he drew his tomahawk and scalping-knife, and was about to deposit them beside the horn, when his eye suddenly fell on a gigantic Indian crouching, as if on the point of springing on him. Like lightning he sprang erect. Then an expression of intense humility and shame covered his grave features on discovering that a large mirror had presented him with a full-length portrait of himself! A sort of pitiful smile curled his lip as he took off his hunting coat. Being now in his ordinary sleeping costume he approached the bed, but did not like the look of it. No wonder! Besides being obviously too short, it had white curtains with frills or flounces of some sort, with various tags and tassels around, and it did not look strong. He sat cautiously down on the side of it, however, and put one leg in. The sheets felt unpleasant to his naked foot, but not being particular, he shoved it in, and was slowly letting himself down on one elbow, when the bed creaked!

This was enough. Big Otter was brave to rashness in facing known danger, but he was too wise to risk his body on the unknown! Drawing forth his leg he stood up again, and glanced round the room. There was a small dressing-table opposite the bed; beside it was the large glass which had given him such a surprise. Further on a washhand-stand with a towel-rack beside it, but there was no spot on which he could stretch his bulky frame save the middle of the floor. Calmly he lay down on that, having previously pulled off all the bedclothes in a heap and selected therefrom a single blanket. Pillowing his head on a footstool, he tried to sleep, but the effort was vain. There was a want of air—a dreadful silence, as if he had been buried alive—no tinkling of water, or rustling of leaves, or roar of cataract. It was insupportable. He got up and tried to open the door, but the handle was a mystery which he could not unriddle. There was a window behind the dressing-table. He examined that, overturning and extinguishing the candle in the act. But that was nothing. The stars gave enough of light. Fortunately the window was a simple cottage one, which opened inwards with a pull. He put on his coat and belt, resumed his arms, and, putting his long leg over the sill, once more stood on his native soil and breathed the pure air! Quietly gliding round the house, he found a clump of bushes with a footpath leading through it. There he laid him down, enveloped in one of Mrs Liston's best blankets, and there he was found next morning in tranquil slumber by our domestic when she went to milk the cows!

Before the three weeks were over Peter Macnab almost paralysed Aunt Temple by a cool proposal that she should exchange the civilised settlements for the wilderness, and go back with him, as Mrs Macnab, to the Mountain Fort! The lady, recovering from her semi-paralytic affection, agreed to the suggestion, and thus Peter Macnab was, according to his own statement, "set up for life."

Shall I dwell on the triple wedding? No. Why worry the indulgent reader, or irritate the irascible one, by recounting what is so universally understood. There were circumstances peculiar, no doubt to the special occasion. To Eve and myself, of course, it was the most important day of our lives—a day never to be forgotten; and for which we could never be too thankful, and my dear father pronounced it the happiest day of *his* life; but I think he forgot himself a little when he said that! Then old Mrs Liston saw but one face the whole evening, and it was the face of Willie— she saw it by faith, through the medium of Eve's sweet countenance.

But I must cut matters short. When all was over, Macnab said to his wife:—

"Now, my dear, we must be off at the end of one week. You see, I have just one year's furlough, and part of it is gone already. The rest of it, you and I must spend partly in the States, partly in England, and partly on the continent of Europe, so that we may return to the Great Nor'-west with our brains well stored with material for small talk during an eight or nine months' winter."

Aunt Macnab had no objection. Accordingly, that day week he and she bade us all good-bye and left us. Big Otter was to go with them part of the way, and then diverge into the wilderness. He remained a few minutes behind the others to say farewell.

"You will come and settle beside us at last, I hope," said Mrs Liston, squeezing the red-man's hand.

The Indian stood gently stroking the arched neck of his magnificent horse in silence for a few moments. Then he said, in a low voice:—

"Big Otter's heart is with the pale-faces, but he cannot change the nature which has been given to him by the Great Master of Life. He cannot live with the pale-faces. He will dwell where his fathers have dwelt, and live as his fathers have lived, for he loves the great free wilderness. Yet in the memory of his heart the mother of Weeum will live, and Waboose and Muxbee, and the tall pale-face chief, who won the hearts of the red-men by his justice and his love. The dark-haired pale-face, too, will never be forgotten. Each year, as it goes and comes, Big Otter will come again to Sunny Creek about the time that the plovers whistle in the air. He will come and go, till his blood grows cold and his limbs are frail. After that he will meet you all, with Weeum, in the bright Land of Joy, where the Great Master of Life dwells for evermore. Farewell!"

He vaulted on his steed at the last word, and, putting it to the gallop, returned to his beloved wilderness in the Great Nor'-west.

THE END.

CPSIA information can be obtained
at www.ICGtesting.com
Printed in the USA
LVHW011256220723
753113LV00005B/73